The Woman in the Woods

by

Jonas Saul

PUBLISHED BY:
Imagine Press Inc.
Ebook ISBN: 978-1-927404-83-6
Hardcover ISBN: 978-1-927404-84-3
Paperback ISBN: 978-1-927404-85-0

Also by Jonas Saul

The Hunt (Twenty-Two)
The Delivery (Twenty-Three)
The Trap (Twenty-Four)
The Ultimatum (Twenty-Five)
The Depraved (Twenty-Six)
The Condemned (Twenty-Seven)
Payback (Twenty-Eight)
The Unknown (Twenty-Nine)
Wrath (Thirty)
The Damned (Thirty-One)
The Game (Thirty-Two)
The Decoy (Thirty-Three)
The Disappearance (Thirty-Four)

The Jake Wood Novels

The Immortal Gene (Book One)
The Immortal Target (Book Two)

Standalone Novels

The Drowning
The Woman in the Woods
The Threat
The Specter
The Mafia Trilogy
A Murder in Time
Frequency of the Dead
Rue (Coming soon)
The Kill Back (Coming soon)

Co-Authored Novels

Collision Course (Written with Gary Ponzo)
There Will Be Blood (Written with Rania Stone)
The Soulless (Written with Rania Stone)

Short Story Collections

Twisted Fate (Tales of Horror)
Twists of Fate (Tales of Hope)

Chapter 1

PRESENT DAY ...

State Trooper Richard Logan of the Oregon State Police listened to the dispatcher confirming the details as he raced to the scene. His sergeant was en route and would meet him there. According to the FedEx truck driver who called in the emergency, an approximately eighty-year-old woman was on the shoulder of the highway—*crawling* was the word the truck driver had used—covered in blood, acting hysterical and irrational.

Hysterical? Irrational? A woman of that age?

Did her husband kick her out of their moving vehicle? Were they camping and got caught by aggressive wildlife? Why would a woman of that age be wandering the shoulder of Highway 58, just east of milepost 73, a desolate area surrounded by nothing but trees and more trees—covered in blood?

Logan came around a long bend in the road doing ninety miles an hour when he saw the FedEx truck.

He keyed the mic. "Trooper Logan arriving on scene."

The cruiser slowed as he braked, the early

morning sun warming the left side of his face as it crested the mountains.

"Copy that. Sergeant Lambert is fifteen minutes out. Oakridge Fire and EMS personnel are ten minutes away."

"Copy that." Logan stopped ten feet from the FedEx truck.

There was no sign of any old woman or the driver. Something about this didn't feel right.

Trooper Logan tapped the butt of his pistol, a reassuring habit. He grabbed his trooper hat off the passenger seat, cracked open his door, and stepped out of the cruiser, the morning air crisp and cool. The cruiser's lights flickered on the roof of his vehicle as he placed his hat on his head. Logan shoved the door closed, adjusted his belt, and stepped forward, the gravel crunching under his boots.

The highway was quiet at this early hour. A finch or a Steller's jay chirped in the trees to his left.

He didn't see a soul, and something in his gut twisted, warning him to be cautious. He slowed his step, the caution bringing his hand back toward his holster.

This wasn't a dangerous traffic stop or a domestic call—at least, he didn't think it was. But where was the driver of the FedEx truck? And where was the old woman he claimed to have stopped to help?

Logan scanned his immediate surroundings. Nothing but trees, shrubs, and more trees.

He glanced back at his cruiser. The lights still

flashed, but no one skulked around the vehicle. Based on cause and effect, he saw no reason to generate the impact on his nerves.

"Officer?" a man called.

Logan jumped at least a foot, landing with his feet spread, arms flailing outward in defense, his right hand grabbing hold of the truck's side to steady himself.

"What the fuck?" he muttered in a forced whisper, happy he didn't yank out his pistol and shoot the guy.

"Sorry, Officer."

A man dressed in a FedEx shirt and brown shorts emerged from behind a tree and made his way cautiously toward Logan.

"You called this in?" Logan adjusted his shirt in a vain attempt to appear like a confident state trooper again and not the startled boy he looked like moments before.

The man nodded. "I'm the caller, Officer. That woman—"

"Trooper."

"Excuse me?"

"I'm a trooper, as in Oregon State Police, O-S-T. I'm not an officer."

The guy stopped a few feet away, his brow knitted in a slight frown.

Logan caught the man staring at his cleft lip, where a small white scar ran up to his nose. "You were saying?"

The man blinked, refocused on Logan's eyes, then

pointed behind him.

"Right, well, when I saw her and pulled over, she crawled into the trees over here."

"She *crawled*? Doesn't that seem a little overdramatic?"

The man rubbed his chin and stared off to the left, his eyes focusing on nothing. Then he blinked and refocused on Logan.

"You're right. It was more like she *slithered*."

Now it was Logan's turn to frown.

He glanced past the man's shoulders but couldn't see any eighty-year-old woman slithering around in the bush.

"What's your name?" Logan asked.

"Bob."

"Bob, what?"

"Bobby Appleton."

Logan's frown deepened. "You're serious?"

"Yeah, I know. Crazy that my last name has apple in it, and my parents called me Bob, but it's the truth. Try growing up with the longest nickname in school. Hey, Bobbing For Apples, how you doin'? What parents often think is cute or funny opens up a world of teasing and bullying for their kid." He shook his head as if still confused about his name decades later.

Logan wasn't sure if he should empathize with the guy and apologize for what happened to him as a kid or sympathize with what his parents did to him—or neither.

He moved a few feet to the right to get a better

view of the trees, knowing all too well about teasing and bullying due to his mangled lip and his surgeries as a small boy.

"You say she *slithered* in there?"

Bob pivoted, gravel crunching under his weight. "Yeah, I followed her for about ten feet, then stopped."

Logan glanced sidelong at Bob. "What made you stop?"

"I didn't want her thinking I was chasin' her."

"Chasing her? Why would she think that?"

Bob checked his watch. "You need my information? I'd be glad to give it, but I must get going soon. You know, deliveries to make."

Chasing her went through Logan's head again. What had this guy been up to? Did he fight with his older girlfriend? Beat her up for some stupid reason?

A bead of sweat formed on Logan's forehead as he glanced unobtrusively at the guy's hands. No wounds, no blood on the knuckles, no redness. Whatever made the mystery woman bleed, it wasn't the delivery guy's hands.

Logan cleared his throat. "My sergeant will be here in a moment. Give us five more minutes of your time, and you can be on your way. That work for you?" There was no doubt that something was wrong with this scene, but Logan couldn't put his finger on it. "Can you tell me what made the woman feel like you were chasing her?"

Bob was irritated by something. He was fidgety

and glancing over his shoulder, and a slight tic had started in his right cheek—like he was biting the inside of his mouth to control something. Pain? Anxiety? Or was the guy biting his tongue to avoid blurting out the truth of what had transpired before Logan's arrival?

And what was that terrible smell? Someone was cooking mushrooms somewhere nearby. How had he not noticed it before?

"When I approached her," Bob said, "you know, to ask if she was okay, she screamed something about me not being real and crawled away, so I stopped following her."

Logan was getting a picture now. There was no old woman covered in blood, no lost soul wandering the desolate highway before nine in the morning. This was all Bobby Appleton and his girlfriend fighting.

He hit her, and she ran, plain and simple. And now he can't find her, and he's afraid she'll die out here. A sudden change of heart had caused Bobby Appleton to call it in.

Everything about the delivery man was nervous now. Mr. Bobby Appleton was visibly shaking, his nerves enduring the aftereffects of adrenaline.

"I tried to soothe her, talk to her," Bob was still talking, "but she wouldn't listen. After a few more steps in her direction, she moved farther into the trees, so I stopped and told her so."

"Told her so?"

Bob shrugged. "I mean, I told her I'd leave her

alone, then backed away. When you pulled up, I was a few trees in, just keeping an eye on her."

"Where is she now?"

Bob pointed. "About twenty feet that way."

Logan couldn't allow Bobby Appleton to leave until this was settled and the entire incident better understood.

"Okay, here's what's going to happen."

Bob nodded, his eyes skirting the road and then the trees. He absentmindedly bit on a fingernail, chewing with anger like it had bothered him for some time, and he was just getting to it now.

"You're going to take a seat in my cruiser and wait for me—"

"Why's that?" The finger yanked from his mouth. "I did the right thing." Bob placed his hands on his hips, his tone defiant. "I called it in."

"Yes, yes, you did the right thing, but until I can understand what's happening, I need you to remain on site."

"I told you I would wait for your sergeant."

Logan moved closer to the man, his shoulders back slightly. "Now look, Mr. Appleton, I'm going to enter those trees and attempt to locate the woman who slithered in there. While my back is turned, I need to know you're safe and in my cruiser."

Bob's face had darkened, and his cheeks reddened. Was that anger? Or guilt?

"You think I had something to do with this, don't you?"

"Did you?" Logan consciously considered the handcuffs or the gun—which would he be reaching for?

"No, I fucking didn't, but I considered driving onward and not calling it in."

"Why would that be?"

"Because of this shit and because I'm working."

"This shit?" Logan stepped closer. He was in grabbing distance now. "Can you elaborate?"

"There's always that chance that whoever calls in a crime is suspected of being involved somehow, and by calling it in, they're attempting to deflect that suspicion."

"Wow, you seem to have it all worked out." Something in Appleton's voice told Logan he was speaking the truth, yet his character was off. If he wasn't involved with what happened here today, the man was guilty of something else. That much was for sure. He would run Bobby's name before leaving the scene to see if he had any priors or warrants.

Bobby said nothing. He just kept staring toward the trees, squinting in the morning sun.

Logan moved closer. "So far, you've given me no reason to suspect you in any crime, Mr. Appleton. I want to talk to the woman in the woods, and while I'm doing that, all I want is for you to wait five minutes in my cruiser. The question is whether you'll do that willingly or not."

Appleton's eyes widened. When he angled his head toward Logan, the sun playing off the side of his face, his clenched jaw was easy to see. The man looked like he would snap at any moment. The throbbing vein in Bobby's forehead told Logan the man was contemplating fight or flight.

Logan's hand moved toward his weapon.

"I'll wait in the cruiser," Bobby muttered.

Appleton spun and stomped toward the police vehicle, opened the back door, then dropped inside.

"What the fuck was that?" Logan whispered to himself.

With Appleton secured in the cruiser, Logan fixed his attention back on the trees at the shoulder of the highway.

The sound of a car approaching in the distance caught his attention. He glanced toward the way he'd come and saw Oakridge emergency vehicles approaching.

The thought of company relieved him. Having reliable witnesses for whatever it was they were about to find had an odd comforting element to it, even though he still couldn't put his finger on what was freaking him out yet—well, other than Appleton's bizarre behavior and questionable use of verbs to describe an eighty-year-old woman's movements.

The ambulance engine revved lower as they slowed upon the approach of the scene on the shoulder.

Logan advanced on the tree line and entered the overgrown branches and shrubs in the approximate area Appleton had pointed.

"Hello?" he called. "Oregon State Police, Trooper Logan in here. I'm moving through these trees toward you."

He waited, then stepped over a fallen tree, forest debris snapping under his boot as he moved deeper into the thicket. The ambulance had come to a stop on the road behind him. He was sure he heard another vehicle approaching, which would probably be the sergeant.

"Ma'am? We're here to help. You're safe now. You can come out."

There was no response.

"Logan?" A female voice called him from the highway. Sergeant Lambert.

"In here," he shouted back in a hushed whisper, recognizing her voice.

"Where?" Sergeant Katrina Lambert had lowered her volume.

"Follow the sound of my voice. I'm only a few trees in."

Footsteps thunked behind him, and then he saw her. Sergeant Kat, her preferred moniker, moved around the same downed tree he'd skirted moments before.

"What'd you find?"

"Nothing yet." Logan turned back around. "Apparently, there's an old woman covered in blood somewhere in here."

"Is that why the delivery driver is in your cruiser? He admit to something nefarious?"

He loved that word, *nefarious*, and made a mental note to ask what kind of books Sergeant Kat read.

"Not yet, but the guy's guilty of something. We find the woman; we learn the story."

They nodded at one another, then separated to five feet apart before moving inward, away from the highway.

"Ma'am?" Logan called again. "We're here to help."

The smell of cooked mushrooms was more potent here, wafting up to him on the breeze. He stopped to inhale it to determine where it was coming from. After losing the smell momentarily, Logan got walking again. Ten feet later, Kat whistled softly. Logan glanced her way to see her gesticulating wildly for him to join her.

Sergeant Katrina Lambert wasn't known for histrionics and over-dramatization in any definition found in any dictionary. When she waved her hand madly, it meant to jump and respond without delay— not to mention he would anyway, as she outranked him.

As he hustled her way, his right hand eased toward his pistol butt again. He counted the number of times he reached for his gun in the past ten minutes and concluded it had been more than in the previous year of duty.

"What is it?" He lowered his center of gravity and scanned the surrounding trees.

"There." She pointed at a dark substance on the

lower leaves of the tree in front of her, then leaned to within inches of his ear. "Something is bleeding, that's for sure."

He nodded and, staying in a crouched position, moved forward.

They found more blood on several leaves on the tree behind the one Kat had found.

They were heading in the right direction.

He stepped around a Douglas fir tree—at least he thought it was a Douglas fir—and stopped when he saw a woman's bare feet.

Instead of waving maniacally at the sergeant, he just stared at the bloody feet and waited. Kat was heading in the same direction, moving around the fir tree on the other side.

Then she saw what Logan was staring at and stopped, too.

The few unprofessional seconds they stared at the body without doing anything was the human reaction to processing what they were looking at. The professional in them both reacted moments later, rushing forth to examine the body for signs of life.

Logan's breath had caught in his throat at the sight of the old woman, and he only started breathing again when he stood over her because he'd yanked out his radio to tell the paramedics to bring the stretcher.

Sergeant Lambert had dropped to her knees and gently placed a finger under the woman's jaw, searching for a pulse.

Kat nodded. "She's alive, but her pulse is weak."

Logan stepped back and turned his head, needing to look away for a few moments, then gave in to that urge.

He called out to the paramedics. "Guys, this way."

They came crashing through the bush, lugging a spineboard. Once she was secured, they'd carry her back to the ambulance, where she'd be strapped to a stretcher, then loaded.

When he turned back to the old woman covered in what appeared to be a thousand cuts, Kat had eased back, too. His sergeant examined the trees beyond the body, looking for who or what did this.

The woman was at least eighty years old, perhaps older. Her feet were bloody, the soles mostly absent of skin from walking a great distance. A couple of toes still leaked blood, and if it weren't for the dried dark blood, her feet would be white due to blood loss. That might help explain the crawling—*slithering*—Bobby Appleton had said to describe the woman's movements.

The woman's hands were black with patches of dark red, as if she'd recently held an easel while painting a terrible version of Dante's Hell on canvas.

There was a butterfly tattoo on her left arm, slightly below the elbow. Other than being covered in dirt and blood, it looked intact.

Logan couldn't say she was wearing pants exactly, but something resembling pants was cinched around the woman's waist, the cloth tattered and shredded like she had crawled a mile through barbed wire.

The woman's shirt was cut and open in several places, revealing her upper body as a mass of open wounds and blood. Even her face looked like someone had pummeled it with solid fists.

Whatever happened to this woman had been devastating and had taken place over some time. She was undoubtedly close to death, emaciated, exhausted, and lacking proper nutrition. The whitish, chalky look on her lips was a clear sign of anemia.

If this woman survived the day and the night, she would need time in a hospital bed wired to IVs filled with more than just saline solution.

Someone called his name from far away. It sounded like it came from the highway.

Why was his hand on his Glock again? What was out here that had spooked him so much?

Sweat had gathered at the small of his back, making him adjust his shirt with his free hand.

Who the hell was calling him?

He blinked several times, and then his gun hand was shoved sideways.

When he twisted in that direction, he was inches from Sergeant Lambert's face.

"I said, step aside, Trooper Logan, and let the paramedics do their job."

He nodded vigorously, moving backward.

Sergeant Kat guided him back to the shoulder of the highway.

"What the hell happened to that woman?" he

mumbled.

"We will find out soon enough."

He snapped sideways. Kat was right beside him.

He had to get himself together. "I don't understand," Logan added. "Something's not right here."

"I'm feeling it, too. Just keep moving. Get back to the cruiser."

At the highway, others had arrived to take over the scene.

Sergeant Katrina ordered Logan to take the FedEx driver in and get his official statement. She would find out who the woman in the woods was, then head to the hospital to interview her as soon as possible.

Logan got behind the wheel and started driving back toward Oakridge while Bobby Appleton protested in the rear of his cruiser.

Within ten miles, he felt better. His stomach had calmed, and his breathing was less ragged.

Appleton talked about losing his job and being blamed for something he hadn't done when they had pulled away from the scene, but now he fell silent.

By the time Logan was in his office, all traces of his anxiety and paranoia had disappeared. Of course, because he was home now, in his territory, his familiar. There was nothing to fear here, nothing to run from, and no reason to grab his weapon.

He took Appleton's statement over the course of an hour and, feeling sorry for the driver, called his boss and told him what happened. Then they had a cruiser drive Bobby back to his truck.

The phone rang before Logan returned to his office.

He snatched it up on the fourth ring. "Trooper Logan."

"Logan, it's Kat." She spoke like she had gasped the words.

"You okay, Sergeant?"

"Meet me at the hospital ASAP."

"Is everything okay with the victim—"

Sergeant Lambert hung up on him.

Logan hopped in his cruiser, flicked on the lights, and headed toward the hospital quickly, skirting as many red lights as he could.

Why hadn't she radioed him to join her at the hospital? Why make it private by using the telephone?

He made it in record time, parked close to the emergency entrance, then ran inside. Sergeant Katrina Lambert was waiting for him near the triage.

When he saw her, he wondered if she was being admitted for something. The sergeant had lost all color. She wasn't just white—her face had turned a light shade of green.

"What's going on?"

She opened her mouth, closed it, then opened it again.

"It's not possible," she finally whispered.

"What's not possible?" Logan glanced around them. No one was paying them any sort of attention.

"The woman from the woods."

"What about her?" Logan nodded at a row of chairs by the back wall. "Let's take a seat. Tell me what you found out."

Kat nodded and allowed herself to be led to the side. Once seated, Logan saw the small file she'd stuffed behind her arm.

Kat glanced down at the file, then back up to Logan, her glazed eyes focusing on him.

"I refuse to believe it."

"Sergeant, what happened? Were you able to identify the woman and find out her story?"

She nodded, but it was barely perceptible like she agreed but wasn't sure.

"I'm freaked out," Kat said, and for the first time since he arrived, he understood what he mistook for shock or surprise was a response to fear. His sergeant was scared shitless and had no idea how to deal with that.

"Start at the beginning, Sergeant. Just tell me what happened."

"The woman is sedated. She's upstairs, on the third floor."

Logan nodded. Now they were getting somewhere.

"I took her prints." Kat glanced around the room, then back to Logan. "Ran them."

"And?"

She raised her head and met his gaze. They stared at each other for several seconds.

"Well?" Logan prodded.

"There was a match."

Relieved, he leaned back and clapped softly. "Good, now we're getting somewhere."

"It's in here." The sergeant handed him the file in her hands. "I had a police records clerk fax it to me here at the hospital."

Logan took it and opened it.

He shook his head when he glanced down at the missing persons report.

"There must be some mistake."

Kat was shaking her head, too. "No mistake. I ran the prints several times."

"Well, clearly, it's impossible." That anxious feeling started in his gut again. How could the sergeant believe such nonsense?

He stared down at the paperwork in his lap.

The woman staring back at him had been missing for several days. The document said she was last seen getting on a train at the Eugene, Oregon, station. Her final destination was supposed to have been Sacramento, California. According to her boyfriend, she was going to visit her dying mother in hospice, but she never made it.

According to the reports, the boyfriend was the last person to see her alive. He was Eugene Police Officer Colton Asher, a man Trooper Logan knew, having worked with him in the past. A few days back at the train station, they'd seen each other when he handed out flyers for a couple of most wanted in the area.

But Colton was in his early thirties, and this woman was in her eighties. It didn't make sense.

The sergeant flicked her fingers. "Check the sheet underneath."

Logan lifted the pages until he saw another missing persons report for the boyfriend.

"Colton Asher is missing, too?" Logan glanced up to gawk at Lambert. "That can't be. I just saw him the other day."

Kat nodded. "He's missing. And get this. When we found her, she had Colton Asher's driver's license in her pocket."

"Holy shit." Logan drew a hand through his hair. "Okay, but that doesn't explain how this woman," he jabbed a finger on the page, "and the woman we found in the woods are the same because they actually *can't* be. It's impossible."

"That's what I thought. Did you see that tattoo on her arm?" When he nodded, Sergeant Kat tapped the paperwork. "Read the part about distinguishing features."

Logan read some of the notes and came to the part about the tattoo. A butterfly on the left forearm, just below the elbow.

"The coincidences abound."

"It's her, Logan. That's the same woman. Impossible, but true."

Kat's eyes were bloodshot, and she still hadn't regained her color. If it weren't his sergeant telling him this, he'd label her as mad.

There was no way he would believe they were the same woman, or he'd have to commit himself.

Several hours ago, the woman they found in the bush was easily in her eighties. Being a senior is something a person can often tell by just looking at them. There was no illusion. The woman upstairs wasn't a day younger than seventy.

He glanced back at the missing persons report in front of him.

The attractive woman who went missing days ago with the same tattoo and identical fingerprints as the old woman upstairs wasn't a day over thirty. Her birthday year listed her as a twenty-eight-year-old when she went missing.

"There's no way that old woman upstairs has aged forty or fifty years in under a week." Logan was shaking his head. "Impossible."

"She hasn't seen this." Kat pointed at the file. "When I entered the room, she was drugged but still awake. I asked her name, details we have on file."

Logan stared at his sergeant. "And?"

"She gave me the name in that missing persons report." Kat eased back to lean on the wall.

Logan grabbed at her, thinking she'd fall. "Are you okay?"

"Yeah, I just need a moment. Feeling lightheaded with this shit."

Logan scanned the lobby but couldn't see a doctor. When he refocused on the sergeant, she seemed well enough, some color returning to her face.

"Tell me what else she said."

"She said the woods were cursed or haunted."

"Cursed or haunted? Which one?"

"Both." Kat lowered her gaze to her lap. "She said the bunker was eating them, one by one. Making them age and disappear. Sucking the life right out of them or something. Absolute delirious shit."

Logan stared at her for a long moment. "Bunker? Eating them? What the hell? If she isn't crazy, we need to verify this story. Her prints will have to be taken and rechecked. Sergeant, if any of this is remotely true, it makes no sense." He glanced around them to make sure no one was listening. "The impossible couldn't happen. I refuse to believe it. There has to be a mistake."

"But prints don't lie, do they?" Sergeant Katrina stood and grabbed the file from his hands. "I've got calls to make, people to inform. And I'll try to find any living relatives. Let's make sense of this fast so we can forget about it and move on."

"I'm all for that."

They strode from the hospital in stunned disbelief, with Logan not forgetting how he felt when he had stopped behind the FedEx truck that morning. He felt horrible, like a sudden attack of anxiety had overwhelmed him. And that terrible smell of cooked mushrooms. It had all dissipated with each mile he drove after leaving the site, but where had that mushroom smell come from? There weren't any houses or restaurants in that area.

Nothing made sense except that something was wrong, that much was for sure, but precisely what it was, he had no idea.

Yet, that woman upstairs had to have some of the answers.

At least, he hoped she did.

Chapter 2

THREE DAYS BEFORE PRESENT Day ...

As she exited the taxi, Anna Valentina clutched her meager belongings in her small carry-on. The cab eased away, and she turned to look up at the sign over the train station building. It said EUGENE DEPOT, and below that, ELEVATION 428 FEET. Did that mean above sea level? Did it really matter that everyone knew exactly how high they were? How was that an important fact?

She moved toward the depot's entrance, her thoughts a jumble of questions, starting with the word *why* and ending with exclamation marks. Her stomach seemed permanently twisted in a knot at the anxiety of what Colton had done. It just wasn't fair—nothing was fair. They were supposed to start a family together and grow old together.

"Fuck it," she whispered to herself outside the station, staring at the tracks and the bushes.

The late afternoon sun peeked through the clouds and washed the area with color, the trees a vibrant green after a solid rain, the building's exterior still wet from the downpour hours ago.

As the clouds released their fury on the area, the hard drops of water pounding the roof of her rental had made packing that much more depressing. She'd cried while it rained, the tide of depression moved by the weight of loss and betrayal and at the reality of what her life had become.

With bloodshot and puffy eyes, she pushed open the train station's front doors and stepped out of the sun. People milled about the depot's interior, some chatting quietly, some on devices, a few sleeping, and two men were playing backgammon in the corner.

One guy glared at her like she'd done something to piss him off. There was a darkness, malice in his expression that sent her a warning to steer clear. He was bald and thick—a lifter—with brows angled downward in a permanent scowl. The man looked like he spent afternoons abducting teenagers off the street and performing unspeakable acts to them in the back of a dark-colored van.

Why the hell was he staring at her, though? The last thing she needed was more trouble in her life, including man trouble, dangerous or otherwise. She'd had enough man trouble to last her a decade. It would probably take that long before she trusted one again, too.

She averted her eyes from the lifter and moved toward the ticket window. With one woman in line in front of her, Anna lowered her carry-on to the floor, then unzipped it to locate her wallet.

Cash in hand, she tapped her foot and waited. The

temptation to glance over her shoulder at the lifter increased to an urge. When she did, the lifter was back to watching the main entrance doors. So it wasn't her, in particular, he was interested in. He was waiting for someone, a traveling partner perhaps. Maybe a blind date from some stupid dating app.

"Ma'am?"

Anna spun back around. The ticket window woman beckoned her forward.

"How can I help you?" She reminded Anna of a hospital triage nurse—bored and disinterested in the human beings that crossed her path. They were one-dimensional beings, a means to an end, nothingness.

Anna shuffled forward, pushing her bag across the floor with her foot. "I need a one-way ticket to Sacramento."

The woman stared at her computer screen, tapped on her keyboard, then stopped to sip from a coffee cup.

"Name?"

"Anna Valentina."

"Spell the last name."

"It's Valentine, but with an A at the end."

The woman paused, her fingers hovering over the keyboard, then typed again. Anna wondered if the woman would make her spell it out in that short lull.

"Your train leaves at five fifteen and arrives in Sacramento tomorrow morning just after six."

Anna glanced sideways at the large clock on the wall. It was just after four-thirty. Her timing was perfect. She'd be out of the Eugene/Springfield area long before her boyfriend—*ex*-boyfriend—would ever know.

"How will you be paying?"

"Cash."

"It'll be fifty-six dollars." The woman smacked her keyboard, still not looking up to see who she was dealing with.

Anna withdrew three twenties and slid them under the Plexiglas divider. Once she got her printed ticket and the change, she grabbed her bag and moved away from the ticket window without a word of thanks. The woman looked up then but didn't stare for long.

After taking a seat near the corner of the station, she slipped her change and ticket inside the bag, then wrapped the bag's handle on her ankle in case someone tried to snatch it. Then she sat back and closed her eyes. She didn't want to face those sitting around her. This wasn't a time to make friends or dabble in small talk. Even though she was about to spend the next thirteen hours on a train heading south, she wanted to be alone more than ever.

How had her life fallen apart so fast in such a short time?

She shook her head to clear the negative thoughts and opened her eyes. Maybe she should get a coffee, stay up late on the train, and do some reading.

Wait, did the train have a dining car? Would she be able to buy something on board? If not, should she have packed something?

The woman at the ticket booth had just sold her a ticket. She didn't offer her any options like first-class or a suite with a bed. Do trains have that sort of thing? Maybe this train didn't, or maybe Miss Uninterested Bitch, who sold her the ticket, didn't care one way or the other about the comfort of the passengers.

Anna got up, unhooked the strap from her ankle, then shouldered the bag and went in search of a coffee.

The lifter was still watching the door, evidently stuck waiting for someone.

From inside her bag, she detected the distant ringtone of her phone, the distinct one telling her it was Colton calling. She wasn't taking any more of Colton's calls. It would be months before she could bring herself to hear his voice, if ever. The lying bastard deserved whatever leftovers he found in Janine's arms. Fuck him and fuck her, too—literally.

Besides a vending machine that dispensed coffee, she couldn't find anything that sold food. That meant there had to be something on the train.

She moved to the window and glanced out toward the parking lot. Could Colton put a trace on her cell? He was a Eugene cop, and he knew people. She was sure he could make that happen if he wanted to find her. And if he saw her, she'd have to face him, talk to him, which held no interest to her. Like the ticket booth woman, Anna could look through the Plexiglas of her life and not want to see it or acknowledge it. That life, the one she yearned for and worked to maintain, resided on the other side now and would soon be gone with the next train.

The phone had to be silenced, so she fished it out of her bag and held down the button to turn it off. If they could trace a phone that wasn't turned on, well then, all the power to them because she wasn't about to throw it away to avoid Colton—he'd cost her enough already.

The clock on the wall said she had twenty minutes left. She jammed her phone back in her bag, opened the door to leave, and made eye contact with the lifter again. A shiver coursed through her. That man gave her the creeps. What was his deal anyway? Why watch the door with such scrutiny that it made people uneasy?

As a train pulled in behind the building, she forgot all about food and coffee. Could that be the one she was supposed to take?

On the platform at the rear of the building, she found an empty bench where she pulled out her ticket to read it. People exited the train while some announcement came over a loudspeaker somewhere, but it was mumbled and spoken so low that she could only discern a single word. The same disinterested employee she witnessed in the ticket booth.

The slip of paper had her name on it, although the woman had spelled it wrong. She'd typed VALENTINE instead of VALENTINA. Was that on purpose because she was being a bitch? Weren't women supposed to stick together? Woman power or some shit?

Anna sighed. The idea of women sticking together had died when her boss, her best friend, was fucking the man she was supposed to marry and have a family with.

"Go fuck yourselves," she whispered under her breath. "Both of you."

"Oh, sorry." A skinny-looking addict had been about to sit on the bench when she spoke up. Evidently, he thought she'd been talking to him.

She raised a hand and opened her mouth to apologize, but nothing came out. Besides, the guy was halfway to another bench already. She let it go and chastised herself to keep her shit on the inside in the future.

Restless and unsettled until the train got underway, Anna rose from the bench and walked the length of the platform to examine the front parking area one more time on the off chance Colton would come barreling in, lights blazing in an attempt to stop her from leaving.

But there were no police cars in the parking lot, and her train was leaving in just over ten minutes.

She marched back to the platform and joined the small line queued to board the train. The bag still on her shoulder, she pulled out her ticket and held it tight.

It was over, finally. Stepping onto the train would be the exclamation mark of her past and the beginning of nothing new. Where would she go after visiting her dying mother in Sacramento? Colton's cheating dashed her dreams of marriage and a small family. She'd be in her thirties soon. The clock was ticking, and she wasn't about to just lie down and get pregnant. It was supposed to be romantic, but like that song said, should she blame Disney? Life sucked, and the sooner she got that, the more she could drink herself to sleep.

A man nudged her arm and pushed past her. The skinny junkie from before bounded up the steps and onto the train. She didn't comment because she had paused, standing there like an ass staring off into space, lost in her thoughts.

When it was her turn, she handed over her ticket to a man who glanced down quickly and then returned it. She took the stairs slower than the junkie.

What was the big hurry anyway? Running wouldn't get anyone where they were going any faster. It was a fucking train—it went as fast as it went.

She meandered along the aisle and opened the door to enter another car. This one had a corridor on the right with open doors that led into small cabins. Maybe she'd take one of those; if someone came, she'd move to another one. She'd be more comfortable in her private alcove if no one came.

The seat by the window offered a great view of the parking area—still no police cars. Good, Colton could stay in Eugene and live the rest of his miserable life with Janine. They deserved each other.

She rested her head back and closed her eyes. Images flitted behind her eyelids as boarding continued. Even though she wanted to stay up and read, she needed sleep, which had been elusive since she found Janine sitting on Colton when she slipped back into the salon to get her jacket.

People walked by her small enclosure several times, but she didn't look up. It was better to appear like she was supposed to be here instead of checking who might be looking in on her.

Eventually, the train got underway with a slight jerking motion to start. They were on their way.

She opened her eyes.

An older man had taken a spot across from her, glasses on the bridge of his nose, a newspaper in his hand. His thin unflattering combover seemed gelled in place as it didn't move with his head tilted down the way it was as he read from the sports pages. Or was it the classifieds he was studying?

Anna glanced away before she got caught staring. The end of the platform eased by as the train picked up speed, and soon they were heading into the Oregonian forest, surrounded by a mountain range whose name she couldn't recall.

When Combover Man looked up, their eyes met briefly. She offered him a half-smile, then fixed her attention back on the countryside. No reason to be friendly and no reason to talk, either. Small talk sucked, and she didn't want to engage in anything remotely close to it.

Anna closed her eyes again to avoid the bitter tears, then pulled her bag closer and wondered what she'd do for the next thirteen hours.

It was times like this when forethought would've come in handy. She should've brought a bottle of something strong to sip on. At least then her sorrows could drown, along with that white-picket fence and two-children family, they'd discussed over the past year.

It was all over, and there was no going back—ever.

Chest heavy, sad for what could've been, she was lulled to sleep by the gentle rocking of the train, her bag firmly in her grip.

Chapter 3

Colton Asher called again, and it went directly to voicemail just like the last five times.

He slammed the steering wheel, and four words came out in a breath of anger.

"Where are you, Anna?"

It was nearing six at night, and he hadn't found her. There had been no note, no goodbye, nothing— just a missing girlfriend. He hadn't made detective in the department yet, but he didn't need to be one to see she'd packed in haste and bolted from their apartment.

Whatever she thought she'd seen at the salon could be explained away, or at least he could try to, but he had to find her first.

Six phone calls later, and none of Anna's closest friends knew where she'd gone. He suspected a couple of them just wasn't going to tell him.

How much did Anna say to her friends? How many of them were lying to him?

It didn't matter. She was gone and hadn't touched the money in their accounts. He'd signed in online and scanned not only the checking and savings accounts but also the credit cards to see if she bought a plane ticket, bus, or train, but there was nothing of the sort.

Not even a hotel room deposit.

Where could she go that would take cash? But the more important question was, how much cash did she have?

Did she take a taxi somewhere? Buy a bus ticket? Train ticket? If she bought one, it would be to see her mother, a trip they planned for next week. Maybe that's all this was. She decided to go early and alone.

If that wasn't the case, she had shacked up with a friend locally and would reach out soon. But he didn't like not knowing one bit.

So, he decided that if she didn't surface by tonight, he'd speak with his supervisor and see if he could file a missing persons report early when he got to work for his shift. That would at least allow him to let his fellow officers know so everyone could keep an eye out for her.

They'd been together for almost five years. All that time couldn't be thrown away for one misunderstanding. He wouldn't allow it.

He rechecked the time. He had four hours before he needed to get ready for work. A trip to the bus and then the train station, then he'd let it go for the night. Maybe someone would remember her face if she had been at either place recently. People forgot faces if too much time elapsed, so he had to stay on it until he located her.

And if he was going to find her, it had to be tonight, or he feared she'd be out of his life for good, and that wasn't an option. They were supposed to start a family.

When his phone rang, he nearly jumped out of his seat. He snatched it up so fast he didn't see who was calling.

"Anna?" he gasped into the phone.

"Have you found her yet?" Janine's voice faltered like she wondered if she should've called. Or maybe she was genuinely concerned for her missing girlfriend.

"Not yet, and why are you calling? What if I had found her and she was sitting with me? How would I explain to you on my screen?"

"I'm worried about her, is all."

"Look, after I've found her and worked everything out, I'll call you, okay? Or I'll get Anna to call you."

"She's going to hate me."

"I'm pretty close to that myself right now."

There was a pause. "You don't really mean that, do you?" Unless she was being insincere, he detected pain in her words.

"Janine, you're her boss and her best friend. What you did was unconscionable, and now she's missing —"

"Missing? You'd call her missing, like filing one of those reports?"

"I'm considering it, yes."

"Wouldn't they suspect you? I mean, isn't it always the husband or the boyfriend?"

Colton frowned and stared out his windshield.

"What are you getting at? I did nothing wrong. It was all you."

"Oh sure, and you didn't kiss me back. Come on, Colton, I've seen how you look at me. And how was I supposed to know Anna would come back in?"

"I gotta go."

"Okay, sorry. Just find her and text me then. You don't have to call. I just need to know she's all right. Oh, and tell her she doesn't have to come in tomorrow if she doesn't want to."

Colton's frown deepened. "Whatever," he whispered into the phone and ended the call.

He tossed the phone on the passenger seat, resisting the urge to call Anna again, then headed to the bus station. Anna's picture was on his phone, and his police ID was in his pocket. He'd get answers before his shift or don the uniform and get answers then.

Someone would tell him where his girlfriend had gone, or heads would roll, starting with Janine's for jumping on him and starting all this shit.

Chapter 4

SOMETHING BANGED SO LOUD it startled her, like someone smashing into her apartment door.

Anna's eyes popped open, and she blinked rapidly to orientate herself.

She was on a train. The sun was still up, beating through the train window, making her shade her eyes. How long did she sleep?

"Tickets, please, ma'am." A man in the train company's uniform stood at the door to her enclosure, a colleague standing behind him, looking in over the man's shoulder. The one holding out his hand for her ticket had thick bushy eyebrows like thin rodents lived above his eyes.

Anna looked away to avoid staring and saw that the balding man who had sat reading the paper when she drifted off to sleep was gone.

She fumbled in her bag for her ticket, scrambling over hastily stashed underwear, containers of makeup —one had popped open, spilling a brush to the bottom of her purse—and her phone's charging cords.

"What's this all about?" She glanced up, pausing her search for a moment.

The man with the eyebrows seemed annoyed. Was

it the question she'd asked, or was he bothered by the drudgery and monotony of his job?

"Ticket verification, ma'am. Routine stuff."

Her attention was back on her bag, which she rifled through until she found the ticket scrunched up and hiding behind her cell phone.

Ticket in hand, she thrust it toward the man.

"Where did the other guy go?"

The train employee continued to examine the ticket. He lowered it to the side and stared at her as the train began to slow.

"The man who was sitting there?" The attendant pointed at the empty seat across from her.

She nodded.

"He was on the wrong train." The man glanced down at her ticket, then back up to her. "It would seem the same fate has befallen you, ma'am. Not only are you on the wrong train, but cabins like this come at a higher rate. I'd suggest you take your seat in the appropriate area when you board the train you're supposed to be on."

He handed her back her ticket and gestured for her to follow him.

"I don't understand." Anna looked outside the window, squinting in the sun. "Why is the train stopping?"

"So that people like you can be removed from this train."

There was something about his tone that spoke to her anger. That *people like you* comment had an immediate effect on her blood pressure. What was that supposed to mean? Instead of debating the finer points of respecting the customer, she chose a different question.

"Where are you taking me?"

"To the exit, ma'am."

She looked outside again. "But there's nothing out here. It's just trees and woods."

The men had moved into the hallway. They exchanged a glance and appeared to be holding back a laugh.

"Ma'am, there is a small substation where—"

"Stop calling me ma'am," she cut in.

The man reared back as if slapped. "Of course, ma—" He stopped, his mouth closing tight. "There is a small substation here where people wait for their proper train. You must embark here as the train you want heads south. At the next station, we are heading east. You won't get to Sacramento on this train. It's a simple case of you got on the wrong train, as did several others."

She was awake enough now to understand. A mistake had been made, simple as that. The train had pulled up to the Eugene station, and she'd just assumed it was the right one. The man checking her ticket before boarding had only glanced at it and waved her on. An easy mistake, one rectified once her train arrived at the substation they were dropping her off at.

Anna rose to her feet and grabbed her bag. "How

long will I have to wait at this substation?"

"No more than thirty minutes. This train was late, and several people boarded it by accident. The train you're looking for was also expected to be ten minutes late. It has since boarded in Eugene and is en route to this station. If you'll just follow us." He stepped back and gestured along the hallway.

Anna moved out of the small room and followed the men through to the next car as the train had almost come to a complete stop. In this car, the seats were full, which led her to believe she was walking through the economy section, the area her ticket would have allowed her a seat.

Escorted as she was toward the group at the other end of the car, one train attendant in front, the other taking up the rear, all eyes were on her. It made her feel like a stowaway, even though she'd bought a ticket.

But what freaked her out was that lifter from the train station in Eugene was waiting by the door, the one who had watched her. He eyed her now as she made her way toward them. The balding man with the combover from her cabin was there, too, just like the attendant had said. The junkie-looking teenager who had cut her off when they were boarding hopped from one foot to the other beside the lifter, clearly agitated about something.

Five train employees surrounded them.

So, the tally was three men and one woman being removed from the train. How safe was that? Did this train substation have employees?

Well, there was no way she was getting off the train with those three unless it was a regular train station with dozens of people milling about. If it was just some drop-off point in the middle of nowhere, being stuck there with those three didn't feel right. How could they do that? What if something happened?

When the attendants escorting her came to a stop by the door, the train also came to a halt with a soft thumping sound. One of the attendants opened the side door and jumped down. He raised a hand to signal someone at the front of the train, then turned back to the four people being taken off.

"This way, please."

The lifter, followed by the addict, and the newspaperman all jumped down the steps and onto the wooden platform.

Anna moved toward the door, glanced outside, stopped, and turned back.

"Are you sure this is the right place?"

Eyebrow Man stepped closer. "Ma'am, you're on the wrong train." His tone had thickened like he was upset with her for such a simple mistake. And evidently, he didn't care for calling her *ma'am* again. "Please exit through that door and wait no more than fifteen to twenty minutes. Your train will come along soon."

When she peered outside again, the other three had moved away from the door, and the attendant on the ground had his hand up, waiting for her to step down.

She swung back to Eyebrows. "But there's no one here."

"This is a transfer station. People move from train to train here. They don't *buy* tickets here."

"I understand what you're saying, but you're kicking me out"—she leaned forward and lowered her voice—"with three other men in the middle of nowhere. How is this possible?"

"We are executing a routine train procedure here, I assure you. The other train has been notified and is aware you're waiting here. If you don't leave soon, I'm afraid they may arrive and hit our stationary train as we sit idle on the tracks." He moved closer to her, pointing at the open door. "Now, if you please."

Anna shook her head. Something didn't feel right. Was this Colton's doing? Was he on his way to pick her up? How many trains pulled into the Eugene station around five in the afternoon that she would make a mistake like this?

"You know what? I think I'll get off at the next station." Anna attempted to push by Eyebrows to take a seat, but he raised an arm to block her way.

"Excuse me." The time for calm was over. She never wanted to be a Karen, but dropping a single woman off with three strangers didn't sit well with her.

"Ma'am, you're considered a stowaway at this point, on this train illegally without a ticket—"

"I bought a fucking ticket—"

"For another train. If you don't exit now, I will be forced to contact the authorities. We would then have to wait here for them, and the lost time would be billed to you." He checked his watch. "Your proper train will be along in just over ten minutes now. So, please exit immediately, as we must be underway."

Several people had gotten up to watch the scene she'd created. She counted five cell phones aimed in her direction.

Ten minutes. She could do ten minutes, even though everything in her gut told her to stay right where she was.

There were witnesses who would not only see her exit the train but also record it. Someone would know if she got off here and anything happened to her. Not very consoling, but something, nonetheless.

The attendant placed a hand on her arm.

She jerked her arm free. "Don't *touch* me. I can walk by myself." She scowled at everyone watching and recording the scene, then turned on her heels and stepped off the train.

The attendant on the ground gave a thumbs up toward the front, then hopped back on.

The massive train started moving seconds later.

Face after face stared out at her from the windows of economy seating. Then the higher-priced ticket area was easing by, but most of those windows were empty.

Having no interest in watching the train gain speed and leave her in the middle of nowhere with three strange men, she turned away and shuffled along the small terminal's wooden platform in search of a vending machine. Tired, cold, scared, and embarrassed, she wanted chocolate, something to soothe her nerves before her real train arrived.

This depot was so remote, it had a small building at the back of the platform that looked like it was built during the last world war. It was no bigger than an average shed in someone's backyard. She twisted the handle on the shed's steel door, but it was locked—of course, it was.

When she turned back around, the train's last car whisked by, and then it was gone, lost to the trees on the right.

Each man had wandered off to their own corners to wait. At least the lifter wasn't staring at her from where he stood near the tracks. The junkie she could take. A swift kick in the balls, and he'd be down. The older man—Combover Man with glasses who had been reading the paper in her cabin on the train—came across as an accountant, or maybe a dentist, definitely someone who kept to themselves—he wasn't there to bother her.

It was the lifter who scared her, the way he had watched the door back at the Eugene station. Like he was waiting for someone to walk through, perhaps someone he was running from. Maybe it was a woman. Maybe Lifter only looked tough, and he was a kitten on the inside. It could be the guy was a victim of spousal abuse. Who knew with people these days?

Everyone had a story, and his actions made her wonder what his story was and who he was on the lookout for.

After a five-minute walk from one end of the platform to the other, she leaned on the steel door of the small shed and waited.

No one had said a word to anyone else as the sun set farther in the west, darkening the area with deep shadows. The tall trees blocked out any chance of sunlight unless it was directly above them, which it wasn't.

The addict-looking guy paced at the far corner of the platform, mumbling something to himself. The lifter now stood in the middle of the train tracks, arms crossed, staring back the way they'd come, probably hoping to see their train arriving soon. And the accountant-like guy was still engrossed in his newspaper. He had plopped himself down on the edge of the platform, his finger pointing to a spot on the newsprint where he followed a story.

Not one of the three of them seemed worried about their situation. Even the pacing addict didn't look concerned—he just looked like he was jonesing for his next fix.

At the ten-minute mark, her stomach growling with hunger and twisting with nervous anxiety, she still hadn't heard a train approaching in the distance. With every second she heard nothing, her anxiety rose to freak-out mode.

The jitters winning; she pulled out her cell phone

and turned it on so if she needed to use it, at least the damn thing would be ready.

Once it was powered up, she couldn't find a signal. Even holding it above her head didn't seem to work. As she walked, Anna moved away from the building, keeping the phone high. Not one single bar could be found from anywhere on the platform. The NO SERVICE notice on the top left-hand side of her screen hadn't wavered.

She stepped out on the tracks and held her phone as high as possible. When she still couldn't get a signal, she dropped it back in her purse and stared at the length of the tracks.

"They filmed that movie out in these parts."

Anna spun around to stare at the lifter. He hadn't moved from where she'd seen him earlier on the tracks, which was about twenty feet from where she now stood.

"And which movie was that?"

"You a Stephen King fan?"

She glanced over her shoulder. Still no train. She turned around to face the man.

"I've read a few of his novels, seen his movies."

"How about the short story called, *The Body*? Ever heard of it?"

Anna shook her head.

"They turned it into a great movie called, *Stand by Me*, which was filmed out here somewhere. This place, these tracks"—he shrugged—"just reminded me of that."

A shiver vibrated her shoulders. The urge to step away from this man made her lift one foot, but she suppressed that urge and gently set her foot back on the wooden railroad tie.

"You sound like a connoisseur of everything Stephen King."

He watched her momentarily, probably trying to assess if she was being sarcastic or offering pleasant conversation.

"I love to read."

He must have decided on pleasant, which was the case.

Then something odd struck her, and she gripped her shoulder bag tighter.

The lifter didn't have a travel bag with him.

She glanced at the junkie. He was bagless, too. The combover guy carried a small backpack, but that was it.

After a brief moment to formulate her thoughts, she faced Lifter.

"No bag? You're traveling rather light. Or is it still on the train we just got booted from?"

He tilted his head slightly to the right, appraising her, then rubbed the back of his neck.

"I travel light. Needed to get out of a situation."

After one more brief look at the others, she said, "So, looks like we have time, and everyone's got a story. What's yours?"

He shook his head and took a couple of steps toward her. "You first."

Familiarity was better than worry. Getting to know the people she was stuck with until the train arrived could work to lower her anxiety. Maybe then she wouldn't be so freaked out by everything unnecessarily.

She glanced down at the railway ties, her eyes glazed over and hoping he couldn't see it in the fading light of the day.

"I'm a hairstylist with a dying mother in California." She glanced up to meet his eyes. He'd moved closer. "That's where I'm headed, to see her."

"I'm sorry to hear that. My name's Rusty Brown. My friends call me Russ."

"Well, I'm happy to meet you under these odd circumstances. I'm Anna Valentina, and my boyfriend —wait, scratch that, my *ex*-boyfriend is a cop."

Russ stopped moving mid-stride. After a moment's hesitation, he slipped his hands in his pockets and stared over her shoulder.

They were still a dozen feet apart, but the change that came over him at the mention of the word *cop* was obvious. His face slackened, shoulders lowered, and there'd been a twitch in his mouth like he was about to say something, then thought better of it.

"You okay?" Anna asked.

He nodded rapidly. "No issue. Just have trouble back home. Asking each other what our stories are got me thinking about it is all."

"Sorry …"

"No need to be. The train should be along soon."

"I'm Jaxon Luke."

Anna jerked sideways and clutched at her chest as the junkie now stood right beside her, his hand extended.

"Geez, lady, I'm sorry." Jaxon rocked his upper body, his hands clasped together as if he was praying.

"It's okay." Anna recovered quickly. "Just didn't hear you approach. I'm Anna."

"Well, I'm pleased to meet you."

They touched hands as if to shake, but Jaxon's grip was non-existent, and his hand was cold and clammy.

"You feeling okay?" she asked.

"Yeah, just don't like it out here. Something's wrong in the air."

"Wrong?" Anna detected Russ moving closer from the corner of her eye. "How so?"

Jaxon stared down the length of the tracks, appearing sad and gloomy.

"The train's not coming."

Those four words made Anna follow Jaxon's gaze along the tracks as the shadows gave way to early evening. Nothing made a sound other than the beating of her heart in her ears. There wasn't even a slight breeze to rustle the leaves on the trees. She held her breath and listened, trying to hold back tears. What had she gotten herself into? Things were moving too quickly. She saw Janine straddling Colton, arms around him, mouth glued to his, then she bolted. She grabbed a bag, packed it, hit the train station, and bought a ticket, and now she was somewhere south of Eugene, probably still in Oregon, all within two hours.

Images of staying the night out here flashed through her mind, and she had to focus on her breathing to keep from hyperventilating, her heartbeat racing now.

"I'd tend to agree." Russ was closer still, no more than five feet from her. Although, for some reason, she felt safer with him closer. His voice was soft, calm. "Not sure if it's coming anytime soon, and without lights out here or any sort of signal that we're here, would the damn thing even stop for us?"

Anna glanced over at the man with the newspaper and the combover. He was on his feet and moving toward them.

"The guy who threw me off." Anna stopped talking, then collected herself and continued. "He said they were alerted about us."

The light dimmed quickly as darkness fell all around them. In the distance, the sun must have dipped behind a mountain because they were bathed in a small amount of light now. Only a tiny white cloud floating overhead still had sunlight on it.

Anna cleared her throat and got ahold of herself. "Should we start walking the tracks?"

"What, like in *Stand by Me*?" Russ snorted. "Not only did they almost get killed running from an oncoming train while crossing a bridge, but they found a body that *did* get hit by the train." He shook his head. "No way. I'm staying right here until that train comes, even if I'm on that platform all night." He pointed at the small wooden deck that led to the little shed.

Coming from the bodybuilder, that was saying something. The rational part of Anna had to agree with him. They should stick together. There was strength in numbers or, rather, strength in his biceps.

"Can anyone tell me what's happening?" Combover had decided to join them. He stepped up beside Jaxon.

Anna pointed at Russ. "This is Russ." She adjusted her arm. "And this is Jaxon. I'm Anna, and we're all waiting for the train to arrive."

"Okay." The man looked at each of them in turn, then added, "I'm Grayson Cooper. Nice to meet you all."

Everyone nodded in his direction as he ran a hand through his thin hair in an attempt to keep the combover in place. The newspaper he'd been reading was clutched under his arm near the pit.

"I understood they said it would be about a ten-minute wait," Grayson said.

Anna nodded, her eyes on the tracks in the distance. "I heard that, too. It's been about twenty minutes, and still nothing."

"I don't like this." Jaxon was rocking his upper body now, head twisting back and forth as if saying no over and over to someone only he could hear.

Anna pulled out her phone and held it up. "If we start walking and use the lights on our cell phones, we could make it back to the Eugene station within a few hours, I'm sure."

In the dying light of day, she caught Russ shaking his head.

"There's no way I'm going back." He spoke those words with such finality that she was sure she was right about him. The man was running from something or someone. Why else was he staring at the train station door so intensely? It made her *need* to know what trouble was left behind in Eugene for him, who was after him.

"Yeah," Jaxon agreed. "Not going back. I got my peeps waiting for me in Los Angeles. Nothing back in Portland for me." He snuck a look at Anna, then averted his eyes.

"So we wait," Grayson said.

She expected him to drop where he was and start scanning the newspaper pages again with his finger, but he didn't.

All four of them stood several feet apart, staring down the length of the tracks that wound north through the Oregon trees, waiting for a train that wouldn't come.

The cold late October evening brushed her skin and made her shiver, churning her stomach. There was a tightening in her chest as she realized what had been bothering her since they'd been dropped off at this substation.

The woods were silent. Not a single bird made a noise. No rodents scampered under the leaves or pine needles on the ground. Not even a plane flew overhead.

There was nothing but the sounds they made.

Worst-case scenarios played through her mind, like spending a night on the ground, staring up at the stars, and waiting for a predator to come out of the woods and eat her.

She glanced left, then right, but now it was so dark she couldn't tell where the trees started and where they ended.

Not being able to see into the trees, though, didn't stop the feeling that they were being watched by something—or multiple somethings.

And she was sure they were being watched.

She could feel it on the back of her neck.

Chapter 5

Colton Asher had no luck at the bus station. He'd checked the schedules, the departures, even the destinations, then asked a couple of dozen people in the terminal if they'd seen Anna, using the current picture on his phone. He spoke with the ticket sellers and a couple of bus drivers, but for all his efforts, he got nowhere.

No one had seen her.

The Eugene train depot was his last stop before getting ready for the night shift and then driving to the police station to clock in. If it wasn't a busy night, he could resume his search to some degree, but that would be limited to the job for twelve hours.

When he pulled in and parked, the train station's parking lot was relatively full. The smell of rainwater still clung to the evening's air from last night's storm. Whenever the wind blew like last night, it made his job more complicated because it set off sensitive alarms in buildings all over town. He'd spent more than half his shift attending false alarms and writing up reports on each one.

If lowlifes had forethought, they'd do their break-ins on those windy nights. Response times lagged up to an hour in some cases, and by the end of their shift, they were leaving some of the alarms unattended, knowing they would be more of the same—false—and knowing the next shift could attend to them.

Colton entered the train station and made his way to the lit-up board showing the expected trains, when they were leaving, and where they were going. Nothing seemed to be headed to the Sacramento area until tomorrow afternoon, so Anna probably didn't use the train. And if she didn't use the train, she'd still be in Eugene. This gave him hope as he could check the local motels before the night was through.

Sacramento had to be her destination if she skipped town. Her mother had leukemia and probably wouldn't make it to Christmas. She also owned a house and had bank accounts, something Anna would have dibs on as an only child. This meant Anna had a place to go and a home to live in without any financial responsibilities. As a hairdresser, she'd find employment by the end of the week.

Race to Sacramento, console her mother at the Wellness Hospice, wait until she dies, then move on with her life far away from her cheating boyfriend— which wasn't exactly true because Colton hadn't *actually* cheated on her. It was Janine who jumped on him, Janine who wrapped her arms around him and forced her lips onto his. Sure, he should have stopped it instantly, but since they were already kissing, several seconds didn't matter, did it? There was no sex, no petting, no tasting each other. Just a prolonged kiss, for fuck's sake. He had no interest in anything further with Janine and would never have fucked her, but Anna *had* to walk in at that precise moment.

A niggling question begged to be asked at the back of his mind. Did Janine plan the whole thing? Everyone knew Janine's ego was huge. She even named her business after herself, Janine's Beauty & Hair.

Maybe that was the whole plan from the start. Call Colton over under a ruse that she wanted to talk about a surprise birthday party for Anna, then call Anna over for some reason. Just as Anna was about to walk in, Janine jumps on Colton and makes it so hot he has to think before resisting, which any man would agree—that's fucking hard with a woman like Janine. She was a knockout, completely fuckable, but not wife material. Whereas Anna was wife material, which is what he wanted—Anna.

Yet, for some reason, she had eluded him all afternoon and evening, and now he was getting worried.

He approached the ticket booth and brought up Anna's picture on his phone. The woman behind the counter seemed quite unimpressed that anyone was approaching for a train ticket. Some people just hated their jobs.

"Excuse me," Colton started, hoping to ease into his questions with a calm, pleasant voice. "I'm a police officer with the Eugene Police Department, and we're looking for this woman here." He pushed the phone through. "Can you tell me if she bought a train ticket recently, like this evening?"

The woman didn't look at him or ask for his ID. She just moved her eyes from the computer screen in front of her and angled her gaze downward to peer at the phone.

Then she nodded slightly. "Yes, she was here."

A flood of relief washed over him. "Oh, thank goodness. Where is she now?"

The woman met his gaze. "Sir, I have no idea where she is. Somewhere south of us, I presume."

"You mean she bought a ticket and is on a train?"

The woman eyed him for a moment like she was deciding how much to tell him or whether she required some legal advice to speak further. He'd heard all kinds of shit on the road, working the night shift.

"She bought a ticket for California—"

"Sacramento, right?"

The woman nodded, her features softening as he proved his worth.

"She got on the train over an hour ago. They'd be approaching Oakland or Sutherlin, maybe even the Roseburg area. They'll pass into the top of California overnight, putting her in Sacramento just after six in the morning."

That was nearing the end of his night shift. Chances are Anna had not called her mother to worry her about them, preferring to give her the news in person. Which meant he could call the hospice and get them to patch him through to Daphne's room, Anna's mother. He could speak with her then, get things sorted out, and be better understood. Anna would believe him and come home. They could be together again and fuck Janine, although not literally.

A sudden lightness came over him, and he blinked several times to avoid the tears welling up at the relief of finding Anna. He'd investigated, and he'd found her. He'd done right by her. She was safe and on her way to visit her mother.

Not only that, he found all this out before his shift started, so now he could concentrate on work and not be stuck visiting random motels all night long.

Maybe he would make detective and surprise them with his bloodhound nose one day.

He profusely thanked the woman behind the Plexiglas, then backed away and ran to his car. There was still time to take an hour's power nap before he needed to get in uniform.

He shook his head while staring off at the darkening sky. Anna was on her way to see her mother. He had been right from the start. That was precisely where he'd thought she'd go.

Maybe that was for the best. They could take a few weeks off and let things cool down, which would give Anna's heart direction.

Colton was sure she'd find her way back to him.

If not, he'd go looking for her.

They were meant to be together, raise that family they'd been talking about. It was everything Anna ever wanted, and now it was all he wanted, too.

They'd be together, after all.
Always and forever.

68

Chapter 6

"Do you feel that?" Anna whispered to Russ.

It was Jaxon who answered. "I feel it."

The guy's voice shook, but Anna suspected it wasn't from fear. He was suffering some sort of withdrawal jitters.

"Yeah, me too." Russ moved closer to her, which didn't bother her one bit now. Her fear of him wasn't as intense as her fear of the unknown in the dark woods surrounding them.

Funny how that worked. Within an hour, the guy she worried about the most was the one she felt the safest with.

The sky darkened further, but it had already descended into a deep gloom where they stood.

"I don't think the train's coming," Grayson said.

She focused on where his voice came from and saw the soft silhouette of his profile. At least he didn't sound worried. She detected something like sorrow in his tone but not worry. Like he was despondent that their train ride was over. It made her consider his story. Where was he going? Who was he meeting, and for what purpose?

A plan was needed. They had to refocus on where

they were and what they would do in the immediate future—like walking all night or sleeping on the grass in shifts so someone could stay awake and fight off wildlife.

"Anyone interested in following the tracks back to Eugene?" When no one answered her right away, she added. "I'm not staying out here all night, that's for sure."

"I vote we wait a little longer." Russ was to her right now. "Didn't they say something about the trains running late? Ours could come along in ten or even twenty more minutes, and debating whether we're staying overnight or walking out of here wouldn't matter."

"True," Jaxon said. "We wait. I mean, at least that's what I'm willing to do."

As they spoke, everyone raised their voices above a whisper until the average volume had been restored. Whatever spooked them from the woods earlier didn't seem to matter to anyone anymore.

"Can we move to the platform then?" Anna tapped the screen of her phone, and after seeing no signal still, she activated the flashlight option. At first, it was so bright after her eyes were used to the pure darkness that she blinked for a moment until her eyes adjusted. "I'm uncomfortable standing on the tracks in the dark, so I'm heading over here."

"Works for me," Grayson said.

She aimed the light to guide her down the slight slope of rocks to the grass, then up onto the small rectangular wooden platform. The three men followed suit until the four of them were standing on the raised wooden area, looking at each other, their faces taking on an eerie *Blair Witch Project* look in the single light of her cell. It made her want to kill the light, but the alternative freaked her out more.

"Now what?" she whispered, more out of nervousness than actually looking for an answer. She was quite aware of *now what* and didn't like any of it. They would have to wait. The train would come, and they'd board it. Or the train wouldn't come, and they would stay the night—her—alone with three strangers.

Another option involved walking the tracks back toward Eugene with however many of them would join her, or at least as far as needed so her phone could jump on a signal and she could call someone for help.

Someone, or did she mean Colton?

The thought of Colton and what he'd done to her —to them—was revolting. She needed to sit down and hold her churning stomach—her *empty* churning stomach. She still hadn't eaten anything and wasn't feeling too good about it.

"Excuse me a moment," she whispered. "I need to sit down."

She raised her phone's light and shuffled over to sit with her back against the shed's wall. Once seated, the three men moved closer to stand near her.

"I'm going to shut this light off to conserve battery."

"Good idea," Russ said.

She hit the button, killed the light, and turned off her phone, but not before checking battery strength. It was sitting at eighty-three percent.

What the hell would she do when it got below ten percent? What would she do when it hit zero and wouldn't turn on?

A thought raced through her mind. In the years when these tracks were built, and people worked out here and camped out here, cell phone technology hadn't existed yet, and those people lived everyday lives. How reliant were we on technology that a cell phone battery's charge sent a shiver of anxiety through someone?

Subconsciously, she placed a hand on her stomach and leaned her head back to stare at the dark sky. The stars were out in full force.

"Wow, can you guys see that?" She pointed with her free hand, but there was no reason to. It was too dark for them to see her hand. "That cluster of stars is the Milky Way, right?"

"I think so," Grayson said from off to her right.

"There's the Big Dipper," Russ added.

She imagined he was pointing at it.

"It's really dark out here," she whispered. "I can't say I've ever been outside in so much darkness."

"Usually, the moon reflects enough light from the sun to guide us a little, but the moon's not up yet." Russ sounded close, which was comforting.

"It will rise soon." Grayson hadn't moved from where he was a moment before. He seemed to be sitting on the platform's edge to her left.

Where was Jaxon?

"You still with us, Jaxon?"

"Yeah." His weak reply came from at least a dozen feet away, back toward the tracks. "You guys smell that?"

Without thinking, Anna inhaled and tried to detect something in the air.

"I got nothing. What are you smelling?"

"I got nothing, too," Russ said.

"I don't know. Something rotten, like burned mushrooms."

"Burned *mushrooms*?" Grayson said, leaning hard on the second word. "Kind of an odd description, isn't it?"

Jaxon cleared his throat. "We're in an odd way, aren't we?"

If there were enough light to see by, Anna and Russ would've exchanged a glance.

This sort of talk wasn't any help in dispelling her anxiety. It only added to it.

"Anyone got the time?" she asked, hoping it had only been twenty minutes or so since they'd been dropped off, but knowing it was more than an hour by now. With each minute they were there, the hope of the train coming to pick them up decreased.

"I don't have a watch, and I don't have a cell phone," Russ said, adding to his mystery. Why wouldn't he carry a cell phone?

"How about you, Jaxon?"

"Same, no watch, no phone."

That made sense. Jaxon probably used any money he got to shoot something up his nose or in a vein. Even though she knew that that sort of thinking was grossly unfair, she couldn't avoid it. One look at the guy and people would declare him a meth head, making her want to know more. Where was he from, where was he going, and how could he afford a train ticket?

"Grayson? You know the time?"

She didn't want to turn her phone back on just for that.

"Who wears watches anymore? I've got a cell phone, but I didn't charge it last night. My phone's in my pocket, but it's dead."

It sounded like Russ sat down beside her. "Don't worry," he said from one foot away. "The train will come whether we know the time or not. Save your cell battery. Don't turn it back on."

There was silence for a few heartbeats, which seemed to make the darkness worse. She couldn't tell if they were alone or not. All she heard was Russ's soft breathing beside her.

"We could sue them, you know?"

"Why? Because the train's late?"

"They shouldn't be allowed to just drop us off in the middle of nowhere at this hour."

"We're not technically in the middle of nowhere. We're in Oregon, maybe an hour south of Eugene by train."

"What do you estimate that is within walking distance?"

"Who knows? Four, five hours, maybe more."

Neither Jaxon nor Grayson had said a word. When they weren't speaking, she had no idea whether they were still with them or not.

She almost laughed at the absurdity of her life now, at the sheer atrocity it had become in such a short time. From a great job with a great man in her life, plans to have children next year, a wonderful place to live, money in her pocket, and food on the table, to have it all ripped away, lost in the Oregonian forest with three men, and no idea how to make it through the night.

If life were a comedy, this was a joke.

If life were serious, this was a tragedy.

Determined to live through it, though, she pushed up off the floor and got to her feet.

"We have to do something. We can't just sit here and wait. I'm hungry and tired, and I want to be *pro*active instead of *re*active. Isn't that what the gurus all say? Be proactive?"

"Yeah, sure." Russ got to his feet beside her. "I'm with you, but I'm not going back to Eugene. There's no way in hell."

His bluntness took her breath away for a moment. What was back in Eugene that he was running from? Since it was probably a topic he wasn't willing to discuss, she asked another question. "Then tell me, why us four? Why would they kick us off the train and leave us here?"

"My name didn't match my ID." Grayson entered the conversation.

After a moment, with Anna thinking about how that bitch back at the train station had spelled her name wrong, she wondered if something so simple could be the case.

"Why would you give them a fake name?" she asked in her most serious tone.

"I was headed to a dentistry convention." If it wasn't dark, Anna envisioned Grayson shrugging here. "I'm embarrassed by it because my colleagues always laugh at me when I go. So, I never give my real name."

Grayson was lying. She wasn't sure how she could tell in the dark, but she could. There was no dentist convention. He was headed somewhere else, like to a gay lover, and he was covering his tracks. Whatever it was, dentistry wasn't part of the picture.

If he was lying about his destination, did that mean he was lying about his cell phone being dead, too?

"How about you, Russ? Did you use your real name?"

He didn't answer right away. No one spoke for almost half a minute. It got to the point that she wondered if Russ had even heard her, but then he cleared his throat.

"I used a fake name, too."

"Dentistry convention for you as well?"

"No, nothing that nice."

She frowned. *Nice?* How the hell could that ever be labeled as nice?

"Then what's your story? I'm sure we'd all like to know."

He waited again before answering. Was he contemplating the truth and how to explain what he was running from, or was he considering a lie?

"I did some bad things in my past ..."

A shiver coursed through Anna. Just when she felt safe with the guy, the truth came out.

"... and now it's coming due."

"Coming due?"

"Yeah, some people are looking for me, and I had to get the hell out of town. They'd have guys waiting at each station if they knew I was on a train. I had to use a fake name."

Then something struck her. "Wait a minute."

"What?" Russ was still very close to her.

"When they asked to see my ticket, they didn't ask me for ID. How would they know my ticket had a spelling error?"

"Maybe you were flagged from the start," Grayson said.

"You mean targeted."

"Depends on how you look at it," Russ added.

"If I was flagged, then it was that ticket booth bitch who did this."

At least the anger rising inside her had warmed her to some degree.

"How about you, Jaxon? Did your ticket have a fake name, too?" When there was no immediate answer, she asked again. "Jaxon? You still with us?"

"Yeah." His reply was weak, and it was from the side of the building that led to the trees.

"Where are you going?" She was so tempted to turn her cell phone on again and light up the area.

"I heard something back here."

A spike of adrenaline laced with fear shot through her stomach, and she had the urge to sit back down.

"What about your name?" she asked.

"I lied, too."

"So, that's it then. Four people with fake names got railroaded, so to speak." She swallowed involuntarily, fear creeping up her backside. It made her want to keep talking. "Why would you use a fake name?"

"Because I'm supposed to take the five thousand bucks my parents gave me and go to rehab. I promised them, and they swore there'd be no more money unless I used it for rehab."

"I'm guessing you didn't go to rehab."

"I didn't. I took the money and ran, but I was heading to Los Angeles to stay with some friends. We'll smoke some weed, but that's it. My buddy's going to get me a job at Universal Studios."

"That's what he said?"

"Yeah, as long as I buy the weed, I'm all set."

Jaxon was still moving, his voice coming from the backside of the platform now, moving toward the trees.

Of all the answers they'd given, she was surprised the junkie's story seemed to be the one that sounded the most truthful. Was everything so fucked up and ass-backward that the junkie could be trusted over the dentist and the lifter?

"Where are you going right now, Jaxon?" she asked. "I can hear your voice moving."

"Something is back here," he said softly. "I'm following the mushroom smell."

"The mushroom smell?" Then she remembered him saying he smelled burned mushrooms. "How can you see where you're going?" She inhaled again, and this time she was sure she smelled something different in the air, something raw like the smell of sautéed mushrooms mixed with something dank, like an underground cellar or a crypt.

"I'm following the light."

This time a chill ran over her skin, raising goosebumps everywhere. She didn't reply for fear her voice would crack.

"What light?" Russ asked, moving forward cautiously.

If she could've hugged him at that moment, she would have, but she couldn't see him.

"The light in the trees straight ahead. It's like a candle burning in a window or the flicker of flames from a fireplace."

To avoid falling off the platform and breaking something useful, Anna pulled out her cell phone and turned it back on. While she waited for it to power up, she remained rooted to the relative safety of the wooden platform.

"Holy shit," Russ whispered from the general area where Jaxon's voice had come from. "He's right. Someone's in the woods."

None of those sentences made her feel especially good. Who the hell would be in the woods in this part of the Earth? No one in their right mind, anyway. Images of horror movies came to her. People lost in the woods and not surviving because they divided their numbers or followed random fires in the trees. No matter how it all played out, this was not a good sign.

Finally, her phone was ready. She typed in her code and saw the battery was at eighty-one percent now.

"Damn it," she whispered, then ran her thumb up the screen to raise the flashlight option and clicked the button. The entire area bloomed with light. From sheer darkness to the light from her phone made her squint again.

All three men stood shoulder to shoulder beside the wooden platform, staring toward the trees.

Without looking at her, Russ waved for her to join them.

Now that she could see, she walked to the platform's edge and hopped down. When she peered into the darkness of the woods, she, too, saw the flame in the distance.

"How far away is that?" she asked.

"A hundred yards," Russ said. "Maybe a bit farther."

They all stared at it, mesmerized. Anna placed a hand over the light to see better in the dark.

"So, what now?"

Russ turned to her. "Well, I, for one, am not going back to Eugene, and waiting here means we may be camping on that platform. I vote we go check it out. You can navigate with your cell's light."

"I'm with you," Jaxon said. "If there's a hotel, I'll pay for the room and dinner with the money my parents gave me."

"Yeah," Grayson echoed. "I'm in. I'd rather not spend the night out here. This place gives me the creeps."

"So." Anna stared at the fire in the distance. "My choice is to join you three or remain here alone in the dark to wait for the train?"

They all turned to look at her.

"Even though I think this is the wrong move," she added.

"Then what's the right move?" Jaxon asked.

She didn't have an answer because she didn't know. And doing something, doing *anything*, was being proactive. Maybe they were right. Perhaps this was a clever play.

"Look, all I'm saying is we're in some sort of a bind, and I have no idea how to fix it—"

"None of us do," Jaxon cut her off.

"But walking into these woods to investigate someone's campfire or whatever the hell that is doesn't feel right when we were told to stay here and wait for the train."

"Do you always do what you're told?" Jaxon's smile looked positively devilish in the light of her cell phone.

"Well, no …"

Russ stepped closer. "I think what he's trying to say is we have to check it out. If it's nothing, we walk right back here and wait until morning. Besides, you were saying we have to be proactive. This is us being proactive."

Using her argument against her was just like a man. But it did make sense. What harm could there be from checking it out? Someone was obviously there. Someone had to have lit that fire. Maybe they'd have a phone. Or maybe her cell would pick up a signal in another area of these woods.

"Okay, you're right. Let's stick together. We check it out. Then if it amounts to nothing, we come back. Deal?"

Grayson and Jaxon moved away, already starting for the trees, their agreement to what she said left to be construed by their actions. Russ turned to follow them, and Anna held up her phone to shine the light ahead for them to see.

After a few feet, Russ glanced back over his shoulder at her.

"Why did you give a fake name on your ticket?"

he asked.

"I didn't. The woman just typed it in wrong. And no one would know my name was spelled wrong as they didn't check my ID."

"Hmmph." He spun back around to face forward.

That response made her think he didn't believe her. So, everyone was lying, and they all thought the others were lying. If she was going to spend the night with these guys, it was starting off on the wrong foot.

But that wasn't what startled her with each step.

It was that burned mushroom smell. The deeper into the trees they went, the stronger it got.

And with that smell came something dangerous.

She was so sure of it. She could taste it as much as smell it now.

Chapter 7

PRESENT DAY ...

Trooper Richard Logan took a seat at the back of the hospital room as two FBI agents spoke with the doctor. Sergeant Lambert requested their presence. She asked for their involvement due to the odd situation involving Anna Valentina's disappearance and the missing police officer from Eugene, Colton Asher.

They had talked to Trooper Logan for over an hour before coming to the hospital. They wanted as much of a picture of Anna Valentina's situation as possible, including every detail he encountered when he found her in the bush.

Logan explained how he knew Officer Colton Asher and had seen him at the train station the other day, but he hadn't seen him since. His relationship with Officer Asher was a professional one only, but he didn't think he was capable of beating Anna. He had never met Asher's girlfriend, Anna Valentina, the woman in the hospital bed.

Doctor Webber moved to the side of the room to check his computer screen while Special Agent

Matthews and Carlson moved to either side of Anna's bed.

With Matthews being female, Logan overheard them say she would take the lead on the questions directed at Miss Valentina.

The doctor nodded at them to go ahead. His patient was ready.

Agent Matthews leaned over the bed, and in a soft voice, she asked, "Anna, are you awake?"

There was no response.

"Anna?"

Still no response.

Agent Carlson glanced over his shoulder to Doctor Webber. "You lowered the dosage, right? Shouldn't she be waking up now?"

The doctor checked something on his computer. "She will wake soon. Give her time."

"Anna?" Matthews tried again.

Logan watched Anna's eyes, but they weren't moving. Even her fingers didn't twitch.

"Remember," the doctor said. "When she does wake, don't overwhelm her. She might only have five minutes in her before she dozes off again."

"We understand," Carlson said a bit too harshly.

Logan frowned, but the agents weren't looking at him. And he wasn't about to say anything as he was invited as a guest, the closest Anna had to family in this area as he knew her missing boyfriend.

"This is my patient." The doctor moved to the end of Anna's bed, his back to Logan now. "I'm allowing this against my better judgment due to the peculiar circumstances of this unique situation, so don't give me attitude. If I deem anything harmful to my patient, I stop this interview, and you can come back in a week."

Carlson gave the doctor a rough look like he was snarling at the man. "We have an officer missing, Doctor. If she knows anything about that, we need to know about it immediately. Not today, not tomorrow, or *next week*. We need to know yesterday. So, let's all act like professionals and get our jobs done."

The doctor crossed his arms. "You have your job to do, and I have mine. Cross me, and I take charge here. Just monitor yourselves accordingly."

Carlson looked away. "Duly noted."

"Anna?" Matthews murmured close to Anna's ear.

The woman in the bed didn't stir.

"It's no use," Carlson whispered after fifteen minutes. "We'll have to come back."

The FBI agents looked at each other over Anna's sleeping form, nodded, then moved away from the bed.

"Looks like you got your wish," Carlson said as they headed toward the door.

When the door closed behind them, the doctor moved back to his screen and made a few notes.

Logan stared at Anna on the bed. What had happened to her? What had she endured in those woods? Who could've beaten her that badly? Could it really be the same girl in the missing persons report?

Or could two unrelated people have the same fingerprints?

He rose from his chair, stretched, and moved closer to the bed. Sedated, sleeping in a near coma state, Anna Valentina looked peaceful—actually, calling her peaceful was a stretch. She was covered in small bandages, bruised all about the face and neck, her lips were swollen, and one of her eyes was poorly swollen but still usable. They'd sponge-bathed her, but the bruises, cuts, and missing teeth made it look like several bulls had run over her in Pamplona.

Something drew his eye downward. Did Anna's finger move?

"Doctor?" Logan whispered.

The doctor glanced over at him. Logan pointed at Anna's hands.

Her right index finger moved again.

"I think she's waking up."

The doctor got to his feet and moved closer. Sure enough, Anna's hand tightened into a fist, then released.

"Is she dreaming?"

The doctor shook his head. "Waking."

Anna's eyelids fluttered moments later.

The doctor moved up beside her head and leaned over. "Anna, I'm Doctor Webber. How are you feeling?"

Her eyes blinked, then shut, then blinked again. She moaned deep in her throat. Probably all the pain was doing that to her. Logan wondered how much morphine the doctor had her on.

Once her eyes adjusted to the room's soft light, she opened them to slits.

Anna was awake.

She mumbled something incoherent, probably from the drugs they had her on. Logan moved around the other side of the bed, still in uniform.

"Anna, I'm Trooper Richard Logan. I'm the one who responded to the call to bring you here."

Her eyes found him but didn't seem to be able to focus.

"How are you feeling?" Logan asked.

Her mouth opened, shut, then opened again, her bottom lip quivering. At least the chalky white shit on her lips was gone as the IVs did their jobs. She had regained some of her color as well.

She muttered something unintelligible.

He had a responsibility to go and get those two FBI agents, but he didn't want to quite yet. This was something he wanted to hear for himself. They could wait ten or fifteen more minutes, then conduct their investigation from there. He had found her, the first responder, so he got to hear what she said first.

She closed her eyes, her mouth working but saying nothing.

A tear slipped past her eyelids, falling to the pillow.

Logan and the doctor exchanged a glance.

Then Anna blinked and spoke again. This time Logan made out every word, but her voice grated like she'd been screaming at a rock concert all night.

"We should have ignored the fire," she whispered.

"The fire?" Logan said, not remembering any forest fire in the area. "What fire, Anna?" He leaned closer. "Who did this to you? Was it Colton? Is that why you had his driver's license in your pocket?"

"We should never have been drawn to the fire. It was evil, pure evil." She cried now, wiping at her tears with shaky hands. "The fire in the cabin. I can't believe that's how it all started."

"Okay," the doctor whispered. "I think that's enough for now. You sleep a bit longer, Anna. We'll be here when you wake."

Anna nodded, lowering her hands to her sides as the doctor approached Logan's side of the bed.

"She said 'the fire in the cabin,'" Dr. Webber said. "Mean anything to you?"

Logan shook his head. "Nothing."

Webber nodded. "When she wakes again and is ready to be questioned, I'll inform you all. But don't expect it until at least tomorrow."

"Those agents won't like that. Officer Asher is still missing."

"I'll see what I can do, but the patient's health is my priority, not their investigation."

"Understood. I'll let them know."

Logan left the room in search of the agents. He planned on telling them what Anna said and adding that she only wanted to talk to Logan, even though that was a lie.

He wanted to be a part of this case until completion, even if he had to lie to get what he wanted.

He had to have something to tell his wife when he went home tonight.

And this story was going to be a doozy.

Chapter 8

THREE DAYS BEFORE PRESENT Day ...

The woods were thick, the ground soft and pliable under her feet. It was slow going for the most part, and not just due to the treacherous terrain of tall grass and thick trees close together. The darkness played a significant role in making them take each step carefully, waving hands in front of their faces to ensure an errant branch didn't take out one of their eyes.

Step by step, the four of them meandered through the trees with minor scrapes and no twisted ankles, which Anna was grateful for as she didn't want Russ to have to be carrying anyone out of there. Russ was the strongest and needed to be their first line of defense if her worries about danger came true.

As they drew closer to the fire that beckoned them, it changed its shape somehow. Well, she wouldn't exactly call it *shape*. More like it changed how it appeared to them.

When they were twenty yards from it, Anna finally understood why it looked different. The fire was inside a building, and they saw it through a low-framed living room window, to be exact. From a distance, all they saw was the light of the fire. Closer to it, the glass gave it an odd perception, like looking at the light through a prism.

Russ hissed for Grayson and Jaxon to stop. Anna slowed to a stop behind them and rubbed warmth into her arms. She certainly hadn't dressed well enough to spend the night in the woods, and her carry-on was becoming a nuisance. She'd switched it two times so far, but both shoulders ached now.

The entire time they moved away from the train tracks, she had cocked an ear, listening for the train's arrival, even glanced over her shoulder several times in search of the engine's single headlight, but she saw and heard nothing behind them.

Even though they'd trudged through the underbrush slowly, she panted for air, feeling out of breath and covered in sweat, which caused the chills.

"I think it's a cabin or something," Russ whispered.

"Looks like it." Jaxon's voice came out jittery. The temperature was working on those raw nerves of his.

"So, we recon the place."

"Recon?" Anna stared at the area where she could barely discern Russ's face in the bit of light coming from the cabin.

"Yeah, they use it in the military. It just means check the place out front and back before knocking."

"Were you in the military?" Anna set her carry-on

down to give her shoulders a rest.

"Why does that matter?"

"I'm just asking because you said recon."

"What, only military types can use that word?"

"Whoa, where's the attitude coming from? That's not what I'm saying at all—"

"Hey," Grayson snapped. "We shouldn't fight with each other."

"We weren't fighting," Anna snapped back. "Just asking for Russ to check his attitude."

No one spoke for a moment.

That mushroom smell had decreased to a tolerable level—or had she just gotten used to it? Either way, she was sensing her emotions on the rise. Anger at being in this crazy situation, paranoia at what was out there beyond the darkness, concern for their safety, and most of all, fear at what was coming next.

They had to be feeling it, too.

Would she spend the night on the forest floor, wrapped in pine needles, curled in the fetal position? Would she end up back at the train platform or inside the cabin? Or worse, which she suspected—attacked by someone, raped, or killed—or raped and then killed? What had she gotten herself into?

Whatever it was, none of this was Russ's fault.

"I'm sorry," she whispered to him. "I'm just feeling a bit temperamental at the moment."

"Me too." Russ moved closer. "I'm sorry, too. No harm meant, no harm done. Now, let's divide into two groups, then walk around the cabin to meet at the front."

"Wait, we shouldn't split up." Anna crossed her arms. This was where she drew the line.

"Anna, we won't be apart long, and if either group encounters anything dangerous, the others are literally right there."

She barely detected him pointing at one side of the cabin.

"Fine, but I don't like this."

"Who does?" Jaxon said from the darkness to her left.

"Who goes with who?" Russ said.

"You and Anna," Grayson whispered. "Jaxon and me."

"Deal." Russ touched her arm, and she resisted the urge to jump away. "We'll go right. You guys go left. See you out front."

Gently, he tugged her forward, and she yanked her arm free this time.

He spun back. "What?"

"One second. My bag." She grabbed her carry-on, shouldered it, and started after him.

A branch cracked, and someone whispered something on her left as Grayson and Jaxon worked their way through the bush toward the cabin. Russ was smoother as he calculated each step, easing branches out of the way and holding them for her.

She wondered what he'd done in his past and what he was running from. A woman? A biker gang? The police? Whatever it was, the man feared what awaited him back in Eugene.

She already had a healthy fear of what they were dealing with, but she still hadn't determined if she should be afraid of him, too.

Everyone had lied back at the tracks in one way or another, and she was sure they had their reasons, especially because they were all strangers and nobody was *owed* the truth, but the circumstances were different out here. If there was indeed something in these woods that was dangerous, then their lives depended on each of them pulling through in some way to make it out of there, and lying wasn't the best place to start.

The question about honesty on the tip of her tongue, she moved closer to Russ, then stopped.

They'd broken through the trees and had stepped onto a weedy area at the back of the house.

Bent at the waist, Russ touched her arm again and moved close to her ear.

"Stay behind me. If anything weird happens, run for the trees and don't look back."

"You expecting something to happen?"

"No, but I don't like this, and if something were to happen, I wouldn't like it more if you got hurt. Understood?"

She nodded, then realized he probably couldn't see her well enough to see her nod, so she said, "Yes, understood."

"Follow me."

Russ started up the side of the house, staying

close to the outer wall. This late at night, their eyes fully adjusted to the darkness; the tiny bit of light from the stars allowed her to navigate okay in the open space by the house. The wall was a darker shadow against the night, the stars blocked by the roof's edge about twelve feet above her head.

Someone was here, that much was for sure—the fire in the fireplace didn't start itself. But would that someone be receptive to four strangers circling their cabin in the dark and then knocking on the door? And for what? To use their phone? Have a bite to eat?

As they approached the front corner, something struck her as odd. Where were the interior lights? Actually, where were the lights in general?

The area appeared void of electricity, as dark as a campsite in the center of the wilderness.

Nothing about this was good, making her stomach knot heavier with worry and hunger.

Russ stopped at the corner and peeked around to the front of the cabin. Then he put a hand near her face and waved her to follow him.

After Russ moved around the corner, she stepped up and came in behind.

Jaxon and Grayson were already standing out front.

They sidled up beside them.

"What do you make of that?" Russ asked.

There was enough light from the fireplace coming through the open front door of the cabin that they could see each other easily now.

"Letting in a breeze?" Grayson said.

Russ shook his head. "It's an invitation."

"Not for us," Anna said in a hushed whisper. "No one knew we were coming."

"Or did they?"

A fresh adrenaline rush washed over her abdomen, making her want to run from this place. Everything in her soul, everything she'd seen in the movies, caused a chant in her head that was shouted over and over.

Run! Run! Run!

But she didn't run because that would mean she'd be alone in the woods. And how fast could she run with her carry-on weighing her down?

"I'll knock." Russ moved forward, then stopped when Jaxon pulled him back.

"You sure, bud?"

Russ glanced down at Jaxon's hand on the inside crook of his elbow until Jaxon removed his hand. Then he looked up at Jaxon.

"Yes, I'm sure."

Russ took the front two steps cautiously. Standing in front of the cabin's open door, he said, "Hello?"

There was no response.

Anna suppressed the urge to step back, keeping her feet planted on the overgrown grass while she watched Russ move two more steps to the door and knock on the wooden paneling to the right of it.

Anna stopped breathing to wait for a response from inside the cabin, but none came.

Russ turned to them and shrugged, his hands out at the side.

"Who are you lot?" a man asked.

A short scream slipped from Anna's mouth at the sound of the man's voice behind them. Jaxon jumped so high he staggered and almost dropped to his butt. Grayson yipped like a little girl and grabbed at Anna.

She was able to stay on her feet while spinning around at the voice.

It was Russ who took action right away. She'd turned to stare at the man holding the rifle when Russ jumped off the front steps of the cabin and moved in front of her.

From the man's age, it looked like he struggled to hold the rifle in place, but there was something in his eyes that was on fire.

"Where did ya come from?" he asked, gesturing with the rifle. "You trying to break into my place?"

"We were dropped off at the train station," Russ said calmly, his hand raised in front of him. "We mean you no harm."

"Then what's yous out here for in the middle of the night trying to enter my home if you mean me no harm?"

"We saw the fire." Russ stopped. "Look, we'll leave. We were stranded and thought you'd have a phone, a place to stay, who knows. But don't worry. We'll leave."

The old man eyed them a few moments more, then lowered the weapon, put the butt in the dirt, and leaned on the barrel.

"Yous need a place to stay?"

Russ nodded. "At least until the morning until we can sort out the trouble with the trains."

"I don't know nothing about no trains, but just over there is the old barracks."

"Old barracks?"

"They tried to turn it into a motel of sorts. I think the younguns call it a hostel."

Anna glanced to the right but saw nothing in the dark.

"You're wondering about electricity." The man stated it without the voice inflection of a question. "There ain't none. We all live in these parts on our own. No lights, no bills, no government."

"Okay, uhm, great. And you're saying the barracks is over there." Russ pointed to the right.

The old man grabbed his rifle. "I'm going in to bed." He nodded the way Russ had pointed. "Just follow this path. It'll take you to the barracks. Someone will set you up. Last I heard, there's no charge."

The man moved past them and up the front steps of his cabin.

"No charge?" Grayson repeated. "How's that?"

The old man turned back to face them. "We don't get visitors in these parts; when we do, we're hospitable. Go on up to the barracks, and you'll see why."

The man spun around, stepped inside his cabin,

and shut the door.

The four of them regrouped in a huddle.

"I vote we head back to the train platform." Anna glanced over her shoulder, but the cabin door remained closed. "Something is wrong here, very wrong. And if the train arrives, we'd never make it back in time running through those woods."

"Anna, the train's not coming." Russ's voice had taken on an edge.

"You okay?"

"Yeah, I just don't like people jumping out of the trees and pointing rifles at me."

"Who does?"

"Look," Jaxon said, even more jittery if that was possible. "I'm going to this barracks motel thing. Then in the morning, I walk to the highway, where I'll hitch a ride to a bus station. Fuck the train."

"I'm with you," Grayson said. They moved away before Grayson turned back. "You guys coming?"

"One sec," Russ said before facing her. "So, what's the plan now?"

"Everything here stinks, and I'm not just talking about the smell. Something's wrong here. I can feel it."

"You know what's wrong, what you're feeling?"

"No, tell me."

"It feels wrong because you're not used to it. If I told you to walk through the woods in an unknown area in the dark with three strangers—men—you'd be weirded out. Doing it without notice has to feel off in some way. But here we are, and it's not just you. All of us are weirded out right now. So, I vote we stick together and go to this barracks thing. In the best-case scenario, we get a room and sleep well, then leave in the morning. Worst case scenario, it's a joke, and we leave and head back to the train platform until morning. That work for you?"

Grayson and Jaxon were still waiting for them. Russ implored her with his eyes or what little she could see of them.

"Fine, but we're out of here at the first sign of danger."

"At the first sign of danger."

She allowed herself to be led forward, away from the cabin with the old man and his rifle, deeper into the trees toward something called the old barracks.

What the hell did that mean? Was this an old US military installation? Had a bunch of hippies or some commune—or worse, a cult—taken over the place?

She had no idea what they were walking into, but something told her the anxiety she was feeling had little to do with the oddity of the situation and more to do with instinct.

Her gut feeling, the hunch that something was wrong, had been trusted in the past. Yet, tonight she was going against it.

And she was sure her defiance would cost her more than an inconvenience.

She looked up at the stars and asked herself, *what the hell am I doing?*

Chapter 9

WAS SHE EVER GOING to get to her mother in Sacramento? How was this helping her in any way? Maybe the answer wasn't to resist it so much. To go with the flow, and see what happens, even though that wasn't her thing. She was the kind of person that made plans and scheduled things. That's why they talked about kids and raising a family. They were planning something. That's also why she pushed the trip to Sacramento up a week when she saw Colton and Janine together. She'd already scoped out the tickets, knew the route, and was ready to go.

So, she kept walking along the path in the trees, even though it felt like they were being watched again. Or was that a universal feeling one gets in the woods at night?

Something rustled in the trees to their left as soon as she thought that.

All four of them stopped, their hands up in some fashion of defense. Some were out at their sides, whereas Russ's were up in front, like a boxer.

"What was that?" Anna asked.

"No idea, but I'm not sticking around to find out." Russ started moving again, and the others followed.

She prayed for light, wondering why she couldn't be traipsing around the Oregon woods with a full moon.

It wasn't difficult to follow close because they weren't moving quickly. The area was easier to traverse as they weren't in the middle of the woods anymore. The ground was hard-packed, and she could even see where it was worn in spots from continued use.

That rustling sound tracked them, keeping pace on their left. Feelings of rage surfaced as she wanted to shout at whatever it was for making her feel threatened. What the hell had they gotten themselves into? The better question was, what the hell had *she* gotten herself into?

Up ahead, a building stood out of the darkness.

The barracks.

From what she gathered in the small amount of light from the moon, it was two stories high, and from the reflection of the stars on the glass panes, both levels were lined with windows.

"Looks like we found it," she mumbled.

"Shhh," Russ whispered back at her.

"Why? Whatever's out there already knows we're here. What does it matter?"

Russ stopped moving, and she nearly bumped into him. He grabbed her and made her face the barracks. The man was so strong she felt like a puppet in his hands.

"*They* don't know we're here yet. And since we

don't know them, we should meet with them unaware of our approach. At least at first." He released her. "Understand?"

Anna brushed off her arms where he'd held her and nodded. "Yeah, sure, this is your show."

That mushroom smell was more intense near the barracks building, but it wasn't appearing to bother any of the others.

Anna scanned their surroundings but saw nothing other than darkness and more darkness. She could determine where the tops of the trees stopped and the night sky started, but that was it.

A metallic knock brought her back to the present.

All three men were at an entrance door twenty feet away when she spun around.

So much for sticking together.

They knocked again, and while waiting, she tried her cell phone. When she pulled it out and hit the power button, she cursed to herself. She'd forgotten to power it down, and now the battery was at seventy-four percent.

She held it over her head and waited for the phone to find a signal, but nothing came. The same NO SERVICE notice sat in the corner where it usually said T-MOBILE.

"Anna, c'mon," Russ said. "Someone's coming."

She powered down the phone this time, slipped it in her pocket, and moved to stand with her fellow stowaways—at least, that's how it was starting to feel since they were tossed off the train.

There was even enough light with the sliver of a moon that had come up over the edge of the tree line to see where they were going. She strode across the last twenty feet to the front of the barracks-turned-motel without looking over her shoulder. With each step, though, she had the feeling of being tracked. Something malicious and hungry had followed them. She was sure of it. Nothing obvious stood out for her to claim this fact other than her gut. It was just something she *knew*.

By the time she reached Russ and the other two, the sound of the door unlocking from the inside came to her. Someone was opening it.

"Good evening," a man said in a deep baritone voice.

Those two words reminded Anna of old Dracula movies, and she almost burst out laughing. From the train to the fire in the cabin to this—what next? Would he quote songs like *Hotel California* and say something about how they could check out, but they could never leave?

"Hello." Russ stepped between Grayson and Jaxon. "We understand you may have a few rooms for the night."

Anna looked past them to the man on the other side of the door. He held a candle up before him, which cast his visage in a ghastly light. He looked as if he was ninety years old, frail, and unwell. How the hell was he even standing?

"We have plenty of room here," the man said, his

tone strong, firm. If she hadn't been able to see him, he would've sounded like a thirty-year-old.

What was this place in the middle of the woods? It had the stirrings of a cult.

Or maybe it was some old person's commune in the bush that was friendly to strangers. Or *not* friendly, which remained to be seen.

The old man with the candle had turned and started away from them.

Without question or discussion, Grayson and Jaxon followed the guy inside.

Russ glanced back at her and shrugged. "Looks like we found a place to sleep." Then he entered the barracks, leaving the door ajar for her.

There was no way she was staying outside all alone tonight.

Anna stepped inside the building and eased the door closed.

Once inside, she rubbed her nose. That pungent mushroom smell seemed to be everywhere. Why was no one questioning it? Was this group of old people perpetually burning something toxic that gave off the scent of cooked mushrooms? If so, they'd been moving closer to the source all night.

Her stomach rumbled with hunger, and her legs were weak from the walking and adrenaline, but she followed the flickering candlelight down the hallway and into a small room.

"Can you tell us about this place?" Russ asked.

"We like to keep to ourselves." The man eyed

them, then fixed his gaze on her when she entered the room. "Please, we are a quiet people. Stay the night, perhaps two, then you're welcome to leave. Just don't recommend us."

Russ laughed like it was a joke while the old man's face remained stoic.

"When strangers pass through, we have no issue with cordiality, the keywords being *pass through*."

Anna moved closer. "Can you tell us what was tracking us back there? Like, what animals live in these woods?"

The old man's head rose a notch. "Tracking you?"

"There was something in the bush on our way here. It moved with us."

"We don't recommend much movement in the dark around here."

"And why's that?" Grayson looked white in the light of the candle.

"There are predators out in them woods. Things that eat humans, like cougars and mountain lions. Best if you all stay inside for the night, then carry on your wayward ways."

"How much you gonna charge for four rooms for the night?" Jaxon asked, sounding tired of the conversation or just tired in general.

The old man chuckled briefly. "Sir, we don't charge for a night's stay. Please, follow me. Pick any room you like. As I said, we're a humble bunch and prefer to be left alone."

"Then why would you help us?" Russ asked the

question on Anna's mind, his tone friendly like he genuinely wanted to know.

"We'd rather offer you shelter for the night than send you back outside to be slaughtered by something wild and hungry. We're not heartless, young man."

Anna couldn't suppress the chill that swept over her this time as she followed them all down a long corridor. The way the man was talking sounded like they were lucky to be alive as they'd just come in from that dangerous wilderness he was referring to.

Everything was beyond strange, and nothing was adding up. The two men they'd met tonight offered strange answers to their questions. There was no cell coverage, no electricity, and they wouldn't accept money for a night's stay. What was she missing? Or was she too tired and hungry to figure it out?

From the scrape of their heels, Anna could tell the hallway hadn't been swept in some time. It made her wonder about the cleanliness of the rooms.

She shivered involuntarily when the old man stopped and raised an arm to point along the hall.

"There is a row of doors along this corridor. Choose any one and spend the night. Feel free to leave at any time. Good evening." He placed the candle in a holder on the wall and then turned away.

Anna glanced down the length of the tunnel-like passageway. When she spun back to the old man, he was gone.

"Wait, where did he go?"

"What?" Russ turned back to her.

"That old man. Where did he go?"

"Who knows? That way, I guess." He pointed back the way they'd come. "Free rooms and no one knows where we are." Russ grinned, his teeth white in the candlelight. "I might stay several nights before I continue south."

"Yeah, I could get used to this," Jaxon echoed from farther down the hall.

Grayson said nothing as he tried one of the doors.

Anna opened the door to her right without another word, but when she glanced into the room, she couldn't see a thing.

"Guys, there's nothing here," Russ said, his voice echoing in the corridor.

Anna snatched the candle from the holder and raised it at the door to her room.

The room was square, a bit larger than a walk-in closet, and completely barren.

"What the hell?" she whispered.

"Sure beats sleeping in the bush," Russ said from behind her, sounding resigned. "And whatever's out there that might eat us, remember?"

He pulled away from her. A moment later, a door closed, then another, then one more.

Anna was left alone in her room, the candle still burning in her hand.

She set it down and moved to the window.

The moon had changed positions in the sky, but it still didn't offer much in the way of light. As her eyes adjusted to the near-total darkness outside, something moving directly in the middle of the clearing caught her attention.

She squinted, trying to better understand what she was looking at.

There was just enough light to see the tops of their heads and the basic outline of their bodies.

It looked like four men standing side by side, roughly thirty feet away in front of the barracks. After a few moments of them talking, evident by how their heads moved from time to time, they dispersed, each moving in another direction.

It was apparent everyone in this commune-like place knew they had visitors.

What was not obvious was what they intended to do with their visitors.

And why the hell didn't that question freak the hell out of the others?

She set her bag on the floor to use as a pillow, laid down on her back, crossed her arms over her chest, and waited for the sun to filter through the window.

When morning hit, she'd be out of this hell town of a commune before anyone knew what had happened.

Her eyes closed, she focused on her breathing, intent on staying awake until daybreak.

She was asleep five minutes later.

Chapter 10

PRESENT DAY ...

The rain covered his windshield as fast as his wipers could wipe it off, making Logan lean forward in his seat to better see where he was going. He'd gotten the call from Sergeant Lambert that some sort of power struggle was taking place at the hospital and that he was required to attend. Apparently, there would be people in the lobby waiting for him.

She hung up before he could ask for more information, but that was usual for Kat. She believed in brevity. Say her piece, get off the phone, call someone else, speak fast, and hang up again. Unless he was standing right beside her, she never chit-chatted.

Logan pulled into the hospital parking lot thirty minutes after he got the call. His shift had started at seven that morning, and Kat called him ten minutes in. It was now creeping up on eight in the morning, and he was about to delve deeper into the Anna Valentina and Colton Asher case whether he wanted to or not.

His curious side was quite interested, but there was something strange or even supernatural about this case that scared the bejeezus out of him, making him think it was better off left alone.

But duty called, and here he was.

He parked close to the emergency doors but not close enough for this rain. Even running to gain entry to the hospital, he'd be as soaked as if he'd gone swimming in his uniform.

Logan glanced up at the clouds to see if there would be a break soon, even though he knew he was delaying the inevitable.

Last night, when he got home and told his wife what had happened to Anna and how the FBI sent a couple of agents over to interview her, she leaned on the side of not believing him about the aging thing since that wasn't possible. Ultimately, she told him she believed what he saw with his own eyes but that there had to be a reasonable explanation.

His gut told him otherwise.

Something happened in those woods that he didn't understand, and whatever it was, aged Anna and took Officer Colton Asher. He hoped they found him soon, too.

The rain pounded the roof of the cruiser without letup.

He glanced at the clock, then decided to run for it.

Hat in hand, he jumped out of the cruiser, slammed the door behind him, and ran for the front doors.

Water soaked through the shoulders of his uniform and ran down the back of his neck.

He shivered when he stepped inside the cool entrance, goosebumps rising on his arms. Once his hat was firmly on his head, he glanced around the lobby, wondering who awaited him.

Several people lingered in chairs near the window. A man and a woman spoke with a doctor near two large admittance doors, and two men dressed in military fatigues sipped coffees while speaking with a nurse.

No one looked at him or moved his way, so he strode up to the woman sitting behind Plexiglas with a sign that read INFORMATION.

"I'm here to see Dr. Webber." He chose Webber because he didn't want to ask for either FBI agent from yesterday.

She nodded, then typed something on her computer.

Someone moved closer to him on his right. He glanced up to see the military guys staring at him now.

"Trooper Richard Logan?" the taller man on the right said, his voice rough, gravelly, probably from years of running a boot camp.

Logan nodded. "And you are?"

"I'm Command Sergeant Major George Miles, and this is Sergeant Major Bruce Atkins."

They shook hands. "Pleased to meet you, gentlemen. How can I help you?"

Atkins gestured to where several potted plants lined a side window.

"Let's talk over there."

Logan followed the men to the relatively private area. Why was the military here for a missing persons case? Couldn't the FBI handle this one? He had so many questions piling up in his head about government experiments gone awry and top-secret shit that led to coverups that he wondered if something would happen to him. Was that what this was all about? Were they going to quiz him on what he knew or saw?

Atkins and Miles stared at him for a moment, sizing him up. What the hell was going on with the intense scrutiny?

Then Miles cleared his throat. "We've taken over the Anna Valentina file."

"I'm curious why that is," Logan said before he could censor himself. "I mean, isn't it a missing persons case?"

"It's not that simple."

Logan pressed his lips together and rocked on his feet. How far would he push back before they shoved him off this case? "Well, that's where I'm confused. She was missing, and now she's found. Case closed."

The men exchanged a glance, then looked back at Logan.

"We want to formally request your help on this case for reasons we can't divulge yet."

He nearly staggered on his feet but was able to hold himself together. Those words were completely unexpected.

"Why's that?" This was a poker face moment if

he ever had one. He wanted to stay on the case but didn't want to appear too eager.

"Well, Trooper, we can't tell you anything until you sign a non-disclosure agreement. Would you be willing to do that?"

Logan looked from one man to the other, then nodded. "I'll sign."

"Great, then follow us."

Miles and Atkins led him to the elevators. While heading up to the third floor, he shivered with the cold as his wet shirt clung to him.

Once off the elevator, they moved along the hospital hallway, skirting around slow-moving patients and nurses.

Anna's room was easy to see as it came up on the left because two men in army fatigues stood on either side of the door, guarding the entrance.

Miles and Atkins strode right past it, all four men saluting one another.

Three doors down, Atkins opened the door to a private office. It looked like they had taken over a high-ranking doctor's office for whatever purpose brought the military here.

Miles moved to the window while Atkins grabbed a black briefcase and set it on the desk. He cracked it open, then removed a small stack of papers and put them on the desk with a resounding thump.

"Feel free to read them thoroughly, but they basically say that everything you learn, say, or do regarding this case is the property of the United States

Government. You are to speak to no one about this case in any capacity. That includes your colleagues at the station, your superiors, friends and relatives, and even your wife. Is that clear?"

What the hell was this? He told his wife everything, even if he wasn't supposed to. He could trust her. Whether they believed that or not, he didn't care. He'd sign whatever they wanted him to sign because now he *needed* to know what the hell was going on. And he couldn't wait to get home to tell Beverly all about this.

He sat on the other side of the desk, pulled his pen from his breast pocket, and started scanning the document. The letterhead was from Homeland Security. The document referenced how the US Army Criminal Investigation Command (CID) was investigating Anna's disappearance and went on with all the usual NDA mumbo jumbo. There were a few penalties for violating the directives set therein, but Logan didn't need to concern himself with that as he wouldn't speak about any of this to anyone except his wife.

With the pen in hand, he paused. "Why me?"

They stared at him, both men standing with their hands behind their backs, their military clothing looking sharp in the light of the doctor's office.

Miles nodded down at the document. "Unfortunately, we can't discuss anything further without your signature, Trooper Logan."

"So, you're saying you can't tell me why the

military is involved? It's a missing persons case where we found the woman beaten up and her boyfriend is still missing. Sure, she's aged in some weird way, but this looks like a domestic if I've ever seen one."

He watched them a moment more, both men immovable statues. This whole top-secret stuff wouldn't scare him off. It wasn't a case of he *wanted* to know. Now he *needed* to know.

They waited him out, so he signed the documents and handed them back to Atkins, who slipped the papers back inside the briefcase, locked it, then placed it behind the desk.

"You were the one who arrived on the scene before your sergeant, is that correct?" Miles asked.

Logan nodded. "Yes, sir."

"And you were in the hospital room yesterday when Anna spoke?"

His stomach dropped a notch, the weight feeling like knots tightening.

"That's correct."

"Both FBI agents weren't present?"

"They were not."

"Good, then we've been able to control the information so far."

"Control the information, sir?" What the hell were they talking about?

"The US Military has taken over this investigation, and we're happy to have you on board. You and Dr. Webber will be the only two civilians involved from this point forward. Sergeant Katrina

Lambert has been notified that we are commandeering your services for an indefinite period of time. Your government will handsomely reward you."

"I see, but why me?"

"Because Miss Anna Valentina refuses to tell us anything unless you are present. We need you, Mr. Logan."

He tilted his head to the side as his muscles stiffened. Not wanting to sound surprised, he said, "I'm not sure I understand."

"Miss Valentina woke up this morning and asked for you specifically. Since we had taken over this case, we contacted Sergeant Lambert and requested your presence. Now that you've signed the NDA, we can all move into Miss Valentina's room and learn more about what happened to her."

Logan got to his feet. "I'm happy to help, sir, but I still don't understand why Anna would ask for me specifically. I didn't know her before she went missing."

"We are unsure as well, Logan, but perhaps she'll enlighten us."

Miles exited the office, and Logan followed him out, with Atkins taking up the rear and closing the door.

Approaching Anna's room, the army men saluted the guards, then knocked as the sentries stepped aside to allow entry.

Dr. Webber pulled the door open from the inside.

"Gentlemen," he said, gesturing for them to enter.

Logan hadn't seen her since yesterday, and already Anna was looking better. She was still old, but the color had returned to her face, and her eyes had life in them. Some swelling had decreased, and the bruising was framed in a jaundiced yellow. Even her swollen eye had opened farther to some degree.

"Would this be a good time?" Miles asked no one in particular.

Anna's eyes found Logan and locked on him, twisting his gut into further knots. What was her plan here? Why involve him?

"Can I have my phone?" she asked, her voice gravelly.

Webber moved to the side and unplugged it from a charger.

"I'm going to speak with Logan," Anna said, watching all the men in the room. "You're welcome to listen, but I will only speak to Logan for now."

Everyone in the room nodded.

"As you wish," Miles said.

She cleared her throat and gestured for Logan to come closer.

"When I found the fence and made it over that fucking rusted barbed wire—" She paused, her hand shaking slightly. "I took a picture of the sign."

She swiped the phone with her thumb, then opened something and handed it to Logan.

He stared down at the sign on the screen and used his fingers to zoom in on the letters. It read, WARNING, then he moved the image and read

MILITARY INSTALLATION. KEEP OUT! Below that, it said, IT IS UNLAWFUL TO ENTER THIS INSTALLATION WITHOUT THE WRITTEN—

Miles snatched the phone from his hand and read the sign with Atkins staring over his shoulder.

Atkins's face seemed to lose all color.

Even though some of this was starting to make sense, he still wondered to himself, *What the hell was going on?*

The military men were staring at each other.

"We have to make the call," Miles said.

Atkins nodded. "Make the call."

Miles handed Anna's phone back to Logan, and both men marched out of the room.

"Mr. Logan?" Anna said, her voice soft and caring.

He nodded her way. "Yes?"

"I asked for you specifically because I'm sure you could smell those mushrooms. Was I wrong, Mr. Logan? Or could you smell the mushrooms where you found me?"

Logan looked over at Dr. Webber, who was in the corner by his computer, watching Anna, confusion painted on his strained face.

When Logan fixed his attention back on Anna, he nodded.

"I could smell mushrooms yesterday morning. Someone was cooking them close by."

A tear slipped out of Anna's right eye. He had the urge to grab a tissue for her but remained rooted to the floor at the side of her bed. He was overtly confused about everything and hoped it would become clear soon.

"How are the mushrooms important?" he asked.

"That's how it starts." She swallowed audibly. "That's how all this started, and that's how it'll end." She wiped a tear, her jaw clenching. "I'm so sorry, Mr. Logan, but I'll need your help to end this."

He stared at her, wondering what he had gotten himself into and hoping it wouldn't kill him.

"I'll help in any way I can," he assured her.

Chapter 11

Two Days Before Present Day ...

Anna woke with a start, jerking upright, a gasp escaping her lips. Disorientation lasted several seconds, but then there was enough light from the morning sun for her to see and remember exactly where she was.

The room she spent the night in was covered in leaves, animal droppings, a thick layer of dust, and general debris. This was no motel by any standard. It was a joke through and through.

Both those men from last night, the one at the cabin with the fire and the one who guided them with a candle to their rooms, were probably laughing all night at their little cozen.

Well, she would see who got the last laugh.

She scrambled to her feet, fighting the soreness of a night spent on a hard flat surface, and grabbed her carry-on bag. Whether or not anyone else was awake, she needed to pee and find something to eat. Maybe there was a natural spring nearby where she could get some water, too. Something, anything for her stomach, then she was gone, out of here, *hasta la vista* baby.

When she turned to leave, the door to her room was wide open. She frowned at it. Had someone come in through the night? She thought she'd closed it. She remembered hearing the three other doors close before entering her room and closing her own door.

Didn't matter now. This commune, or whatever it was, was history as she bought a train ticket and headed back to the train station to wait for whatever train was coming because trekking through the Oregon forest and staying in random communes was not only ridiculous, it wasn't getting her any closer to Sacramento.

She exited her room, glanced along the hallway at all the closed doors, then turned left toward the exit. Outside, she looked back up at the building in the daylight. It looked exactly like what she would expect for an army barracks in the middle of the trees, hidden away from society, except for one thing.

It was far creepier than any barracks she'd ever seen before.

There wasn't a single window intact, all broken over the years of abandonment—that included the window of the room she'd slept in.

There were sections of the roof where it had caved in, and some of the sidings had come loose, piling up haphazardly on the ground around the base of the building.

She ran a hand through her messy hair at the strangeness of the situation. She studied the door she'd just exited, then counted the windows along the wall until she got to the room she suspected she'd slept in.

Wasn't that window intact when she stared through it last night? She was sure there was glass there—double damn sure, because she remembered watching some three or four men chatting among themselves in the dark in the middle of the clearing.

At that thought, she spun around and stared at the clearing.

There is nothing there now, just an open space surrounded by trees, overgrown by wild grass and weeds.

What the fuck is going on here? What is this place?

After a moment, her bladder urging for release, she wandered over to a tree on the side of the clearing, where she lowered her pants and, with one hand on the tree, squatted to pee while keeping an eye on the building.

When she was done, she lifted her pants, fastened them, and started back toward the barracks.

How could the window be broken out when it was there last night? Wouldn't she have heard the glass shatter?

The answer was simple. She had only thought she was looking out a window from the outside. It was dark, and with a window frame, why wouldn't she just assume there was a window there, too?

She strode back inside the side door of the barracks, marched along the hall to her room, and glanced inside. The floor was littered with leaves and a thick layer of dust, just like it had been earlier. It also had a disturbance in the debris on the floor where someone had left footprints and a definite impression of where that person had laid down for the night.

She backed away, feeling deep in her soul that something was wrong with this place, something more than meets the eye. Either that, or she was losing her mind because she trusted what she saw.

Back outside, she stared at the broken window on the room she'd spent the night in.

"Good morning," a man said.

Anna nearly jumped out of her skin. She leaned against the building to regain her breath as she looked over at Russ, his head peeking from the window next to her room.

"Crazy place to spend the night, eh?" His smile was undeniably cute but also quite irritating at that moment. How could he be so happy to have slept in this horrid, disgusting building?

"Sure, crazy enough that I won't be spending another night in it."

"Oh, come on, it wasn't that bad." He lifted himself onto the sill, then hopped over to stand beside her. "Out in the trees, being one with nature."

She pushed off the wall, able to stand on her shaky legs again. "I didn't sign up for the adult adventure program. I signed up for a ride to Sacramento, which I intend to get to today."

"Yeah, understandable." He glanced downward, kicked at something on the ground, then back up at her. "So, you're leaving?"

She frowned and tilted her head. "How is that not obvious? It was late, and it was darker than Satan's butthole out here, so yeah, okay, I'll stick with you guys when it's that dark. But since right now is no later than seven or eight in the morning, there's enough sunlight for me to make the Canadian border on foot, so, therefore, I'm leaving."

"Will you at least wait until the others wake up and ask who's going where? I wouldn't want you walking out there alone. Mountain lions aren't nocturnal."

"What's that supposed to mean?"

He raised his hands. "It just means things can happen to you in the daytime as much in the night. It'd be better if at least one person left with you is all."

"Wait, you're not leaving?"

They stared at each other briefly before he blinked and glanced away.

"No, I think I'll stay here for a few nights, figure some shit out."

"Figure some shit out? What's that supposed to mean?"

"Doesn't matter right now."

"Well, then, answer me this. How will you eat, drink water? You a hunter?"

"I know a thing or two about surviving in the wild, which berries to eat, which to avoid. I can make it a week out here without too much trouble, perhaps longer."

She nodded in an exaggerated way. "You think you could find me some berries for breakfast before I leave? I don't know the first thing about wild berries other than they make you sick, and I'm famished."

"Sure, but let's wake the others first and see if they want to come."

Russ backed away from her, then turned and moved to the window directly beside his making big steps to get his feet above the foliage that had grown up alongside the building's outer wall.

"Hey, Grayson. You up?"

A mumbled reply came from inside the building.

"How about you, Jaxon?"

When there was no reply, Russ moved closer to the next window, presumably Jaxon's room.

"Jaxon, you still sleeping?" He placed a hand on the wall, leaned in to get a look, then turned to Anna with a deadpan stare. "He's not there."

"Try the next one."

Russ nodded, pushed off the wall, and moved to the next window. After looking in, he faced Anna and shook his head.

She spun in a circle, studying the tree line in all directions. "Where would he have gone?" She asked that question, thinking it didn't matter to her situation as she was leaving soon anyway. If the junkie kid wanted to wander off in the trees somewhere, then so be it.

The door on the side of the building smacked open, making her jump.

"Sorry," Grayson said. "Didn't know it only had one hinge." He stretched and yawned. "That floor is too hard to sleep on."

"Did you see Jaxon?" she asked him.

Grayson shook his head mid-stretch, then lowered his arms. "No, but I heard him earlier."

Russ was making his way toward her. "Heard him? What's that mean?"

Grayson rubbed his eyes and shrugged. "Not sure, really. I was asleep for the most part. It sounded like he found something because he yelled the word *Bingo*. That's what woke me. I listened for another minute or two before falling back to sleep but heard nothing else but talking."

Anna stepped closer to him. "Heard nothing else but talking? What's that supposed to mean? Was he chatting up the old guys?"

"It sounded like he was on some kind of stairs." Grayson scrunched up his face. "Maybe I was dreaming."

"Stairs?"

"Like on steps." Grayson glanced up to the second floor. "Maybe he found a room up there?"

Russ followed his gaze, then stepped back to appraise the top.

"Jaxon!" he shouted. "You up there?" When there was still no reply, he glanced at Anna. "I have a bad feeling about this."

"Me too."

"We need to find him, then search for food."

Anna shook her head. "Nuh-uh. I don't want to be a party pooper here, but I'm leaving. I have to get to Sacramento today, preferably."

"How far are you going to make it on your own? You're starving and thirsty, and you have no idea when the next train is coming." He took a step closer to her. "What if you make it to the train station by yourself, but no train comes for a couple of days?" He was shaking his head. "Just help me find Jaxon. Please give me a half-hour at most, and then I'll personally find you food and walk you to the train station. The worst case is, if it's eight in the morning, you'll be there by noon, promise."

She hated being grilled by anyone but hated it more because he was right. Without saying it directly, she was being selfish. Even if it was borne of fear and longing and several things that didn't make sense, she was being selfish. What if Jaxon needed their help? She could give Russ a half hour, even an hour, but then selfish or not, she was leaving.

"I'm sorry. You're right. I'll help." She glanced around them once more. "Any idea where our host from last night went? The jokester or prankster or whatever it is they call themselves nowadays?"

Russ and Grayson shook their heads at the same time while surveying their surroundings.

"Haven't seen him," Grayson said. "Just woke up."

She guffawed. "We're probably on YouTube now or TikTok."

"What makes you say that?" Russ asked.

"The guy in the cabin last night said this was a motel or something. We get here, and we're shown to our *rooms*"—she said this word with air quotes—"which is just an abandoned building where we slept on the floor in dirt and filth. This was a joke played on us, and I'm angry about it. Before we leave, I want to go to that cabin and give them a piece of my mind."

"Deal, but first, we find Jaxon."

She nodded. "Of course. I've already agreed to that. Where do we start?"

Russ shrugged. "I say we look for stairs. If Grayson thinks he heard Jaxon on the stairs, we search this building first. That work for you guys?"

Grayson moved toward the open door he'd just come out of, agreeing to what Russ said by his actions.

Anna turned to Russ. "That works for me, but then I need to eat soon."

"We're all hungry. Find Jaxon, then locate berries. You have my word."

"I'll hold you to it." She tried to smile, but it fell flat as Russ had already turned away.

They re-entered the abandoned barracks building and started up the dim corridor, the morning sun not yet over the trees, light filtering in through each room's broken window.

Trepidation grew inside her with each step she took.

Something happened here many years ago, something terrible. Otherwise, why would the government leave such an expensive secluded army base unguarded?

When those old men and their group—cult or commune, or whatever the hell they were—found these buildings and took them over, was that what they called squatter's rights?

Whatever was going on, she didn't like it one bit. From the moment they stepped foot on this land, something had been bothering her, and now she knew what it was.

That burned mushroom smell had a source, and there was no way someone cooked mushrooms every minute of every hour.

It was making her sluggish, already making her feel tired even though she'd just woken up within the last half hour. It was also making her feel dizzy.

Or was that the lack of food? She couldn't remember the last time she ate. Maybe it was lunch yesterday before she'd walked in on Colton and Janine about to have sex. She hadn't eaten in almost twenty-four hours if that was the case.

She hoped they would locate Jaxon soon because she needed Russ to find her food. She needed something to stave off the dizziness. Otherwise, she'd have trouble navigating her way out of the forest.

She wondered how long she could go without eating.

Then she wondered if she'd ever make it to Sacramento.

Chapter 12

Colton Asher finished his uneventful shift, changed into civilian clothes, then raced home to make some calls. His personal phone sat plugged into the cruiser all night and was still at one hundred percent battery life. He might have checked it a dozen times per hour, but Anna hadn't called, and she hadn't responded to any of his text messages.

Rationally, all that meant was she'd spent the night on the train with her phone off so she could sleep. It was going on eight in the morning now. She would have already gotten to Sacramento, taken a taxi to the hospice, and was probably sitting with her mother at that very moment.

He took a deep breath while staring out the bedroom window he had shared with Anna, then dialed the hospice. They answered on the second ring.

"Wellness Hospice, Sacramento, how can I direct your call?"

"I'm looking for Daphne Valentina's room, please."

"Who may I say is calling?"

"It's her son-in-law, Colton Asher."

There was a pause, then, "Son-in-law? I've met

her daughter. She's even coming down next week. I must've missed something, but I didn't know she was married."

"Well, we're not married yet." He cleared his throat, already feeling like he screwed this up. "Call me her *future* son-in-law."

"Your name, sir?"

Even though he'd just told her, he repeated it.

"It's a bit early. Some of our guests are still sleeping while others are eating breakfast—"

"Actually, since you've met Anna, she's the one I'm looking for."

There was another pause. Colton saw the woman in his mind's eye, mouth open, eyes staring at nothing, debating what she should say.

"Anna isn't due for a visit until next week, as I just said, but I can't be discussing these sorts of things over the phone—"

"Anna's missing."

"What?"

"I'm her boyfriend, and I'm a cop in Eugene, Oregon. She bought a train ticket to Sacramento last night, and as far as I can tell, she got on that train. Since then, nothing. So, I'm calling to see if she arrived safe, that's all."

"Sir, I can't really …"

"I know, I get it. But you just admitted to knowing Anna, and you said she's expected next week. That tells me you didn't see her today."

"I didn't say that—"

"So you *did* see her today?" His volume rose, hopeful.

"Mr. Asher, I can't discuss things like this over the phone—"

"Ma'am, when I file the missing persons report, and I assure you I will, I'll tell them Anna was heading there before she disappeared. When this breaks in the news, I'm not sure you want your hospice all over the front page—"

"You have a nasty habit of cutting me off, and now you're threatening me? The nerve of some people. Good day, sir."

The phone smacked down in his ear.

"Shit, that didn't go too well."

He glanced around the room, contemplating his next move. This development left him no choice. Anna wasn't returning his calls, hadn't arrived in Sacramento yet, and wasn't in Eugene as far as he could tell.

She could be almost in Los Angeles or even headed toward New York by now. Who could really know where she'd gone? But she could also be lying in a ditch, dying somewhere. He needed to get to her fast, which would require some much-needed help.

The kind of help an entire police force could offer.

It was time to fill in the missing persons report and claim it was entirely out of character for her. He'd tell them about the train and get the authorities in Sacramento out looking for her, too.

Then he'd go back tonight to interview that train

station woman who sold Anna her ticket.

Someone had to have seen her somewhere.

If she was still alive, how could he suspect otherwise? He would find her if it were the last thing he did.

She had to know the truth: he didn't cheat on her. Janine set him up. It didn't look good, but it wasn't how it looked. He was innocent.

Once he found Anna, he'd plead his case.

But he had to find her first.

Chapter 13

ONCE THEY WERE BACK inside the barracks hallway, they had to step over dead rats and a couple of field mice as the three of them moved along the hall.

Anna mumbled a few moans and grunts, steering clear of their tiny bodies.

"I wonder what that's all about," Russ whispered, pointing at another one for Anna to step over.

"What, what's all about?" Grayson asked from up ahead.

"Dead rodents."

Anna grunted again. "Don't they just die sometimes?" As soon as she said it, she knew it sounded stupid. They were prey, and if they'd just died somewhere, tiny scavengers would've come and cleaned up their carcasses by now. Birds played a part in that, too. Yet, since getting off the train last night, she'd seen or heard no wildlife, unless whatever was tracking them before they entered the barracks was wildlife. But something told her it wasn't. She was sure it was those men she'd seen huddling in the clearing before they'd all slept.

"What I'm saying is," Russ said, "why not run back outside? Why die here? Unless someone left behind rat poison, there's no reason for these rodents just to stop and croak here. And why haven't they been eaten already?"

Anna would have to conclude the same thing with what little she knew about the life of rodents. "That is weird."

Up ahead of them near the end of the hall, Grayson stopped at a wooden doorway on the left. There were two more doors past this one that looked like they probably opened into more rooms, but this particular one had a sloped ceiling above it, which probably meant there were stairs behind it.

"Not sure where this leads," Grayson whispered as if talking to himself.

"Open it." Russ gestured with a nod. "Then we'll find out."

"Wait." Anna picked up her pace. "What if the old guy from last night is in there? Shouldn't we knock first?"

This constant tension was getting to her. This place, the strange men last night, the windows in the rooms she thought she saw when there was nothing there. How could she not feel a breeze on her face when she stared out her window before sleeping last night? And where were the old men who fucked with them? Those rodents, too—what Russ said made a lot of sense.

She didn't want to open that door. She didn't want to look behind door number one, door number two, or any fucking door in this entire area. All she wanted to do was go back to the tracks, then walk back to Eugene if she had to. Wandering deeper into the barracks was a mistake on every level.

But Grayson did precisely what she didn't want him to do.

He knocked.

He grabbed the handle and swung the door open when there was no answer.

Russ and Grayson leaned forward and peered inside.

"Shit," Russ whispered. "That sucks."

"What?" she asked, unsure she wanted to know.

He turned to face her. "It's a staircase leading upstairs, or what's left of a staircase leading upstairs."

"Yeah," Grayson said, closing the door. "No way Jaxon went up this way."

"If he even went up," she added.

"Are you saying he went down?" Russ asked. "Like a basement or something?"

"I'm not saying anything." She shook her head. "Just saying we should go outside and look for him." She wrapped her arms around herself. "Not feeling so good in here at the moment. And that fucking smell of burned mushrooms is getting to me."

To Russ's credit, he moved closer and gently touched her arm. "It'll be okay. We'll be outside in a few minutes. As long as we're all together, nothing will happen."

That small gesture was enough to calm her. She glanced at the floor, embarrassed by her neediness but grateful for Russ's kindness.

Russ turned back to Grayson. "Is there anywhere else he could've gone?"

"How should I know? I got to this crazy place at the same time you did."

"You're right. Of course. Why don't we head back outside—"

Something banged against metal deeper along the hallway behind one of the two doors left.

"Oh shit," Anna mumbled, her lower lip quivering now. "I don't like this. I think I'll wait outside." The hair on the back of her neck rose—she could literally feel it stiffening.

"Anna, please." Russ held a hand up. "Stay with us. I don't want anyone separating from the group until we're out of here."

"Why? You're scared, too?" She hoped he'd admit it so she wouldn't feel so alone.

"No, it's just we don't know what we're up against. Once we know, we can decide the next step."

"Oh, I've decided already what I'm—"

"Guys," Grayson said in a grunted whisper. "Jaxon may need our help. Chattering on as we are isn't helping him or us."

"You're right." Russ pushed forward, shouldering past Grayson. He grabbed the first door he came to and tore it open. It collapsed in his hand, and he had to jump aside as it hit the opposite wall making such a loud bang in the small corridor that Anna let out a short yip and jumped on the spot, a hand rushing up to cover her mouth.

Someone had removed the pin in the door's hinges. It had only been suspended in place. Now the fallen door separated Russ from Grayson and her.

"Who would do that to the door?" Grayson asked the question on Anna's lips as she couldn't find her voice yet.

"Who knows?" Russ grabbed the door and pushed it up to lean against the wall. "And who cares?" He turned to the last door.

This wasn't good at all.

The last door was steel and seemed to be reinforced.

"That," she gasped, inhaled, and tried again. "That one looks locked. Be careful." How stupid did she sound when she was scared? Or did she level up to terrified? And if it was terrified, then she didn't care how ridiculous she sounded. They needed to leave and run like their lives depended on it. Everything was wrong with this place, yet she had no physical evidence to back it up.

Russ inspected the hinges first, looked over his shoulder at them, nodded that they were intact, then moved to grasp the doorknob.

She wanted to ask him to knock, but if someone was waiting on the other side of the door—which she suspected because who made the metal banging sound about a minute ago?—they had to know someone was coming after that hinge-less door smashed against the wall and made a considerable racket.

Russ twisted the knob and pulled the door open slowly. "Well, I'll be damned." He forced the door open all the way.

She wished he hadn't chosen those words in particular.

Russ glanced over his shoulder, a broad grin on his face. "Just as I suspected." There was a hint of happiness in his tone.

"What is it?" she asked, already inhaling the rank air from below. This was the source of that burned mushroom smell they'd endured since last night.

"It's the stairs to the basement, the bunker, or whatever the army calls their hidden tunnels underground."

"Oh, Russ," she said, her voice quivering. "I swear, if you go down there, I'm leaving."

"Anna, you heard something clang in there." He pointed inside. "Jaxon might've taken these stairs and fallen. I'm not leaving until we go down."

"I'm with you," Grayson said.

"You want to wait here?" Russ asked her. "Or come with us?"

"Can't you just shout down and see if he's okay?"

"Sure, but that wouldn't satisfy my curiosity. This is my chance to see what's down here before we all leave this place."

"Then go. I'll wait. There's no way I'm going down there."

Russ slipped through the door without hesitating. Grayson offered her a thin-lipped smile, then followed

Russ through the door.

She listened to the clanging of their footfalls as the men descended what sounded like a metal staircase, then the clanging stopped. They must have reached the bottom.

Their voices filtered up to her like the sound was coming through a tunnel.

After one glance over her shoulder to make sure no one was standing at the end of the hall watching her, which she was sure was the case, she dropped her carry-on bag on the floor and, ran for the door, slipped inside, then started down the spiral staircase.

Being alone up there seemed worse than entering the bunker with the two other men—until she made it back to the train tracks. Being alone wasn't an option she wanted to entertain.

"Guys, wait for me," she shouted, but they were already gone.

Chapter 14

PRESENT DAY ...

The hospital had become oppressive to him.

Logan wasn't sure how else to describe it. He needed out. He needed air.

All day in his uniform, feeling grimy after the rain that morning, and yet no one was willing to tell him when he could head home to change. Apparently, he needed clearance from either Sergeant Miles or Atkins.

Logan had overheard Dr. Webber protesting to Command Sergeant Major Miles about his patient being moved.

Moved? Where were they going to move Anna? Some secret facility or a laboratory to study her rapid aging?

It wasn't just something in the air. Logan could feel the change coming. More military staff were in the hospital that afternoon. More personnel were coming in and out of Anna's room, even though she slept most of the day away.

Atkins had called him in to speak with her when she woke. Before falling asleep again, Anna told them about the barracks and described what she could about the area. Some hallway that led to a metal spiral staircase. A bunker with rooms or something. Then she dozed off without talking about Colton or who beat her so severely.

Were they looking for her boyfriend armed with an arrest warrant? Or was Officer Asher caught up in what had gotten to Anna Valentina—that thing that aged her, whatever it was?

Until she told them more, they were in the dark.

But that didn't stop Atkins and Miles from making their own moves. They had made *that call*, whatever the hell that meant. And once that call was made, the entire atmosphere at the hospital changed.

He wasn't allowed to make a phone call without one of them present. He wasn't allowed to leave the building. They'd update him soon on sleeping arrangements, but since they'd commandeered him for an indefinite period of time, apparently, that meant they *owned* him. He wasn't going home that night.

Logan understood to a degree. They needed him close for when Anna decided to start talking as she continually requested his presence, but he didn't care. A night's sleep and a change of clothes would do him good.

As the sun set, he strode down to the hospital's main entrance and glanced outside at his cruiser. The back of the parking lot was lined with military vehicles, with more arriving as he watched.

"What the fuck is going on?" he whispered out

loud.

Thoughts of alien life filled his mind. A new Area 51, maybe? Or perhaps it was an experiment gone wrong, like the Philadelphia Experiment, where people disappeared.

Wait, was that just a movie, or was it a real experiment? Sometimes fiction and reality blurred for him as he read so many novels in his spare time.

Whatever was going on, it was big, and he was at the center of it, a place he didn't want to be anymore. A bystander was something more up his alley, but he had no desire to be in the thick of things this serious.

Someone tapped his shoulder. He jumped and spun around to see Sergeant Major Atkins behind him.

With a hand on his chest, he gawked at Atkins. "Shit, man, I was lost in thought. Scared the fuck out of me."

The main lobby area was relatively quiet as the military mobilized outside the hospital. Unless someone had an emergency, they weren't coming to this hospital at the moment.

"We're shipping out, Trooper."

"Shipping out?" Logan moved to face the man. "What does that mean? It's over?"

Atkins stared out the windows at the parking lot. "We're taking this show on the road."

"You guys are all leaving?"

Atkins looked at Logan, his gaze hard. "This is just the beginning, Trooper. We're moving Miss Anna Valentina to a secure location where our own doctors will assess her. From there, we'll deal with whatever comes up."

"So, where do I fit in?"

Atkins watched him for several heartbeats. "You are requested to go home, speak to no one, change into civilian clothes, pack for several days, then return here for further orders."

"What should I tell my wife, sir? She'll want to know where I'm going."

"Tell her the truth. The US government has hired you for a short while, and you'll be gone until the job is complete. Nothing more, nothing less."

It was Logan's turn to stare at Atkins. His wife was his confidante, his listener, and his lover. How could he say such generalities to her? She'll be hurt and probably concerned for his safety because of his lack of forthrightness.

"Is there a problem, Trooper?"

Logan shook his head. "No, sir, just mulling over the proper words to honor the NDA."

Tell them what they want to hear. Then do what he needed to do.

"CID Detective Sergeant Ray Smithers will follow you home and bring you back here before we move to the secure location." Atkins nodded at a man standing behind Logan. "You have one hour, Trooper."

Logan glanced at Smithers, then back to Atkins. "Secure location, sir? Where are we headed?"

Atkins broke into a smile and smacked Logan's shoulder. "Well, it wouldn't be that secure if I told you, now would it?"

Then he walked away, headed toward the elevators.

"Sir," Smithers said, gesturing toward the door. "Your cruiser is this way."

Logan watched Atkins push the elevator button, not a care in the world. What had he truly gotten himself into? Why did he have to answer that emergency call?

Being locked away at some secure facility did not feel like fun—a secret place far from his wife, his life, and his career.

What could they think happened to Miss Valentina to be orchestrating such a huge maneuver? What the hell was going on?

Logan turned to follow Smithers out of the hospital, the first stirrings of fear developing in his stomach. This was too much for him. Robberies, assaults, thefts, parking tickets, and speeding tickets were all things he was hired to deal with. This was out of his league and, thereby, out of his realm of comfort.

Already contemplating what he needed to do for the past hour, he realized Atkins had given him a chance to do just what was required. He would go home, shower, change his clothes, and then do what was necessary to find out what happened to Miss Valentina, and everything would end.

He'd signed an NDA, so what he saw didn't matter. He was on their time, so Sergeant Lambert wasn't expecting him back for several days or longer.

Smithers followed in a nondescript black SUV while Logan drove the cruiser home. When he pulled into the driveway, he didn't see his wife's car. Maybe that was for the better. At least he wouldn't have to attempt to explain his way through his absence. Katrina could tell his wife what she needed to know. It wasn't ideal, but it was undoubtedly easier for Logan.

Smithers said he'd wait in his vehicle while Logan spent fifteen minutes inside the house.

"Give me twenty minutes."

Smithers stared up at the house, his eyes moving from window to window, then he turned to Logan. "You can have twenty."

Logan ran inside and took a quick shower. Then he filled a backpack with necessary items like snacks, water, a flashlight, and an old phone that he kept charged in case he needed to call emergency services. It had no cell plan, but it didn't need one to call 911.

He slipped his weapon inside the backpack.

In total, he used up twelve minutes of his twenty to get prepared.

Then he left the upstairs lights on, exited the house from the back, and locked the door behind him.

Minutes later, he was a block away, the backpack bouncing softly behind his shoulders as he trudged up the road.

Free from the eyes of the military, free from Atkins and Miles, he made his way to the train station to find out what Maggie might know. She sold everyone their tickets. She had to know something.

Besides, the night he saw Colton Asher at the train station, Asher had slapped the Plexiglas in front of Maggie and said something about a guy getting on Anna's train, whatever that meant. Maggie had been the one to upset Colton that day, so she had to know something.

Logan was determined to find out whatever was going on, and he would do it on his terms.

Fuck the military and its rules.

Fuck 'em all.

Chapter 15

TWO DAYS BEFORE PRESENT DAY ...

Colton filed the missing persons report and made sure the Sacramento Police Department was notified that a police officer's fiancée was missing and presumed to be in their area after departing the train that morning, then he went home to get some sleep. However, rest proved more difficult than he expected. He tossed and turned until around nine, then got up and showered.

Sleep wouldn't come until he heard from Anna and knew she was safe. That, or he dropped from exhaustion.

So, he booked off the following two shifts, giving him five days off work in a row as he was due a three-day break after the weekend.

When he called the station, there was still no news on Anna.

He got himself a large coffee and a burger to go, his usual breakfast on the night shift, then drove back to the train station, hoping the woman he spoke to the day before was working again this afternoon.

He was in luck.

Several people were in line buying tickets when

he entered the station. He got in line behind them and waited.

If Anna was avoiding him, then fine. It would suck, but he could live with that after what she thought she saw. Not returning his calls to tell him to stop calling and leave her alone wasn't going to fly, though. She can't buy a ticket to Sacramento and not show up at the hospice. That became suspicious and warranted the missing persons report.

Neither her credit cards nor banking had been touched, as he had signed into their accounts online and saw no activity.

So where are you, Anna?

The odds were nothing terrible had happened to her, and she was fine. Maybe she got off the train in Redding or somewhere closer and was waiting to return home after regretting her decision to leave. Perhaps she had stashed enough cash to live a week without using their banking.

There were a lot of *maybes* and not a lot of *for sures*.

Until he discovered the truth, he'd never let this lie for one simple reason: closure. He'd had two serious relationships in the past, and both had ended without proper closure. He had no idea why people did that to each other, but he wouldn't let Anna go without a conversation, at least. He needed to hear her voice and know that she was okay. If she called him from Utah, Missouri, Texas, or even Montana, fine—as long as she called. He'd cancel the missing persons file the moment he heard she was okay, even if she told him to get the fuck out of her life.

The last ticket buyer moved aside, train ticket in hand.

Colton eased forward, pulling out a copy of the report he'd filed on Anna.

"I'm back," he said to the woman behind the Plexiglas. "And I brought this with me." He slid the paperwork through the booth's opening. "This is the missing persons report for Anna Valentina, and as far as we can tell, you were the last person to see her alive."

He chose those words on purpose. The subtext of guilt often got people talking, which is precisely what he needed today.

The woman behind the counter only glanced at the document, then slipped the paperwork back through the slot.

She leaned close so only Colton could hear her speak. "Meet me at the side counter." Then she pointed, then was up off her chair and moving. "Mary, can you tend the ticket window?" the woman said on her way to the side counter.

A tall brunette, presumably Mary, sauntered over and took the seat at the booth that was just vacated.

Colton didn't hesitate. His hope was renewed afresh as it was apparent this woman knew something. Otherwise, why drag him aside like this?

She beat him to the little access door, unclipped it, and swung it open for him to join her.

"I'm Maggie Werner." She held out her hand.

He clasped it. "Officer Colton Asher." When they shook, her hand was cold and clammy. Once their hands dropped apart, he fought the urge to wipe his off on the leg of his jeans.

"Follow me," Maggie said.

She led him into the back, where they walked through a break room with a small white fridge and a table cluttered with three lunch boxes, then into what looked like a mudroom with mops, buckets, and brooms. At the back door, Maggie shoved it open and held it for Colton, the sunshine blinding him.

Before he had a chance to wonder if she was kicking him out of the building, he stepped outside, and she closed the door behind them. Without a word, she leaned against the wall, produced a pack of Camels, and lit a cigarette.

"Smoke break?" he asked.

She shook her head, inhaled deeply, held it, then sent smoke through her nostrils in a double stream.

"I just started my shift but needed a smoke to tell you what I know."

Colton's nerves fired up, sending a worry to his stomach in the form of acid.

"I'm listening."

"Anna was here yesterday."

"You sold her the ticket, right? You said that yesterday."

She nodded, then took another drag on the Camel.

"After you left"—her first three words saw smoke

emanating from her mouth like she was chewing fire —"I asked around."

"Asked around?" Colton placed his hands on his hips, hoping she'd speak faster but not wanting to rush her.

"I called the train she was on and the one she was supposed to be on."

"*Supposed* to be on? I'm lost. What the hell does that mean?"

Maggie nodded like she understood how lost he probably was, glanced down at her cigarette, tipped off the ashes, then dragged on it again.

Colton wanted to smack the cancer stick from her hands so she could stop focusing on that and focus on telling her story.

She met his gaze and held it. "You have to understand something. We have a lot of trains come through here, and sometimes they're late, and sometimes there are two coming in around the same time."

"So, you're saying she got on the wrong train? Is that what happened?"

Maggie nodded, looked at her cigarette again, then dropped it and stamped it out.

He wanted to pat her on the back for making the right choice. Now maybe they could get somewhere with this little chat.

"Once the mistake was discovered, they dropped her off about an hour southeast of here."

"Dropped her off?" His voice rose an octave.

"How can they just *drop her off?*"

Maggie raised a hand for calm. Probably a good move because he was breathing heavier by the second.

"Hear everything first, then get mad."

"Too late. Already mad."

"I get that, but you gotta listen in order to find your girl."

That sounded like something a kidnapper would say. What the hell had Anna got herself mixed up in?

"Go on," he whispered, his temper in control—for now.

"There's a substation on the line where we drop people who have the wrong ticket. They're never there for more than thirty minutes and usually only five or ten."

He opened his mouth to ask where it was when Maggie raised her hand for quiet.

"And then the right train comes along, and they hop on it."

"So, that's what happened to Anna? She hopped on another train, and she's in Atlantic City now? Or Jacksonville?"

"Listen, she was dropped off once her ticket was verified and told to wait for the correct train to come along, which was supposed to be about fifteen to twenty minutes later. I assure you, we've done this in the past to get people going on the right trains. If there's a waiting period longer than an hour, they drop them in the next city, but the logistics are often much more challenging in getting those people to the right train later on."

"So, she got on the right one then?"

Maggie shook her head. "The train that she was supposed to be on, which was heading to Sacramento, pulled to a stop at the substation, but no one was there."

"Oh, my fuck …" Colton whispered. Heat rose around his collar, and his eyes blazed with anger at the incompetence of the train staff. He leaned in close to her. "Where is this substation?"

She pointed south. "Almost one hour that way."

"Accessible only by train, right?"

She nodded. "No roads in that area. Nothing out there." Then she moved a few feet to the right and pointed at the tracks. "See that train right there?"

He nodded vigorously.

"It's headed south and leaving in fifteen minutes. I can get you on it and have them drop you off at the substation."

"How do I get back?"

"Find Anna, then hop on the train heading toward Redding, which will come through half an hour later. Take a bus home from Redding." She shrugged. "At least you'll find her if she's still out there."

Maggie's face was lined with worry. Was it personal guilt for having sold Anna the ticket, or was she worried about a lawsuit?

"If it's just a matter of a train transfer gone wrong, why pull me out here? Why not call the police station and tell them what you told me?"

"Let me ask you something. When you go to the police station to start your shift, is there a list of most wanted or something for you guys to keep an eye out for?"

He frowned at her. "Yeah, we've got a system like that. A list of license plates of stolen vehicles, too. What's that got to do with Anna?"

"Have you heard of a man named Grayson Cooper?"

Colton's frown deepened. "No, I haven't. But something tells me you're going to tell me about him."

Maggie slipped a hand into her pocket and pulled out a folded piece of paper.

"Cops were here a few hours ago, dropping these off. I just started my shift and only saw it, like, ten minutes before you walked in."

"What is it?"

She handed it to him. Colton unfolded the paper and recognized it immediately. It was a Department of Corrections Most Wanted document, which listed the usual stuff like age, race, weight, date of birth, all the way down to the guy's eye color. There was a mugshot, too. It also stated why the Department of Corrections was looking for the guy. In Grayson Cooper's case, he was wanted for sexual abuse and attempted sodomy of a minor. It went on to state that Grayson Cooper was *probably* headed to Redding, California, to meet an underage girl he'd been in contact with online while posing as a fifteen-year-old male youth. The underage girl's parents had called it in, and the search for Cooper had started at the train station.

Colton looked at Maggie, the worry in his gut making him sick. "How is this connected to Anna?" He folded the paper and passed it back to her.

"As I said, I spoke with the ticket guys on the train last night, the ones who verify each ticket, so I knew who to call when I got this Most Wanted thing. They told me they dropped off four people at that substation, Anna being one of them. So, I called to ask about this Grayson asshole." She tapped the paper in her hand. "In fact, I just got off the phone two minutes before you walked in."

"I'm listening. What did they say?"

"Well …" She paused to take a breath.

Colton saw her hands shaking. Whatever she had to tell him was hard on her. A buzzing under the skin of his knuckles made him want to punch something. He placed his hands behind his back to wring them in private.

"This Most Wanted document thing," she flicked the hand holding the paper, "was also sent to the train personnel. My guy from yesterday, who said he dropped off four people at the substation, recognized Grayson Cooper's face from this sheet. He's easily identifiable with that combover."

"Are you saying he was one of the three others dropped off with Anna at some substation in the middle of nowhere?"

Maggie nodded, then kicked at something on the

ground. "We didn't sell a ticket to anyone named Grayson Cooper, though."

Colton shot his hands out to the side and raised his shoulders. "So he used a fake name. Happens all the time."

She kept nodding. "That's what we think."

"And you didn't think to call this in?"

"My boss *is* calling it in. As soon as we got off the phone, he called your department two minutes before you walked in."

Colton spun in a circle, gazing up at the sky, baffled at how things could go so wrong so fast. "Anna got dropped off at your substation with a convicted sexual predator, a man wanted on sexual abuse charges of minors—"

"None of us are responsible, mister. We're just doing our jobs. I didn't see this Cooper guy myself, and we didn't sell a ticket to anyone with that name. I'm just telling you what our ticket guys told me and offering you a free ride to the substation."

"The ultimate case of cover your ass."

Maggie spun around, ripped open the back door, then slipped inside quickly. Before the door closed, Colton followed her. From behind, he saw her wiping her eyes. Sure, she was upset, but he was, too. And until he found Anna, he would hold these people personally responsible.

"Which track am I on?" he asked as they moved through the lunchroom again, headed toward the front.

"Track number one," she mumbled, her voice

broken slightly by emotion.

When they stepped back out front, he stopped at the sight of four officers walking through the seated area.

"Hey, Logan," he called and started his way.

Trooper Richard Logan had assisted him several times when a suspect fled in the middle of the night, hitting the highway south of Eugene. Logan was a dedicated state trooper, always alert and ready for anything, but most of all, he didn't bicker over territorial bullshit. They were all on the same side, and Logan acted like it.

"Asher, how you doing?"

They gripped hands to shake, their other hands slapping shoulders.

"What's going on here?" Colton asked. "Looking for that Grayson Cooper guy?"

"Cooper?" Logan shook his head and handed Colton a Department of Justice Most Wanted sheet just like the one he'd read out back moments before.

"Looking for a man named Rusty Brown. Aggravated assault charges with a baseball bat. Skipped court yesterday afternoon. A bench warrant is out for his arrest." Logan glanced around the sitting area. "We were asked to drop these at all egress points out of Eugene. Seen him around?"

"Can I borrow this?" Colton asked, a sinking feeling in his gut.

Logan nodded and stepped away. "Keep it. We got lots."

Colton returned to the counter and slipped the paper under the Plexiglas to show Maggie.

"Seen this guy recently?"

Maggie blanched, all color leaving her face. When she looked up to meet Colton's gaze, he knew she'd seen him.

"He was here yesterday. Acted weird, like he was on something. Bought a ticket, but one second, I don't recognize that name." She tapped on her keyboard, then shook her head. "That name isn't in our system."

"Was he on the train with Anna, too?" Colton couldn't help his voice rising.

"He sat over there." Maggie pointed. "He watched the doors, then left."

Colton slapped the Plexiglas with his hand, making Maggie jump. "Did he get on Anna's train?"

"I don't know," she wailed, clearly upset now. "I'm pretty sure he left around the same time."

"Oh fuck," Colton shouted through clenched teeth. "Get me on a train headed to this substation, *now*!"

After Maggie gave him a free ticket, he marched to the side door and looked back.

Trooper Logan was watching him, concern on his face.

Chapter 16

WHEN ANNA GOT TO the bottom of the spiral staircase, she stopped. The sides of the tunnel were concrete and looked strong, despite the spider cracks covering them.

What stopped her were the candles.

Strung along the walls, about five feet from the ground, were evenly spaced candles. Someone had lit them all the way to a fork in the tunnel. The side heading to the left was dark and appeared to be a dead-end, something left unfinished after they abandoned the barracks. But to the right, candlelight emanated deeper into the tunnel.

Grayson and Russ stood at the entrance to the lit tunnel on her right, just around the corner.

"Guys, did Jaxon light all these?"

"Who else?" Russ said, his voice a fading echo.

"What is this place?" She started toward them, the cool, damp underground air seeping through her skin, causing a chill.

"Many army bases are equipped with bunkers." Russ looked away to glance down the tunnel in front of him. "You know, in case they're bombed."

She stopped a few feet away and peered down the

length of the tunnel in front of them. It only went as far as three candles, about twenty feet, and then it faded to black.

"This place is creepy," she whispered. "We should leave."

Russ turned to her again, his brows knitted. "You think that old guy from last night has a man cave down here?"

She shrugged out of nervousness, her eyes on the darkness beyond where the light couldn't penetrate. "Well, if he lives at the bunker, he must live somewhere, right?"

"Do you feel that?" Grayson asked, taking a step forward.

"What?" Anna squeaked out, already stifling the urge to bolt for the stairs.

"There's a soft breeze coming up from the tunnel."

"Yeah." Russ nodded. "I feel it and smell it."

Anna could smell it, too. The most rank version of the burned mushroom smell so far. Whatever was at the end of these tunnels had been generating that odd smell since they got off the train last night.

"You guys ever watch any seventies horror movies?" she asked.

Both men turned to her and shook their heads.

Russ said, "Well, I saw *Planet of the Apes* and a few Charles Bronson movies. How is that relevant?"

"There's one called *Don't Look in the Basement*, and I have to say that applies here. My vote is we wait upstairs for Jaxon."

Russ took a step back to look her up and down. "Wait for Jaxon? I thought you wanted out of here."

She wondered why Russ seemed so aggressive today. For some reason, it made her angry. "Okay, well, if you guys wanna walk along abandoned tunnels, go for it. I've been dragged into this farce too long. I'm leaving." She turned and stomped toward the metal stairs.

"You're going to walk all the way to the train tracks alone? Is that it?" Russ's voice echoed longer in this bunker tunnel, the louder it was.

"Guys!" someone shouted from much farther away.

All of Anna's anger dissipated at the sound of Jaxon's voice. She spun back to face Russ and Grayson, the candles flickering slightly in the soft breeze.

"Guys!" Jaxon called again.

"Yeah?" Russ shouted. "We're here."

"Wait, I'll come to you."

So, they'd found him. That made Anna happy, although she didn't feel too happy. Standing in the abandoned tunnel made her feel like they were in the maw of a giant beast, waiting for its jaws to close. Instead of moving back to stand beside Russ and Grayson, she moved to the base of the spiral staircase. When Jaxon emerged from the darkness at the end of the tunnel—she had no idea where he was, except that's where his voice seemed to be coming from—she would be the first one up those stairs.

"Here he comes," Russ said for her benefit. "He's carrying a candle."

"Where have you been?" Grayson asked him in a soft voice.

"I found food." Jaxon sounded overjoyed. She didn't know him too well, but this was definitely a different side to Jaxon. He seemed jubilant, more lively than the junkie last night, who looked like he was starting to feel strung out while waiting for his next fix. Of course, she'd stereotyped him, but who wouldn't judge a super skinny guy with terrible teeth, hollowed-out cheeks, and wild eyes?

Anna frowned and tightened her lips, her tongue moving around her dry mouth at the mention of food. As much as she wanted to hear those words, she couldn't believe it. How the hell could Jaxon have found food down here unless he was stealing it from that old man who told them they could crash there for the night?

"How could you find food down here?" Russ asked the question that was on her mind.

"MREs were stored in a room just over there."

"MREs?" Anna asked.

Russ glanced her way. "It stands for Meals Ready to Eat. Militaries worldwide use this version of compact food for their soldiers."

Jaxon stepped into view at the corner of the tunnel, and Anna could tell something was wrong with him immediately.

"What happened, bro?" Russ asked, easing back from Jaxon.

Grayson was already on his way to the staircase; his head turned back to watch Jaxon.

The junkie looked like a scarecrow of his former self. The transformation was intense, and it happened overnight.

"What the fuck?" Anna whispered as she hit the first step and started up, hoping to make it without falling now that her limbs were shaking.

"What are you guys talking about?" Jaxon stopped at the corner where the tunnel angled to the right, one arm holding a batch of five or six silver packages, the other hand holding a candle. "I already ate. These are for you guys."

Russ was halfway to the staircase when he said, "Come on up to ground level so we can eat up there."

Jaxon nodded. "Sure, works for me."

That over-excited tone grated on Anna's nerves. She'd only briefly met Jaxon last night, but this was someone else. Maybe he was high. Did he bring some kind of drug with him?

Russ continued talking to him. "Then you can tell us all about what you found down here."

"You guys won't believe it." Jaxon giggled.

Anna reached the top without incident, grabbed her carry-on bag, and started down the long corridor toward the outside. Grayson followed, then Russ, and finally Jaxon.

Once outside, at least ten feet from the barracks

door, Anna scanned the area but didn't see anyone. The sun was higher, indicating it was closer to nine or ten in the morning now. She was losing time, but that wouldn't be a problem—yet. She'd leave this dreaded compound within minutes as soon as she learned what happened to Jaxon.

Grayson joined her, then Russ.

The three of them formed a semi-circle watching the door as Jaxon stepped outside into the sunlight.

"Hey, guys, what's the big rush?"

Russ stepped forward, just like he'd done last night, like he was offering himself as a shield for Grayson and Anna.

Then Grayson edged up beside her, uncomfortably close.

"What's the big rush?" Russ repeated. "Just kinda spooky down there, is all."

They stared at Jaxon like it was their first time seeing him.

"Gone swimming, did you?" Russ asked.

Anna hadn't thought of that but also didn't think the water had done what they were witnessing.

Jaxon shook his head and glanced down at his body, the first wave of confusion crossing his face. "Do I look wet or something?" He didn't sound upset, just completely unaware of what they were staring at.

"Take a look at your arm, bro."

Jaxon set the silver packages on the ground at his feet and lifted his sleeve to the elbow.

"Wow, different air down there, I guess." Jaxon's

voice held a quality Anna couldn't pin down. A mix of wonder and amusement, but also a dash of resignation, like he was okay with what he was looking at.

When Jaxon looked back up at them, his eyes were alight with life, his smile wide, rotten teeth on display.

Jaxon had to be high on something that energized him like he'd taken a heavy dose of uppers.

"Dude," Russ said. "Did you say you ate some of those?"

Jaxon looked down at the silver packages, then back up to Russ. "I couldn't sleep, so I searched for that old guy, hoping he'd share whatever he was cooking. Someone is making a tasty mushroom dish close by, and I'm starving, man, you know."

Russ nodded. "And?"

"I found that staircase and was sure I heard him down there."

Anna recalled the metallic clang they all heard before heading down to find Jaxon, although it wasn't Jaxon, as he was much deeper in the tunnel.

Then what drew the three of them below ground?

"So," Jaxon continued as he stared at the skin on his arm. "I saw the lit candles, grabbed one, and wandered through the tunnels calling his name. I must've fallen asleep down there. When I woke up, I found these, ate a batch, and here I am." He picked up the packages from the ground and examined them, then let his hands drop to his sides. "Maybe the air down there is wet. Or do they call it humid?" He shrugged. "Oh well, I have no idea what happened."

Yesterday, Jaxon looked to be in his late teens, maybe early twenties. At first glance, she would estimate him to be at least forty, perhaps fifty years of age, this morning. The only thing that hadn't seemed to age overnight was his eyes. They were still strung out and youthful.

Or was it possible she just hadn't gotten a good look at him?

What Jaxon couldn't see without a mirror was his hair. He'd gone mostly gray overnight.

"Did you check the expiry date on those things?" Russ asked.

"Of course, but they don't stamp these packages with expiry dates."

"They don't?" Grayson asked.

Jaxon shook his head. "The time stamp on MREs is always the inspection date. Also, these things have a shelf life of five years at least, but when kept in cooler conditions, like that bunker down there, they've been known to still be edible up to and over ten years."

"How do you know all this shit?" Russ asked.

If Anna weren't watching Jaxon's face, she would've missed it. After Russ spoke, a flicker of doubt rushed across Jaxon's eyes as they refocused for a moment, then he blinked, and it was gone. To the casual observer, they would've just seen Jaxon blinking and looking up to answer the question, but something deeper was going on for Jaxon.

"My brother was in the army. Brought some of

these home once for us to try. I hated them, but man, when you're starving, they do the trick."

Russ and Anna exchanged a glance, while Grayson just kept staring at Jaxon like he saw a ghost.

"Then tell us what the inspection date is on those things," Anna said, feeling stronger on solid ground, the sun beating down on her.

"They're just over ten years old, but there's another way to tell if they're edible."

"Oh, yeah." Russ stepped forward to take one from Jaxon. "How's that if it smells or has green stuff growing on it?"

"There's an inner lighter circle and an outer darker circle on each one. You're good to go as long as the inner circle is still lighter than the outer one. When they've gone the same color, you need to back away. So, I opened ten and found at least six to be edible. These are all from the edible batch."

He handed one to Grayson and reached out with one for Anna.

She hesitated, then her stomach made up her mind for her. She adjusted her carry-on so it wouldn't slip off her shoulder, stuck out her hand, and snatched the silver packet from Jaxon's grasp.

Russ tore into his, smelled it, then sampled a corner. "Not bad, actually."

Grayson did the same. "Lighter inner circle," he said, then bit into the MRE.

Anna opened hers, sniffed it, then recoiled from the disgusting odor, her gag reflex kicking in. These had to be where that burned mushroom smell was coming from. The rest of the MREs were likely rotting underground and causing some sort of methane or gas buildup, which was exhaled through vents built into the bunker somewhere. There was no way she could put any of that gross fake food in her mouth.

"How many of these things are down there?" she asked.

"A few thousand, maybe more."

A few thousand? That sounded like enough to emit such a noxious odor all the way to the train tracks.

Jaxon watched as the other men ate their MREs. "Tonight, we sleep in the tunnels," he declared matter-of-factly.

"Oh," Anna piped up right away. "No one told you."

"Told me what?"

"We're leaving." How could he not know that, or at least suspect it? "We bought train tickets to specific destinations. Grayson is supposed to be at a dentist convention. I'm going to see my mother in a hospice, and Russ is—"

"Staying for a few nights with Jaxon," he said, cutting her off with his mouth full. He swallowed, then turned to her. "I'll help you get where you're going, but Jaxon's right. If there are thousands of these things, then I've got all the food I need, and I'm sure those old guys, wherever they are, could use some help around here. I might just stay a week or two."

"Right on, man!" Jaxon pumped a fist in the air. "I can handle company."

"What about you, Grayson? You staying, too?" Anna faced him, not happy with the idea of traveling with him. Something about the guy was giving her the willies.

Grayson was nibbling on his MRE. The gleam in his eye as he stared at the hard-packed army food made him look hungry, yet he still appeared reserved, even nervous to continue to eat.

Grayson swallowed and looked up. "Well, there's no use going to my convention now. Even if I got there this afternoon or evening, Sunday is the slower day. I would rather just head home if you want company." He stared at her oddly, immediately making her feel uncomfortable. It wasn't something she could put her finger on. It was just a feeling.

"I don't want to walk those tracks alone, so yeah, come with me." She didn't add that she wanted as far away from this place as she could get, as soon as possible. If Grayson tried anything when they were alone, she'd bash his head in with a rock and leave him on the tracks.

After a glance at Jaxon with the impossible physical changes that had taken place overnight, she was ready to leave. Actually, she was prepared to leave when she woke up, but that got delayed.

"Then it's settled," Russ said, opening another MRE package to eat.

She watched him, her mouth watering at the idea

of food while still unable to stomach eating one of those things.

"So, we're leaving now?" she asked, as no one seemed to be in a hurry.

"You guys go ahead," Jaxon said. "I'm heading back underground to search through more of the rooms in that bunker. I found at least a dozen crates left behind." He was already moving away. "Time to explore."

"You sure that's a good idea?" she asked. "Going alone down there?"

"Absolutely." He laughed a short burst. "No one's out here. Why wouldn't I be safe? All the bad guys are in big cities."

"I wouldn't be too sure about that," she mumbled to herself.

Jaxon didn't seem to hear her as he spun around and headed for the side door of the barracks.

"I'll come to join you soon," Russ shouted after him.

"You escorting us back to the tracks?" she asked.

He shook his head. "Just to the cabin we saw last night. From there, you and Grayson will be fine." He glanced up at the clear sky above. "There's lots of light. You'll be able to see your way back through the trees without an issue."

She adjusted her bag on her shoulder. "You're not concerned with what you just saw there?"

"Saw where?"

Her eyes widened. Was she the only sane one left

in the group? "Jaxon looks as if he's aged twenty years overnight, perhaps more. Come on, don't tell me you didn't see that, too." Controlling her tone was tough as she let some of her shock at his stupidity come through in her voice.

"That didn't happen, couldn't have happened." Russ shook his head. "We all must've missed something last night."

"What?" Her hands went to her hips in defiance. "How absurd. The guy stood right in front of us before the sun went down last night, and he didn't look like that."

"Anna, you're upset." Russ moved closer. "Understandably."

She eased back a few steps until he stopped.

"I'm not going to hurt you."

"Then stay where you are."

He glanced at Grayson, raised and lowered his eyebrows, then turned back to her.

"Anna, did we really get a good look at him last night? We got off the train. We were all upset. Then we headed into the trees and saw the cabin with the fireplace, and then we came here. Look, all I'm saying is, aging twenty years overnight doesn't happen in our laws of physics and shit. So, it *didn't* happen. Something else rational *did* happen. I just don't know what that is."

"Me neither, and thank you for explaining it to me, Mr. Scientist."

"You don't have to be bitchy about it."

She spun away from him, a hand over her mouth to cover the quivering lower lip. Being emotional in front of strangers was so embarrassing.

"I'm sorry," she said, her back still to him.

"Maybe it's time we head to the cabin. Then I want to go after Jaxon and see if he's okay."

She spun back around to face Russ, her eyes glazed over. "What if it happens to you?"

"You mean, what if I age overnight?"

"Yeah, what if you come up from that dungeon and you're fifty, or worse, sixty years old? Then the day after, you're a hundred, and you're dead? Then what?"

"Well," he chuckled, "that won't happen, but thanks for your concern."

How could men be so stupid? Then an image of Janine straddling Colton flashed through her mind, and she understood the answer to that question. Men were absolute fucking idiots, and she was so done with them. She'd been done with men for years, but she kept giving them chances like a stupid girl living in a grown woman's body.

She glanced down at the tattoo of the butterfly on her left arm. When her father walked out of the house, and their life, when she was fourteen years old—almost fifteen years ago—she decided the butterfly was apt. Like a snail, the caterpillar wormed his way into her mom's pants, produced Anna, then spent fourteen years changing on her mother. He cheated on her, drank all night, and yelled at her mother most days until finally Anna woke and her father was gone one morning. Just like a butterfly, he grew wings and fluttered off.

She'd struggled with relationships at an early age, as she was drawn to men who wanted to have some fun, then take off like her father. Some would credit Freud for his insight into her life years before she was born, but Anna wasn't buying it. Her father taught her that most men wanted one thing, and that was it. Once they got it, they were gone unless they were the loving, relationship type. It was only a matter of time. How many men were relationship types? She figured the percentages were in the low one or two points, certainly not high enough to matter to her anymore.

She stared at Russ and Grayson for several more heartbeats, then said, "I'm leaving." She stormed off. "You coming, Grayson?"

"Right behind you."

Fifteen minutes later, they saw the same cabin from last night emerge from the trees along the path in the distance.

She slowed her pace. Something was different about it this time. From a distance, she couldn't quite put her finger on it, though.

Grayson and Russ were chatting fifteen feet behind her, taking their sweet time along the trail. The odd laugh here and there, but she couldn't pick up too much of their chatter. The bodybuilder guy and the combover dentist sounded like old friends for no particular reason. Was that what they called male bonding? One of her ex-boyfriends called it that when he argued about going to poker night. That same poker night where they weren't actually playing poker—they were in a strip club in Portland until one in the morning.

From about thirty feet away, the cabin from last night didn't look lived in at all. The front door was still open, just like it was about twelve hours ago, but there was no fire inside. There was a reason for this—because it looked like no one had lived in this cabin for many years.

The wooden exterior walls were rundown, and in places, there were holes as big as bowling balls where she could see inside the rundown building.

Seeing the cabin and the state it was in last night, then seeing it again this morning, didn't make any sense whatsoever. Or did they just *think* they saw a solid cabin in the darkness, and now with the light of day, they could see all of its blemishes?

She slowed to a stop in front, her mouth hanging open.

The boys were still chatting about a baseball team—something about the Blue Jays and the Yankees.

"Guys?" she said.

Her voice had no effect. Russ said something about the early nineties and how the Jays won the World Series.

"Guys!" she screamed and twisted around to stare at them, cutting Russ off mid-sentence.

Both men gawked at the cabin.

"Yeah, just what I thought," she snapped. "You think we didn't see how old this place was last night, too?"

Russ muttered something, his mouth moving, but she didn't catch it.

"Someone," she said, "please tell me you saw the fire last night, the old man leaning on the rifle."

Grayson closed his open mouth and nodded. Then Russ was nodding.

"It looked," Russ started, then tried again. "It looked lived in."

"That's what I thought." Anna moved up the steps. "Hello?" she called.

When there was no response, Russ clumped up the steps behind her, then moved past her and into the cabin.

Grayson followed him.

Before going inside, Anna scanned the woods but saw nothing moving except a few trees. A soft breeze had picked up, bringing with it that sick mushroom-burning smell.

Something struck her as odd. Where were the insects?

Not a single mosquito had tried to take her blood, and not a single fly had landed on her arms. There were no black flies, horse flies, deer flies or bees, hornets, or wasps. She hadn't even seen a spiderweb in the trees.

Anna glanced up into the sky but had failed to see a single bird roaming above the treetops since they'd arrived.

The only evidence of any wildlife had been the moving around in the bush last night. The old man at the barracks had warned them that some kind of cat was out there, roaming for food, but they hadn't seen it. All she'd seen were a grouping of men in the clearing, watching them before falling asleep in that disgusting barracks building.

Whatever was going on, they needed to get out now. They needed to run for their lives. She felt that literally.

"Anna?" Russ shouted.

She ducked at the sudden intrusion into her thoughts, then moved toward the door and stepped inside.

Russ and Grayson were standing by the fireplace or what was left of the fireplace.

Russ had his arm up. He pointed at the living room window.

"We saw the fire through that window, right?"

Her stomach dropped at the thought. Something was wrong with this place—*everything* was wrong with this place.

"We have to get out of here." Her voice seemed distant but firm enough.

"Anna, it had to be another cabin." Russ was talking stupid again. Why did she have the sudden urge to smash him in the face?

"This was the cabin, Russ. Don't attempt to rationalize what cannot be rationalized."

"Look," he pointed at the fireplace, "no one has had a fire in there for years. It's covered in an inch of dust, which falls naturally." He glanced up at her. "They couldn't have put out the fire, cleared the area, then added this dust."

"What about the window?" she asked. "Or lack thereof?"

"That's got me, too." Grayson scratched his head.

Anna continued, "Last night, I saw the fire *reflected* through the cabin's back window. It's what drew us to the cabin in the first place after it got dark."

"Well, then." Russ shrugged like it was no big deal. "Since there's no windowpane in that frame, you didn't see it reflected through the glass in this cabin. It had to be another cabin." He swung his hands outward. "Look around you, people, and you will see absolute evidence that no one lives here." Now he laughed, and it made him sound nervous. "So, I go with the evidence. This wasn't the cabin."

Now she really wanted to smack the man. It was that sort of stupidity that got people killed in horror movies.

"Is or isn't, doesn't matter. I'm leaving. Right the fuck now." Anna stepped back twice, then turned and marched out of the cabin, down the steps, and over to the side where they'd approached it from last night—or where they *thought* they approached it from.

It had been dark, almost absolute dark, but she was pretty sure this was the place. The front steps and the door placement—all easily taken in last night from the firelight emanating outward—were exactly as she remembered. Even the pathway they'd walked out to the barracks building was similar in the daylight.

None of it mattered, though. The train tracks were directly behind the cabin, about a hundred yards away, maybe more to her right. The woods were thick, almost impassable, but doable in the light, especially since they did it last night in the dark.

"Thought you were leaving?" Russ said as he exited the cabin.

"I am. I just wanted to take another look from out here."

"Well, I'm happy you didn't run for the trees."

The wind had picked up more, the upper sections of the trees behind the cabin swaying. She pushed the hair out of her face and wrapped it behind her ears.

"This starting to freak you out now, too?"

He stared at her a moment. "Somewhat. So much that I want to leave now. I think we've seen enough evidence that all four of us should probably vacate this area."

"Yeah," Grayson said. "I'm with you on that, but I'd like to know where those guys from last night are. If this is some huge prank, why not jump out and laugh and be done with it?"

She narrowed her eyes at him. "You think this is a prank?"

"I didn't say that. I said *if* this is some sort of prank."

She glanced from Russ to Grayson, then back to

Russ. "Okay, so we're all leaving. Let's get going."

"Not without Jaxon." Russ walked past her, heading back toward the barracks.

"You're kidding, right?"

He stopped and looked back, a scowl on his face. "You mean you'd just walk away and leave Jaxon alone?"

"Well, no," she stammered. "It's just, we need to leave, and it was obvious he was quite happy with the barracks dungeon or whatever that thing was down there—"

"Bunker."

"As I said, whatever, and this is yet another delay in leaving."

"Then go. No one's stopping you." Russ turned away from her and continued toward the barracks.

Grayson followed him.

Both men moved farther away with each step, and she hadn't had a chance to tell them about the lack of insects or birds. They were leaving her alone by the empty, unused cabin, alone to fend for herself in this strange place.

The wind picked up even more, causing a howling creepy sound to roll through the trees behind her.

It brought with it a sound.

She cocked her head slightly, tilting her ear up to listen.

It sounded like a train.

She spun around to face the trees behind the cabin, but it was so thick all she saw was green and semi-darkness where the sun didn't penetrate too well.

Something screeched from that direction, like brakes being applied.

Then it was gone.

"Guys, did you hear that?"

She had goosebumps roaming over most of her body's flesh, so much so that she hugged herself and glanced back at the retreating men.

They were nearly forty yards away now and about to disappear around a bend in the path.

She'd be completely alone out here.

It was likely close to lunchtime, so there was still plenty of time to leave in the daylight.

Get Jaxon, then leave.

Decision made, she bolted after Russ and Grayson, her bag bouncing against her arm, the strap digging into her shoulder.

They had just disappeared around the corner when she heard a man shouting.

She redoubled her pace, groaning at the stupidity of being alone out here.

Then that shout came again, but she was sure she knew what he was saying this time.

It was her name sailing to her on the breeze— someone was calling her name.

She ran harder.

Chapter 17

COLTON ASHER GOT ON the train, double-checking that he was on the right one with that ticket woman, Maggie. To reassure him, Maggie even came out and spoke with two train staff, who were official-looking guys, pointed at Colton, then nodded.

They were dropping him off at the substation. Everyone was on the same page. Perfect.

From there, he was on his own. His phone was sitting at ninety-six percent, which would hold the charge all night. The burger and coffee for breakfast would keep him most of the rest of the day if needed, and he wasn't working tonight, so he was all set to spend the afternoon and evening looking for Anna.

The train pulled out minutes later, and he tracked it on his maps app on the phone to see where they'd end up.

Almost an hour later, as the train began to slow for him to exit at the substation, he lost service coverage, and his map stopped updating his current location. The train cruised what felt like ten more miles but was probably only two or three, moving slower and slower until it stopped, the brakes squeaking intermittently, and still, he had no service.

"Shit," he mumbled under his breath when the train suddenly stopped, its brakes protesting.

The people in the car around him were glancing out the windows, probably trying to see why they'd stopped in the middle of nowhere.

He was asking himself that same question. How could they be so inept at dropping off a woman with three other men to wait unattended for the next train in the middle of nowhere?

An attendant strode toward him. "Sir, this is it."

"Figured as much."

Colton slipped his phone away and rose from his chair to follow the attendant.

One minute later, he stood on a small wooden platform as the train started the arduous task of getting back underway and up to speed.

He jumped off the platform and stared into the trees behind it.

Way too thick to traverse. He stared along the track line but saw nothing out of the ordinary.

While waiting for the long train to pass by to check the other side of the tracks, he jumped back onto the platform and examined the wood for signs of blood or hair or any indication a struggle had occurred.

There was a small maintenance shed of some kind. He tried the door, but it was locked. He banged on the door several times, then placed his ear to it to listen.

Nothing.

The last train car was easing by his position.

He waited a moment, then when it disappeared down the tracks, he jumped down from the platform and walked across the tracks. The other side was just as dense and thick. Actually, it looked double the thickness.

Nothing jumped out at him. There were no signs of a struggle, no discarded clothes, no nothing.

"Anna!" he shouted in the rising wind. Then he called her name again and again, mostly out of frustration.

If she had walked the tracks, they'd pick her up south of this location or back in Eugene. But if she entered the woods on either side, she may be lost, hence why he was here. He had to find her.

After another check of his cell phone and finding no signal, he slipped it into his pocket and marked the sun's position. As long as he kept it at his back and left shoulder going in, then it would be at his chest and right shoulder going out.

He was ready.

So, he chose the woods behind the wooden platform as they were thick but manageable. The other side was worse, much worse.

He had brought his service pistol just in case some wild animal were to get too close. He'd kill it and explain the gun's usage later.

Anna was missing, and he intended to find her.

Then get them both home safe.

There were no other options because this was all

his fault, and if something happened to Anna, it was on him.

If she hadn't walked in on Janine straddling him, Anna wouldn't have pushed up her trip to the hospice in Sacramento.

He needed to do better. He *could* do better.

If only Anna gave him a chance, he'd show her.

As long as she was still alive.

Colton pulled out the Department of Justice sheets on Rusty Brown and Grayson Cooper and studied their faces. Then he folded them up, slipped them into his back pocket, and headed for the trees. After ducking to avoid a thick branch, he pushed more out of his face and entered the throng of greenery.

The tracks disappeared from his view in moments, and he was completely immersed in the Oregon thickness.

Even the sun didn't touch the bed of this section of the forest.

Chapter 18

PRESENT DAY ...

It was nearing eleven in the evening when Trooper Logan made it to the train station on foot after leaving his cruiser and Detective Sergeant Ray Smithers at his house. Surprisingly, he wasn't that tired yet, which was good. He'd need his strength for what he intended to do.

During the entire walk over from his house, he avoided the main streets, kept to the shadows, and maintained a steady pace. If this was going to work, it had to be tonight.

Once inside the nearly empty building, he read the board that listed the trains coming and going. The last passenger train left the station in half an hour, heading north toward Washington State.

Staff were mopping the floor, and the woman behind the ticket window was tapping away on her screen, probably playing Solitaire until her shift ended.

He moved to the ticket booth, leaned close to the Plexiglas on his right arm, and nodded.

"Maggie, right?"

The woman jerked her head his way, a frown causing a series of wrinkles to crease her brow.

"I recognize you," she said.

"State Police, Trooper Richard Logan."

"Right, you were here a few days ago dropping off those Most-Wanted flyers."

He nodded. "That's what I wanted to talk to you about."

Her face lost some of its color as she adjusted herself in her chair. "How can I help you, Officer?"

There was no need to correct her use of the term *officer* as he technically was a cop. He just preferred to be called a trooper.

"I saw you speaking with Officer Colton Asher that night."

She nodded. "Other cops came asking about him already."

"Figured as much, but I want to know why he was here."

She shrugged, avoiding eye contact. "Bought a train ticket. Headed toward Redding." She eased out of her chair as if she wanted to leave.

"Maggie, that's not entirely true."

She stopped moving, then slowly met his gaze.

"Maggie," Logan said, drawing out her name. "He came asking about Anna Valentina, didn't he? When I gave him the Rusty Brown flyer, he showed it to you, said something, slapped the Plexiglas, then bolted from the building. Why don't you tell me what you know before I haul you in on some ridiculous charge related to Miss Valentina's disappearance or even Officer Asher's disappearance? I mean, after all, I can verify you were the last person to see that cop alive, am I right?"

If Maggie had any color left in her face the moment before, it was gone now. Her eyes darted left and right in their sockets, and her hands fidgeted at her sides.

"Come to the back. I'll tell you everything."

"That's all I want to hear." Logan moved to the side, where Maggie unlocked an employee door and let him in the back. She guided him into the staff lounge, then down a hallway to a back door, where she stopped.

"I didn't do anything wrong," she started.

"Then why did you look guilty back there?"

"Because I don't want to be responsible for bad things happening to good people."

"How could you be responsible?"

"What I'm about to tell you is what I told Colton, and now he's missing, too."

She looked on the verge of tears.

"Look." Logan raised his hands. "I have people missing, and I'm trying to get to the bottom of it. Just tell me what you know, and we'll go from there. No one is holding you responsible for anything." *So far,* he didn't add.

Maggie started talking. Five minutes later, he knew what he had come here to learn.

"How do I get to this substation?"

"The last train headed that way left over an hour ago. Nothing until tomorrow morning now."

"That won't work. I need to get there tonight."

She shook her head. "There aren't any roads in that area. You can't drive or walk to it unless you follow the tracks."

"How far is it?"

"Thirty, maybe forty miles south. Maybe closer."

It all started to come together for him. Anna got dropped off with Rusty Brown, Grayson Cooper, and probably one other passenger. Then Colton went out there looking for her, but only Anna made it out of the woods—so far, and that FedEx driver found her and called it in.

Then what happened to the others?

They had to be still out there somewhere. Maybe Grayson was trying to have fun with Anna when Rusty attacked them. Rusty was wanted for aggravated assault, after all. He probably saw Colton Asher, who would've identified himself as a cop, and thought he came to bring him in.

Something happened in those woods, and Miss Valentina paid the price.

But what made her age so fast?

"I need to get out there now. Are there any extra trains, an engineer that'll drop me down there?"

Maggie shook her head. "I'd do anything to end this shit, but there's no one here. Just the cleaning staff and myself. We're closing up in less than twenty minutes to go home. Staff returns at five in the morning. Take the train then."

Logan leaned back against the wall and stared up at the ceiling. "No, I need to get out there now."

"Why? What happened? Has something come up?"

He opened his mouth to tell her about Anna, then closed it. He'd signed an NDA. Questions would already be asked regarding his conduct after ditching Smithers at his house. He didn't want a violation of the military NDA on his record, too.

"I just need to get to that substation as soon as possible."

"Well, unless you're willing to wait until breakfast, you'll have to walk the tracks to get there."

He pushed off the wall. "Then I'll walk the tracks. How long could it take to walk that far?"

"You're crazy. You'll be walking all night."

At least the military guys won't find him on a train track in the middle of nowhere during the night.

"Any trains due to be on that particular stretch of track tonight? Something I should watch out for?"

She shook her head. "None."

"Then I'm walking. Point me in the right direction."

She stared at him momentarily, then pushed open the door they stood beside and stepped out.

They were on the back platform where people waited for their train.

Maggie pointed along the tracks toward a wall of blackness where the light was swallowed by night.

"Jump down and walk that way. Depending on how fast you walk, it'll take you most of the night." She looked up at him. "My guess is you'll do it in five or six hours if you push hard, seven to eight if you take it easy."

He nodded at her, and without another word, Logan jumped off the platform and started walking along the tracks, placing each foot on the wooden ties in the center.

The back door closed behind him as Maggie slipped back inside the building.

Within a few minutes, he was surrounded by darkness, leaving the light of the building behind him. He withdrew his gun and slipped it into the back of his pants to feel more secure. Then he grabbed his flashlight from the backpack and gripped it tightly in his right hand.

Every so often, when he heard something scampering along in the woods, he flashed his light that way, shouted something, and kept walking.

After two hours of walking into the woods along the tracks, he stopped for a five-minute break, retrieving some snacks from his pack. Cashews and raisins, with some water. He sat on the side of the tracks to eat, took a piss, then packed everything up and started walking again.

Quite a few hours later, as the sun colored the sky in the east to his left, the outline of the substation came into view.

He'd made it. When he found Officer Colton or

any of the others, and he called it in, he'd have to answer to the military guys. Yet, he didn't work for them, nor did he sign up for this shit. He was a state trooper, and he had a fellow cop missing. It was his job to find him as much as anybody else's.

If he didn't find anyone, maybe what was here would lead him to what happened to Miss Valentina.

Ultimately, he hoped this wasn't a fool's errand because, without results, he'd have difficulty justifying his actions to Miles and Atkins.

The small shed-like building on the platform was locked. He flashed the light around the area but saw nothing out of place. After a short investigation of the site, scanning the trees, and studying the platform and area immediately surrounding it, he concluded nothing had happened there.

In fact, there were no signs anyone had been out here at all.

What if they didn't get off at this substation? He failed to ask Maggie if there were more than one. Maybe there were two, and he stopped at the first one, not knowing there was another one ten miles away or something.

The sun had moved higher, offering him more light to move about more freely. It hadn't crested the mountain yet, but he didn't need the flashlight to see where he was going anymore.

He jumped off the substation platform and moved behind it. Back there, it got darker again with the coverage of trees, so he flicked on his light.

Footprints, or what looked like indentations, were on the ground in the grass.

His heart rate increased as he looked around.

Someone had been here recently, and since this location was in the middle of nowhere, this had to be the spot.

"Hello?" he called.

What if Colton was hurt? What if he couldn't move?

"Hello?" he called louder, then tilted his head to listen.

It struck him as odd that he didn't even hear an animal scurry away in the bush. He hadn't heard any animals for the past hour or so.

A creepy feeling came over him, raising goosebumps on his flesh.

What the hell was this place?

That's when that smell hit him. It was the same mushroom smell he'd detected by the side of the highway when he first moved into the trees to find Miss Valentina.

Who was out here cooking mushrooms? This situation just went from creepy to weird.

"I'm coming into the trees," he said. "I'm with the Oregon State Police."

Then he took several tentative footsteps away from the tracks, moving deeper into the woods. The flashlight was necessary as none of the sun's early light reached below the canopy of thick trees.

"Anyone here?" The sound of his own voice

startled him.

He moved deeper, and with each step, the scent of those mushrooms grew thicker until it smelled like they had been burned while someone was attempting to sauté them.

Flashlight in hand, he spun in a full circle. There was nothing but trees, bushes, and small patches of grass.

He had no idea what he was looking for or if he'd find anything at all.

So he kept moving away from the tracks.

Could that abandoned military base be in here? What if Miss Valentina stumbled upon something the military wanted to keep secret, hence their heavy presence?

That had to be it. There was a secret out here, and they intended to keep it.

Something moved to his right.

Startled, Logan spun that way and saw a man in full military fatigues, a large weapon in his hands, staring at him.

"What the fuck, man?" Logan gasped for air. "You scared the shit out of me."

"We've been asked to bring you to the command post."

Logan glanced around and saw four other men in uniform. "Where did you guys come from?"

"Sir, this way." The soldier gestured for Logan to move to his left.

"Do you even know who I am?"

"Yes, sir. You're Trooper Richard Logan. You've been assigned to help with the CID investigation. Our superiors are waiting for you, sir." The soldier now stood a few feet away, his arm up and pointing to Logan's left.

He exhaled heavily, then turned that way. Two men led the way, and two took up the rear, with Logan in the middle.

They walked through the trees until a fence came up on their left. Along the fence, he saw several signs similar to the picture of the sign on Miss Valentina's phone.

Some of the compound to his right still sat in semi-darkness as the sun couldn't penetrate those areas until it was directly above them due to the thickness of the trees.

The inside of the fence intrigued him. What was in there? Or rather, *who* was in there?

Before facing forward, Logan caught something moving behind a tree.

He slowed, then stopped, eyes riveted to that tree.

"Sir, we have to keep moving."

"I know. One sec. Someone's in there."

"Sir, nothing is beyond this fence—"

"Look!" Logan pointed at the man who stuck his head out from behind a tree.

By the time the soldiers followed his finger, the man had jumped back behind the tree.

"There's someone in there." His voice sounded more urgent this time.

"Sir, we see nothing. We must continue."

"But ..." He glanced at all four soldiers in turn. "Do you have people on the inside?"

"Sir, to our knowledge, there is no one on that side of the fence. Now, we must continue."

They didn't see anything, so they chose not to believe him. Fine, he would report what he saw to Atkins or Miles when he got to them.

They started moving again. Five minutes later, without any of them speaking a word to each other and Logan wondering how much trouble he was in with Miles and Atkins for giving Smithers the slip, they arrived at what looked like a temporary military base camp in the middle of the woods.

It swarmed with men in uniform and was well guarded by fully armed sentries posted every dozen feet or so.

His escort soldiers led him to a white trailer, where the lead man stepped up a small set of stairs and knocked.

Command Sergeant Major George Miles opened the door and stared at Logan.

"As much as we need your help, I do not appreciate your games."

"It was no game, sir. I'm looking for a missing officer."

"As are we." He gazed at the four soldiers. "Return to your posts." They saluted him. He saluted back, then faced Logan. "Come in. We must talk."

Logan moved up the steps as Miles eased to the

side. Atkins was seated at a table, a map spread out before him.

"We are in quarantine mode," Atkins said without looking up. "This temporary command post is organized and set up close to where Anna jumped the fence. You shouldn't have dumped Smithers, but we expected it. You don't have the discipline we live with day to day."

"She jumped that fence?" Logan asked, ignoring Atkins's discipline jab. It would do him no good to spar with these men as they'd undoubtedly win intellectually. "I want to go in there." He also neglected to tell them he saw a man hiding behind a tree.

Atkins looked up from the map as Miles took a seat opposite him.

"Logan, if you go in there, you won't come out."

He frowned at how serious they sounded. What could possibly be inside that fence line that was so scary?

"Anna came out." Those words sounded like a weak retort as soon as he said them.

The military men exchanged a glance, then looked back at Logan.

"She's the only one. Ever."

Chapter 19

Two Days Before Present Day ...

Anna caught up with Russ and Grayson just as they were about to slip inside the door that led along the barracks corridor.

They both stopped to address her.

"You okay?" Russ asked.

Anna bent over, hands on her knees, gasping for a breath after running the whole way. Her carry-on bag slipped off her shoulder and dropped to the ground, the strap snagging on her wrist.

"I ran," she gasped, inhaled, "to catch up." She pushed off her thighs and stood, untangling her wrist to leave her bag on the ground. She arched her head back and inhaled deeply. "Someone was calling my name."

Russ made a face and looked askance at Grayson. "We certainly didn't."

Anna's breathing was getting back under control, but she felt heat rising to her cheeks now. In this area, out front of the abandoned army barracks, the wind had died down to almost nothing, the surrounding trees having broken it. Under normal circumstances, they'd be able to hear a cricket in the bush, a plane overhead, or even the buzz of a bee, but there was nothing. Absolute silence except for the sounds they made. Like they were living in a bubble, how is it that neither of these men noticed any of this?

"You must've been hearing things," Russ added.

"No, I know what I heard. It carried to me on the breeze. Maybe it was coming from the train tracks area. The likelihood of us being declared missing by now is a real possibility. People could be out looking, like search parties and shit."

"Okay." Russ pointed at the barracks. "I'm going in there to get Jaxon. Then we'll leave. But first, let's take one minute to break down what you just said."

She placed her hands on her hips. "Break down what I just said? How so?"

"You said someone was calling your name on the breeze, right?" Russ held up his hands. "What breeze?" He looked at Grayson. "Do you feel any wind or even a slight breeze outside?"

"There's one over there by that cursed cabin." Anna jabbed her right arm behind her, pointing the way they'd just come.

"Anna dear, a breeze or a—"

"Don't, *dear* me." For some inexplicable reason, the hostility level inside her had gone nuclear. Sure, they were under a lot of stress, and sure, they were dealing with something they were all trying to explain away, but fighting with each other about it wouldn't help. Yet, she wanted—no *needed*—to be mad at someone, and that someone seemed to be Russ at the moment.

Then it came to her why.

She had been ready to leave as soon as she woke up, yet she was still here. It was like Russ was in league with whatever was working against them so they could stay here.

"Obviously, you're angry." Russ held both hands up in front of himself, chest high. "But let me tell you something. This isn't my fault, so don't attack me. I'm stuck in this place, just like you."

Anna couldn't hold his gaze. He was right. She was angry, furious, in fact, and scared. Now would be a good time to apologize, but she chose not to. Later, she'd apologize profusely when they made it out and were walking along the tracks with this place in their rearview mirror. But for now, all she could do was nod his way, at least acknowledge what he said, and tighten her lips to keep from saying anything else.

"There's no breeze, Anna. There's no one out there calling your name, and if there was, then by the time we get Jaxon and start back toward the cabin, they will have found us. So, everything's okay, and we'll be out of here within the next half an hour or so. Cool?"

She hated when guys said *cool*. The word men complained about with women was *fine*. When a woman said she was *fine*, guys read that to mean she wasn't fine. When guys said *cool*, it wasn't cool at all. It was something they said to patronize a woman and keep her from losing her cool.

Russ backed away, then turned and entered the door to the barracks.

Grayson offered her a half-smile, then followed Russ inside.

Her head on a swivel, she took in the surrounding area. Did she want to be alone out here? It wasn't the wild animals she was afraid of because, after all that had happened, she was starting to believe that none lived in this creepy area.

The thing or person that was watching them was what freaked her out. She could feel it like it was a soft touch on the nape of her neck. It wasn't just a gut instinct; it was more like killer intuition. The feeling one gets before an attack is something humans were more in touch with back when they were hunter-gatherers. She would put money down that they were being watched by something malicious that intended them harm, something cunning and ancient.

While the clearing was the size of an average playground on any suburban street in America, there was nothing to see that would instill fear. Yet, being alone out here in the sunshine freaked her out.

"Anna!" Russ shouted.

This time she was sure someone was calling her name. But even though his voice was coming from inside the barracks, it startled her enough that she lifted off the ground, a short screech rushing from her mouth.

"Come quick!" Russ added.

Decision made—she *was* going inside and couldn't do it fast enough.

Even as she entered the door to race down the length of the corridor, someone shouted her name from the outside again, somewhere behind her. It wasn't Russ because Russ was in front of her.

But she refused to give it another thought. Whoever was yelling for her outside the barracks, whether they sounded like her ex-boyfriend or not, had to be a figment of her imagination.

Russ was right. No one was here looking for them this early in the morning. They'd only been dropped off last night, and perhaps only twelve to fifteen hours had gone by so far. Not enough to be declared missing yet.

Colton would know she was gone, but what the hell did he expect after what she saw him doing with her boss, Janine? That alone would not motivate him to search for her, and even if he did, he wouldn't already be here, in this particular section of Oregon, walking these exact woods. The odds were improbable.

Whatever was outside was that thing that was watching them, and it was trying to scare the shit out of her, but she wouldn't let it.

"Anna," Russ called again as she reached the top of the spiral staircase.

"I'm here," she shouted down.

On the top stair, she paused. Russ and Grayson stood at the bottom, their faces white in the candlelight.

"What is it?" she asked, afraid of the answer.

"It's Jaxon."

She took one more stair, then stopped, not trusting her knees to hold her for the short trip down the winding steps.

"What about him?"

"We can't find him, and there's no exit."

"What?" She shook her head to clear it. "So, he came back up for some reason. Otherwise, he's down there. People don't just disappear."

Russ shook his head. "We've looked everywhere. He's gone."

"Probably smart of him. He bolted from this place. So, come on up, guys. We should leave, too."

Russ was still shaking his head, a hand on his stomach. She hadn't noticed it before, but Grayson also had a hand on his stomach. And now his face wasn't just white—it seemed slightly green.

"What happened, Russ?" She lowered to her butt, not willing to keep standing on the steps. "Just tell me."

"You remember Jaxon saying there were more rooms down here that he wanted to explore?"

She nodded, her lower lip trembling in fear now.

"Well, you must see what's in the last room."

She shook her head. "No, I think we need to leave." Her voice rose an octave, surprised fear could do that to her. "Please, can't we just go and never come back?"

"Anna, none of us are leaving until we all see what's in that final room. Then we *have* to leave to inform the authorities."

"Inform the authorities?" She nearly gasped the words. "Inform them of what?" Her mind raced at what could be in that last room.

Russ waved a hand and turned away from the bottom of the stairs.

"Follow us."

Grayson looked ready to puke. They eased apart when the two men moved deeper into the bunker's tunnel. They were probably afraid to spew on each other in case one of them did vomit.

Maybe it was that sick mushroom smell. It was so intense down here, she felt like she was in the underbelly of a rotting whale.

Although, there was no way she would sit alone on the top of the staircase down here. Waiting outside with the sunshine was one thing, but it was way too creepy in here.

She used the railing to haul herself to her feet, then clutching it with both hands, she descended foot by foot, step by step.

"Wait for me," she muttered, her voice shaking. "Holy fuck, this is stupid," she whispered under her breath, then shouted, "Wait up!"

She reached the bottom of the metal stairs and ran to catch up, knowing what she was about to see would change her life in some way, some dark and horrible way.

She grabbed her phone and hit the power button to take a picture of whatever it was, then rounded the corner and fell in behind Russ and Grayson as they headed toward the darkness at the end of the tunnel.

Chapter 20

COLTON HADN'T GONE FAR before seeing a cabin's outline through the trees. He called Anna's name again, then pushed through the shrubs and underbrush faster. His ankle landed on a thick root and twisted off of it painfully, making him lose his balance. He dropped to the side, arms out to protect his face, but that wasn't too effective. A branch the thickness of an average man's wrist clipped his cheek and dug with the pressure of his weight as he fell.

Warm liquid seeped out and down toward his ear as he landed on his back, looking up.

"Son of a bitch," he whispered to himself, already holding his cheek with his right hand. It came away with blood on it.

"Damn it."

Colton pushed up off the ground, then used the offending branch to drag himself to his feet while holding his cheek with his free hand. He tested his weight on the ankle first, then gently stood on it. It wasn't bad, but it could be mildly sprained, which meant it would become swollen and make navigating through this area a nightmare.

The laceration on his cheek wasn't big enough to

require stitches, but it would bleed until it clotted.

He wiped the blood from his hand on his pants and pushed through the last bit of forest, paying more attention to the ground and mainly relying on his good foot.

The cabin looked deserted years ago. The windows were all broken out, and the exterior was worn with the weather and age. It was obvious no one lived there anymore and hadn't for at least a decade, perhaps longer.

He limped to the front of the cabin, saw the wide-open door, and then moved closer to look inside. More of the same—desolate and would probably be considered condemned by city standards.

He pivoted on his good foot as the breeze died down slightly and listened to the area.

Had he heard something?

There was a rhythmic thumping to his right, like someone running off in the distance. By the time he turned around, he couldn't hear it anymore. Well, there'd be no running in his near future, but he could still move around. A cane of some kind would help.

He scanned the trees until he found what he was looking for. He approached one particular tree, grabbed the branch where he wanted to make the break, and leaned downward. After a slight struggle, the limb snapped off in his hands.

Around three feet in length, the thick branch now served perfectly as a makeshift cane.

He wiped the blood from his neck where it tickled

him, already feeling the flow having slowed, then limped onto a small path out front of the cabin and started along it.

There was no sign that Anna or anyone else had come through this area, but he had to be certain. Another half-hour, maybe an hour more of searching, then he'd head back to the tracks and try the other side.

"Anna?" he called again, just in case she was nearby. The wound on his cheek ached when he opened his mouth to speak.

"Anna?" he tried once more, listening to the silence of the woods, then decided to keep going without shouting to give his cheek a break.

There had been no answer, leaving him no choice but to keep moving forward.

That and the feeling someone was here.

He just knew it.

Chapter 21

Anna rounded the bunker's corner to follow Russ and Grayson, her phone in her right hand, with no idea what to expect.

Both men stopped at the extent of the light, the threshold where the darkness started at the end of the tunnel.

"Since there are no lights beyond that point," she said. "Do you guys have any candles?"

"We have candles. We were waiting for you so we could light them. Don't want to waste wax."

Grayson was unreadable, but there was something on Russ's face she couldn't discern. Was his wild-eyed, open-mouth-stunned look his way of showing surprise, or was it fear? Whatever it was, she didn't like it. They'd seen something that made them call her down here—again—and not only could she *not* handle that disgusting, intense mushroom smell down here, but she was also supposed to be on the train tracks, already walking back toward Eugene, where she'd complain profusely to the train company and then their head office. A lawsuit was not out of the question. Maybe this little debacle would make her rich.

Not wanting to see a body, she asked, "Is it

Jaxon? Is he dead?"

Russ shook his head. "We told you we can't find him. He's not down here." Then he added, "Dead or alive, I assure you."

She put a hand on her chest and exhaled. "Good, I don't want to see dead bodies today."

The men exchanged an odd glance.

"What?" she whispered. "Are there dead bodies down here?"

Russ shook his head again. "No, but something as equally disturbing."

Anna slipped her phone into her back pocket, then moved up and stopped in front of Russ. "Then why do I have to see it?" She hated the squeak in her voice.

"One person can hallucinate, maybe even two, in some twisted shared world of illusions. But adding you to the mix will make us believers."

She scrunched up her face in a dramatic scowl. "What's going on?"

"Follow us. You'll see."

They each took a candle, with Russ having two in his hands, and lit them on the nearest sconce suspended at the height of about five feet along the wall. After Russ handed her one, he led the way into the darkness at the end of the hall.

Anna followed; her empty stomach and weakened legs from no nutrition, and an overdose of adrenaline begged her to walk the other way, but her curiosity drove her onward.

Russ slowed, then stopped in front of a large

wooden door that had seen better days. Down here in the dank, musty air, the doorway had deteriorated. It still sat on rusty hinges, and Anna estimated another five or ten years before it would tear loose of those hinges and smack down to the bunker's floor.

Russ stared at her, his face cast in an eerie yellow light from the candle he held inches in front of him. "You know this place was an old army barracks, right?"

"Well, I don't *know* that, but we assume as much."

"It was, trust me."

"Okay, fine, it was."

He pushed the door open and stepped a few feet inside.

Anna followed, her candle held high to see as much as possible. Grayson and Russ had stopped by the door to wait by the sounds of their footsteps, or lack thereof.

On the right, the edges of crates stacked high against the wall took shape as the candle's light hit them. She moved deeper. With every step, there were more and more crates. When she stopped and raised her candle over her head, she saw the crates stacked over ten high, with the eleventh and twelfth lost to the darkness above.

"How high do these go?"

"As high as we're able to see," Russ said. "Probably fifteen, maybe twenty deep, perhaps more."

She moved farther among more and more stacked

crates.

"What are all these for?"

"Turn toward the middle."

Anna stopped, then did as she was told. More crates were stacked on her left. "It seems endless."

"After about twenty-five in a row on the left, there's an opening where you can move to the next aisle, then the next."

Anna stopped and turned back to Russ and Grayson, who were still standing by the door, their candles making it look like they were floating heads in a sea of darkness.

"So, what are you saying? The military built this to train their soldiers, then forgot about a room and left behind all these empty crates?"

"Anna, they're not empty."

She scanned the crates again, then looked back at Russ. "How do you know that?"

"Over there, on the other side of the wall you're standing by, we opened about ten of them."

"You opened them?"

"It appears Jaxon was here before us, as he had already opened four crates."

Anna moved down the aisle to get to the opening in the middle and turned left as Russ instructed. She wanted to see what was in the open crates.

"You gonna tell me what's in 'em all?" she asked.

"How about you see for yourself and then tell us? Again, we want to know we're not seeing things."

That sounded like an odd request. "But you've

already seen what's in them, right?" She found the section where the crates stopped to create an aisle in the middle, then skirted the last ones and crossed the small aisle to move to the far wall stacked high with the same rectangular-shaped containers, which were all made of some sort of wood and steel.

"Guys, maybe this place wasn't abandoned too long ago." Then an idea hit her as she moved back toward the front. "Wait a second. Is this where Jaxon found those MRE things?"

"That's the room across the hall. We're going there next."

"Well, then, I'm convinced the powers that be must've forgotten about this place and left all this junk behind, which is something I'd like to do pronto."

When she reached the front of the row nearest the door, there were four crates with their tops torn off, exposing whatever was inside. Before lifting the candle high enough to see the contents, she eased closer to the crate itself and read the description painted in block letters on its side.

There were a series of letters and numbers like M1 and 5T and a lot number. She read the word FUZES, and in the middle, near the bottom, it said 2-CARTRIDGE for 105MM.

Slowly, she turned to face Russ and Grayson. "Are these weapons?"

"Look inside any one you want. You'll see."

Reluctantly, Anna lifted the candle over the edge as melted wax descended onto her fingers, then glanced inside an open crate.

"Oh my fuck," she whispered, switching the candle and wiping the wax off her hand and onto her pants. "This is a huge cache here. Why would they leave all this behind? Guys, there are hundreds and hundreds of weapons, assuming all these crates are full."

"Okay, so we're not hallucinating. That's what we saw, too." Russ waved at her. "C'mon, Anna, there are more rooms."

"What?" She followed them across the hallway in a daze, where Grayson pushed open another sizable wooden door.

The moment that door opened, she gagged and fought the urge to vomit. Grayson was already stepping back, and Russ hadn't approached.

"What the fuck, guys?" she said, moving away from the door, a hand over her mouth and nose.

Russ had covered his mouth, too. "Just hold your breath, then go inside," he said, his voice muffled through his hand. "Trust me. You're gonna want to see what's in there."

She moved closer to him. "Is the room as large as the weapons one?"

He nodded. "I'd say it's roughly the same size. You only need to see the first few boxes, though."

Anna nodded at him, inhaled that disgusting mushroom smell twice, then held her breath and stomped into the room while Grayson held the door open.

Her candlelight revealed boxes piled toward the ceiling that went on past the limit of the light. They were lost to the back of the room, just like the weapons crate room.

Something terrible happened here, and she didn't like this one bit. Why would the government leave all this behind? The possibility of them forgetting it all didn't make sense to her. Didn't they do proper inventories of these sorts of items? What if kids wandered down here, or worse, a rogue biker gang or members of the mafia? They would have access to a massive cache of weapons that could arm a small militia.

Boxes sat open to her left. The words MEAL, READY-TO-EAT, and INDIVIDUAL were written along the side of every box. Then below that was, DO NOT ROUGH HANDLE WHEN FROZEN. The date on the top of the box lid that sat open was barely legible, but she could make out 1981.

That was impossible.

Didn't Jaxon say something about them being ten years old and still edible? If these were from 1981, then they were forty years old.

Her lungs protested for air. Before she was forced to breathe in this room, she hustled over to the boxes, raised the candle, and glanced inside.

What she saw made her gag reflex trigger. She stumbled backward, almost fell, then ran for the door. As soon as she exited the room, Grayson closed the door, and all three of them retreated to the lighted area of the bunker corridor.

"What the fuck, guys?" Anna gasped, panting for air that made her want to throw up. They had to get back to the surface soon, or she'd never be able to eat mushrooms again.

"We thought we were seeing things, but we wanted your opinion because you didn't eat any of that shit."

Anna was shaking her head in disbelief. "Those ready-to-eat meals Jaxon gave you guys were in silver packages. The ones in there didn't look silver. They were a darker shade of brown or something."

"And the ones in there are many decades old," Grayson added. "Which is why we're fucked."

"Fucked?" Anna had steadied her breathing. "How so?"

"Did you see the state they were in?" Russ asked.

She nodded. "Yeah, petrified and completely rotted out. Gone to dust or some shit, whatever they call it."

"Exactly. Basically, not edible is an understatement."

"Then what did you guys eat?"

"We don't know, so we kept investigating and found one more room."

"Oh, no. I'm done down here. This is out of control. I'm leaving."

"Anna, please. We feel like we're hallucinating this." Russ gestured with a wave. "Look in this last room, then we go topside and discuss it on the train tracks on the way home."

"Topside? You make it sound like we're on a boat."

"Aren't we? Alone out here like this? But instead of rough water, we're on shaky ground."

"Cute." She sneered at him. "Just tell me what's in the last room and save me all the trouble."

Russ shook his head. "No way. I'm convinced we're hallucinating, just like we hallucinated that cabin last night and the old guy leaning on his rifle. He held one of those rifles in his hand." Russ pointed at the weapon's door. "I think we hallucinated panes of glass in the barracks last night, too, because before I fell asleep on the floor of my room, I swear there was glass in my window. This morning, I wake up, and I can tell the glass had been broken out decades ago as the barracks fell to rot and ruin."

Grayson was nodding. "Me too. I saw the same stuff."

"So you both believe me about the cabin now?"

Russ tilted his head sideways. "It's not that we *didn't* believe you. It's we didn't *want* to believe you." The men exchanged a glance. "We suspect the two old men from last night were also an illusion. And that nothing lives here, well, nothing human."

The pit in her stomach lowered to her bowels, loosening them. The urge to run for the spiral staircase was overwhelming, but she didn't run because she didn't want to be alone.

"What are …" she stammered, "you saying?"

"Just look in that last room, and then we'll find Jaxon and get the hell out of here. Although, we recommend we take a souvenir from that final room so people will believe us."

"A souvenir?"

"Trust us. When you see what's in there, you'll have no issue with us taking some."

They all stared at each other for several seconds, then she switched the candle to her other hand and started back toward the darkness at the end of the bunker's tunnel, already regretting her decision.

"Let's get this over with and then get the hell out of here."

"We couldn't agree more," Russ said.

Chapter 22

THE PAIN IN COLTON'S ankle slowed him down and pissed him off. How could he be so careless to twist his ankle in the backwoods like this, far from any vehicle, help, or even cell coverage, all while looking for a missing person?

If he found Anna, which he intended to do, and she was hurt, how could he ever be expected to carry her out now?

Colton leaned hard on the cane he'd made from a branch, trying to take all the weight off the damaged ankle. He breathed in deeply to try to control some of the pain.

What about painkillers? Why didn't he bring any with him in case Anna was hurt? If there had been any forethought, he'd have food, water, and painkillers so he could take some and stop for a bite to eat soon. He wasn't hungry yet but would be in an hour or more.

With each step, he pushed forward, the cane sinking slightly into the soft ground.

Nearing the end of the small path, the area widened to a large clearing where the edges of a building came into view.

A rush of hope spilled over him, and he picked up

his pace, hobbling along like a penguin with a broken leg.

More of the building came into view, which dashed his hopes that it would lead to anything. At the mouth of the path, he stopped to catch his breath and stare at the building's two stories of broken windows and general broken-down façade. The place reminded him of a native residential school from the sixties or an abandoned army training place. Whatever it was, there were no signs of life for at least two or three decades.

"Shit," he muttered to himself, then slammed the branch he was using as a cane into the ground several times.

This was the wrong way. What would ever make him think Anna was in here, walking around these trees? She probably waited for her train, then when it didn't come, she started up the tracks, walking away from Eugene in the hopes that the next stop wasn't too far.

That had to be it. There was no way she'd walk back to Eugene as long as he was there, the cheating ex-boyfriend. He'd screwed up big time, and now Anna was lost, possibly forever. This was all his fault, yet he could do nothing about it.

He adjusted himself to turn back toward the cabin and, ultimately, the train tracks when he heard something moving around in the bush.

After a quick scan of the area, he saw nothing. No leaves billowed in the slight breeze, no wild animals snorted or made any sort of movement, and no humans stood watching him. He would've sworn he was all alone if he hadn't heard that noise.

"Hello?" he called. "I'm a cop with Eugene Police. You can come out now."

Again, there was no movement from anywhere.

"Anna?" he called again.

What if it wasn't Anna? They had a pervert and a violent offender on the loose, with one of them on that train with Anna and the other *suspected* to have been on that train with Anna. What if they did what they wanted to her, discarded the body, and now needed him gone? Out here, alone, if he learned that was the case, he would probably kill them both and bury their bodies deep in that abandoned building. There'd be no witnesses, and not too many people would be able to find this location.

Without delay, he withdrew both Most Wanted posters from his pocket and unfolded them to study Rusty Brown's and Grayson Cooper's faces again in detail in case either man was wearing some sort of disguise.

A rustle from the trees to his left made him jump back and rest on his bad ankle—a huge mistake. He squealed in pain and dropped to his butt, the Most Wanted papers flying from his hand.

"Motherfucker," he blurted out as he grabbed for his gun.

Weapon ready, his foot radiating pain up his leg, he waited for a few heartbeats to catch his breath while keeping the gun up in front of him.

When no one tried to jump him, he rolled onto his hands and knees, slipped the gun back into his waistband, then pushed upward using the makeshift cane to support his weight.

From his knees, he got onto his good foot, hopped around in a circle while holding his breath at the pain in his ankle, and pulled out his weapon again.

"Who's there?" he called into the bush. "I'm armed. This is the Eugene Police. Come out with your hands up."

Something moved again, but this time he saw a branch swat back in place. Someone had been holding it down and had just released it.

Colton had broken out in a full-body sweat with the pain. If he had a mirror, he knew his face would be blood red with the strain of being upright.

This was no good and getting worse by the second. He needed to do something, and he knew what that was—he needed to get back to that train station platform and wait for the next one to come along, then bring help.

The Most Wanted papers had scattered with the breeze and were now slowly surfing over the grass in the clearing, moving away from him.

Fuck it. He didn't need them anymore.

He studied the trees again, looking for signs that someone was watching him but saw nothing.

One thing was for sure. If it were Anna, she would've made herself known. So, whoever was out there meant him harm. Otherwise, why continue to hide?

Which led him to believe it was either Grayson Cooper or Rusty Brown.

"Hey Grayson, hey Rusty, I know you're out there. So, here's what we're going to do. I will head back to the train tracks and let the other cops I brought with me know that you're in here. Then fifty officers will comb these woods until we find you. That work for you assholes?"

He wondered if his bluff would draw either of them out, but he was rewarded with only silence.

Colton shrugged. "Suit yourself. Heading back to the train tracks now."

He leaned on the cane, jumped forward, the gun still in his other hand, then repeated the process so that his injured foot wouldn't touch the ground at all.

Before he got three steps, something or someone rattled the bushes again. He almost didn't look because of how high school it was all becoming, but he couldn't miss the chance to see who or what was fucking with him.

Leaves moved, disturbed by something more substantial than wind, but he saw no one standing there.

"Fuck you guys," he said and turned back around quickly.

Something like a wall hit him in the side of the face. He felt himself falling, the cane and gun leaving his grasp to break his fall.

He landed hard on his right shoulder, punching the air from his lungs as if he'd been hit with a solid tackle in football. A moan escaped him as he rolled onto his back and raised his hands to ward off another blow.

A crazed-looking gray-haired old man stood over him with a thick chunk of wood the length of a baseball bat. The guy looked coked-out and high on something while scratching at his arm.

"I'm a cop," Colton muttered, his mouth not working well from the blow. His face was numb, and he tasted blood where his teeth had mashed the inside of his cheek.

"Step away and let me get up." The words came out like he'd just returned from the dentist, and his mouth was still frozen.

If the guy's hair had been fluorescent green instead of gray, the guy would have been a dead ringer to Jared Leto's Joker in *Suicide Squad*. Even the sclera of the guy's eyes was so bloodshot they looked like they'd been painted in red streaks.

The guy widened his mouth in a full-teeth grin—some of his teeth were missing, and the others had darkened to look like little brown chicklets—and brought the chunk of wood up over his shoulder.

"Hey," Colton said, inching backward on his shoulder blades, hands up before him. "You don't want to do that. I'm a fucking cop."

"All the more reason," the old man grated out the words, then swung the club.

Colton took the blow in his left forearm, hearing something crack.

The pain didn't come right away, but the momentum of the blow caused him to roll partially onto his side.

When he glanced back over his shoulder, the wood was descending again.

He opened his mouth to scream, but it was cut short when the wood contacted his head.

Then everything turned off, even the rush of pain.

Chapter 23

Just as Russ and Grayson promised her, Anna found another door farther down the hallway past the room with the weapons. This door was smaller and wasn't made of wood. It reminded her of something she would find on a submarine with steel bolts lining the outer edge and a circular handle in the middle. There was a keypad, which had been rendered useless years ago as several buttons were missing with age. Another indication that the keypad wasn't needed was that the door sat ajar.

She pushed it open, wondering what had gotten Russ and Grayson into such a state of panic about this final room. What could be so important after finding a huge room filled with weapons?

The candlelight made its way into this room, and again there were more crates, but these were sophisticated, cleaner looking. They were much smaller rectangular boxes with strips of wood through the middle for extra support. Curiosity overwhelmed her, and she had to see what was inside right away. What could be so heavy that these smaller boxes needed such an expertly-crafted box? Lucky for her, someone had already opened a few of them on her left.

She moved that way slowly, lowering the candle until the contents were easily visible.

Then everything Russ said about taking some with them became apparent.

This massive room, filled with dozens of crates—probably hundreds, but her candle couldn't penetrate the room too deep—held a fortune.

In each box were ten gold bars.

The years had been hard on the building and the contents held within, but the gold hadn't decayed in any way. It simply had a thick layer of dust on it.

This was a treasure beyond imagination. She seemed to recall that one bar of gold was worth over half a million dollars, perhaps more. So, that meant one box of ten bars would be worth millions, and there were dozens and dozens of boxes in here.

But that wasn't possible. How were they all here, and where did it all come from? There was no way the military would abandon this property and leave such a fortune behind unattended.

She grabbed one of the gold bars and attempted to lift it.

"Each one weighs slightly north of twenty-five pounds," Grayson said softly.

Anna dropped it back in the box. "How the hell am I expected to carry one of these things out of here?"

"You're the only one with a carry-on bag." Grayson kept his voice down like they were in a vault of some kind, and he didn't want to alert anyone to their presence. "I forget where I left my bag, or maybe it's by the cabin." He glanced down at the gold, then back at Anna, his eyes alive with greed. "Besides, there was nothing in my bag but bathroom stuff like toothpaste and deodorant. So, we figure your straps will carry the weight of two of these bad boys at least, and both of us are prepared to carry one each up to your bag. Then we leave and tell the world what we found."

"What about Jaxon?"

Russ shrugged. "If we see him on the way, we include him in our plan. If we don't, we'll pick him up when we return in a few days. It doesn't matter to us as he's already stated he wanted to stay behind for a bit, which means he'll still be here when we return."

"Besides," Grayson cut in, holding his candle up to his face. For some odd reason, the way the candle lit his face, he looked like he was auditioning for that movie, *The Blair Witch Project*. "We know he's seen this room already and these bars. Several are missing from that box, and he neglected to tell us about them. All he offered us were moldy MREs while trying to pass them off as edible."

They exchanged an odd glance between them again. What else were they planning?

Russ stepped forward. "Anna, Jaxon tried to poison us. That's what we suspect he was up to with those MREs. And we're feeling weird."

"Yeah, really weird." Grayson nodded behind his candle.

"Weird, how?" It was amazing what greed did to the body. She was listening to them, but all she could think about was the room filled with gold and how much of it she could hoard for herself. The urge to leave was still there but diminished to the point that it wasn't that urgent. Getting her hands on ten or twenty crates was what was urgent now. Even that horrid mushroom smell was suddenly tolerable. But saying that Jaxon tried to poison them snapped her back to the here and now.

"We feel sick, older, and tired," Russ said. "Like the poison of whatever it was, he fed us is weakening us. And you didn't eat any of that shit, so you're safe to keep walking out of here if something happened to us. You could get help for us."

"Oh guys, I don't think he would try to harm us in any way." Anna swept an arm over her shoulder. "There's enough of these things that we could all never work again if it were divided four ways."

That strange look crossed between the men again, and it reminded her that they needed to get back outside in the sunshine. Sure, this place had gold, but it was creepy as hell and was changing them somehow.

"The thing is, we don't think it's the gold that's manipulating him."

She frowned and glanced down at her candle. It was half gone already. They were running out of time and light. She still had her cell phone, but her battery was probably at fifty percent by now.

"Then what's got Jaxon all messed up if it isn't the gold?" she asked.

"Whatever's living down here." Russ fixed her with a hard stare.

That sentence sent a shiver through her and made her want to forget the gold and run.

"What does that even mean? The rats and mice in the hallway upstairs were dead. There's nothing else down here." She paused, then asked, "Is there?"

"The hallucinations we were talking about. Something's wrong here, and it's gotten inside Jaxon. Whatever it is and however it works, we feel it might be in us, too."

"You guys are talking crazy shit. There's nothing here but a building filled with old military stuff and gold. Come on, guys ..."

"You really believe that?" Russ whispered.

They waited for an answer, so she decided on the truth. "No, I'd say there's something definitely wrong with this place, but I don't believe in the supernatural, so maybe it's just a bad vibe. Like something you'd feel in the basement on a tour of that prison called Alcatraz or even while touring Auschwitz. When something emotionally shocking happens in a specific place over time, I suppose it can leave behind negative psychic energy. If there's anything down here other than that, it's an animal or human. There's nothing else."

"And that line of thinking can get you killed," Grayson said. "Open your mind to other possibilities, or it'll be opened for you."

"What's that supposed to mean?" She fixed her gaze on him, her scalp prickling, her heart rate picking up. "That sounded like a threat."

Russ moved even closer, forcing her to lean back into the wall. "What he's trying to say is, we're so convinced something's alive down here and working on keeping us here that we're worried it won't let us leave—ever."

She wanted to laugh as the two men in front of her acted like little boys, but she caught the look in Russ's eyes and understood how serious he was. Laughing wouldn't be appropriate at a time like this.

"You're spooked. I get it." She lowered the candle from her face area. "But nothing is stopping us from putting one foot in front of the other and walking away from this place. We made it to the cabin earlier. We can do it again."

"Then let's test your theory," Russ said. "We will carry one bar each, then place them in your bag and head for the tracks. No more distractions, no more delays. Even if we see Jaxon, we'll ask him to join us or stay behind, but we're leaving. No discussing it, no negotiating, no nothing. Exit strategy number one and the only one. Deal?"

"Deal. Grab your gold, gentlemen, and let's be off."

Anna started forward as Grayson and Russ slipped deeper into the room behind her to grab one bar each. When they exited the room, their treasure in their arms, the trio headed for the turn in the tunnel leading to the spiral staircase and the outside.

"You guys," she said, shaking her head. "You really had me going there for a second."

"That wasn't our intention," Grayson said. "There are too many illusions or hallucinations—call it whatever you want, for my liking."

"I agree," Russ said from behind her. "Too many."

At the corner, they turned as a unit, then suddenly stopped.

Jaxon was sitting on the bottom step of the spiral staircase, resting back on his elbows.

It was the only way out of the bunker.

There was enough sunlight filtering down from the open doorway above the staircase to see all the changes that had taken place in Jaxon's face. The man looked positively old now. If she hadn't met him yesterday at the substation platform when he looked to be in his early twenties, she'd never have believed it. She would swear he was at least seventy-five years of age now.

At this rate, there was no way he'd live another day.

"Jaxon," Anna started, unable to control the wobble in her voice. "We were looking for you. We should all leave."

He smiled, and his grin made him look maniacally insane.

Russ stepped up in front of Anna. "She's right. Dude, you don't look so well."

Anna caught sight of Jaxon's hands. There was something like a dark liquid on them. What the hell had he been up to? Was that blood?

Grayson moved around Anna on the other side. "We're leaving. Are you coming?"

In the better light filtering down the metal stairs from the front entrance to the bunker, Anna also saw changes in Russ's and Grayson's faces, making her step back. Both men had gray hair in patches now, and there were wrinkles in their skin where there weren't any that morning.

What the hell is going on?

She lifted her arms, examining them closely. Veins were riding high under her skin. Unless she was seeing things, even her skin was aging before her eyes. She wished she had a mirror to check her hair, her face.

"You're all leaving, are you?" Jaxon asked. The guy spoke like an old man, his voice frail and brittle.

"Look, Jaxon," Russ said. "Whatever you're dealing with, we're dealing with it, too. It's an illusion, though. All of this is an illusion. Those men from last night weren't real. That cabin we found, the one with the fire raging in the fireplace, isn't lived in. This place ..." He paused and looked back at Grayson, then Anna, his hands out at the side. "This place is alive with something evil."

Jaxon laughed, his shoulder vibrating like he was hiccupping, then he coughed and stopped laughing.

"I used to need my fix, always getting high." He

leaned forward and glared at them. "I was headed to Los Angeles to get high with my friends, wander through life, and see where it took me."

"Then let's get out of here so you can do just that," Grayson said.

"But when I found that last room, the one beyond the room with the gold, I knew this was my new home."

Fear covered Anna like a blanket, and she had the sudden urge to sit down. Her hands trembled, her mouth went dry, and her throat felt like it was clenching shut.

"What room?" Russ asked, his voice tentative.

"The final one, the one with all my friends."

Russ and Grayson exchanged one of those guy glances like there was a shared understanding among them.

"There are no friends," Grayson said, stepping closer still, his voice soft and in a higher pitch like he was speaking in falsetto. "This place has a hold on us all, a grip that's hurting our bodies, our minds."

Jaxon couldn't smile wider at this statement. "You're missing the point, gentlemen. This place is the best high I've ever had. Better than cocaine and more addictive than heroin. I'm not leaving, and neither are you three." He slipped one hand behind his back, and with the other, he pointed at what Grayson was holding. "Is that my gold?" Jaxon pushed up from the stairs to stand. "Are you stealing what I found?"

With one hand still behind his back, he

approached Grayson. Anna stepped back and moved to remain behind Russ, who incidentally thrust his free arm out to cover her.

"Jaxon," Grayson whispered. "We *are* leaving, with or without you."

Jaxon shook his head in an animated way that looked positively gross and scary at the same time. He looked like a geriatric with Parkinson's Disease on speed. When he finished shaking his head, he brought out the hand from behind his back. In it, he held a weapon.

He pointed it at Grayson's stomach area.

"As I said, no one is leaving, especially with my gold."

Russ bent over to set the gold on the bunker floor, as did Grayson.

"Jaxon," Russ started. "There's enough gold for all of us and then some."

"Says the guy who didn't find it and can't claim it." Jaxon sneered at him.

"It's all an illusion," Grayson said, turning to Russ and Anna. "I'm sure of it. Maybe he found that gun in the back somewhere. No way it still works."

"Want to see if it does work?" Jaxon asked. "Want me to test it out?"

"No," Russ said, his hands up. "Don't start shooting people. We can walk away from some things, but not that."

"Then listen to what we're going to do since I'm the one with the gun."

"We're listening."

"We're all going to the farthest room in the back as a group. In there, you'll find rope. Russ, you'll tie up these two, but leave Grayson's hands free. He will tie you, and I will tie Grayson's hands."

"What's the point?" Russ asked. "Why don't we just leave, and you keep everything down here?"

Anna nodded vigorously. She'd listened to this entire exchange trying to find her voice but was too scared to say anything.

"The point is," Jaxon whispered. "My friends want you to stay for several days. Then it'll all be over."

"What'll be over?" Grayson asked. That soft voice from moments before was replaced with something harder and angrier.

Jaxon lowered his head but kept his eyes on Grayson, a smile still pasted to his lips. Anna noticed that Jaxon had lost some teeth since yesterday. Maybe they were enduring some sort of radiation poisoning times ten.

"All of it will be over," Jaxon said. "Everything, which is just the beginning."

"Beginning of what?" Russ asked. "You're deluded and talking in circles."

"Shut up," Jaxon shouted. "Too many questions. Just do as I say and start walking toward the back."

"It's an illusion," Grayson said, glancing back at Russ again. "I'm convinced even his gun is a fake, so fuck this." He turned to face Jaxon. "And fuck you."

Then he started forward, and Jaxon leveled the gun at him.

Russ shouted, "*No!*"

The weapon fired, and Grayson dropped.

Anna fell, too, her nerves jumbled in a way that her knees were too weak to hold her upright any longer.

Grayson had been wrong about the gun being an illusion, and he paid a heavy price for that error—one that may cost them all.

Chapter 24

PRESENT DAY ...

Logan stared at Miles and Atkins, his eyes moving between the two men in the command trailer. "What are you talking about? What does 'no one ever made it out' mean?" He left his mouth open.

Miles exhaled. "Take a seat. You want coffee, tea?"

Logan nodded. "Coffee, black." He slipped out of his backpack, placed it on the floor, then sat opposite them.

Atkins grabbed a radio beside him. "Bring three large black coffees to our trailer."

"Copy that," came over the radio.

"I don't drink it black," Miles said.

"You do today, sir." Atkins nodded at him. "You'll need it."

They eyed each other momentarily, then both looked at Logan.

"What's going on here?" Logan shifted in his seat.

"You signed that NDA."

"I did."

"You speak to anyone on your expedition through

town?"

He went to shake his head, then stopped. "I spoke with Maggie at the train station. She sold the tickets to Valentina."

"Why speak to her?"

"Because I saw Officer Colton talking to her the other day. He was upset about something, then he left the train station and now he's missing. Thought maybe she could tell me what they talked about."

"Officer Asher likely learned that Anna took the train out here, got off, and went inside this restricted area. He followed her and is still in there somewhere."

"Then I reiterate. We need to go in there."

Atkins shook his head. "Not going to happen."

Now Logan was getting angry. "And why's that?"

"Because we've lost hundreds of good men inside that fence."

Logan looked from one man to the other, then leaned back in his seat.

"How would something like that happen? What are you talking about?"

A violent knock sounded on the door.

"Enter," Miles shouted.

The door opened, and a man in uniform stepped in with three coffees on a tray. He placed one in front of all three men, saluted, then backed out of the trailer, the empty tray in hand.

Steam rose from all three cups. Logan was the first to grab his and take a sip. For US Army coffee, it was damn good.

"That NDA was a blanket form." Miles stared a hole into him. "Do you understand what that means?"

"Of course I do."

"What we're about to tell you stays here. Nothing ever gets repeated unless you're speaking directly to us."

Logan nodded. They were deadly serious. "Understood."

"This area served as a base of operations in the late seventies," Atkins started without delay. "When they finished the construction of a bunker under the barracks building in 1980, there was a huge celebration."

Logan drank more coffee as Atkins continued talking.

"During the celebration, we received a radio call for help."

"Help?" Logan repeated. "From a military training base in the Oregon woods? What sort of help would they need?"

The military men stared off to the side, neither one looking at him for a moment.

Miles cleared his throat. "It was a distress call. Some sort of seismic activity was reported, and then the line was cut off."

"Did the US Geological Survey pick up the seismic activity?"

Miles shook his head, his hands wrapped around his coffee cup.

"So what happened?"

"A dozen armed men drove out to this site in response to that call for help."

"What did they find?" Logan's leg bounced with anticipation.

There was a pause as if they were deciding what to tell him and what to leave out.

"We don't know."

Logan frowned and jerked his head back. "How is that possible?"

"Because when others came out to this area thinking there was a hostile situation, they came in hot, with their superiors staying back to monitor the situation from the road."

"What road? There's a road that accesses this place?"

Atkins shook his head. "The road is long gone, but there was one once. It came in off Highway 97."

"What happened to the road?"

"Once this base was permanently fenced in, they bulldozed the road and planted adult trees to cover any sign that a road ever existed."

Logan watched the men for a moment, then drank more coffee. It burned the roof of his mouth, but he barely noticed.

"Okay, so tell me what that emergency response team found. Bodies lying everywhere? What was it, a chemical spill? Radiation accident? An experiment gone wrong? What?"

"They found nothing but a dirty, empty barracks. Not a soul in the place—all nine hundred men gone."

Atkins glanced down at his coffee.

Miles picked up the ball. "We have over five thousand army bases housing our troops, with Fort Bragg being one of the most populated with upward of a quarter-million soldiers on site. This base here in the Oregon woods was brand new back in 1980, so only about eight hundred men occupied it when we received the call for help. We lost the team that came to their aid, too, and then we lost everyone who crossed that fence after that."

"Lost them to what?"

Both men shook their heads. "No one knows."

"Holy shit."

"No truer words."

They sat in silence for a few moments.

Logan couldn't believe what he was hearing. All this time living in Eugene, he had no idea a place like this existed. "You think there's a hole in the earth or something swallowing men whole?"

Miles shrugged. "Your guess is as good as mine, Trooper. We have zero knowledge of what's on the other side of that fence. All we know is that no one ever leaves once they go inside."

"Miss Valentina did."

"And that's why we're here. We formed a small team of psychologists to speak with Anna, learn what she knows, what she saw, but she won't speak freely without you."

He squirmed in his seat. "I have to admit that makes me uncomfortable. I'm unclear of the nature of her attachment to me."

"We are, too, but right now, we're willing to entertain it as we have to end this, whatever *it* is."

"If no one knows what's in there, how can you end it?"

"We learn what Anna knows, then decide from there. Although, we have some options."

"Like?"

"Let's discuss those when needed," Miles said. "We don't want to jump to conclusions."

"How did Anna get in there in the first place?" Logan asked. "I mean, if the road was bulldozed and there's a fence surrounding the place, why would anyone jump that fence to enter a secure US Military base?"

"Since the 1980s, when this base was closed and the fence was built, we maintained a no-fly zone over the area and had satellite footage to watch the fence. There's an area on the train tracks side where overgrown trees hide the fence. It looks like it fell down years ago."

"And it was never fixed?" Logan lifted his coffee, then set it back down without taking a sip. Someone shouted an order outside. A horn blared somewhere.

"No one could see it from the sky, and no one was ever authorized to come into the woods to check it. Over the years, the satellite photos got logged and filed, and that was the end of it."

"And now people are missing."

"If Anna hadn't gotten out, we'd never have

known."

"Since no one knows what's in there, I'm assuming what happened to Miss Valentina is also a mystery."

Atkins nodded. "She claims to have no idea how she aged forty to fifty years in the few days she was missing."

Logan released the pent-up breath he was holding. "You guys know this sounds like some kind of Scandinavian thriller where something wakes up when the ice thawed or an outtake from *The Thing*?"

"What we do know is it's based in reality. This isn't fiction, and remembering that will do you well."

"I'm under no illusions, sir. But something is alive in there. That would make the most sense."

Miles raised his right eyebrow. "How would you know that?"

"Because I saw a man watching us from behind a tree."

"Illusions."

"Illusions? How so?"

"We see people beyond the fence all the time, mostly at night."

"Who are they? Does anyone ever try to help them over to this side?"

"No one is over there. Whatever is at work in that abandoned barracks has the power to conjure images, something to lure more people beyond the fence."

Logan's mouth hung open for a brief moment. "Are you saying it's an intelligent creature of some sort? Something that lures its prey like a cat toying with a mouse? Or maybe a black widow spider killing and eating her mate after the fun?"

Atkins scratched at his temple. "What we're saying is we don't know, don't understand it, and can't allow it to continue."

"How do you know we're at a safe distance right now?"

"No one on this side of the fence ever went missing."

"So then, at least we know it can't jump too high, whatever it is." Logan couldn't mask the irritation in his voice. Or was that fear seeping in?

"I think it's time we go speak with Anna," Miles said. "She wants to tell us more about what she saw and kept asking for you."

"How did you know where I was?"

"Smithers followed you to the train station, then onto the tracks."

Logan frowned. "How is that possible?"

"That's his job, to follow people undetected. He was tasked to keep an eye on you, and that's what he did."

Miles got to his feet, leaving his barely touched coffee on the table in front of him. Atkins got up, too.

"We must speak with Anna Valentina." Atkins moved past Logan. "We have things in motion to ensure this ends tonight."

"What kind of things?"

"Once we speak with Valentina, we will decide on

a course of action."

Atkins opened the door and stepped outside. Logan followed, leaving his backpack on the floor of their trailer.

They escorted him to a large white trailer with a red cross on the wall beside the door.

"You took her from the hospital to bring her here?" Logan asked.

"Trooper, don't sound so surprised." Miles stared back at him. "The information she may possess is too valuable to this operation."

They entered the medical trailer and moved toward the only bed in the center of the unit. Two men and one woman in white lab coats tended to Anna, with one of them helping her eat.

Anna was sitting up, her mouth moving with what looked like pink yogurt on her spoon. Despite all the bruising and swelling, she looked even better today. Her eyes brightened at the sight of Logan.

"You're back," she whispered.

He nodded her way. "I'm here. You doing okay?"

She took one more spoonful of yogurt and then set it aside. "They've been treating me well, and I'm feeling stronger by the hour. I can even walk on my own now. Although, I don't like being this close to that fence."

Logan glanced back at Atkins and Miles. "I'm sure none of us feel too comfortable this close. Have you told them everything? Like, what's in there? What's behind everything? Or do you know?"

"I was telling them earlier how there were four of us in total."

"Four?"

Anna nodded. "We were going to leave, but then Russ convinced me to stay behind to find Jaxon."

She went on to explain about the abandoned cabin and how it seemed like an illusion. How they went down a spiral staircase into the bunker and found all sorts of weapons that had been left behind to rot.

"You said there were four of you." Logan waited for her to nod. "Have you given these men their names? You mentioned Russ and a man named Jaxon. Who else was there?"

"Grayson, too."

"Okay, so it was you, Rusty Brown, Grayson Cooper, and this other person named Jaxon? Have I got that right?"

She nodded.

"Did you see your boyfriend at any point? Colton Asher?"

"What?" she sat up in bed. "Is he missing, too?"

Miles stepped around Logan. "We think he went in looking for you. Trooper Logan bumped into Officer Colton at the train station when dropping off flyers for Rusty Brown's bench warrant. Did this all start there, at the train station?"

Anna's lower lip trembled as she stared off to the side.

"What's the matter, Anna?" Logan said.

"I just remembered that first day."

"What about it?"

"I could've sworn I heard what sounded like a man calling my name. It could've been Colton." Her eyes refocused, and she stared up at Logan. "Was he there? I mean, was he really there looking for me?"

"We don't have any proof, but Colton is missing, and we suspect he went looking for you."

"There's only one way to end it all," Anna whispered so low Logan couldn't hear what she was saying.

He stepped closer. "I'm sorry, I didn't hear what you said."

Anna edged off the side of the bed and tried to stand. "I have to go back in there. I have to kill it."

The doctors moved fast. They secured her arms and eased her back onto the mattress.

"Kill what, Miss Valentina?" Logan said, loud enough to be heard over her protests.

"I need bombs, I need bombs ..." she mumbled over and over.

Atkins's phone rang, and he eased away to take it. As the doctors tried to comfort Miss Valentina, Logan stepped back to stand near Atkins.

"Yes, sir," Atkins said into the phone. "I understand, sir. Nineteen hundred hours. Confirmed, sir."

He tapped his phone's screen and looked up at Logan and Miles.

"The US Air Force will drop bunker busters into the barracks at seven this evening. The approval has been granted. It will destroy the barracks and whatever's underneath it by dusk. Then we can all go home."

Anna screamed behind them. "Send it all to Hell!"

Chapter 25

TWO DAYS BEFORE PRESENT DAY ...

Colton Asher's eyes fluttered open to a world of pain, but that wasn't the worst of it. The headache and the all-over-body agony caused a moan to build in his chest and escape from his mouth. How could a body hurt so bad?

The ankle felt stiff and swollen to twice its standard size. His left arm couldn't move as the elbow or something close to that area was broken. Both cheeks were aching one where he bumped a branch when he fell on his twisted ankle, and the other when he got clubbed by that old guy.

All the training to be a cop, self-defense classes, and the workouts at the gym reduced him to this—a broken, bleeding mess. He couldn't walk out of here now if he tried. Only one leg worked and one arm, but he'd need his eyes to see where he was going, and every time he opened them, the light raised the volume of his splitting headache.

Was there a way to put his arm in a splint without causing too much pain? Would that make him pass out again?

To sit and do nothing, wallowing in his misery, he could remain on the ground and wait to die of starvation.

Or he could do something, start moving and try to figure shit out. A line from one of his favorite authors came to him. Something about being busy living or busy dying—choose one.

Of course, he'd choose living, but every movement created waves of pain on top of the thudding undercurrent he was already tolerating *without* moving.

He opened his eyes as far as he could and glanced around. He was still where the guy clubbed him, at the mouth of the path, a clearing to his left and an abandoned army building to his right. Maybe that's where the guy lived. Would there be others? Did he have Anna down there?

Colton rolled his head the other way slowly to look up the path toward the cabin. He couldn't see the cabin from where he lay but knew that beyond it was the train tracks and a ride home, then off to the hospital—eventually.

All he had to do was get up on his good leg to leave the area so he could report what had happened here. An entire platoon of cops would descend on this place and clean it up. That was his best move. He came in search of Anna, got fucked up, hopped out of the trees while broken and bruised, and lived to see another day. If Anna were here, the cops who raided this place once he got out would find her. He was done, used up, and broken.

He closed his eyes and focused on his breathing. This wouldn't be pretty, but when he pushed up to stand, and the pain washed over him, he had to stifle the scream that would follow. The last thing he wanted was to alert that old guy with the club. If he came back swinging, Colton knew he wouldn't be able to defend himself too well.

"Actually," he muttered without moving his lips. "I didn't defend myself too well when I had the use of both arms."

After two deep breaths, he gritted his teeth and propped himself up using his right arm.

There was more pain, but not as much as he expected. The left arm ached badly where the bone had snapped, but it had a numbness about it, too.

While he rested on his right elbow, staring at the front of the two-story building, a loud crack cut through the air from somewhere, startling him.

Then someone screamed. It sounded like a woman's scream.

Colton had heard gunshots before and knew exactly what they sounded like. It was often mistaken for firecrackers going off, but this was no firecracker.

And that scream could've been Anna.

He laid back down and patted his belt for his weapon.

It was gone.

His eyes widened.

His belt was missing, and along with it, his

handcuffs.

"Motherfucker," he whispered. "That old guy stole my weapon."

Colton leaned back up on his right arm and glared at the building. The old guy who clubbed him was in there with his service pistol, and now Colton was sure Anna was in there, too. How could he go back to the police station and explain how he lost his gun while not on duty and it was used in the commission of a crime?

A broken arm? A twisted ankle? That was all that held him back?

That was a lot, but he couldn't hop to the train tracks without at least going to the building first to see what the hell was going on.

He'd go armed, though. That branch he'd been using as a cane. He'd take that and enter the building slowly. He'd control the pain, hone it, harness it into something that fueled rage, and he'd wallop the old guy so hard, the geriatric fucker wouldn't stand a chance.

In a perfect world.

But he had to try.

Colton pushed himself into a sitting position, keeping his broken arm in front of his stomach. Pushing up with his good arm, he eased his uninjured leg under him and sat up on his knee.

The swollen ankle touched the dirt softly, causing a wave of white-hot angry pain to flow through him. He fought it, his forehead covered in sweat, eyes closed. It began to subside after a minute, and his heart rate slowed again.

He added weight to one knee, then pushed up on his good foot and hopped twice to maintain balance.

Success—he'd done it. He was upright with only a minor bump. He hopped once more, almost lost his balance—which would be tragic and extremely painful —and realized he wouldn't make it too far without that improvised cane.

After a short search, he found it in the bush five feet away. A couple of calculated hops, and he stood over it.

Not wanting to get back on the ground, he pivoted at the waist lowering his upper body and kicking out his sprained ankle to grab the cane.

His fingers wrapped around it, and he swung back up.

A dizzy wave made him lose his equilibrium momentarily, and he needed to jab the cane in the dirt to remain upright. The dizziness passed within seconds, and now he was standing on one leg, the branch cane in his good hand, ready to move across the open field toward the building in search of Anna and his weapon.

He hopped once, leaned hard on the cane, then hopped again.

As his luck would have it, his good foot landed unevenly. He tried an emergency jump to the left to avoid falling as he shifted off balance, but it was useless.

Colton dropped hard, landing on his broken arm. The bone moved under his flesh—he felt it move, grinding against the other piece to which it was once attached—creating a massive amount of searing pain.

When his ruined ankle smacked down on a chunk of root sticking out of the ground, he didn't feel it because he was already unconscious.

Chapter 26

Curled in a ball on the floor of the bunker, Anna wept. She had never been close to a gunshot victim, never heard a real gun go off. Sure, her ex-boyfriend Colton was a cop, but she had never been in his cruiser dealing with the shit he dealt with during their relationship. Her weapons at work were a pair of scissors, a blow dryer, and clippers.

She moved inward, bringing her knees up to her chest, wanting to disappear and escape this hellhole. She kept her back to the wall as her body shook uncontrollably. Her lips were dry, and her hands clammy as she stuffed them in her armpits.

Why did Russ insist on coming back for that lunatic? Now he was going to kill them, too. They were all as good as dead.

Grayson had dropped hard. Then he'd screeched in pain as blood flowed freely from his leg wound.

Did Jaxon aim only to wound Grayson? Because by the looks of it, Grayson wouldn't die from the leg wound if they could stop the bleeding. Walking out of here was out of the question for Grayson, but would he die? Probably not.

Grayson had dragged himself to the wall where he

leaned against it, unwrapped his belt from his pants, and was just now tying it around his leg above the wound, mumbling and cursing under his breath.

Jaxon had watched without expression. The guy was seriously deranged. When they got home—*if* they got home—there was a lawsuit in this for sure. How could the train company drop four strangers off without outside help and no cell coverage at an unknown location?

Russ pleaded with Jaxon to put the gun down, but all that did was make Jaxon aim it at him, so Russ closed his mouth and edged closer to her as Grayson wrapped his leg.

"What now?" Russ asked.

Anna stared up at Jaxon, the gun still in his hand. Was this the end? Was it their turn for a bullet now?

Jaxon took his free hand, slipped it behind him, and produced two handcuffs pairs.

He tossed one pair to Russ, then slipped the other pair back in his pocket.

"Cuff your left wrist to Anna's right wrist."

Russ stared briefly down at the restraints in his hand, then back up at Jaxon.

"Where did you get these? They're like brand new, man."

The gun moved in his direction, then Jaxon took a step closer.

"Bullet in the leg or handcuff on the wrist." Jaxon's voice had suffered as much as his body with whatever aging process he was enduring, but when he spoke those words, they came out monotone, like he didn't care either way. "Currently, I'm willing to give choices, but that compassion will end soon."

Russ was definitely invested emotionally in which choice he'd prefer as he slipped his wrist into the cuff, clicked it closed, then turned to Anna with the open side of the cuffs.

"I need your right arm."

Without hesitation, and having no desire to be offered terrible options by Jaxon, Anna unfurled herself from her ball of despair, sat up, and thrust out her right arm. Russ clipped the handcuffs on her wrist, securing them together.

Then he stared at her momentarily, sending some sort of message with his eyes. If it was meant to be comforting, she wasn't feeling it.

After a moment, they both glanced up at Jaxon for the next step.

"Grayson," Jaxon whispered. "You bad, bad boy." He tsked with his tongue while staring down at Grayson, shaking his head. "There was never any dentist convention, was there?"

Grayson's white face jerked up to glare at Jaxon. The man's glasses kept slipping on his nose, and his combover had flopped down one side of his face. Anna wondered if Grayson would ever leave this place as his odds had decreased dramatically. That metal spiral staircase would be hell on one leg.

When Grayson didn't respond, Jaxon kicked the leg with the bullet wound. Grayson gritted his teeth and leaned his head back, fighting against the pain, moaning deep in his chest.

"Why'd you go and do that?" Russ asked, his tone indignant.

"He's not going anywhere on his own," Jaxon said as if speaking to himself. He swept the area with his eyes, then refocused on Grayson. "You'd never make those stairs with one good leg while dragging the other one the way it is. Hiding in here won't save you, so we'll leave now." He leaned closer to Grayson. "But if you try to hide"—Jaxon's smile was a mask from a horror movie—"I'll find you down here. I have my ways." He tapped the tip of the weapon to the side of his head.

Jaxon stood back up to his full height, twisted around to face them, then gestured toward the spiral staircase with the weapon.

"You two, on the other hand, are leaving this dungeon."

A spark of hope rose from her abdomen. Could he be joking? What was his end game here? Leaving, as in *leaving* the area? Or just the building?

"Come on," Jaxon said. "Get on your feet and start up those stairs."

Russ scrambled to his feet but remained bent over, his wrist attached to Anna. "Come on. We need to do as he says."

Anna stretched her stiff legs, then angled her body and managed to get up with her right arm cuffed to Russ.

They stood side by side, their wrists linked, and waited for instructions from the guy with the gun.

Jaxon moved toward the spiral staircase. "Both of you will go up these steps, down the hall, then stop just outside the building. I'll be right behind you."

They moved to the stairs, and with each step, Anna was reminded how hungry and thirsty she was, having not eaten since before getting on the train yesterday.

She wiped her eyes with her free hand and glanced back at Grayson. The gold bars remained on the bunker floor scattered around his fallen form, once a dream of riches, now misery wrapped in fear.

Greed changed people, and it had altered Jaxon, not to mention whatever physical changes were taking place. He wouldn't be alive by tomorrow at the rate he was aging. Maybe that was how they escaped him. All they had to do was wait him out.

Russ started up the steps first, leaning back as far as he could while still ascending, his left hand awkwardly tethered to her. She held her cuffed hand over her head to ease how far down he had to bend, and together they moved upward, step by step.

Jaxon came behind them but didn't start up the steps until they were over halfway. Probably worried they'd kick him back down.

At the top, Russ led her along the corridor, the afternoon sun coming through all the broken windows in each room lighting their way.

The air up here was much better. Clean and fresh.

The scent of burned mushrooms was still cloying and disgusting, but moving away from the source made a huge difference.

They stepped outside as a single unit at the end of the corridor and stopped on the wild grass a few feet from the door.

"What now?" she whispered.

"We wait, see what his plan is, then I kill him."

Anxiety rose in her at the thought of further violence, more tension.

"I don't know how much more of this I can handle."

He shot her a stern glance. "You'll handle everything because you want to survive. That's how this works."

Jaxon stepped outside and marched past them. "Follow me."

They did as they were told while Jaxon watched them over his shoulder.

He led them around the end of the building to an overgrown area they hadn't been to yet, then stopped by a tall, weathered pole sticking out of the ground.

Jaxon produced the other set of handcuffs and clipped one end through a small eyelet about two feet off the ground, then waved them over with his gun hand.

"Russ, or should I call you Rusty?"

Russ narrowed his eyes. "Russ works."

Rusty? Anna wondered. Why would he say that?

Jaxon stepped back a few feet, the weapon resting

on his thigh now. There was never a moment when they could rush the guy, never a clear time to jump him. He always stayed five to seven feet away or farther, which gave him time to react with the weapon if needed.

"Russ, take your free hand and place it in that open cuff that's attached to the pole."

Russ glanced at the pole, then back to Jaxon. "You don't need to do this, man. We could just leave, and you can have all the gold to yourself."

Jaxon frowned as if confused about something. "You think this is about the gold?"

The sun beat down on Anna's neck, its warmth soothing after being in that dreadful bunker for so long. She wished Jaxon would just let them go. Whether the sun or the moon guided them, she wasn't afraid to walk those tracks until she hit civilization again. They just needed to be away from this place. Staying here was worse than what they'd find out there.

"I don't care about any fucking gold," Jaxon continued. "This isn't about *gold*." He said the last word with such contempt that it sounded like he hated the thought of wealth.

"Then what's this all about?"

Jaxon used the gun to point at the open handcuffs. "It's about you putting your fucking wrist in there and closing the cuff, or I shoot you in the leg and then cuff you myself. That's what this is about. In the cuff with or without a bullet makes no difference to me."

Russ raised his hands, yanking hers with him. "Okay, okay, I'll do it. Just thought we could figure something out, work on a plan." He moved to stand beside the pole and slipped his wrist inside the open cuff. A moment later, Russ was secured to the pole, and Anna was bound to Russ.

"There's nothing to work out," Jaxon said, slipping the gun into the back of his pants. "There's you, then there's me, and soon it'll be all of us."

"What's that supposed to mean?"

"You'll see," Jaxon whispered as he pulled out some folded pieces of paper. "Here, take this." He offered the papers to Anna. She took them. "Read what's on those pages, so you know who you're tied up with and why I shot Grayson." He walked by her and tapped her shoulder like they were friends. She recoiled from his touch, but Jaxon didn't seem to notice. "You'll thank me later," he said, walking around the bushes back toward the barracks.

Anna took in the area, breathing rapidly. This was their chance. Jaxon was gone. They had to find a way out of the cuffs so they could run and then bring help back for Grayson.

"What'll we do now?" she asked, breathing out the words. "He's gone. We have to get out of here."

Russ yanked on the cuff connected to the pole. "Not sure we're going anywhere too fast."

She moved around him to examine the cuff; the papers Jaxon gave her held tight in her grip.

"Can't we break it off somehow?"

"Not these cuffs, unless you have superhuman strength. These are police-grade shit."

She shot him a glance. "Police grade?"

He nodded.

"How would you know that?" Then she held up her free hand. "Wait, don't answer that. The question I want to be answered is, how did Jaxon get his hands on a gun and police handcuffs that look brand new? He wasn't traveling with a bag. Only Grayson had a bag, and he seemed to have set it down somewhere."

Russ studied the perimeter of the clearing on the other side. "Who knows? Maybe a few cops came through here looking for you or me, and he jumped one. I have no idea."

"First of all, we were just outside half an hour ago. We would've seen cops. And secondly, why would they be looking for you or me?" Something in his tone bothered her, reminding her of what he said yesterday about bad shit he did in the past coming back to haunt him. Was he referring to that?

Their eyes met.

He shrugged. "You know, missing persons and shit. You didn't make that train. I didn't make that train. People were expecting us. It's been twenty-four hours, at least. People are going to come looking for us." Then he looked away and glanced off into the distance again. "Who knows?"

Anna glanced up the length of the pole and recognized it as an old flagpole. This was where the military would raise the American flag when they occupied this base. It was quite old and leaning to the side slightly, but the damn thing didn't look like it would come out of the earth too easily. Besides, the cuff was inside an eyelet, probably where a rope was once tied to secure the flag. Even if the pole came out of the ground, they'd have to carry it with them wherever they were going, and that wasn't happening.

Desperate to leave, Anna repeated, "We have to break these cuffs somehow."

Russ glanced down at their wrists. "That isn't going to happen, Anna. They're too tough."

Frustrated, she blew out air and scanned the area at their feet for a rock, but they were surrounded by weeds, wild grass, shrubs, and the trees stood about five feet away. There was nothing they could use even to attempt to pick a lock.

Across the clearing were more trees, and that was it. She couldn't even see the barracks from where they were as it was around a corner behind thick shrubs.

"What now?"

"We wait." Russ nodded toward the ground. "Come on, sit down, and let's see what he handed you."

Anna looked at the folded pages in her hand and frowned. In the moments with the gun, the handcuffs, she hadn't wondered or even cared about the papers Jaxon had handed her.

Russ dragged her arm down with him as he dropped to the ground, so she sat, too, and crossed her legs. Using the top of her thigh, she unfolded the first paper with one hand and read Grayson Cooper's name.

"Holy shit," she whispered. "Look at this." She handed the paper over to Russ. As he read it, she opened the second sheet.

Rusty Brown's name was written on the top, with a mugshot photo of Russ gracing the front.

Before handing it to him, she read the list of crimes, the aggravated assault charge, and that he was wanted on a bench warrant for skipping court. It was dated yesterday.

When she looked up, he was staring at her.

"My question is how Jaxon got ahold of these," Russ said.

"You want to explain this?" She held up the sheet and shook it.

"I got nothing to explain to you. Besides, I already told you some bad shit in my past was fucking with me today."

"Skipping court is *you* fucking with your past, isn't it?"

He exhaled sharply. "Whatever. Tom*ay*to, to*mah*to."

"Am I in danger here? I mean, they drop me off with Grayson Cooper, a fucking convicted sex addict who likes little girls, and Jaxon, who's deranged beyond help. And now I find out you're on the run from the law for almost killing a guy with a baseball bat, according to this document."

"Yeah, well, he may or may not have deserved it.

You certainly don't. There's a difference, and that difference is as wide as the Red Sea parted by Moses." He leaned closer. "And Grayson wouldn't touch you. You're almost thirty years of age, which is too old for the likes of him by the looks of this document."

"So that leaves Jaxon as my most dangerous adversary."

Russ was shaking his head.

"What?" she asked.

"Jaxon is a junkie who has been possessed by whatever's in this place. You have to fear this abandoned barracks, not Jaxon."

"Yeah? Okay, so tell me, what's in this place?"

They eyed each other for a moment.

"Something old and evil. It wants our bodies and our souls, and it's winding up for the kill as we sit here and debate what to fear."

"Oh, great, so we're dead no matter what?"

"As defeatist as that sounds, yes."

"Well, I'm not giving up. I'm getting out of here no matter what."

"You can't make promises from Hell."

"Is that where you think we are?"

"Pretty much."

"Then I'll start praying."

"Pray for me, too, because I've never believed."

Chapter 27

PRESENT DAY ...

Trooper Richard Logan was given a bunk in one of the empty trailers at the back corner of the temporary command post. It was a quieter area surrounded by trees. They fed him a decent lunch, then he laid down, leaving the authorities to plan out their evening strategies. Having spent the night walking the tracks, he fell asleep in under a minute and rested for several hours without interruption.

There was a loud banging that finally woke him up. At first, he thought it was a dream, his awareness was a fog of reality, but when he sat up in bed, he remembered all the horrible details of where he was and what was happening.

Someone banged on his trailer door again.

"Trooper Logan, you're needed in the command trailer."

"Okay," he muttered, still feeling half asleep.

Everything in his gut told him to lie back down and sleep, but something kept him upright. What would Atkins or Miles need from him? More talking with Miss Valentina? That didn't make sense, as she seemed to be discussing her time behind the fence quite freely when he wasn't around. He'd have to ask Anna directly why she required his presence to talk about what happened to her since that wasn't entirely true. So far, he'd avoided that question as he had wanted to be as close to the investigation as possible, which was something he was growing to regret.

So then, what did Miles and Atkins need that was so pressing? Why couldn't he sleep longer?

He checked the time. It was coming up on five in the afternoon. He took a deep breath and got to his feet.

"Trooper Logan?" the man outside said, evidently waiting for him.

"I'm here. I haven't gone back to sleep."

"How long, sir?"

"How long what?" He tried to keep the irritation from his voice but failed.

"Until you're ready, sir. You're needed in the command trailer immediately."

He glanced down and saw that he was still wearing civilian clothes. He'd fallen asleep without changing or disrobing.

Other than a piss, he was ready.

The door smacked open, almost hitting the soldier. "I need a piss and a coffee. Then I'm ready."

The soldier, no older than twenty-five, stepped back. "That can be arranged, sir. Piss anywhere, and there's coffee in the command trailer."

Without a word, Logan moved to the back of the

trailer and was pissed while the soldier waited behind him.

"Lead the way," he said after finishing and moving up beside the man in uniform.

Something had changed as they strode across the mass of trailers and SUVs. The mood? The atmosphere? He wasn't quite sure, but something was different, and it stirred fear around the edges of his calm demeanor.

"What happened while I slept?"

The soldier didn't speak.

Logan slowed, then stopped and faced the man who had also stopped several feet ahead to look back.

"What? Happened?"

The soldier glanced around them to see whether they were being watched or not.

"People are missing, sir."

"What do you mean, 'people are missing'?"

"Look, the sergeant major will be able to explain —"

"I want you to explain so I have an idea of what I'm walking into over there."

"All I know is some of the soldiers cut through the fence line, while others ran up to the opening on the train tracks side."

"And?"

"They never came back."

"Why were they entering a restricted area? Is there a lack of discipline at this base?"

"Gold," the man whispered, barely discernible.

"What did you say?"

"We heard there was a room in the bunker filled with gold bars—hundreds of them."

"And what? People thought they could run into that place," he jabbed a finger toward the fence, "and steal it all without the government noticing?"

"I'm sorry, sir. I can't speak for the missing soldiers."

"Missing?" Logan stepped closer. "You mean they never came back out?"

The soldier shook his head. "No, sir. We've lost over forty men and one woman today."

"Forty!" Logan shouted. "What the fuck!"

"Can we please continue? The sergeant is waiting for you, sir."

Logan turned to stare past the fence and into the trees beyond. He couldn't see any abandoned buildings from where they'd set up the temporary base camp, but he could smell that ugly mushroom shit. Who the hell lived close enough to be constantly cooking mushrooms?

And what the hell was in there?

"Sir?"

Logan nodded and followed the soldier to the command trailer without another word.

Logan guessed there had to be over a hundred men and women stationed here when he laid down. Since he woke up, the population at the base had decreased by over half in his estimation, and several more official-looking vehicles had arrived. They were now parked in a row on the narrow path the army had created as a makeshift road through the trees on the south side.

When would they pull out of the area? If the Air Force was still coming to drop bombs on the barracks in the next few hours, wouldn't they want to be clear of this area?

Several uniformed men stepped from a trailer on the right and strode to the trailer where Logan had met Miles and Atkins that morning.

The soldier was leading him that way. He stopped at the base of the stairs.

"Is Atkins or Miles in there?" Logan asked, nodding toward the door of the command trailer.

The soldier watched him. "Both are, sir."

The door opened, and Command Sergeant Major Miles stood there, waving Logan inside. When he entered, five other men he didn't recognize crowded around a table, staring down at what looked like a map of the area.

Miles nudged Logan's arm and leaned in to speak to him. "Army personnel have arrived from Washington to take over the situation. We'll be working alongside them, and we've apprised them of your situation and how you're connected to Anna Valentina. You have full clearance on my say so."

Logan nodded, wondering what Miles meant about his connection to Miss Valentina. There was no *connection* to Anna in any way. Why still play that game?

Full clearance? Why would a state cop get all this high-ranking top-secret clearance? Something bothered him about everything that was happening, but he still couldn't put his finger on it.

He had to consider that it was based on Anna's request that he was here and involved in such a way. He'd never met the woman in his life before responding to the emergency call on the side of the highway. Her motivation eluded him, but he'd ask her about it soon.

Several men nodded their way when they saw him standing beside Miles.

There weren't any seats available, so Logan leaned against the wall to listen, trying to understand what they were saying.

"We don't know what's in there," a white-haired man said sternly. "Or what's causing the disappearances."

A man with shiny, heavily oiled hair smacked the table. "The investigative team in HAZMAT suits came out and were whisked away. Where are they now, and how come I wasn't informed of that?"

Logan leaned closer to Miles. "HAZMAT suits? What's he talking about?"

"They sent five men into the bunker under the barracks."

"What? Why?"

Miles hesitated a moment. "We're missing a few soldiers."

"A few?" Logan turned to face him. "How many?

Thirty? Forty? More?"

Their eyes locked for a moment. "Over fifty."

"How is that possible?" Logan spoke in a forced whisper, his hands tight at his side, suppressing the urge to scream at Miles.

"We don't know." He shrugged. "The lure of easy money."

"Has anyone claimed that they saw someone inside the fence?"

Now it was Miles's turn to be confused. "See someone inside the fence? What are you talking about?"

"When I was being escorted here this morning, I saw a man hiding behind a tree inside the perimeter of that place. Maybe someone's in there cooking mushrooms and drawing people in to kill them or some shit."

"That all sounds ridiculous except for the mushroom thing. We can all smell it."

"What happened to the HAZMAT team?"

"Only two of the five came back out. They took photos of what's in there, then somehow made it out alive."

"Really?" Logan said, his voice rising. He detected several men glancing their way. "Only two? What's in there? What did they see? Did they tell you what happened to the other three?"

"They found weapons in one room and cases of dried food in another. Also, they got photos of the room with the gold bars."

"Gold bars?" Logan gasped. "Are you fucking kidding? No wonder you've got soldiers going AWOL. This is a scary setup, and the promise of gold is too tempting. Are you aware of how much money each bar is worth?"

Miles moved closer until his mouth was close to Logan's ear. "Keep your voice down, or they'll kick us out of here. Two men in here outrank me."

"Did anything happen to the two men who came back out? I thought Anna was the only one to leave this area alive."

Miles eyed him a moment, then leaned close again. "They came out—" He cut himself off, then added, "Aged."

Logan narrowed his eyes. "How old?"

"Twenty years older, perhaps more."

"How long were they in there?"

"Enough time to walk to the barracks, find their way to the bunker, examine the rooms and take photos, then walk back out. Several hours tops."

"And nothing attacked them?"

"We think it's something airborne, something that works on us in a way that we age in a couple of days, then die. That's why no one ever gets out alive. We'll need scientists here for years to study the air, the atmosphere."

Logan shook his head. "No, that can't be. At the first sign of aging, I'd run for the fence. There has to be something else in there. Besides, where are all the others? Why aren't they bolting from the place, their arms laden down with gold?" He stopped talking and just shook his head. "Something else is in there, and it's alive. Whatever it is, it's devouring humans in some unique way."

"Are you a reader?"

Logan frowned. "Ferociously so."

"Well, you read way too much. What you're talking about is fiction. Doesn't happen. If we can't see it, there's no monster."

"Are you religious?"

It was Miles's turn to frown. "No."

"The argument, if you can't see it, there's no God, doesn't work. He's there. You just have to have faith."

"You a Bible thumper, Logan? You trying to convert me?"

"I wouldn't consider myself a crusader, but I believe in God, and he has our back."

Miles chuckled softly. "Well, I wouldn't have pegged you as a religious nut, but we'll find out soon enough what's down in that bunker." He glanced back at the table and the men surrounding it. "The Air Force is coming, and the bombs they have will be strategically dropped right at that spiral staircase and in the surrounding area. Before detonating, they will penetrate over twenty feet of concrete and up to one hundred feet of earth. Whatever's in there won't live through the night."

Logan scoffed. "And no one is worried that it's beyond our scope of reasoning? I mean, I think it might not be an animal, something that bleeds and dies. What if you're unleashing whatever's in there? These bombs could set it loose on the rest of Oregon, then the rest of the States."

"No, that is not one of our fears. This attack will kill it, whatever it is."

Logan crossed his arms. Several of the men around the table lowered their heads. They'd gone quiet as they listened to Miles and Logan talk.

Miles spoke freely, the need to whisper over. "Miss Anna Valentina will be dead within weeks, perhaps sooner. Her attending physicians have informed us of this grave news. There's nothing we can do to stop that now. Whatever is in there already killed her. She just doesn't know it yet."

The white-haired man jabbed a finger at the map. "Whatever's stealing all these poor souls must be destroyed."

Miles nodded and turned to Logan. "And that's why we're sending in bunker busters to destroy it."

"There's got to be a better way," Logan said.

All the men in the trailer shook their heads in unison.

"No, we kill it," White Hair said. "This ends in two hours."

Having forgotten about getting a coffee, Logan stepped out of the trailer and stopped ten feet away to stare past the fence.

The mystery confounded him. He was a state trooper, dragged into this mess for no discernible reason other than a dying woman's request, and now he felt like he was the only rational one here.

He had to talk to his wife. At least to tell her he was okay. When she got home last night and saw his cruiser in the driveway, but her husband missing, she'd worry and call the station. Sergeant Lambert would have explained where he was and that he'd be back soon, but Logan always told his wife everything himself. This just wasn't right.

The cell phone he grabbed last night was still in his back pocket. Non-disclosure agreement be damned. This was his wife. She had a right to at least know he was okay, and she should hear it from him.

When he turned on the cell, he couldn't get a signal. But then he recalled it didn't have a plan anyway. He could send a message through emergency services, which was something he shouldn't be doing anyway.

"Fuck," he whispered, staring up at the overcast sky.

"You okay?" Miles asked from behind him.

Logan spun around. "Yeah. Fine."

"You don't look fine. You look scared."

"Maybe I am."

"We all are Trooper. We've lost a lot of men today. Over half of them called here to work on this operation are gone, probably for good. That's a lot of homes to visit to inform their families they're gone when these boys weren't at war."

They stood in silence for a moment.

"How's Miss Valentina?"

"Holding up well. But she doesn't like the Air Force dropping bombs on that bunker. She said it's a mistake."

"Then don't do it."

"An eighty-year-old civilian can't advise us and then alter military strategy based on that advice. Don't be ridiculous."

Logan pivoted back to stare beyond the fence. "I'm worried about what's in there."

"Me too."

"It's something evil. Something truly evil."

"If you believe in that sort of thing."

They stared at the trees and shrubs of the Oregon forest on the other side of the fence while something stared back. At least, that's how Logan felt.

Like he was being watched.

Chapter 28

Two Days Before Present Day ...

Colton Asher was sure he heard Anna calling his name through his fog of pain. It had to be her. Otherwise, there's no way he'd try to get up off the ground. Any sort of movement was torture, and he'd decided to sleep it off if that was possible.

But then he heard her call him again.

Colton opened his eyes and saw dirt. He was lying on his stomach; his broken arm was stuck under his chest. To roll off would be an insane choice. To push up with his free hand would be more maddening, hence the conclusion that any sort of movement was a testament to how insane he had become. Therefore, he wouldn't move until some ambulance came for him—one equipped with strong painkillers.

Yet Anna was calling for help.

"Sir?"

Colton jumped at the sound of a man's voice behind him, then squeezed his eyes shut and clenched his teeth to wait out the wave of pain that shot through him.

"Sir, I'm so sorry."

Colton blinked and turned slowly to look at a pair of running shoes to his left.

"I didn't know, sir," the man added.

"Know. What?" Colton forced the words out of his mouth, past his tightened jaw.

"That you were with Anna. I had no idea."

He twisted his head up farther but could barely see the guy's waistband without rolling onto his back, and he still wasn't prepared—or brave enough—for that move yet.

"You always … just attack people? Without provocation?"

"Sir, with all due respect, this is my property, and you were trespassing."

The guy sounded remorseful, at least, which gave Colton hope that this was over and he'd found Anna, and they'd get the help they needed.

"I'm an old man," the guy continued. "I stay fit working my fields out here."

Colton closed his eyes and focused on his breathing. To leave, he was going to have to get up, and to get up, he would have to endure the maddening pain of lifting himself off his broken arm.

"When I saw four people," the guy continued to try to explain away his actions, "walking through my field yesterday, I stopped to ask them what they were doing. The one tough guy mouthed off, then ran."

Rusty Brown? Colton wondered.

"There was another guy with glasses who was older. He seemed pretty creepy the way he was watching the woman. Anyway, he bolted for the trees."

Grayson Cooper?

"And then there was some strung-out punk and your girl, Anna."

"What happened? To them?"

"I gave them shelter and food. It's too dark out here at night, and I live like the Amish, sir, with no electricity or lights. Anna twisted her ankle, so she is waiting until tomorrow to leave, but now that you're here."

Colton lowered his head to rest his forehead on the dirt. He'd gone the right way; he'd found her. She was alive and well and resting in this guy's place.

"Where is she now?"

"Waiting for you. I told her some guy came wandering onto my property with a gun, so I knocked him out and took his weapon. I called the police, but they won't be here for a few hours."

"Hours? Why so long?"

"This place is hard to get to. No roads in or out, just the train tracks, and it's quite a walk through these trees."

Neither one of them spoke for a moment.

"You hungry, sir? Need a drink?"

"I'd like to see Anna."

"Then you'll have to get up."

"She can't come here?"

"No, sir. She's not able to walk on her twisted ankle. Too swollen."

"My ankle is just as …" he stopped to let a wave of pain subside, "as bad."

"But with my help, I can take you to where she is."

"Your help? You broke my fuckin' arm."

"But, sir, you were trespassing. And I'm sorry for that."

"I identified myself as a cop—"

"I've got food on the stove. It's mid-afternoon. When the sun drops, and you're out here alone, bleeding, unable to defend yourself, it's just too dangerous, while Anna will be safe—"

"Okay, I get it, I get it. We're going to see her, and not the other way around."

"We need you to get up and get moving. In my home, we can wrap your wounds. I've got painkillers, too."

He felt around with his good hand, but more than his gun was missing.

"Why'd you take my utility belt, gun, and handcuffs?"

"As I said, I didn't know who you were, but now I do."

Frustration made him crazy. If he were in better shape, he'd knock out a few of the guy's teeth.

"I'm a cop."

"Yeah, geez, I know that now. But why are you alone?"

"Because I came out here looking for Anna."

"Without backup?"

"It was a hunch. I'm off duty."

"Well, your hunch paid off. Good for you. But you must admit, it was stupid to wander onto someone else's property armed and alone."

"I identified myself immediately."

"I'm old, hard of hearing, and we're going in circles." The guy released a frustrated breath. "I know you *said* that, but guys say a lot of shit to get out of a beating."

"You didn't just beat me. You broke my arm and knocked me out."

Footsteps thumped lightly beside him as the guy stepped away. "Looks like you want to wallow in self-pity instead of getting up and going to see Anna."

"Okay, okay, you win."

"C'mon, let me help you up."

The man moved closer on his good side.

"Gently," Colton muttered. "It's going to hurt like a bitch. I fell on my broken arm."

"I can see that. We'll go at your pace. As soon as you're in my home, I'll give you something for the pain, and we'll splint that arm. Then you and Anna can leave here together when the authorities arrive."

"Yes, okay, that would be good."

This nonsense was over. All he had to do was get up, fight the pain, and let this guy help him. It was his chance to *grow a pair* or *be a man*, as people liked to shout at weaker men.

The guy's hands slipped gently around the biceps of Colton's good arm.

"On the count of three, I'll lift, and you get up on your good knee. Then we'll do it again and get you onto your good foot. Ready?"

"Let me breathe a bit first."

"Breathe all you want."

Colton took several short bursts of air, then nodded, even though that flared a headache.

"Ready," Colton whispered, knowing a monsoon of hell was coming.

"On the count of three."

Colton nodded.

"One, two, three."

He clenched his stomach and brought his knee under him as the old guy lifted upward. His broken left arm dangled out away from him, moving in a manner that caused a fire-hot agony.

A groan formed in his abdomen, forcing its way up and out his mouth. He didn't want to scream. He didn't want Anna to hear him whine.

He blinked and orientated himself. The guy's hands still held his arm, keeping him balanced.

"Thanks," he whispered. "That wasn't as bad as I thought." His cheeks still hurt from the blows, but they weren't anywhere near the pain in his broken arm. The swelling was enormous, too. Doctors would have to perform surgery to get things back in order. Metal pins or screws would probably be needed as well. It didn't matter right now, though. Right now, he had to get to Anna, then swallow a dozen painkillers, and get the fuck out of here, away from the crazy old guy.

"One more time," the guy said. "We need you up on your good leg. Instead of using that branch as a cane, you can rest on my shoulders. We'll go slow."

Colton nodded in three short bursts. "Got it. Count of three."

"One, two, three—"

As he moved upward, he got his good foot under him and pushed.

Then he was standing on that good leg, his body leaning heavily into the old guy.

"You sure you can hold my weight?"

"I got you, don't I?"

"It'll be easier as I get the blood flowing into this leg."

"Doesn't matter. We haven't got far to go."

They started off, the guy walking slowly, pausing until Colton hopped solidly and stayed upright. Then another step, and another. Soon, they'd made it halfway to the old barracks building.

"Where's your place?"

"Inside there."

Colton frowned. "*Inside* the barracks?"

"Yeah, when I bought this place from the army, I didn't want to spend the money fixing their building. The damned thing is nearly condemned. So I built onto their back area and inside their bunkers."

"Bunkers?" Colton couldn't believe what he was hearing. "You live underground?"

"Man, you're going to love it."

"How so?"

"You've heard the term *man cave*?"

"Sure, everyone has. But usually, it's a converted garage or a renovated basement with a big screen TV and a beer fridge."

"Not out here. I've got the ultimate man cave. You'll see."

They continued in silence for several more steps before Colton asked the guy a question.

"You know my name, but I haven't been properly introduced to you."

"I'm Jaxon."

"Jackson, like Samuel, the actor?"

"Sounds the same, but mine's spelled with an X."

"And you live out here all alone?"

Jaxon laughed. "No, I've got friends, dear friends."

They made it to a side door, hopped inside the barracks building, and started down a long corridor with dirty rooms to his right.

"Such a waste to let this all go to ruin."

"Yeah, I didn't want to spend the money or time fixing everything. And for what? I wasn't going to be staying in here."

Something seemed off with the guy like something was wrong with his eyes. They didn't match his face, as if he'd aged while his eyes stayed young. Age is often revealed in the eyes. With that being the case, this guy was still under fifty or forty years old, but his pallor and skin elasticity made him look eighty at least.

They reached the end of the hall and stopped at a door that opened to a spiral staircase leading downward.

"What's down there?" Colton asked.

"My man cave, where Anna is waiting for you."

That didn't feel right for some reason, so he turned and shouted down the stairs. "Anna, you down there?"

He waited for a response, a wild mushroom smell emanating up to him.

"I wouldn't do that if I were you."

Colton spun around to glare at the guy. "And why's that? I can't call for Anna?"

"When I left, Anna was sleeping. You wouldn't want to wake her. Better to surprise her."

"And how am I supposed to get down there with a fucked-up ankle and a broken arm? The stairs are too narrow to go down side by side."

"I will be right behind you. Just twist your good arm back, and I'll offer support. I got you."

"No, I have a better idea."

Jaxon stepped away from him. The expression on his face became something akin to irritation. Why was the guy so determined to get him downstairs? And what was that horrid mushroom smell?

"Why don't you go get Anna and bring her up here? That way, I don't have to go down or return later to leave. That makes the most amount of sense." Colton shook his head. "Taking these stairs in my condition is stupid."

"Suit yourself, but Anna wanted to see you, so I told her I'd help you down." Jaxon moved to the top of the stairs.

"Also," Colton said. "I'll need my gun, cuffs, and wallet."

"Yeah, it's all in the man cave. You'll have to come down—"

"Dude, it's right there in your waistband." Colton pointed at the butt of the weapon sticking out of Jaxon's pants.

"Sir, that's *my* gun. Yours is downstairs."

"Pull it out. Let me see it then."

Jaxon placed his hands on his hips. "You're really not here for Anna, are you?"

"What's that supposed to mean?"

"She's right down there," Jaxon jabbed a hand downward, "and you're not willing to take a few stairs to see her."

"A few stairs? Is that what you call this?" He couldn't help his voice from rising. Ever since he'd gotten off that train, his life had been one mistake after another, and now he stood in front of an armed stranger who wanted him to go into some sort of dark bunker alone and injured. Something told him that he'd never come back up if he went down those steps.

Yet, this guy knew about Anna. So she had to be down there. Otherwise, how else would Jaxon know her?

"Colton?" A woman's voice called from below.

"Colton?"

"See, there's Anna now." Jaxon shook his head. "Some boyfriend you turned out to be."

Colton hopped forward and pushed Jaxon out of the way.

"Coming, honey," he called out to her.

He grabbed the railing, hopped down one step, then lowered his hand on the railing, gripped it tightly, and hopped down another step.

On the third step, Jaxon whispered, "You're going too slow."

The man placed his hands on Colton's shoulders, then shoved him hard.

Colton panicked and tried to hold on, but his body twisted over his good hand, and gravity did the rest. He lifted over the railing, teetered on his stomach, and felt one more shove from Jaxon as he pushed on Colton's right thigh.

Then Colton was in the air, falling.

It lasted all of a second before the ground opened up a new world of pain to him, a level of pure agony he had never thought imaginable.

Something else broke in his body; something ruptured. His breathing became ragged and filled with hurt. His ribs were probably separated somewhere, and something was wrong with his knee now, too. Any movement of his leg was excruciating. The wrist on his good arm had shot out to help break the fall, but all it did was snap backward under his weight.

Colton had no idea a body could scream in agony

as much as he was.

Something moved him, and he screamed.

The old guy was there now, kicking his leg.

"You doing okay, cop?" Jaxon asked, then he laughed. "You liked that imitation of Anna's voice?" He laughed harder.

Colton would never consider murdering anyone, but if his body wasn't in such bad shape, he would have gotten up and killed Jaxon. If anyone deserved it, it was this guy.

"My friends can imitate voices," Jaxon said. "You liked Anna's? Good impression, huh?"

"Fuck you," Colton said, his consciousness wavering in and out.

Jaxon grabbed Colton's broken left arm and straightened it.

The pain was unreal, absolute pure Hell.

Colton screamed, his vision blurred, and he almost fainted.

The old guy was dragging him along the bunker's floor, everything in his body on fire now.

"You'll like my friends." Jaxon wailed with what sounded like joy. "They're *dying* to meet you."

Then he laughed—Jaxon's laugh was the last thing Colton heard before losing consciousness.

Chapter 29

"A MOMENT AGO, YOU said, 'something old and evil.'"
Anna looked over at Russ. "You want to explain that last comment? What's it supposed to mean?"

"Did you know that the first dinosaur bones weren't discovered until the early 1800s?"

"And that has to do with this, how? Russ, we're supposed to be thinking of ways to get the fuck out of here. I don't want a history lesson."

"Just listen for a minute." His handcuff jangled against the flagpole as he shifted his position. "Guys like George Washington, a founding father of this great nation and the first president, had no idea dinosaurs ever existed. Whoever lived before the early 1800s had no idea—no one knew."

Anna stared off at the distant trees as she thought she heard someone talking over that way. "Okay, didn't know that." She turned to face Russ. "Are you saying there's a dinosaur underground?"

"No, I'm saying there are still things undiscovered about this place we call Earth."

"Yeah, like what?"

"Well, I can't answer that because it hasn't been discovered yet."

"This isn't a time to make jokes. We need to figure a way out of this place." She felt a tear of despair rise in her eye and blinked it away. She didn't want to completely lose it yet.

Russ leaned forward. "Anna, you're not listening to me. I have a theory, and it may not get us out of here, but at least it'll help us understand what we're dealing with."

She tugged lightly on the cuffs and scanned the trees yet again. "Unless a bunch of rescue guys come charging through those woods, I don't see us getting out of here anytime soon, so enlighten me with your theory."

Russ cleared his throat. "As I said, we just discovered dinosaurs, and on Earth's timeline, that's considered quite recent. What if there are other things, deeper things, that live closer to the core—"

"Right, and they can live at over five-thousand degrees. It's fucking hot down there."

"Okay, fine, maybe not the core. All I'm saying is, we don't know everything about this planet, and it's not unheard of that something else may live here with us."

She wiped her face and opened her mouth to speak. "Are you saying some *being* is doing all this, some living thing?"

"What I'm saying is, the communion of the beast is upon us."

"'Communion of the beast.'" She nearly spat the words, staring at him like he'd lost his mind. "Where did you come up with that shit? What the hell's it supposed to mean?"

"Those MREs weren't really ready-to-eat meals, were they?"

Now he had her interest. She at least wanted to see where he was going with this.

"No, the ones we saw in that bunker room were vastly different than the silver-packaged ones you three ate."

"Right, you didn't eat one, and you're barely aging."

She had forgotten all about that, but now in the sunlight, Russ looked even older. Certainly not as bad as Jaxon, but she thought his skin was more wrinkly. She checked her arms and hands, then mumbled a few curse words under her breath.

"Whereas," Russ continued, "I look at least twenty years older now, and so does Grayson. We all saw how much of that shit Jaxon was eating. He's aged the worst of us, making me suspect he won't make the night."

"I was thinking the same thing when I saw Jaxon. I hope he brings us the key before he dies, though. It would be shitty to be tied up with you for days listening to these theories and end up dying of starvation."

Russ scoffed at her. "I think I'm onto something here. That mushroom smell is the key, wherever it's coming from. When we ate the MRE, it's like communion, you know, the body of Christ, except this shit is from Hell, and we ate the body of Lucifer, hence communion of the beast."

"And what, it's taking our souls now?" Her tone sobered somewhat as she wondered if he was onto something.

"Let's say for a second that I'm right. Then what we ate has accelerated the process, which is physically evident—we can see it with our own eyes. I also figure all that stuff we found in the bunker wasn't abandoned. It's all there because no one ever left this place alive."

She shivered, not wanting to believe what he had just said. How could that be possible? It was just another piece of land, wasn't it?

"Then where are they?" she asked.

He watched her eyes for a long moment. "They're all gone, long gone, but something of their souls lives on here. Those old men we bumped into last night were an illusion. For some reason, it can pull that shit off at night, but illusions might be see-through when the sun is up, and it's bright." He shrugged, the cuffs jangling. "Who knows? I mean, I'm guessing here."

"Really? Well, is that the best you got? Any other theories, wild guesses?"

He leaned forward, yanking the cuff attached to the flagpole.

"Remember what Jaxon said? 'There's you, then there's me, and soon it'll be all of us.' What do you think he meant by 'all of us'?"

"I have no idea."

"I think this place is a soul eater, and unless we break these cuffs and start running now, we won't make the night."

"Now I'm scared. Thanks."

"What, you weren't before?"

"Yeah, but hearing it said that way." She stifled an internal moan but had to wipe her eye. "All I wanted was a family."

"What?"

"A family," she snapped. "But Colton fucking cheated on me, and I bought a train ticket a week early."

"You're here because your boyfriend cheated on you?"

"Yeah, with my boss, no less."

"Damn, a shitty reason to die."

"Is there ever a good one?"

"Point taken."

They fell silent for a few moments. Anna was sure she heard voices again, then someone grunted. Maybe Jaxon was bringing Grayson to the surface because it sounded like someone was on the metal spiral stairs leading to the bunker.

"You're still young enough to have kids."

She held out her arm. "Look at me. I'm twenty-eight going on forty. Shit, you're practically sixty years old by the look of that gray in your hair."

"Yeah, and because Jaxon ate a lot more of that MRE shit, he's nearing one hundred."

"Then what will happen?"

Russ shrugged. "Not sure, unless this being or entity or whatever we want to call it, needs our life source to fuel its own needs. I mean, if that's the case, we'll be dead before we know what happened."

"If that's the case, whatever's down there could escape and take more …" she drifted off. "Wait, what the hell? You got me talking like you now."

"Yeah, you're thinking, analyzing shit. Once we understand it, maybe we can defeat it."

"Defeat it? Sounds like a tall order." She held up their cuffed hands. "Besides, we get out of these cuffs, I'm running. I won't be defeating anything except my ability to run a marathon on my first try."

"Let me tell you something else, another little theory of mine."

"No, I'm done talking theories."

"Why, because they're close to the truth?"

"No, because they're a waste of time."

"What else we got but time?"

Russ laid back and stared up at the clouds as they drifted by. She watched him as his eyes darted from one cloud to the next, wondering what he could be thinking.

"Tell me about the baseball bat attack."

"Thought you didn't want to talk anymore."

"Oh, don't be so overdramatic. I didn't want to hear any more theories on Hell and some soul-eating dinosaur monster."

It was several more minutes before Russ started talking again.

"They'd let a convicted registered sex offender loose on some sort of day pass in our area. Then, six months later, he was in a halfway house or some shit. The locals heard about it and protested with signs that read, NOT IN OUR NEIGHBORHOOD. Anyway, the authorities assured everyone he was rehabilitated, but I don't believe you can rehabilitate assholes like that. If they haven't been castrated, as long as they still have their balls and they're producing semen and testosterone, a sex offender will re-offend. No doubt in my mind."

She waited for him to continue, not wanting to interrupt.

After a moment, he started talking again.

"My worst nightmare became a reality." He sounded choked up. "My seventeen-year-old sister lived two blocks away from this released sex offender asshole. I warned her over and over to watch her back. I gave her pictures of the guy and showed her where the asshole lived. We went through drills and how to ward off an attacker. To punch him in the throat, go for the eyes. To call me if she was nervous or for any other reason."

Anna wasn't sure she wanted to hear the rest.

"Then, one night, I got the call."

"The call?"

"Yeah, caller ID said it was my sister. All I could hear was whispering and muffled screams like someone had a hand over her mouth when I answered. Then grunting."

"Oh no …"

"I jumped in my car and drove the ten minutes to her house."

"You didn't call the cops?"

Russ had to pull her cuffed hand up to wipe at his eyes. "No, I wanted the guy all to myself. My sister is tough. She could handle ten minutes, which was my irrational thought at the time. Or actually, I wasn't thinking at all. It was just blind rage."

"So, what happened?" she asked, thinking she still didn't want to hear the rest.

"I burst into the house, saw a baseball bat and glove on the floor by the front door, grabbed the bat, and busted into my sister's room. I saw the guy on top of her, my sister's shirt already off, and I whacked the guy endlessly."

"Shit, they should give you an award for that."

"No, I'm going to jail for sure."

"Why?" she blurted out. "You saved your sister? How could any jury not have sympathy for you?"

"I didn't save shit."

"How so?"

He wiped his face again. "It was her boyfriend. He'd just come back from baseball practice, and they were alone, just getting frisky. She had dialed my number accidentally when taking off her pants—a butt dial. The whispering and moaning were real, but no one was in distress. They were just feeling each other up. And now her boyfriend has to eat through a straw and will never walk again. I was lucky they lowered the charge from attempted murder for a plea deal. Then I panicked and ran for the train on court day."

Anna bit her lower lip. The pain and guilt Russ had to be enduring, not to mention what his sister's boyfriend was going through, was a tragic situation, a complete tragedy for everyone involved.

"I'm just one of the good guys who took the wrong road, and I'm still making bad decisions."

"How so? You stepped in front of me and put your arm out to protect me when Jaxon had the gun. I saw what you did. You're one of the good guys, full stop."

"Yeah, well, tell that to the judge."

"I will if you get us out of here."

"I'm sorry, Anna, but I don't think we're going anywhere anytime soon."

"Now, who's sounding defeatist?"

"Jaxon is too far gone, taken by this thing, this entity that's sucking the life from us like a vampire or whatever the fuck. He's taken Grayson with him. Next, it'll be me because I represent the most physical danger to stopping Jaxon, but it won't come for me yet. He's waiting, or it's waiting."

"Waiting? For what?"

"For me to age further and become weaker, but also for nighttime."

"Why nighttime?"

"Because that's when this thing has more power to do its magic. As I said, those old men from last night were nothing but a shared illusion. The fire in the cabin, the intact windows in the barracks—all easy for this thing to conjure when it's dark, and we can't see its imperfections."

"You're scaring me right now."

"I'm not trying to. Just telling you how I see it."

"Can we not talk for a few minutes? You know, catch a breath?"

"Sure."

She watched the clouds now, wondering how high in the sky they were, how easy it was for them to drift by and leave the area. If the handcuffs weren't removed, how would they ever leave?

Could buying a train ticket literally set her on a path to her death? It couldn't be. She refused to believe that. If so, then what was it all for? How random was it that a good guy like Russ and a nice girl like herself were caught up in a mess like this?

After about ten minutes of silence, she rolled her head toward him. "You said you had another theory. You still want to tell it to me?"

He rolled his head to face her. "You sure you want to hear it?"

She nodded. "Yeah, the silence is more maddening. I feel like cattle waiting our turn in the slaughterhouse."

"I won't comment on that to avoid making you feel worse, but I'll sum up my other theory in a few sentences."

They both stared back up at the sky.

"Everything is either alive or dead."

"Wow, that's brilliant. Well said, Russ. Truly."

He laughed, and out here at that moment, it sounded musical. "Okay, wiseass, let me finish. Plants are considered living things, so they don't rot as they're not dead. A tree knocked over in a storm will rot because it's not alive anymore. We rot when we're dead. The wood they use to build things is pressure treated, so the rotting process takes decades or longer. Get the picture."

"Yeah, alive equals no rot, dead equals rot."

"Basically, yes. So, I believe we're spiritual beings having a human experience."

"I've heard that said before somewhere."

"It's a famous quote. Anyway, the spirit inside keeps our flesh and blood from rotting. As soon as we exit our body, dust to dust, ashes to ashes." She detected him turning his head to face her. "Still with me?"

She nodded. "Go on."

"To feed our bodies, we eat things that were once alive or, in some cases, still are."

"What? No, I don't eat anything alive."

"Do you eat salad? How about a steak? These are things that were nurtured in nature, raised with spirit, and offered to us as nutrients—live residual nutrients—for our bodies to sustain our individual lives."

"I'm not sure where you're going with this, but so far, I'll agree that plant life is called that for a reason and that we eat meat, which was alive just before we ate it."

"Keeping all that in mind, I want you to think of a

parasite. It lives off the host and consumes what it wants until the host dies."

"You think this thing in the bunker is a parasite?" She averted her gaze from the sky and turned to stare at him.

"All I'm saying is, everything that's alive will do what it must to stay that way. We all aim for sustenance in our own way, sucking the life from cattle and extinguishing the life from spinach and broccoli. What if this thing is on a different level, one that we don't or can't comprehend? What if it needs the spirit in us instead of the body?"

Anna shivered. "That's nightmare-inducing, Russ. Shit, you're scaring me. Spiritual cannibalism? Really?"

"Just think about it. If our best attribute is our spirit, which offers us up to a hundred years in a body, keeping all that rot at bay, then why not steal that for its consumption? We measure food in calories. A nice skinless chicken breast offers us roughly two hundred calories. Once we expend those, we need more food." He leaned up on his elbow to look at her. "What I'm saying is, how would a spirit eater measure the calories of a soul? And if sustained, wouldn't that soul offer the spirit eater decades and decades of life as it would to the original owner had the soul not been taken?"

"Where the hell did you come up with that?"

"Remember when I talked about communion?"

She nodded. "Yeah, you called it a communion of

the beast or something."

"And we saw those old guys last night who aren't real?"

She continued to nod.

"Well, I figure those guys are souls this thing took, and it can reanimate them at will, but it's not perfect at the reanimation bit, so it does it at night. Our bodies won't give it lasting energy, but our souls will."

"Okay, great. This sucks. And here I thought, if we died, at least we had a chance at Heaven. Now I'm hearing even our souls will be stuck here in the belly of some soul-sucking, spirit-stealing parasite."

"I didn't say it was a fact." He laid back down. "I said it was a theory."

She tried to calm her breathing because this shit was really scaring her.

"What if you're right?" she whispered.

"Then we're fucked."

"Gee, great. What I mean is, if you're right, where did this thing come from?"

"That's what I meant when I was talking about dinosaurs. What if we haven't discovered things yet, and they found one of the ancients when they built this military base and that bunker? People disappear without a trace all over the world. You've heard of the Bermuda Triangle, right?"

"Yes, I did a research paper on it in high school. It's also called Devil's Triangle."

"Ships and airplanes have disappeared for years in the Bermuda Triangle, never to be found again.

Whatever happened to Amelia Earhart? How about Jimmy Hoffa? I mean, who really knows?"

She blew air out her mouth in nervous exasperation.

"What I'm saying is," he continued. "What if this is a Bermuda Triangle on land? I mean, why haven't there been any planes overhead? Where are the flies, the bees, and the bugs? Dead rats and mice line the hallways of the barracks. It's calling out to them, then stealing their tiny souls, leaving their bodies to rot. There are no birds. Unless this place is polluted with radiation, which I highly doubt, or the rest of the state of Oregon would already know about it. That leaves me to conclude that something here is beyond our scope of imagination, and it's got its parasitic fingers into Jaxon's soul."

"Damn, Russ, that's making some sense."

"My worry is if it moves."

"*Moves?* What the hell does that mean?"

"I mean, what if it gets enough souls to become mobile? What if this parasite walks out of the woods and enters Eugene? On day one, half the town is eighty years old. Day two, they're dead, and this thing has more souls, more spirits. Then off to Portland. The next stop is the State of Oregon. Then north to the State of Washington or south to California? Choices, choices."

"The way you talk about it." She rubbed her empty stomach. "I feel sick."

"Me too."

"I don't have it in me to be a hero, but can you think of a way to stop it or kill it?"

"No, haven't got that far yet."

"Russ!" she snapped at him like he was a petulant child. "Don't come up with all these theories and possibilities without at least one option to stop it. So not fair."

"Well, if I'm right, and this thing exists on souls, then not feeding it any more souls would certainly help."

"Great idea," she said too loudly. "Let's get up and leave. Tired of this place anyway, and I'd love to keep my soul right where it is, fully intact."

"You know what I mean. If it's a soul parasite, and you asked how to stop it, then we must find a way to escape and tell the world what we know."

"Okay, sorry. I can get snotty when I'm afraid." She touched his hand with the one that was cuffed to him. "I like that idea. Escape and tell the world. But how?"

"I'm thinking."

They dropped into silence again. After about five minutes, Russ turned to her.

"There's one way."

"Which is?"

"When Jaxon takes the cuffs off to lead us back to the bunker, which I'm sure is his plan, I try to overpower him, and you find a way to run."

"So, sacrifice yourself? That's your plan?"

He nodded.

"No way. That plan sucks. Try another one."

"Look, Anna, we are limited on time. I'm still strong, but I feel that shit inside me, working on me, aging me. It's already taking what it wants. I'll die by tomorrow, but you've got a fighting chance. You didn't take the communion. You didn't eat that body-of-the-devil MRE shit."

She couldn't stop the water rising in her eyes this time. Tears slipped over her eyelids and ran down her temples to the grass.

"This is about survival now," he continued. "One of us has to get out of here, and that must be you. And if it's already dark and you're running, don't let the parasite scare you as it conjures up old men with rifles. Think of them as holograms. Run right through them. If you could run with your eyes closed, that would be better because if this thing detects you're leaving, it'll throw everything it's got your way."

She expelled a shuddering breath she'd held for a few moments.

"Where do you think this thing came from?"

"No idea. Outer space? Maybe it crash-landed here millennia ago. On our planet, we eat animals once they're dead and the spirit is released. On their planet, maybe they do it the other way. Release the spirit and eat it first. Who knows? All I know is this aging thing isn't natural, and Jaxon was twenty years old yesterday when we got off that train. He isn't twenty anymore. So, I could be wrong about everything, but none of that matters. All that matters is you getting out of here alive, and if you're willing to run like your ass is on fire, I'm willing to die to give you that chance."

"Why would you do that?"

"Because I'm going to die here anyway, so it might as well be worth something."

"And if I don't make it?"

"Anna, if you don't make it out, you die, too. Or you'll live here in Hell, scaring wanderers for centuries as they meander onto the abandoned premises of this army barracks that's become the eating domain of a rather powerful spirited parasite."

"In other words, I'll die and go to Hell."

"I'd say that about sums it up."

"Then I'll run."

"I was hoping you'd say that."

Chapter 30

THE AFTERNOON WANED ON, with Anna and Russ taking bathroom breaks as best they could. Discussions on everything to escape, murder, ex-boyfriends, and the court system, mixed with existentialism and thoughts on why humans existed in the first place, kept their minds off the obvious—they were tied to a flagpole. At the same time, something possessed Jaxon into shooting Grayson, and now he was holding them hostage.

Anna had dozed off during a lull, but it couldn't have been more than ten or fifteen minutes.

"Hey," she said, rubbing her face as fatigue made her eyes heavy. "When's this nightmare going to be over?" She stared at his face in the waning light of the setting sun. Russ had aged at least another ten years while cuffed to the flagpole. Her own flesh revealed some aging on her part, but certainly not as much as him.

"No idea, but I suspect this nightmare will end tonight." He glanced down at her and smiled.

She looked up in the sky and saw the sun on its course toward setting for another day. Her stomach churned at the thought of their situation and the helplessness of it all.

"Have you come up with any more theories or ways to get out of this?"

"Not yet, but I've got a couple of things brewing."

"Like what?"

"I'd prefer to keep them to myself until I figure out a few more details." He stared off at the trees as if his eyes weren't seeing anything, unfocused.

"Mister Talkative has had a change of heart."

He smiled, then resumed his thousand-yard stare.

Their situation was dire, but something more than that was bothering him. "Has anything changed? Did you hear from Jaxon while I dozed?"

He shook his head. "I heard some talking, but nothing else, really. He knows where we are, and we're not going anywhere. He'll be back when he's ready."

"If he doesn't die first."

"True, there's that."

She eyed him for a moment, studying his face. "You sound different, more somber. You okay?"

"Just contemplating my life."

"In situations like this, shouldn't we be contemplating life and how to keep it?"

"Sure, I'm with you there, but this is more of a meditative, philosophical state. I'm just not sure how to beat this thing unless I kill Jaxon."

"Kill or be killed," she mumbled.

He glanced her way. "That's what's on my mind, but isn't that worse on some level? To steal someone's life? Am I forfeiting my soul by taking someone else's life?"

"Too philosophical for me. Just stay alive, and if taking out the guy trying to kill you is what it takes, then do it and worry about your soul later. Getting us out of here is the only answer."

"Yeah, but at what cost?"

"Russ, you can't roll over and die, either."

He swiveled his head back and forth as if frustrated she wasn't listening.

"I'm not giving up, but let's say I find a way to beat the guy, and we walk out of here; what do I have to go back to? A sister who despises me for destroying her boyfriend's life, a court system with an arrest warrant out on me, and a prison cell with my name on it for at least ten to fifteen years, possibly more? Wow, that sounds like a great deal. Kill a man in cold blood to go on and win life in a cage."

She used her free hand to touch his shoulder in a soft gesture of comfort. "Hey, I'm sorry. Things got shitty for you. I understand that. But whatever happens tonight or tomorrow will define you. Don't let that one accident, a miscalculation, be your life's work. That's not you. Saving your sister *was* you, and saving us *is* you."

He lowered his head to stare at the grass, then nodded softly. "I've got too much fight in me to give up and too much attitude to let him win, but there's a side of me that doesn't want to go back." He glanced sidelong at her. "I mean, what the hell for? I've lost everything."

She rubbed his shoulder, her hand working in circles. "I'm so sorry."

"Maybe that's why I'm here."

"What? Why?" Caution in her tone. She wasn't sure she wanted an answer.

"I set this path for myself. Created a life back home that crashed and burned, so I could fight here with nothing to lose."

"Is that what you think? Because if so, then you're talking about a cosmic plan and shit. Back to our chat on existentialism."

"Well, if life has meaning, then it has to mean something, right?"

"Yeah, get us out of here and go on to live the life you want. No one will know you escaped this place. I can tell them Jaxon killed you down here. Once you're dead to the authorities, you can change your name, get a haircut, dye your hair, and live on until you die of old age one day on a beach in the Bahamas."

"Sadly, my death will likely happen a week or two after getting out of here anyway."

"Back to being defeatist, are we?"

"Okay, so what's the point? What are we doing here? Gonna just sit and wait to die?"

Russ didn't move for a moment, then he turned to her, his eyes roving up, then down.

"I'm going to do everything I can to figure this shit out while I still can. I'll fight Jaxon, fight this thing, whatever it is, and do my damnedest to get you

out of here. Whatever happens next"—he shrugged—
"I'm okay with it because I know I did my best."

"Well, I'm not okay with it. I want you out of here
with me—"

"Good evening," Jaxon said, coming around a
bush to stand and stare at them from fifteen feet away.

Her stomach dropped at the sight of him. This
was it. The fight was on for their survival. The waiting
had been agonizing, but now it was bittersweet. No
more waiting for Jaxon to arrive. Someone was going
to die soon; she could just feel it.

"How are you two holding up?" he asked as if
they'd all been going through the same ordeal.

Jaxon moved out of the shadows, and Anna had to
suppress her gasp. It couldn't be the same man. He
had to be at least one hundred years old now. Besting
him wouldn't prove difficult as his muscles had
atrophied, and his shoulders were hunched slightly
forward as if their weight alone was too much to carry.
The body fat had fallen off in chunks, as if he'd been
stricken with some sort of thinning disease, leaving
behind a veined skin wrap to cover his bones. Lips
parched, sallow complexion, sunken cheeks, and nary
a tooth, Jaxon looked positively horrid, yet his eyes
still held life as well as something else.

Evil.

There was a maliciousness to his eyes as they
stared back at Anna and Russ like something lurked
behind them, all-seeing. It made Anna shiver when his
eyes took her in, swallowing her.

"It's almost over." Jaxon moved closer. "For me."

"I can see that," Russ said, easing sideways to move in front of Anna. "You feeling okay, man?"

"Never better, actually."

"How do I get some of that?"

Jaxon smiled, revealing gums turned brown with age. "In time, brother, in time."

"What are you doing?" Anna whispered to Russ. "Do not sacrifice yourself for me."

He looked back at her over his shoulder. "Trust me. I think I've figured this thing out, what it wants, and how it gets you."

"Then tell me so we can do the opposite and kill it."

"I will. Soon."

Jaxon stepped closer. "What are you two whispering about?"

Russ turned back to Jaxon. "We're just concerned for you, is all."

"There's no need to worry on my account."

"Have you seen yourself?"

"Why would someone second guess a state of bliss?" Jaxon moved even closer, and the sun set farther. "Why would I *check* how I look when life couldn't be better?"

Russ shrugged. "If you say so."

Anna stared at Russ momentarily, wondering how long it would take him to look like Jaxon. Probably by the morning, or perhaps later in the day tomorrow, but he was heading there, that much was for sure.

Was hope something they could entertain? Or was it too late to ever escape this place?

Then a thought struck her. Was it the communion of the beast, the eating of the MREs, that did this? Or was it that disgusting burned mushroom smell they'd been inhaling since they arrived? Jaxon had taken in more of that pungent smell than any of them had, spending so much more time in bunkers than all of them. Russ and Grayson had been closer to that smell in the bunkers for more extended periods than Anna. Maybe that had something to do with their aging issue.

"I came up to say goodbye," Jaxon said.

That fickle bitch called hope stirred in her gut. Was it truly over, or was Jaxon just fucking with them?

"Where are you heading?" Russ asked, sounding genuinely curious.

"To stay with my friends. I've waited long enough. Lived a lifetime waiting, in fact."

"I can see that."

"But first, I need someone strong to take my place." He moved closer and now only stood five or six feet away. "It's a temporary position, at best, but —"

"How about Grayson?"

Jaxon focused on Russ. "He's currently indisposed."

"Why? Because you shot him?"

Jaxon smiled wide again, revealing the disease inside his mouth. "That bullet wound was the least of his worries. He could've survived that."

The hope that had stirred in her stomach vanished with reality. *Could've survived that* inferred he hadn't survived after all.

"I was thinking someone like Colton Asher." His eyes landed on Anna when he spoke.

Anna glared at him, speechless at hearing her ex-boyfriend's name spoken by Jaxon.

"How do you know that name?" she asked.

Jaxon frowned as if the answer was obvious. "I know that name because he's here, enjoying a cup of Earl Grey in my office with some friends."

"Bullshit." Anna spat the word. "You read my mind, or better yet, the thing that has possessed you to read my mind."

Jaxon moved his head back and forth, his eyes closed, hands behind his back.

"Colton came looking for you." Jaxon maintained his broad smile. "How sweet, right?"

What she felt at hearing that statement was unfamiliar. Relief that he had found her so fast, annoyance that he'd taken it upon himself to come after her in the first place as if they were still a couple, and dread at what Jaxon had likely done to him.

It all came back to her. This was her fault she was in this mess, her fault Colton had fallen prey to Jaxon, and her fault they were all going to die.

Colton may have cheated with Janine, but he didn't deserve to die for it. His betrayal immensely hurt her, but that was because she loved the man.

She'd wanted a family with him, babies, a house, a life. Deceit came at a cost and a loss, but not a life. That was too steep a price.

"What have you done to him?" Each word was measured, cold, and direct.

Jaxon's shrug was grotesque. She no longer cared what happened to the aged junkie. He shot Grayson, tied them up all day long like cattle, and now he'd done something unspeakable to Colton, something unforgivable. She just knew it. The first chance she got, the anger rushing through her veins was enough to choke the life out of Jaxon.

"I've done nothing to your man but offer him a cup of tea while he waited for you to join him."

Russ moved even farther in front of her—at least as far as the cuffs allowed him to. "She's not going anywhere with you."

"I'm afraid you don't get a say in the matter." Jaxon stared him down. His hands slowly lowered to his side, the weapon in his hand.

"I'll go," Anna whispered. "I need to see Colton."

Russ snapped his fingers. "So that's where you got the handcuffs and the gun?" Russ held Anna back. "You saw Colton and removed his weapon and cuffs before we bumped into you at the bottom of the stairs, which implies that Colton isn't waiting for Anna somewhere while sipping tea because you already dealt with him in order to have his weapon. A cop doesn't just hand those things off to strangers in the woods."

Anna pulled on the cuffs. "Russ, stop. I'll go."

"No, he's taking you to it, whatever it is."

"Anna, Russ, I will have to ask you both to remove your shoes and socks, then toss them to me."

"Fuck you," Russ shouted, spittle coming from his mouth.

Anna reared back at the violence of Russ's protest, her eyes wide.

Russ glared at Jaxon. "Tell me, why should we do anything you tell us to do?"

"Because I'm holding the ultimate negotiator." Jaxon raised the weapon. "And I'm asking nicely. This thing in my hand won't ask as nicely."

Anna started untying her shoes.

"Anna, wait," Russ said. "We can't do everything he tells us."

"What option do we have? He'll shoot us otherwise."

"Then let him shoot us. I'd rather bleed out in a minute or two than be taken by what's in that bunker."

She stopped to glare at him, her eyes bulging. "Russ, if Colton is down there, then he may need me to make sense of all this." She lowered her voice so only Russ could hear her, barely a whisper. "And we could use a cop on our side."

"If he's still alive."

"I assure you, Anna," Jaxon said, his tone soothing. "Your man is still alive. Come, be a family again. Join him for a chat and a cup of Earl Greyson."

"'Earl Grey*son*'?" Russ repeated. "What the fuck

is that?"

Jaxon shook his head as if confused. "I said, Earl Grey, as in tea."

"Right, of course you did."

Jaxon stared off at the sun as it dipped below the trees. "The dark is coming." He turned back to them, focusing on Russ. "Give me your shoes and socks. Then I take Anna to Colton. Once they've seen each other, I will bring you down, too."

"Good luck with that," Russ said, then spit. "Fuckin' junkie."

Anna started in on her shoes, kicking them off. She slipped her socks down and off, then stuffed them into the shoes.

"Here." She held them up.

"Toss them toward me."

She did as she was told. They landed and rolled a couple of times, one of the socks slipping out to lie on the grass.

"Now you, Russ?"

"Come get them yourself."

Jaxon raised the weapon to aim it at Russ. "I don't have the time to convince you to do as I ask."

"Neither do I, evidently."

"Russ, please." Anna pulled on his shoulder. "Don't get shot over this."

He glanced back at her. "And what, die of old age tomorrow? Those are my choices?"

"There's a lot that can happen overnight. Just think about it. Then do as he says."

Russ looked back at Jaxon, then Anna. After several seconds, he huffed out a breath and untied his laces.

Jaxon lowered the weapon.

Once he'd removed his socks, he didn't just toss them toward Jaxon; he threw them. One went wild, but the other hit Jaxon's thigh, causing the man to smile at Russ.

There was a moment of heightened tension before Jaxon slipped the weapon away behind him, probably in the back of his pants as they do in the movies, and produced the handcuffs keys.

He pointed at Anna. "I need you to inch away from Russ as far as you can go until your hands are suspended out sideways."

Anna moved as instructed, anticipating a protest from Russ that didn't come. Once their hands were raised, Jaxon approached and slipped the key in to release her.

She expected Russ to snatch at Jaxon somehow, but he just sat there with a scowl on his face, glaring at Jaxon.

Freed from the cuff, Anna moved sideways, then got to her feet gingerly, mindful of standing on the softer grass as her feet were bare now. When she turned around, Jaxon had put the key back in his pocket, and the gun was in his hand again.

"What's to stop me from running?" she asked.

"A bullet in the back, not to mention you'd have very sore feet. You wouldn't get far."

"How do I know you actually have Colton in the bunker?"

"I figure the gun and the cuffs, as Russ mentioned, would be enough proof, but I brought this along just in case you asked that."

Jaxon slipped his free hand in his pocket without taking his eyes off Anna, then withdrew a card and handed it to her.

She took it and examined the front.

It was Colton's driver's license. She pocketed it and met Jaxon's gaze.

"Take me to him."

"Right this way."

"Anna," Russ said, his tone hard, even harsh sounding. "Don't trust this asshole. I'm worried I'll never see you again."

She stumbled on her bare feet after stepping on a small pebble, righted herself, and glanced back over her shoulder.

"I'll see you again, Rusty Brown. Just keep working on those theories. I'll be back up to chat about them soon."

Jaxon laughed at that as he pushed her forward, the gun held at his waist.

He laughed until Anna entered the abandoned barracks as if they'd just said the year's best joke.

She didn't care what Jaxon found so funny. All she could think about was how many bullets she could take and still be able to crawl out of the bunker because, before long, she was going to attack Jaxon and kill him.

It was the only way to escape.

Jaxon had to die.

Chapter 31

PRESENT DAY ...

Trooper Richard Logan spent an hour visiting Miss Valentina before he got something to eat—slop that resembled a wet hamburger but was more like a disgusting meat pudding—and then headed to the trailer to watch the Air Force maneuvers on TVs set up for that purpose.

Speaking with Anna about why she requested him in the first place got him nowhere. She claimed to have never made such a statement.

Then why was he here? Would Anna lie to him? Or was it Miles and Atkins who wanted him here for some reason? If so, what could that be?

Be careful what you wish for was never more true. He had wanted to be a part of this investigation from the start, and now he was all the way in, so how could he complain? But finding out who and what was behind him being at a secure military facility would go a long way in learning the why.

Although, would it matter anymore? The Air Force pilots were scheduled to fly overhead with enough bombs to create a crater in the earth very soon.

According to the military elites, it would be dead soon if anything were alive down there.

He'd argued with Miles and Atkins for nearly an hour about destroying the barracks while their people were inside, begging them to consider the lives of the soldiers who had gone AWOL. They'd confirmed that over half of the soldiers and investigators at the command center had gone missing, most of them suspected of being inside the fence line.

"How can you blow up the barracks with your own people in there?"

"What you're missing, Trooper, is that whatever's in there needs to be destroyed, and if anyone is still somewhere beyond the fence, they're likely dead by now."

"See, that's my point. You said, 'likely dead by now,' but you don't know."

Atkins thumped the table with his fist. "If they aren't dead now, they'd be dead by tomorrow. The destruction of the barracks will happen on schedule. Everyone who went AWOL in search of gold, or whatever the fuck the reason was, knew what they were doing. We're here to erase this place from existence. Make no illusions about it; that will happen tonight whether we lose more people or not."

As the clock ticked closer to the bombing that afternoon, the army counted nine more deserters. They all ran into the fenced-off area and were never seen again.

Anna protested the bombing to Logan, who sent

her claims up the ranks, but it all fell on deaf ears. This wasn't the way to kill whatever it was that lurked in the bunker. She mumbled something about it being from another planet or that it was from before our time, and it knew how to survive.

Her argument was based on its location—stuck underground. If it wasn't bound to live in the bunker, then why didn't it come up and kill entire towns? Weren't they afraid the bombs might release it upon the world and that they were falling into its hands, doing exactly what it wanted of them?

Anna Valentina explained to Logan that there was one way to kill it, and she knew exactly what that was.

"Tell me how it can be killed, then," Logan said.

"By beating it at its own game." Anna spoke in detail about what she saw, heard, and dealt with, and what she thought would kill it.

Logan tended to believe her and took her claims to Miles and Atkins, but they denied her request and ordered the jets to release their payload without delay.

At the back of the trailer, Logan watched the TV screen mounted near the ceiling. The pilots of the two planes radioed in that they were nearing the site.

"Less than one minute and counting," the soldier operating the radio said, loud enough for the fifteen high-ranking officers and one state trooper to hear.

The tinny voice of the pilots responded that they had the location locked in and were proceeding with the bombing.

"We're not too close to the target site, are we?"

Logan asked the soldier beside him.

The man seemed to have a permanent scowl, so Logan didn't take it personally when he turned his way and shook his head. "They're bunker busters, sir. They detonate underground strategically. If we feel anything, it'll resemble mild seismic activity."

Logan nodded once. "Gotcha."

Scowl Man looked away, his eyes back on the TVs.

The TVs displayed what the cameras mounted on the planes revealed, which showed the terrain as they approached the barracks. The tops of the trees flew by on-screen as the aircraft flew over them, and in the distance at the top of the screen, the long roof of the two-story barracks building surrounded by thick trees came into view. There was a clearing in front of the barracks, which was likely where the army uprooted trees to train their troops.

The aircraft moved closer, the radio chatter confirming data coordinates. It was nothing Logan needed to pay attention to. He just wanted to see what would happen after they released their payload.

On camera, shown to all the men in the military trailer on the fifty-inch screens, movement on the ground could be clearly seen.

So, the soldiers who went AWOL were still alive and had grouped in the clearing.

Logan rose to his feet, his eyes locked on the TV screen as the aircraft flew closer.

In the seconds it took for the planes to fly over the

barracks and drop their munitions, the movement was easily recognizable as men, women, and children. They were all standing there, looking up at the approaching planes, their hands raised to block out the setting sun.

There had to be over two hundred people on the grounds of the abandoned army barracks.

Logan's mouth opened in shock as the pilots veered off course.

They had aborted the mission.

Atkins grabbed the radio, jamming it close to his mouth. "This is Sergeant Major Bruce Atkins. I'm ordering you to drop your weapons on the location as ordered."

"Sir," the pilot said. "There are soldiers and civilians on-site, sir. That wasn't the understanding. We were destroying an abandoned army base, sir. I'm not killing Americans today."

"There is no one there," Atkins shouted. "The barracks is abandoned and empty. Drop your fucking bombs. That's an order!"

Riveted to the TV, Logan blinked, then stared at Atkins. The man was insane, furious.

It was several seconds before the radio clicked, and they heard the reply.

"Negative, flying back to base, sir. No Americans will be killed today."

Atkins threw the radio out of his hands and ran for the door, smashing it open and launching himself outside. Most of the officers trailed after him.

With the realization that the bunker would remain intact—for now—Logan felt the urge to tell Miss Valentina. She needed to hear it from him.

He stepped outside to find men in uniform fighting. Men shouted at each other about the chain of command and following orders.

Someone said they weren't at war on Oregonian soil, so everyone needed to be more lax.

Logan stayed at the rear of the angry group of men as they all stared past the fence and shouted expletives at each other during the debate about what to do next.

Undetected, Logan approached the medical trailer to see Miss Valentina. She had to know what had happened, but he also wanted to ask about the people he saw on the aircraft's camera. Who were all those men, women, and children? If the military lost forty, fifty, or even sixty people over the last twelve to fifteen hours, how were there a few hundred people in the clearing in front of the barracks?

He knocked lightly on the medical trailer door and waited.

When no one responded, he knocked again.

After he waited the appropriate time for a response and didn't get one, he tried the door.

It was unlocked.

He eased the door open. "Miss Valentina? It's Trooper Logan."

The trailer was empty.

Anna Valentina was gone, and the medical

personnel attending to her were gone, too.

Logan stepped back outside to scan the area.

Would Anna go back inside that fence line after struggling so hard to leave? No, as much as nothing else was making sense here, that made the least amount of sense. There was no way Anna would go back into that hell voluntarily.

Then where was she?

After staring in all directions, looking for any sign of movement—so many of the personnel had deserted the area that he was hard-pressed to see anyone walking around on this side of the fence—his eyes stopped on the large, camouflaged trucks that were parked in a row. What were they storing in those trucks? They weren't there when he'd laid down earlier in the afternoon. When he'd been woken up and escorted by the soldier to the command trailer, he hadn't noticed them.

The back door of one of them swung in the soft breeze.

Was someone inside it?

The sound of the men arguing by the fence just outside the command trailer had dimmed somewhat. Although, that mushroom smell had gotten stronger, making him wonder what it was they were all breathing.

Something rattled in the back of the truck, the one with the back door open, so he started that way. Whoever was in there might have seen where Miss Valentina had gone.

When he got to the rear of the truck, he peeked around the open door.

Anna Valentina grunted with the weight of a wooden crate in her hands. A dolly sat a few feet in, with two crates already on it. Due to her advanced age, she moved slowly, and he saw her wince in pain.

"Miss Valentina?" Logan said, unable and unwilling to hide the surprise in his voice. "What are you doing?"

"Taking these bombs inside the fence line. If those fuckers won't blast it from the sky, I'll walk down those stairs myself and take them into the heart of the bunker."

Behind her, the back of the truck was filled with wooden crates, all marked with decals that read EXPLOSIVES on them.

"You can't possibly take these crates on your own all the way to the barracks. You're in pain, and you're —"

"Old?" She set the crate down, then leaned on the dolly's handle. It looked like she was going to cry. "That thing took everything from *me*." Her voice rose on the last word. "Just look at me. I no longer have the allure of a twenty-eight-year-old woman, and I'll never have children now. My fantasies of having a family were always just that—fantasies." She kicked the bottom crate in anger. Logan winced, hoping that kick wouldn't cause whatever explosives were in there to blow up. "It took Russ, and he was a good man." Logan wanted to remind her about the bench warrant but refrained from interrupting her tirade. "It took Colton, my only real chance at a man in my life, even though he cheated." When she peered at him through tear-covered eyes, he saw the anger on her face. "I know I'm being selfish, and I should act more selfless because that thing in there took hundreds upon hundreds of people over the years, but it has to end today." She lumbered to the end of the truck, a slight limp on her right side. "If those Air Force guys are too scared to drop their payload, someone has to do it. I will take dolly after dolly in there until I have enough to blow it sky-high. Then I'll stay behind and detonate because I'm as good as dead anyway." Her voice weakened, her anger already dissipating. "No use waiting a few weeks in bed to die. Better to go out with a bang, as they say." She clutched at her ribs. "This ends tonight. It has to."

Logan blinked, his eyes drying out from staring at her raw determination, courage, and strength.

"One dolly after another will take all night. You don't have the energy for that."

She stared at him, a single tear lowering over her cheek. "Then help me."

"How about we just drive the truck in? You know, smash through the fence and end this thing the right way."

Anna kept staring at him. "You can get the keys to this huge truck?"

He stared back at her, his eyes unwavering. "I can do that." After saying the words, he wondered how the hell he intended to steal the keys to a US Military vehicle and then drive it through the fence undetected. His career would be over, not to mention the charges that would be brought against him. What would his wife say?

"What happened to your medical staff?" he asked. "Your trailer is empty."

"When the Air Force aborted, they ran past the fence and headed for the bunker in search of the gold bars down there."

Logan nodded like he understood, but he didn't. What was the fascination with everyone wanting to enter the abandoned barracks after all the horrors they knew existed down there? Something aged people unnaturally and killed everyone who ever ventured inside that fence. Only Miss Valentina ever made it out —and she was eighty years old now.

"Looks like we should follow them." He scanned the crates. "And take this payload with us."

Anna held out her hand. Logan took it.

"What would your wife say?" she asked.

Logan choked up a moment, then looked away to formulate his thoughts. When he turned back, Miss Valentina was watching him with concern on her face.

"She would be proud of me. This is my Bruce Willis moment from the movie *Armageddon*. She'd hate it but understand."

Miss Valentina nodded, pulling her hand back. "Technically, it's *my* Bruce Willis moment because I'm staying behind, but you can tell her it was yours when you get home to her."

He nodded vigorously to avoid speaking. His emotions would make his voice crack, and that shit wasn't tough enough for a moment like this.

"Logan?"

He stopped nodding and stared at her, his heart in his throat.

"Go get me the keys for this beast. Once I blow this thing apart, please go home and hug that wife of yours. You have a family. It was all I ever wanted."

He stepped away in time to avoid her seeing his tears, then ran for the command trailer.

Chapter 32

Two Days Before Present Day ...

That revolting, unpalatable, pungent, burned mushroom smell seemed even thicker as Anna descended the spiral staircase in front of Jaxon, her grip firm on the railing. The steps sported small metal prongs to facilitate grip, but all they did was dig into her soft bare feet painfully. When Anna reached the bunker floor, the cold seeped up her legs, making her shiver.

"Head down the hallway to the right," Jaxon instructed.

"What's in the one to the left?"

"A dead end. Nothing of interest to us."

Jaxon kept at least ten feet from her, so she couldn't make any sudden moves and overpower him in any way. For an old guy, he was still spry, making those stairs without hesitation and keeping pace with her without protest.

Since yesterday, her body had weakened, but it still functioned well under the circumstances. It was amazing what a day without food could do to her. She had read about ketosis, where the body would use fat reserves when there was no nourishment for an extended period, but what would happen at the forty-eight-hour mark without eating? How about the seventy-two-hour mark? Desperate measures would have to be taken to stay alive soon, but none of that would probably matter. She planned on being far away from this place tonight or tomorrow at the latest.

When she rounded the corner, the area was lighted well. Similar to the previous time, the candles were new and lit. She passed one on the right and stared at it, wondering if those were illusions, too.

At the extent of the light, where walking any farther would place her at the darkened end of the tunnel, she slowed to a stop and waited for Jaxon to catch up and give her more instructions.

"What are you waiting for?" he asked from behind her shoulder. "Carry on to the final room on the left."

"But I can't see where I'm going." She turned to face him. "You want me to stumble along in the dark?"

"When you enter the darkness, it will be taken care of for you."

She frowned. "What the hell does that mean? What will be taken care of?"

Jaxon had stopped a few feet away, his eyes alight with life. This was where he was his best, where his soul would rest forever. He was home. She could see that now.

"My friends run this place. They'll guide you in.

Just walk."

Anna didn't have a choice. It was a bullet from Jaxon's gun or walking into the darkness to meet his friends, whatever the hell that meant.

"Why are you doing this?"

"Doing what?" He shuffled his feet.

"Forcing me to come here. Why not let us go?"

"Because I've found the fountain of youth and want to share it with my friends."

She turned back to face him, unable to stop the smile on her face.

"Fountain of youth? That's funny, coming from you. Have you seen yourself lately?"

"Youth is a state of mind—"

"Oh, come on, Jaxon. You're dying, and you think this place, or whatever lives here, will allow you to keep living?"

"I'm not sure a conversation will convince you." He gestured with his gun hand. "Start walking. You'll see."

She stared at him for several heartbeats, moving her tongue around her dry mouth, then turned back to face the darkened end of the tunnel and started walking.

One foot in front of the other.

The darkness swallowed her, and immediately she felt a sense of well-being, like she was supposed to be here. In this area of the tunnel, the mushroom smell was less harsh and more pleasant. Most importantly, she could see where she was walking without the aid of a candle.

When she was in this area with Russ and Grayson, they had candles lighting the way, and she hadn't felt this sense of belonging.

What was this place? What dwelled in this section of the bunker?

"Anna?" a man called, his voice eerily similar to Colton's. "Anna, is that you?"

"Colton?" she called back, still walking forward.

Straight ahead, a large opening, roughly the size of a standard garage door, beckoned to her. It felt like it called to her, soothing in its nature.

Somewhere deep in her consciousness, she was aware this was a trick, like being somewhat drunk but still able to process rational thoughts. Feeling heady with the dank fungi smell, which made it easier to comply, she continued toward the open maw at the very end of the tunnel, Jaxon several steps behind her.

"Anna," Colton stepped out of hiding from behind the door. "Please, come join me in here."

The loathing she felt for her cheating ex-boyfriend rose to the surface, snapping the spell cast by whatever was manipulating everyone down here. It, whatever it was, might think she wanted a family more than anything else in the entire world, but she didn't want one if it meant achieving that with Colton Asher. He wasn't family now. He was disowned the minute Janine sat on him. He was an asshole.

"Why Janine?" she asked, unable to control the distaste for him in her tone.

Colton's lips parted in a teeth-revealing smile, his hand on the edge of the door, his shirt falling open slightly.

"Whatever do you mean, my love? She's your boss, and she was inappropriate. Nothing happened."

Anna slowed, then stopped five feet from him. This wasn't Colton. This was a mirage, a hologram. However this thing was doing it, she had no idea, but one thing she did know was that whatever was down here was powerful and beyond her imagination.

To move forward, to enter that garage door, meant she would never leave this place. Her mind would slip, be lost to *its* will, consumed, and gone forever to the other, darker side. Perhaps after going to that darker place, she would become a hologram, too.

Colton reached out, his hand hovering in the air. "Join me in here. Even just for a little talk."

That's when the noise hit her. It rose steadily until the sound was unmistakable.

Dozens of people, perhaps more, were laughing, chatting, and having a party behind Colton. Lights rose in the darkness beyond, illuminating the faces of those who had gone through this passage before.

The pull, the urge to step inside, to come in from the cold, overwhelmed her, and she stepped closer against her will. Only Colton's face stopped her. She wanted nothing to do with her cheating ex-boyfriend, nothing at all. If this thing brought Colton here to entice her inside its lair, it had made a grave error, literally.

"Please enter, Anna," Jaxon whispered from behind her. "We'll always be together. You'll have what you want. We're a family in there."

"Yes," Colton said, his hand still beckoning. "We'll be a family forever. Isn't that what you always wanted? A family?"

Her eyes watered, knowing they were playing with her, but wanting to walk through that door more than anything she'd ever yearned for in the past. The pull was more than she could resist, the urge becoming a need. And all those people sounded so happy. She recognized the music of Lana Del Rey playing in the background—her favorite.

"Come to me," she said to Colton, forcing the words out. "Step out here, and come to me."

"Why?" Colton frowned, his smile never wavering. "This is where the fun is, where your family is. We are waiting for you."

She shook her head and closed her eyes, but the yearning didn't decrease. The volume of Lana's song, *Born To Die*, increased from somewhere beyond the door.

"Anna?" Jaxon said, having moved beside her now. "Why aren't you going to your family?" Jaxon was forced to move closer to be heard over the party.

Eyes closed, standing two arm's length from the opening, she said, "Because I need Colton to make an effort."

"I am making an effort," Colton said. "I'll show you the splendor of this place once you join me."

Splendor? Colton didn't talk like that. This wasn't him, yet it looked just like him.

She opened her eyes and stared at her ex-boyfriend, her resolve strengthening.

"How do I know it's really you?"

"Ask me anything you want."

Jaxon stepped in front, turning back to stare at her face. "None of that matters. I've got this"—he tapped her shoulder with the tip of the gun—"and I'm telling you to go inside that door to be with your family."

In this light, Jaxon was a grotesque version of an old man. She had no idea how he was still standing.

"He's right, Anna," Colton said, his voice loud enough to be heard over Lana's soothing voice. "Come to me."

"Tell me where my mother is." She stared at Colton. "Where is my mother?"

That pasted-on smile didn't flinch. It was his eyes that appeared unreal, like they were hard to animate. It was difficult to tell exactly what was wrong with his eyes in this light, but something was different, like they were clouded over in a white glaze.

"Your mother is in the Wellness Hospice in Sacramento, California."

Jaxon had watched Colton, waiting for an answer. Now he turned back to Anna. "Happy now? Can we join the party, your family?"

It was Anna's turn to smile. "Of course, it's time."

The tension of the moment seemed to relax Jaxon when he heard those words. He glanced over at Colton and nodded as if to congratulate him on successfully dragging her through the gates of Hell or whatever was beyond that door.

Anna planted her feet to prepare. "It's time to remove Colton from my life forever."

She lunged hard and shoved Jaxon sideways with everything she could muster, all the anger at her situation, all the pent-up rage knowing she may never get out of here alive.

The man was feather-light and literally launched into the air. The gun flew from his grasp, spinning wildly, lost to the open door. Jaxon hit the bunker floor hard, wincing as something likely snapped. One of his hips? Ribs?

The music behind the open door was too loud to hear whether he broke anything, but that wasn't important. She was more interested in the handcuffs key.

By the time Jaxon landed in a heap on the floor in the corner, she was on him, arms flailing. She hit him several times in the face, a mix between slaps and punches. Ever since grade school, she hadn't been in a fight, but seeing Colton's cheating face brought up a wave of anger that she couldn't quell, nor did she try.

Defeated, mumbling nonsense, Jaxon bled from his nose and mouth, nearly dead now.

Behind her, the music stopped, but the voices didn't.

She ignored the people at the door and rummaged through Jaxon's pockets for the key. Once she found it, she pocketed it and got to her feet.

The door was filled with faces, a dozen, two dozen, maybe more. Colton was gone, as whatever was orchestrating this charade had realized—too late —that he was the problem and not the solution.

Jaxon moaned at her feet.

"You want in there?" she shouted. "Then get in there."

She dragged Jaxon to the edge and almost stepped in herself—that need, the urge, hadn't decreased. Only her anger had kept it at bay.

After lifting his shoulders until he was in a sitting position, she spun him around until his back faced the door, then she released him.

Jaxon dropped backward, his upper body falling past the door's threshold.

A brief moment later, something she couldn't fathom happened.

By the time Jaxon had landed half in, half out of the door, his lower body was dragged inside with extreme force, so fast that one of his shoes tore off. One second he was there; the next, he was gone.

Anna stepped back, horrified at what might lie beyond that open door.

"My family is in Sacramento," she shouted. "Colton Asher isn't family. He's a cheating, disgusting son of a bitch. So, fuck you!"

The faces in the door disappeared and were replaced by something monstrous.

She was still moving backward, almost out of the

darkness and back into the candlelight at the end of the bunker, when something from another world watched her.

An eye hovered about ten feet above the ground inside the door. Surrounded by darkness, it glared at her maliciously.

Something that might be considered a mouth opened below the eye and released a roar that deafened her in the confines of the bunker. She dropped to the floor, hands covering her ears, and screamed, but she couldn't hear her own scream.

If that thing was any louder, she wondered if it would cave in the bunker the American military had built all those years ago. Dust rose in the air, and the floor vibrated gently.

Anna rolled away against one of the walls, keeping her hands over her ears. When she reached the light of the candles, she got to her knees, then her feet, and turned back to face the darkness to make sure it wasn't slithering out to snatch her ankle and drag her back toward its lair.

But all she saw was darkness.

Without hesitating further, she turned and ran the length of the tunnel, fueled by fear, her anger dissipated.

When she rounded the corner, she was running so fast she didn't see the man standing in her way.

They collided, knocking her to the floor. She mashed her elbow and rolled twice before stopping and holding onto her wounded arm.

She glanced up at who towered over her, hoping Russ had broken out of the handcuffs.

"Where might you be going, young lady?" Grayson Cooper asked. "Don't you know no one leaves this place—ever?"

Chapter 33

Rusty Brown pulled on the handcuffs so often that his wrist was red and bruising. If not for the pain, he would have continued for hours until the cuffs weakened and broke, but that wasn't likely to happen anytime soon. So far, they'd shown no signs of wear at all.

He'd tried to slide his hand through by wrapping his thumb toward the center of his palm, but it was no use. Without a key, he was stuck to this flagpole.

The last of the sun's light filled the sky in the west, yet there was some hope. The moon was rising a notch earlier this evening. Perhaps there would be more light to deal with whatever was coming their way.

He waited with his back to the flagpole, knees up in front of his chest. For what, he had no idea, but whatever it was, it had to come quickly. The aging process was working on him like it got Jaxon. Anna had been spared to some degree, but the vibrant twenty-eight-year-old now looked like she was approaching fifty.

This area was sucking the life out of them, draining them of their existence and lifespan. And then, as he explained to Anna, it would presumably take their spirit, their soul.

The stars overhead held no answers. He stared up at them, thinking that whatever they were dealing with had come from another planet or universe. This wasn't natural or aligned with the laws of physics everyone defined the world by.

He was adjusting himself to find a more comfortable spot when something vibrated the ground, causing him to stop and listen.

What sounded like a tremendous roar—if he could call it that—emanated from the bowels of the Earth, somewhere under the old barracks building. The kind of noise that would startle birds from the trees, but this area didn't have any birds.

His heart picked up speed as he scanned the darkness around him. What was out there, coming for him? Did it have Anna already? Was he the last to be taken by whatever lived in the bunker?

"This can't be happening," he mumbled to himself. "This isn't real. None of this was real."

Something moved in the bushes to his left.

"Who's there?" He spoke in an authoritative voice, but nothing responded.

The way the handcuffs were secured to the eyelet on the flagpole, he couldn't stand without bending over. Defending himself would be limited with only one arm free.

"Anyone there?"

He waited for a response, but nothing came.

A sweat broke out on his lower back and forehead as his heart rate steadied.

Whatever was in the bushes moved again, but this time it moved quickly, disturbing bushes in a row.

"Hey," he shouted, more out of fear than anything else.

"It wasn't your fault," a female said from somewhere to his left.

He frowned, gasping in breaths. "What?"

"It wasn't your fault. You were only doing what you thought you needed to do."

It was impossible, but that voice sounded eerily close to his sister's.

"Jen? Is that you?" He sat, open-mouthed, staring at the dark bushes, the light in the sky all but gone.

"I love you, Russ. I will always love you."

It was Jen's voice, no doubt in his mind. How had she found him?

Wait, this wasn't real. It couldn't be.

Tears leaped from his eyes. Real or not, those were the exact words he'd wanted to hear from her ever since that fateful night when he pulverized her boyfriend with a baseball bat and ruined everyone's life.

He'd also lost his sister that night and would do anything to have her back in his life.

The bushes parted, and someone stepped out into the clearing about fifteen feet from him. This person was almost six feet tall, which meant it wasn't his sister he'd been talking to. It wasn't Jaxon, either.

"Who are you?"

"My name is Colton Asher. I'm with the Eugene Police Department, and I came here looking for Anna, my girlfriend."

Relief swept through him as he yanked on the handcuffs. "Can you undo these things, get me out of here?"

"Tell me where Anna is first."

"I don't know," Russ said in a rush. "You have to hurry. Jaxon came and took her down into the bunker. I don't know what happened to her. Undo these, and we'll go together."

The figure moved closer until Russ could barely make out some of the features of Colton's face with the light of the moon. The man was moderately attractive with strong features. Didn't Anna say the guy had cheated on her, though?

"Wait, how did you find us?" Russ asked.

"I asked around the train station with Anna's picture. They told me about the substation and the transfer that was supposed to happen but didn't. So, I walked in by an abandoned cabin and found this place."

"You came at night? Without a flashlight?"

"I came this morning but got lost. I'm here now."

"Okay, who was that girl talking to me from over there a few moments ago?" Russ pointed toward the bush.

The figure in front of him shrugged. "I'm talking to you now, but before I heard you and spoke up, I didn't hear anyone else."

"Okay, whatever. Just take these things off, and let's go find Anna."

"That sounds like a fine idea, but I think I'll wait."

"For what?" Russ snapped, sounding harsher than he intended. "I'm sorry, I'm just frustrated."

"It's okay, but I met someone else here first, and I'd love to hear what he has to say about all this."

"Buddy, you don't know what you're talking about. If you met someone here, they might be an apparition. Things aren't as they seem in this place."

"How's that, Rusty?" Colton crossed his arms.

Russ debated telling him about the old guys from last night, the fire in the cabin that was never there, even though they all saw it—a shared illusion. Then he realized it wasn't worth it.

"Wait a second." Russ eyed the guy. "How do you know my name?"

"Based on what I can see in this darkness, you're Rusty Brown. A bench warrant was issued for you after you skipped court the other day."

"Fine, I'll answer to that. Uncuff me and take me out of here. Take me back to Eugene and place me under arrest. You got me. It's over."

"Not that simple. I have to determine whether or not you hurt anyone else—"

"I didn't hurt Anna," he cut in. "If that's what you're thinking."

"We'll know soon enough, but there is something

else."

"What's that?"

"You were supposed to go to court because they were going to drop all the charges against you. Not showing up is a failure to appear, which brings its own charges."

Russ stared at the figure in front of him for several seconds. "Bullshit. Why would they drop the charges?"

"Your sister and her boyfriend declined to proceed. Your lawyer—"

"A piece of shit."

"Fine, but your lawyer fought for a lesser charge and got it thrown out completely. I came for Anna but knew you might be out here, too. Once we figure out what's happening, you'll leave here in my custody, and you can start your life again."

Russ stared at the guy, trying to process what he was saying. Could it be possible, or was the guy lying for some reason?

He shook his head. "What the fuck?" he whispered to himself, then louder, he added, "Dude, you're not even real."

"As real as I'll ever be."

"Then come here. Let me touch you."

"An odd request coming from you. No, I think I'll stay here and wait for the other guy."

"What other guy?"

"Grayson Cooper."

"Yeah, right. Grayson was shot and long gone by

now."

Russ could see the man shaking his head back and forth.

"He has a leg wound that bled copiously, but it was only a graze."

"A graze?" Russ tried to keep the skepticism out of his voice but failed.

"Yeah, like tore the skin open but didn't enter his leg or create an exit wound."

"Okay, where is Grayson now?"

"Searching the barracks for you and Anna to help me take you both out of here."

"Again, I call bullshit. You're imaginary, and Grayson will be, too, if he actually shows up."

"Suit yourself, but I'm not armed, and I don't have handcuff keys, so we're waiting for Grayson no matter what."

"And he's got handcuff keys?"

The guy was nodding. "He took them off some old guy he called Jaxon before Jaxon croaked and died."

Russ gaped at the guy. "Are you saying Jaxon is dead?"

"Yes, I saw the man myself. He had to be over a hundred." Colton shook his head.

"Then where's Anna?" Russ felt like they were going in circles.

"You're a strange one, Mr. Brown."

"What?"

"I just told you Grayson is looking for Anna. We

haven't been able to find her."

The bushes moved on the barracks side; then another man stepped into view.

Grayson.

"Tell me you're real," Russ said.

"What?" Grayson stammered. "Of course, I'm fucking real." He approached, his hand out in front of him. "And I got the key for the handcuffs from that asshole, Jaxon."

Grayson dropped in front of Russ and grabbed the cuffs.

"Holy shit, dude, you are real."

Grayson looked at him. "What are you on about? Why wouldn't I be real?" He glanced over his shoulder. "Colton, Anna is in the bunker. She's injured. Go to her, and I'll come in a moment."

"She's injured?" Russ said.

"How do I get to the bunker?" Colton asked.

"Take the hallway in the barracks to the end, then take the spiral staircase to the bottom. You'll find her in a room, the one that has lots of gold bars."

Colton moved fast, disappearing in the dark in the direction of the barracks, the bushes moving aside as he brushed them.

Russ stared at Grayson. "But, I saw Jaxon shoot you. I thought you were dead."

"He freaked me out with that bullet, but it was nothing more than a flesh wound. I'll need stitches, but not until I'm back in town." The cuffs opened, and Russ yanked his hand free. "It still bleeds a bit, but there's hardly any pain."

"Wow, man, I can't believe we're actually leaving this place."

"Me neither." Grayson got to his feet. "Wait, where are your shoes?"

"Jaxon made us take them off and tossed them aside."

"Can you find them in the dark?"

"Yeah, they're right over here."

Russ moved to where he saw Jaxon toss the shoes, then searched the ground until his hand bumped them.

"Got it."

"You'll move better with your shoes on."

"Agreed."

The emotions and feelings he was experiencing were overwhelmingly euphoric. They were getting out. Jaxon was no longer a problem. The police were here. Maybe they could stop the aging process or at least slow it down. Or perhaps they only looked this way and weren't *actually* getting older.

"Hey, was that cop real?" Russ was working on his second shoe now.

"Real? Oh, right, you mean like those old guys from last night."

"Yeah, was he like them or real?"

"He was real. The cops found us, Russ. We're getting out of here."

Shoes on, Russ jumped to his feet, surprised his body responded so well. He felt spry and ready to do whatever it took to get out of this horrible place.

"Then let's go," Russ said. "Back toward the tracks? Or is there another way?"

Grayson moved closer. "You can run any way you want, but I'm not leaving without Anna and Colton." Grayson turned and started toward the barracks.

Russ started after him. "Well, are we waiting up here? I mean, I really don't like the idea of going back down there."

"You do what you want, but I'm going down. I can't wait up here while Colton may get lost. Also, Anna is suffering. Colton may need help with her."

"Suffering? What the hell happened to her?"

"Jaxon beat her bad. I found her unconscious and covered in blood." Grayson looked back over his shoulder. "That's why I came up to tell Colton, so he'll go down. He's younger and stronger than me and can carry her up if needed."

"Carry her? I'm strong enough to help."

"Then follow me down one more time before we leave this place."

Russ hesitated, his gut warning him about something, then nodded. If Anna were in trouble, he'd go down. Grayson was trying to help, just like the Grayson he knew from earlier. The guy was as real as the day is long, too, because he had touched him. There was no way Grayson was an illusion.

The man had a slight limp but nothing that would impede his exit from this place, and in the little light of the moon, Russ could tell that Grayson had aged about as much as he had.

"Okay, we go down, get Anna, then leave, right?"

Grayson had entered the long corridor to the barracks when he stopped and spun back to face Russ.

"What do you mean by right? Can you think of any reason to remain here?"

Russ hesitated.

"That's what I thought." Grayson turned back around and continued down the corridor. "We get Anna, carry her up, and walk out of this place during the nighttime. I'm not staying another day here. No fucking way."

"That's what I'm talking about," Russ said, feeling the warmth of hope course through him, even as the mushroom smell deepened.

They reached the top of the spiral staircase, with Grayson headed down first.

Russ turned around, feeling like they were being watched, but no one was there. It had to be an irrational fear that this place gave off. Whatever happened, they had to get out of there. They had to escape at all costs.

There was enough light to see each step as he followed Grayson down. Someone had lit the candles along the walls of the bunker.

He glanced over by the wall on the concrete floor and saw the small spatter of blood where Grayson had been shot.

The man in front of him didn't even bat an eye as he strode toward the tunnel that led to the weapons and gold rooms.

Just before Russ followed him along the length of the tunnel to the right, he noticed a new splattering of blood to his left.

"Hey, Grayson, what happened here?"

"I think that's where Jaxon beat Anna."

Russ clenched his fists in anger. "If only I could get my hands on that junkie."

"Too late," Grayson said, walking backward. "He's already dead."

Grayson spun around and headed toward the end of the tunnel.

"Anna?" Russ called. "You down here?"

Grayson stopped and glanced back at Russ.

Then Colton materialized from the dark at the end of the tunnel. "She's in here."

The two men strode toward Colton.

"Grab a candle," Colton said.

Russ didn't hesitate. He snatched a candle from its holder and walked with his other hand in front of it to protect the flame from extinguishing. They passed the weapons door, then continued to the door that led to the gold.

That's where Russ stopped. "Where is she? Which room?"

"In there." Colton pointed.

Russ couldn't see a room in the direction Colton was pointing, so he moved forward, edging inside the rim of darkness.

That's when he saw a large door roughly twenty

feet high and fifteen feet wide at the back wall of the tunnel.

"Hey," he said, slowing his step. "I didn't see that before."

"What?" Grayson whispered beside him. "I certainly did."

"No, that wasn't there."

"We just didn't go far enough."

He glanced at Grayson, holding the candle up to Grayson's face. "Dude, I'd remember a door that big."

Something was wrong with this entire picture. Why would Jaxon beat Anna, only for Anna to flee inside a large door at the end of the bunker?

"I heard her crying in there," Colton said. "I'm going after her."

"No, wait." Russ reached out, but Colton took the four steps required to pass the threshold and moved inside the room at the end of the tunnel.

"Guys?" Colton called, his voice echoing oddly like he'd entered a cavernous room. "I'm going to need some help here. Bring the candle. I can't see shit in here. Just feeling my way around."

"Grayson," Russ whispered. "I don't feel good about this."

"Good about what?" The man was right beside him now. "Good about helping Anna get out of here?"

"No, there's something wrong with this scene somehow."

"Like what?"

Russ went into panic mode, every ounce of

anxiety ratcheting up beyond levels he'd ever felt before. It made him want to run and never stop running.

"Guys?" Colton called. "You coming?"

Grayson moved forward, but Russ grabbed his arm. "I wouldn't."

Grayson ripped his arm out of Russ's grip. "Wouldn't what? Help a friend in need? What kind of man are you?"

Grayson disappeared inside the large open door.

Now Russ stood alone in the corridor, holding a candle close to his face, a full-body sweat covering him.

"You guys found her yet?" Russ asked.

"No," Grayson said. "We need the light. Come in with that candle."

Everything in his body told him not to enter that room. Even if he wanted to, he didn't know if his feet would respond to the command to move in that direction.

"Russ?" a female voice called. "Is that you?"

He opened his mouth to respond to Anna, but Colton was already shouting.

"Keep talking, Anna," Colton said, his voice resonating throughout the bunker. "We need to find you."

Russ moved closer to the doorway, the candle held high. "Anna?"

"Russ," she said. "I need your help. I'm hurt."

"Colton and Grayson are in there. Keep talking so

they can find you."

Grayson's face appeared at the door. "Hey, either come in and help or give me that candle so we can find her."

Russ hesitated. He stood one meter from the door and didn't even want to extend his arm to give the candle to Grayson. For one, it would be too close to the open door where that horrid mushroom smell emanated from, and two, if he gave up his candle, he'd be left standing in the dark.

"Really?" Grayson said. "I uncuffed you only to learn the bodybuilder guy is spineless? Get in here and help us find out what Jaxon did to Anna."

Grayson's face disappeared back into the room.

"It can't be that bad," he muttered to himself.

He had touched Grayson. The man was real. This wasn't an illusion. And Grayson had just come back to the doorway for the candle, meaning he wasn't harmed or dead in there. So, what sort of danger could be hiding behind that door that was freaking him out so much?

He stepped forward as if his feet had a will of their own.

"Russ, please," Anna called. "Please come to me."

The yearning in her voice was what did it. He knew the story of Anna's boyfriend and how he cheated. To be left alone in there with that man would bother Anna. Of course, she wanted the man she had been tied up with to help take her out of there.

Anna wanted Russ, and she was calling for him.

His sister had needed him, and he answered the call.

That one ruined his life.

This one could offer him redemption.

"Russ?" Her plea was more than he could handle.

He moved one more step closer.

A hand shot out of the impossible darkness from inside the last room of the bunker.

As he passed the candle over, his hand crossing the threshold by mere inches, he realized this wasn't a door after all.

This entire section was where a wall used to be. A concrete slab had been removed from the back wall of the bunker.

What had it revealed, though?

Something latched onto his hand. The candle died out.

He had the urge to yank his hand back, but whatever gripped him tightened, crushing bones.

The second his mouth opened to scream, whatever had him in its grip yanked inward with extreme force.

It pulled so hard his arm tore at the shoulder, ripping clean off.

Panicked, teetering forward from the violence of that pull, blood squirting from where his arm had been attached the moment before, he fell facedown just inside the room.

Something grabbed his shoulders and dragged him inside.

He never had a chance to scream as his body was ripped asunder, his soul freed from its restraints.

Chapter 34

PRESENT DAY ...

Trooper Richard Logan made his way back to the group of soldiers by the fence. The argument had stopped, and many officers and soldiers had dispersed.

Miles's stern voice emanated out of the open command center door. It sounded like he was arguing with someone on the phone about following orders.

After waiting several heartbeats, knowing he had to do what was right here, Logan stepped inside the command trailer and stopped by the door.

Miles was on the phone, and he had one soldier standing guard by the table. They were the only two in there. There was no sign of Atkins or the other high-ranking officers or soldiers.

They couldn't have all gone over the fence. Logan refused to believe it. Some of them probably left the site to head back to the city.

Miles saw him and raised a finger for him to wait.

"I understand, sir, but this place must be destroyed. Send the planes back and do the job you've been ordered to do." His neck was corded with veins, his face red. Miles clutched the phone in anger, then threw it across the trailer, where it shattered into chunks of plastic and batteries.

"Fuck them, fuck this, and fuck everything!" Miles shouted. He spun toward Logan. "What do you want?"

"Where is everybody?"

"Gone, they're all gone."

"Where?"

"Who the fuck knows?" Miles tossed his hands in the air, then slapped his waist when they came back down. "Some deserted and ran for the woods, too afraid to maintain their position. Some jumped the fence and ran for the gold, thinking if little old Anna Valentina could make it out alive, they could, too. And the others, led by Sergeant Major Atkins, took up arms and went to shoot down whatever the fuck it is that lives in that bunker."

"They think something lives in there?" According to Anna, something *did* live down there, but Logan felt it best to play dumb here.

"You think I know what's in there? I have no fuckin' clue, Trooper."

"That's not what I meant—"

"Something has to be in there. It took Anna's life from her, but no one has a clear picture of what we're up against."

They stared at each other for a long moment.

"Am I needed any longer?" Logan asked, a plan forming in his head. "There's no cell coverage out here, and I haven't spoken with my wife since yesterday morning before I went to work."

"Are you saying you don't want in on the gold inside that bunker? Not going to make a run for it?"

Logan placed his hands on his hips. "Sir, how many of those that went inside have you seen or confirmed have come back out again toting gold bars?"

Miles glanced at the soldier, who stood to the side, then turned back to Logan.

"No one has come back out to our knowledge."

"Just as I thought. Does that answer your question about me running for gold? I want to go home, see my wife, hug her."

"Then go," Miles said, flicking his hand toward Logan. "You're clear of the site. Everyone else is gone. This mission is shut down. Shit, we've lost almost everyone. Just go and keep your mouth shut."

Logan stood there a moment longer, stunned at how easy it was to be told he could leave, that his presence wasn't required anymore.

Miles crossed his arms over his chest. "Was there something else, Trooper?"

"My cruiser is back home in my driveway as I spent all night walking here. I figure you have several spare army vehicles on-site as so many personnel have taken off. Think I could borrow one to get home? You know where I live. I'm sure you can have someone come pick up the vehicle later. Does that work for you?"

Miles nodded and pointed at the soldier. "Take

him to the key box; let him take home whatever he wants."

The soldier saluted Miles, then stepped outside the trailer to wait for Logan, who was still staring at Miles.

"You did your best, but whatever's in there is powerful. Perhaps the best anyone can do is build a bigger, stronger fence."

"You think we should build a wall?"

Logan detected sarcasm in Miles's tone but didn't blame the man in his current state of frustration.

Logan glanced at the soldier, then back at Miles. "Just get out while you still can. Get far away from this place. Tell everyone there was a nuclear spill or something, and save as many lives as possible by blocking in whatever's down there."

Without waiting for a reply, Logan stepped from the command trailer and followed the soldier to another smaller trailer that held a variety of tools, ropes, and plastic crates. The soldier had a special key to access this trailer.

Once inside, he opened a metallic box on the wall and gestured with his hand to take any set of keys Logan wanted.

He stepped closer and examined the tags attached to each set of keys until he found the right ones.

Munitions vehicle.

He pocketed the keys, nodded at the soldier, and wandered back across the grass toward the truck where Miss Valentina waited. One glance over his shoulder told him the soldier was headed toward the command trailer.

When he got to the munitions truck, Anna was sitting on the back, her legs suspended in the air.

"Did you get them?"

He nodded, pulled the keys from his pocket, then held them in his open palm.

"Good. Help me down, and let's do this."

Logan got behind the wheel once Miss Valentina was settled in the passenger seat. Logan didn't see a single person during the entire time it took to settle in the cab and start the engine. It was like they were the last two people in the abandoned army post.

"I can't see the barracks from here," he said. "Which way?"

"Through those trees." Anna pointed.

"You think the truck will make it through there?"

"It'll make it. Trust me."

Logan put it in gear and started forward.

"You'll have to give it some gas to smash through the fence."

Logan got it up to twenty miles per hour. With thoughts of Indiana Jones racing through his head, he pushed the gas pedal down and rammed the fence, the large truck barely feeling the impact as it drove over it.

The uneven ground proved relentless, though, causing him to break out in a sweat with the fear of the dangerous cargo in the back accidentally detonating while on their way to the bunker as they bounced from one hole to the next. A thick tree scraped the side of the truck before they dipped to the right into another depression in the ground.

In the headlights, he saw several men running ahead of them. Another man chased them with a rifle. A gun fired somewhere. A man shouted.

"What the hell is going on? This looks like complete bedlam."

"Don't worry, and don't forget." Anna touched his arm. "I made it out alive, remember?"

"Yeah." He bobbed his head in agreement. "True."

It looked like they were getting close to a clearing up ahead. He thought he saw a body lying in the bush to his left. He slowed the truck when he saw two more bodies. From the driver's seat, it was clear that both men had been shot in the head.

"What the fuck happened here?"

"It's okay," she whispered. "It all ends with us, this truck's payload. We'll get through this. You have to ignore what you're seeing and keep driving."

"Are you okay?" Logan glanced over at Anna as she clung to the handle on the truck's ceiling by her head.

"Yeah, just get us there. Don't stop for anything."

After fifteen minutes of slow-going and fancy maneuvers to circumvent large branches and thick trees, Logan drove them into a clearing where the two-story barracks building came into view on the left.

"Holy shit," he whispered. "That place looks

creepy as hell in the dark."

She glanced at him. "That's exactly what I think it is."

"What? The creepy part, or the Hell part?"

Anna explained what she thought was in the bunker as Logan drove across the clearing and backed up to the last window of the barracks building, which would put them the closest to the spiral staircase Anna spoke of several times.

Soldiers wandered around the premises as if in a daze, but it was getting harder to see anyone as the light from the sun was almost gone behind the trees.

"We have to hurry," Anna said. "It owns the night."

Goosebumps rose on Logan's arms as he placed the truck in park and killed the engine.

"Did you say it *owns* the night?"

She opened her door, then turned back to him. "For some reason, that's when it's the strongest— when darkness falls." Then Anna eased herself down and walked out of view, leaving her door open.

The headlights still on, Logan stared out the windshield at nothing, the smell of burned mushrooms even stronger this close to the barracks.

This was his defining moment, what his life had culminated to. It was his do-or-die moment. The *do* part wasn't so bad, but he didn't want the *die* part.

Yet everything he'd heard about this site so far made him believe he'd never leave here alive.

Whatever or whoever ventured this way never

ventured elsewhere again.

Exiting the truck and making his way to the back, he wondered what his wife would put on his epitaph.

His biggest regret was not being able to say goodbye to her.

Maybe he'd do what hundreds before him couldn't do. Perhaps he'd become just like Anna. Age a bunch of years in the few hours he'd be here, then find a way out. At least he could die at home with his wife.

They could write his epitaph together.

Anna was gone by the time Logan got to the back of the truck.

"Anna?" he called, keeping his voice low. When he got no response, he spoke louder. "Anna?"

Cold steel pressed into the back of his neck.

Logan raised his hands as his stomach clenched, and his bladder suddenly needed to release.

He knew the feel of a gun on his skin when it touched him.

Chapter 35

Twenty-Four Hours Before Present Day ...

Anna coughed.

She rolled over and coughed again, liquid rolling past her split lips.

Blood, so much blood.

Not able to see it in the absolute darkness, she could taste it in her mouth, on her lips—smell it, too.

Grayson had been real, or *un*real, as it were. The man was known to the authorities and is currently on the run. He groomed young girls under the auspices of being a teenager himself, according to the Most Wanted poster's list of charges against him. Grayson was a criminal through and through and creepy as hell.

They'd have to add a violent criminal to his list of crimes after beating her half to death.

Anna could barely move her mouth from the pain. Several teeth were loose, and she'd lost a few. The aches and protests from her aging body made her want to lie down and wait for death.

Weak from lack of nourishment, in defiance of her body's need to not move, she rolled to her side and got up on her hands and knees.

Heart racing with the effort, teeth tightened in pain, she breathed heavily and waited for the wave of pain to subside.

Grayson's last words to her before using her as a punching and kicking bag resonated through her head.

Don't you know no one leaves this place—ever?

Was that possible? If she started for the exit and headed toward the train tracks, would anyone *real* attempt to stop her? Or would it only be hallucinations moving in her way?

Several of her ribs had to be broken or at least cracked, but she pushed upward slowly until she was upright, then got to her feet.

Even though she aimed to move slowly, her equilibrium suffered, making her sway on her feet for one scary moment, hoping there was a wall nearby for support. Dropping to the hard bunker floor would be torture at this point, and she wasn't sure she'd be able to rise to her feet again.

She stepped forward, her battered hands in front of her in search of a wall or a door.

Remarkably, the weight of her phone in her back pocket gave her hope. If there were any battery left, she'd be able to get a signal once she got far enough away from this place.

Another step forward, then another, and she stopped, blinking in the dark.

Her phone. Shit, why didn't she think of it before?

She eased the device out of her pocket and turned it on.

The screen was cracked in several places, which made sense after being thrown to the hard floor of the bunker by Grayson, but it worked.

After rubbing her thumb upward on the screen, the flashlight app button appeared, one of the cracks snaking through it. She tapped it, and the light clicked on.

A wave of hope washed over her. She'll be able to walk out of here after all.

The wall of the room was still three feet away, the door off to the right.

Grayson had dragged her into the weapons room when she was semi-conscious. Her phone said it was just after three in the morning, and her battery was at twenty-three percent.

She had to hurry.

Waiting until the sun came up wasn't an option.

Anna moved toward the door and soundlessly slipped out of the room barefoot. She aimed the light toward the back of the tunnel, saw the huge garage door-like opening, then glanced away quickly to avoid being drawn back toward it.

They'd all gone through to the other side now. She was sure of it. She had to get upstairs and over to the flagpole to free Russ and leave.

When she touched the pocket with the handcuffs key, it was gone.

"Shit!"

Grayson must've taken it when she was unconscious. What else did he do when she was out of it? Being a fucking pervert, he could have done anything he wanted.

She avoided thinking about that and moved up the tunnel of the bunker toward the end, where the spiral staircase led to the surface, one cautious step at a time. Someone had not only extinguished the candles, but they'd also removed them, too.

The corner came quickly. She eased around it to see Grayson sitting on the bottom steps, and the knot in her gut tightened.

"I already told you there's no leaving this place," he whispered in the dark, staring at her.

She was too weak to fight him before, and now she was a wreck, so unless he volunteered to move, she was stuck down here with him.

"Please," she whispered, barely moving her mouth for the pain. "We need to leave this place. It's evil."

Grayson laughed, the echo reverberating off the dead walls of the chamber, chilling her.

Options raced through her mind, but none seemed to make much sense. She leaned on the wall, weakening by the moment, her resolve growing dim.

"Please, Grayson, this place isn't good. Let's leave together."

"Isn't good?" He got to his feet and moved toward her. "Then tell me, what is good on this fucking planet? Huh? Tell me that."

She shook her head slowly, her free hand coming up to ward him off.

"Don't," she whispered, tears springing to her eyes. "Don't hit me again."

"There's nothing good here," he went on as if he didn't hear her, "nothing but a dirty planet and me. What's religion? Nothing but faith in something unproven. What's science? Politics? War?" He scoffed deep in his throat. "All malfunctions in a world of shit, ruled by idiot children who have no idea what cause and effect actually means."

"Okay," Anna whispered, nodding. "Just please —"

"Please, what? Help the human race survive? Offer pointers while I'm trapped down here?" He moved closer. "You people disgust me. You make automobiles for convenience without understanding how you're polluting your planet. You make plastics without considering the long-term ramifications of how it'll affect your oceans." He stopped to stare at her from about two yards away. "What a waste of time. Why am I preaching to you, a nobody that'll die down here?" He shook his head. "You *were* nothing, Anna, and you will *be* nothing."

She waited for what he would say next, but then he turned and retreated to the bottom step of the spiral staircase to sit.

"You're not leaving," he whispered.

"But, Grayson, I must leave." She pushed off the wall. Kick him in the balls, hit him in the throat, something—she had to do something to get past him.

"Have you ever read any poetry?" Grayson asked.

That stopped her, the cell phone's flashlight aimed at the floor. What the hell was he talking about now?

"How about Robert Frost's *The Road Not Taken*?"

She shook her head. "No."

"That poem was widely misunderstood."

To keep him talking as she edged closer, she said, "How so?"

"We all have choices in this life, and we think those choices matter, but they don't. Nothing matters."

"What do you mean, nothing matters?" She moved even closer to the stairs, staring at the top as if it was salvation itself. If only Grayson would move and she could ascend, she might be saved.

"Frost basically spoke of the futility of choice and the belief that we all think we have endless possibilities in life. All that does is keep what's real at bay."

"What's real?"

"That we are born, we live, and then we die, and whatever happens in between is pointless. All those terrible decisions, missed appointments, spousal fights, getting the kids dressed on time, being late, yelling, arguing, just being, fucking up, and learning lots or learning nothing—none of it matters when you're dead. The clock keeps ticking, people keep repeating shit, and on and on it goes until your fucking sun explodes or some meteor smacks into Texas and ends life here in a cloud of fuckness."

"That sounds so depressing," she said, stepping closer. "Probably why I don't read poetry. Can't really stand the stuff."

Grayson glanced up to meet her gaze. "So, you'd rather believe in a God that doesn't exist? Really? Religion? That's your fix?"

"Well, who's to say God doesn't exist?" She was close enough to kick him in the face now.

"A baby born from a virgin? Isn't that how the story goes? Then when Jesus dies and ascends to Heaven days later, you're told to believe in him to have everlasting life or die and go to Hell. People symbolically eat his flesh and blood—a bit morbid, don't you think?—and ask him to remove evil from their lives, something inherent in all humans—believe me, I know. All this because a woman made from a man's rib ate an apple—a forbidden fruit on some enchanted tree, and since when are apples forbidden? —after being told to eat it by a talking snake that a fallen angel manipulated? You've got to be kidding? What a bloody stretch. Only people in need of asylums would ever believe a fairy tale like that as truth or take it on faith." He laughed and shook his head. "The whole human race is deluded, mad, and disposable."

She moved in front of him, her hands shaking with resolve, the phone's light aimed at her feet. It was either die down here or get past Grayson and leave this wretched place, and she wasn't about to have her story end this way.

"Then I must need serious help because I believe in God and all the beauty in this world. Also, Frost sounds depressed or something. Perhaps he needed religion because all those agonizing decisions I make in my life while I'm here do have meaning."

"Yeah? To who?"

"To me."

She lunged forward, her knee coming up to hit Grayson in the chest or, better yet, under the chin.

But she missed entirely and fell to the bottom stair, scraping the skin off her knee.

Grayson had been there one moment; then he'd disappeared the next.

She almost dropped her phone. With it held tight in her hand, she spun around in search of the man, a groan of pain escaping her lips.

Grayson stood several feet away, smiling at her.

She aimed the flashlight at his face to blind him, but he didn't move.

The light went right through him.

An illusion—all this time, he was a fucking illusion.

She started up the steps, favoring her sore ribs, limping slightly at the pain in her leg while blood leaked down past her ankle.

"You won't get far," Grayson taunted from below. "Others are waiting for you up there."

"Bring them on, asshole."

She reached the top and started down the corridor that led outside without pausing. Off to her left somewhere, the sound of a group of men chanting something grew louder and louder.

All that mattered was getting to Russ and then

getting the hell out of there, provided they found a way to free him from the handcuffs. Together, they'd have a story to tell that no one would believe.

Once she emerged from the corridor, there was enough moonlight to see a group of men to her left lined up, staring at her, rifles cradled in their hands. They chanted some military song under their breath, getting louder and louder.

"Stay away from me," she shouted as she moved farther from the barracks.

"Stop, or we'll shoot," one of them yelled.

Those words alone made her stop. Even though she was sure it was likely another illusion, when a group of armed men ordered her to stop moving, she stopped.

Shaking with fear and adrenaline, she raised the phone.

The light didn't stop on their bodies as they pressed closer to her—it went right through them to illuminate the ground they walked on.

Another illusion.

She exhaled and wailed out a cry of exasperation.

"Fuck you and your pink elephants," she whispered to the thing, or whatever it was that continually orchestrated these phantasms.

Anna moved around the bush on her right and stopped short of the flagpole.

Russ was gone, the handcuffs still attached to the pole, the one that held his wrist lying open on the grass.

She glanced back over her shoulder, but the military men were gone.

They were replaced by women and children, standing in a long row. Kids of varying ages, clinging to their mother's hands, a scowl on every mother's face.

"You get to leave," one woman said. "That luxury wasn't afforded us."

"Yeah," said another. "We're bound here."

"But," yet another said. "So is she." That woman pointed at Anna. "Just look at how old she is. I'm taking bets she doesn't make the fence line."

"Fence line?" Anna murmured. "I didn't see a fence."

A few of them laughed, and then they all joined in. The laugh turned maniacal, then outright insane, like she was listening to several witches screeching as they spoke of toil and trouble over a cauldron.

She had to get out of there before she lost her mind.

Thoughts of Russ and his whereabouts evaporated from her mind. She had to go, save herself, so she pushed on, the phone out in front of her, hoping the battery lasted until she got free.

A man popped up on her left, then another on her right. They spoke to her, but she ignored them and trudged on, her energy waning as she walked.

Exhausted and in pain, hopes of ever leaving this place dimmed with each step.

A group of young boys, no older than ten years of

age, formed a line up ahead, hands joined.

She turned to the right to avoid them and kept walking.

With no idea where she was going, she kept moving, knowing that each step took her farther from the barracks, the bunker, and whatever lived down there. Even if each step didn't offer her salvation, a way out, at least she'd get far enough to leave that thing behind and be able to die in peace and not be resurrected as an apparition for those who come later.

So she pushed on, finding strength where there was none. Finding strength like her mother had after battling cancer for years, soldiering on as her quality of life deteriorated, because that's what people did, whether it was meaningless or not.

A large tree offered a spot to rest for a few moments. She turned off the flashlight to save the battery, which now said it was seventeen percent. It wouldn't last the night, but it got her out of that hell hole.

After a few minutes, she got moving again as she needed to walk while she had battery life left. Once her phone died, she could rest longer and wait for sunrise.

She had to assume they were all dead. Grayson was real when he beat her and stole the handcuffs key. He probably freed Russ, then went where Jaxon went. Whatever lived under the barracks took them all, body and soul, and reanimated their images to lure others down to the bunker. Like when it worked on Jaxon that first night. Then it beguiled Jaxon into bringing them into the fold, which started with eating those fucking MREs, yet she refused—which was probably the only reason she was still alive.

When she moved into a small clearing, that group of boys was there again. They stood off to the left, their arms locked together this time.

Was it guiding her on a certain path, leading her out? Or scaring her away from the exits?

Twenty steps later, she came to a tall fence. The top of the fence was wrapped with barbed wire.

"What the hell is this?" she whispered to herself.

"The only way out, Anna," Russ said from beside her.

Anna jumped at the sound of his voice, her free hand going to her chest.

"What the—where did you come from?" Then it dawned on her that he was an illusion.

She raised the light to check.

It went right through him.

"This is it," he said. Then he pointed. "Look."

Anna followed his finger. A deer grazed off in the clearing.

"Is that real?"

Russ nodded. "That's real."

"Why are you helping me?"

"Because you're already dead, and hope is comical."

"Comical?" She stared at him opened-mouthed.

Russ glanced down at her feet, then back up at her

face. "You're nearly eighty years old by the look of things. Spent too much time unconscious in that bunker, smelling my essence, allowing me to shorten your telomeres."

"Shorten my what?"

"In human language, telomeres are caps that protect chromosomes. As you age and cells divide, telomeres get shorter, which leads to aging. My essence leaches yours, speeds up this process, which allows me to live and you to die. It's like when an inactive muscle atrophies, only a million times faster."

She gawked at him, knowing she was speaking to what was buried beneath the barracks. "You're insane."

"On the contrary." Russ smiled. "When I take one of you *people*, I take your past, thoughts, and feelings, and I even acquire your knowledge, which gives me a better understanding of your world, the world I helped create."

She leaned on the fence, utterly exhausted. "Why?"

Using Russ's mouth, it told her why.

It told her everything.

She fought the urge to drop to her knees and give up now. It was useless; it was all useless.

But it was unfair, too. All of it couldn't be for nothing. There had to be a greater purpose. What if this thing was lying, having also garnered that ability from humans? What if it was simply an abomination, just like Russ had said, something from before the dinosaurs were discovered, and all it needed was a nuclear weapon shoved up its ass to end its body-snatching existence?

Determined to leave and not allow this *thing* in Russ's body to manipulate and confuse her further, she slipped her phone into her back pocket, stuck both hands in the fence, placed her right bare foot in one of the holes, and heaved herself upward.

"I wouldn't do that if I were you," Russ said. "Better to stay here, and when the sun rises, you can crawl back to safety in the barracks."

"Fuck you," she grunted as she lifted herself closer to the barbed wire.

"You're dead anyway, Anna. Come on back down."

The fence wire dug into her palms and the balls of her feet, but she did her best to ignore the pain.

This was her last chance to get out, to be free.

The barbed wire at the top presented a problem. When she reached it, no matter where she gripped, it cut the skin along her forearms, making her moan in pain.

She considered rolling over it and falling to the other side, but the impact with the ground would be too much to continue moving out of the trees.

With a firm grip on the top of the fence, her right arm bleeding in several new places now, she brought her right leg up and carefully straddled the top as if she was about to sit on a horse.

Aware the wire was cutting the inside of her

thighs but knowing she was already halfway over the fence, she changed hands and lifted her left leg over to the other side, tearing her pants as she went. She started to lower her body on the free side, but the barbed wire dug too deep into her left forearm, making her scream.

Everything in her wanted to let go and jump off the fence, but an inner strength made her hold on for a moment more. She lowered a foot, blindly found a spot to place it, then lowered the other one. When she was four feet from the ground, she let go, hoping nothing would break and her sore ribs could manage the impact.

The ground came up fast, smashing into her, forcing a grunt of air out of her mouth. Her right leg twisted under her but, thankfully, didn't break.

She had made it to the other side.

She eased her phone out of her pocket without sitting up and swiped up for the flashlight.

Above her was an old metal sign rusted with age. Her flashlight illuminated the sign, and before her battery lowered too much more, she snapped a photo of the sign.

It read, WARNING, then below that, it said, MILITARY INSTALLATION. KEEP OUT! Farther down and in smaller print, it said, IT IS UNLAWFUL TO ENTER THIS INSTALLATION WITHOUT THE WRITTEN PERMISSION OF THE INSTALLATION COMMANDER. AUTHORITY: INTERNAL SECURITY ACT, 50 U.S.C. 797.

She missed reading the final lines of the photo as she rolled onto her side and glanced back through the fence.

Russ was gone.

Completely exhausted, she tried to get to her feet but stumbled and dropped to her knees. After resting for several minutes and controlling her breathing, she started crawling.

She crawled for an hour, and then the sun began its ascent in the sky, and she was able to see where she was going.

Depleted of almost all energy, she resorted to crawling on her stomach at times, moving inch by inch, wondering if she'd ever make it out alive.

Maybe that thing had already killed her, and she just wasn't giving in yet.

She closed her eyes for a short break, but the sun was higher in the sky when she opened them. Not wanting to check the time on her phone, she pushed up and kept crawling.

The sound of a vehicle in the distance gave her hope.

She pushed on, covered in a mix of dirt, blood, and pine needles, until she reached the edge of a highway.

Then a FedEx truck came to a stop on the shoulder.

She crawled back into the bush to escape the direct sunlight and waited. For all she knew, the delivery driver could just be another illusion.

But then the FedEx driver called the police.

401

Chapter 36

PRESENT DAY ...

"What are you doing here?" a man asked, his voice familiar.

Logan swallowed. "I brought this truck of explosives in so we can blow up that bunker, along with whatever's in there." After no response, he said, "Atkins, can I turn around?"

The gun retreated from his flesh. "Turn around then."

Logan lowered his hands to his side and looked over his shoulder as he wheeled to face Atkins.

"What's going on here?"

Atkins eyed him with suspicion. "We're removing the gold. Once it's secure, I'm taking this rifle into the last room of the bunker, and I will kill it."

"It? Have you seen it?"

"Felt it only. Smell it, too, but I haven't seen it."

"And you think a rifle will kill it?"

Atkins glanced down at the weapon in his hands and shrugged. "Not sure, but I'll fire every bullet I've got trying."

"How about you get the gold and leave Anna and

me to take all these explosives down into the bunker?"

From the glow of the taillights, Logan saw men walking the length of a hallway inside the barracks. Each man held what looked like bars of gold.

"Hey," Logan said. "Tell each man bringing up the gold bars to take a crate of explosives back down when they go for more gold."

Atkins smiled up at him, some sort of insanity already taking place in the man's eyes. After a career in the army, his life was dedicated to serving his country. To watch him give it all up for a few bars of gold when it was his job to kill whatever was in the bunker was a tragedy. Logan couldn't imagine what Atkins was feeling or going through or what drove him to do what he was doing now. Could it be as simple as greed, a strong aversion to avarice, borne from years of service that bred entitlement?

Atkins turned away from Logan, shouting new orders at his men. They were to empty the explosives from the truck and place them all deep in the bunker, crate by crate. No man was to walk down to the bunker without explosives in hand. Then, when they came back up, they were to carry two gold bars each, one in each arm, and place them on the rear of the truck.

When Atkins was through ordering his men to get to work, somewhere from deep inside the building, a scream filled with pain or terror emanated up to them, making Logan shiver in fear.

"What the hell was that?" he whispered, his voice

cracking once.

A soldier walking by stopped and stared at him. "Get used to it. Someone went into the wrong room."

"Which is the right room?"

The soldier didn't answer as he moved away, lost to the darkness several feet away.

"Anna?" Logan called again, only able to see to the extent of the taillights.

"Right here," she said, her voice weakening.

Anna stepped around the corner of the truck.

Logan moved closer, his hands out to grab her if she fell. "Are you okay?"

She nodded. "Just tired. Let's get this over with so you can leave."

"There's a room downstairs that a soldier—"

"There are many rooms downstairs," she said, cutting him off.

"A soldier said there's a wrong room and a right one."

Anna nodded as she leaned against the back of the truck. "There's only one room that everyone should avoid. The rest of the rooms are safe."

"Are you sure?"

She met his gaze and held it. "Logan, I've been here before. I entered the rooms, saw the gold and abandoned weapons, and got out. I lived to tell. You will, too."

Soldiers had gathered behind them at the back of the truck per Atkins's instructions. Both Logan and Anna moved aside as men began lifting crate after crate of explosives out of the back. Like ants taking food to their nest, all walking in a row, the soldiers moved the explosives to the bunker below. There had to be twenty men still alive, most aging and some in their fifties now. Moments later, they surfaced from below laden down with gold bars, then placed them on the back of the truck and grabbed more crates.

In the short time it took to lower the explosives to the bunker, they were able to build several piles of gold in the back of the truck. The keys were still in Logan's pocket, as Atkins hadn't asked for them yet. He just had the men bringing up gold and taking down bombs.

With five or six crates left on the truck, out of reach and stuck deep by the wall of the cab, Logan escorted Anna to the side door of the barracks. She clutched the doorframe and stopped, looking back over her shoulder at the night beyond.

No one was around. The place looked deserted now.

"You okay?" he asked.

"I'm feeling very old right now. Being back here, smelling that sick mushroom scent on the air. I just … felt much better back in the hospital." She stared into his eyes. "When they brought me to the temporary command post, and I could smell it again, I knew it was working on me."

"Is it the smell that ages you, like whatever's in the air?" Logan asked, wondering how it might be affecting him.

"That scent does more than age you."

"What else does it do?"

She leaned into him. "It coerces you and makes you *want* to find the source until you end up in the bunker, a victim to the spider's web."

"I have no urge to go down there other than to ensure those explosives are in the right place. Then we all leave."

She stared at him in the doorway. Where had all the soldiers gone? They still had to be down in the bunker.

"I won't be leaving, Logan. Someone has to stay behind to make sure this place blows apart."

"I allowed you to think that you'd stay behind when we were back at the camp, but I'm not leaving you down there, Anna. That's no way to die."

"I'm afraid you won't have a choice. This thing has aged me ten more years since I've been back near its presence. Even if I wanted to leave, I'd be dead by the end of the week, possibly by tomorrow."

"Then let's go and get this done immediately so we can leave right away."

At the top of a spiral staircase, Anna took a deep breath, then started down one step at a time.

Men milled about below them, hard to make out by the candlelight. Without the help of Atkins's men, Logan wasn't sure how he would've been able to carry all those explosives down to the bunker on his own.

Sometimes, some things just worked out in his favor. He contemplated whether that was divine intervention or not. God had to be watching over them, steering their hand.

Halfway down the narrow staircase, someone shouted, making Logan jump and spin around to see what was happening. A weapon fired rapidly from somewhere deep in the bunker, then another gun blasted. More men screamed, one sounding like he was in horrible pain, then the scream was cut off instantly.

"Anna," Logan shouted, stopping on the stairs above her, already turning to head back up. "We can't go down there."

She glanced back at him. "There's no other way."

"Didn't you hear that?"

Panic rose in him until he felt he *had* to run and screw the consequences. He worked for the state police and had seen many things during his time as a trooper, but what was happening in the army bunker was something he knew would change him forever if it didn't kill him first.

Self-preservation kicked in. It was time to leave— now!

"We have to go," he shouted.

Someone screamed again. Then a man shouted orders to get back. Logan recognized that voice as Atkins's.

Anna blessedly took a step back toward him, then waved a hand for him to come closer. He leaned in to hear what she had to say.

"Before I jumped the fence, Russ came to see

me."

"Anna, look, we have to leave this place—*now*!"

She shook her head. "But it wasn't Russ who came to see me."

He frowned. "Then who was it?"

"Russ was already dead. It was an illusion of him."

"Oh shit, that's not good, Anna."

"The hologram of Russ was speaking for it, whatever *it* is that lives down here."

"Are we leaving?" He felt desperate enough to leave her behind, already rationalizing how old she had become. Maybe it was for the better. He didn't want to die down here. He needed to get back to his wife, his life.

She grabbed his lapel and pulled him down to her face with surprising strength.

"Russ told me what's down here."

"Have you told the others?"

She shook her head. "No one would believe me."

"What?" Logan's voice hit a pitch so high he had no idea his voice had that sort of range.

Two uniformed men ran for the base of the spiral staircase and started up toward them. There wasn't much room, but they could still edge past Anna and make Logan lean out over the railing to get by.

"Run," one of the men shouted in Logan's face. "Get out of here."

"I'm trying." He turned back to Anna. "So, what is it? What's down there?"

"Beelzebub, the Devil himself."

Chapter 37

ANNA REACHED THE BOTTOM of the metal stairs before two more men came around the corner, covered in blood. Another weapon discharged deep in the bunker, and both men dropped, sliding on the black concrete of the bunker floor, a smear of blood forming a trail from their short slide.

It sounded like absolute mayhem around the corner.

Logan lurched down the last few steps to get out of the way as others ran around the corner.

"Atkins!" he shouted. "What the fuck is happening?"

He grabbed Anna and moved her to the wall on the right to keep her out of the line of fire. Then he edged forward until he could peer around the corner and see what was happening down the bunker corridor to his right.

Candles lit the wide hallway on both sides. He counted eight armed men in military fatigues. They formed a semi-circle in the middle of the chamber, all facing the darkness at the end of the tunnel, their weapons raised at their waists.

One more lowered his weapon, turned, and ran

toward Logan and Anna, where they hid behind the wall.

Atkins spun toward the soldier and fired multiple times. The man dropped hard, his legs sporting new holes as he screamed and clutched at his right knee, blood spurting through his fingers. The torturous scream, something Logan suspected he'd hear in his nightmares, was abruptly silenced by one of Atkins's bullets to the head. The soldier dropped back onto the concrete, his body overcome by death seizures.

Atkins spun back around to face the darkness.

None of the other men moved.

"Atkins?" Logan shouted. "Anna and I are coming down. Don't fucking shoot us."

"You have safe passage," Atkins shouted back to Logan. "None of my men will raise their weapon toward you."

Anna walked out around Logan and marched toward them.

Logan ran after her. "What are you doing?" he snapped. "Stay behind me."

"No," she shouted, her voice echoing throughout the corridor. "Too many dead, too much pain. This ends now."

She slowed by the men, then slipped through their ranks and turned around to face Atkins. Logan moved up beside her.

"What's going on here?" she asked.

Logan stared at Atkins. The man was covered in blood—someone else's blood, and his eyes were glazed over with madness. Half of his remaining soldiers had blood on them as well.

"Something is in that final room," Atkins said, his voice monotone, with an edge of madness to it.

"I've been here before," Anna said. "I've walked these rooms. There's nothing dangerous down here but that mushroom smell."

Atkins took his eyes off the darkness at the end of the tunnel and focused on Anna. "It's alive. Something strong and evil."

"It's all in your head. An illusion and I can prove that to you."

"How?" Logan gawked at her.

She ignored him and pointed at Atkins. "Do you have a flashlight?"

Atkins nodded and retrieved one from his army fatigues. He handed it over.

Anna flicked the switch and turned to aim it at the back wall.

Logan followed the light to stare at a hole in the bunker wall that was at least ten feet wide and maybe fifteen feet high. Pure darkness lay beyond that.

"See?" Anna said, holding the light on the hole in the wall while glancing back over her shoulder at Atkins. "There's nothing but darkness. The illusions don't work with light. That's why it doesn't happen when the sun's up."

She handed him back his flashlight. Atkins lowered it, the beam aimed at the floor.

"Atkins," she said. "Raise that beam. Aim it at me

to watch something."

Without a word, Atkins raised it again, the beam on her face. Anna squinted in the light but didn't protest.

She turned away and moved to one of the crates of the explosives stacked by the wall. With whatever strength she still possessed, Anna grabbed the crate and started walking toward the opening at the back of the tunnel.

"Anna, no!" Logan yelled at her. "Don't go in there."

She stopped at the door, Atkins's light illuminating her like the headlights of a car.

"I know what I told you, Logan, and I'm right. It is the Devil down here. But Lucifer comes in many forms; in this case, he's somehow stealing souls through this portal. Blowing it up kills his chance to continue to do that. These explosives need to go in this room as deep as they can go."

"Don't go in there," Atkins said. "Something ancient roams that darkness. We saw it."

Logan snapped his head toward Atkins. "What did you see?"

"One large eye, scales for skin, a mouth wider and bigger than the trunk of my old '75 Monte Carlo, and that baby I owned was called a boat." His bulging eyes slipped sideways to stare at Logan, unable to blink in terror at what he saw. "That thing in there had teeth double the size of a great white shark, and they seemed sharper than any guillotine ever used." He looked pale in the candlelight, his face slack. "My men were torn apart in seconds, shredded like paper, their bodies yanked inside that hole in the wall, screaming until their heads were ripped from their bodies, and they could scream no more."

Logan needed to vomit. The thought of how his luck had run out, how a state cop was in an army bunker with a monster from some other world, cut him to the core. He should be in his cruiser, pulling people over for speeding and arresting people for being drunk and disorderly. This bunker wasn't in his job description anymore. He'd made the mistake of thinking he could be some hero and save the day. What a fool he'd been.

"There's nothing in here," Anna repeated, then turned and walked inside the room, the crate of explosives in her hand.

As much as Atkins aimed the light into that darkness, they had lost her.

"Anna?" After Logan didn't get a response, he called again. "*Anna?*"

She stepped back out into the light, her hands empty. "See? There's nothing in there. It's all an illusion." Anna grabbed another case, then limped to the hole in the wall, and was lost to darkness once again.

The men all stared at each other dumbfounded. Their semi-circle loosened as men leaned on their rifles, with two moving to the wall to sit.

"Well," Atkins shouted. "You can't expect Anna,

in her advanced age, to carry every crate inside that hole. Let's go, men. There are over thirty crates of explosives. Get them inside. Then we leave, blow the place, and we're all rich. Actually, richer now because only a few of us are left."

Some of the men grumbled something, while the others didn't move to help.

Anna emerged from the hole in the wall, moving slower now, grabbed another case, and started back toward the dark hole.

"Can I get some help?" she asked. "Stop being pussies."

Several men moved past Logan, determination and fear on their faces. They grabbed a crate each, then started for the dark hole in the wall.

Anna came out in front of them. "Go to the back of the room. It's dark, but there's a candle burning where I stacked the other crates."

They nodded and moved past her, entering the darkness without hesitation.

Logan watched the remaining men stare at the hole, waiting for a scream, a fight, a weapon to discharge, but nothing happened. After a moment, one of the men spoke from inside the hole.

"Found the candle," he said, his voice hollow from the cavernous room and distance. "Can we get some help here?"

They all looked at Anna, who gestured toward the opening. "Let's do this, then get out of here."

Three more men moved forward, grabbed crates,

entered the darkness without hesitation, and then disappeared.

Only Atkins and two soldiers were still there. They waited several moments longer before Atkins handed Logan the flashlight and grabbed a crate.

"If you two do not help," he said, addressing his soldiers, "you will be killed when we come out. If you run, we'll find you and kill you. No one leaves without their share of the gold. Otherwise, you're a liability. Now, grab a crate and get in there."

Atkins faced the hole in the wall, crate of explosives in hand, then stepped forward and was lost to the darkness.

The two soldiers looked at each other, fear radiating off them, then they grabbed a crate each and started for the open maw at the end of the bunker tunnel, leaving Logan alone.

He aimed the beam at Anna, that terrible mushroom smell intoxicating down here. He coughed once when he tried to talk, the smell cloying at the back of his throat.

"I thought you said …" His voice trailed off when Anna disappeared in the light's beam. She was standing before him, his eyes seeing her clear as day, then as the direct beam of the flashlight crossed her body, it showed the wall of the bunker.

He moved the beam aside and saw her watching him. Then he aimed the beam back at her again, and she wasn't there. The beam hit nothing but the dirty wall of the tunnel.

An illusion, an apparition. Anna had used the word *hologram*.

"Guys," he shouted as the two men were about to enter the door to that insane darkness. "Don't go in there—"

The first man couldn't stop in time. He was already passing the threshold when something dragged him all the way in. But it didn't drag him so much as catapult him inward. First, his shoulders jerked forward, like something had latched on and yanked the man. Then his upper body shot forward so fast his feet rose to chest height before being lost to the darkness beyond.

The second man dropped the crate at the threshold of light, pinwheeling his arms backward to arrest his forward motion at the sight of his comrade's feet near his face one millisecond before.

A drawn-out "Noooooo" slipped from Logan's mouth as he stood seven feet from the opening in the wall, immobilized with fear.

The last man, leaning back, even stepping back now, his face a mask of absolute fear, never stood a chance that close to the hole in the bunker wall.

Whatever was in that final room exited the several feet needed to take hold of the soldier around his waist. He glanced down, his hands already working on getting the snake-like tentacle off his midsection.

A huge eye emerged from the darkness, close to the bunker's roof, at least nine feet high, followed by the rest of its face, which angled away from the eye.

Logan was already stepping backward, the flashlight raised and aimed at the final soldier.

The man was lifted off the ground, his feet thrashing wildly in the air, his shoulders arched back like a gymnast about to perform a contortionist trick.

Two things happened at once.

One, the soldier's body broke in half like the sound of a large branch snapping in the forest, and two, the thing that held him came into the beam of the flashlight, enough that Logan viewed part of its face.

In that face, he saw an ancient evil, something double the size of a Tyrannosaurus Rex and looking just as vicious but with the head of a one-eyed lizard and the mouth of an oversized piranha. It radiated evil and intelligence. In those few seconds, Logan stared into its eye. He saw that it knew him, would take him, and would cause him to go absolutely insane in the process.

No god would allow a maleficent entity of this nature to roam the earth. Something that inspired madness, darkness at depths untenable by the human brain, something that caused madness by sight alone. Medusa and her head of snakes—only this creature didn't turn anyone to stone. It turned their insides to jelly. It broke them mentally, then physically, and ate them whole, devouring them, body and soul, in one swallow.

How Logan understood all this in the seconds upon laying eyes on the beast mattered little to him. What concerned him the most was running, surviving, or at least attempting to.

Stuttering random sounds as he staggered backward, Logan watched as the thing eased farther out into the corridor.

When Logan turned to run, he tripped over the body of the soldier Atkins had shot in the legs, falling hard onto his hip. He rolled once, got to his hands and knees, then shot up to his feet and scrambled away.

The creature was close behind, almost entirely out of its cave, swallowing and becoming darkness as it came.

Somewhere near the back wall, Anna's hologram cheered it on, screaming for Logan to run, but that he couldn't hide. Then she laughed like she was trapped in an asylum.

At the corner where Logan turned toward the spiral staircase, he glanced back to ensure it wasn't too close.

The thing opened its trunk of a mouth and tossed the dead soldier in, chewing his remains with grotesque crunching noises as it rose higher on feet that didn't resemble cloven hoofs. It looked more like the feet of a centipede, each one sporting the kind of hair that reminded Logan of the backs of tarantulas.

But even as he stared, mesmerized and feeling the stirrings of shock settle over his system, the thing changed shape with the darkness, folding into it, like it was part of the dark, creating the dark, one with it, *conjuring* the dark.

Then the beast thing was gone from the middle of

the corridor, forming into what Logan could only imagine was a hungry darkness. It moved along the tunnel toward him, extinguishing candle after candle on the walls as if light was unable to survive in its wake.

As Logan forced his legs to move and fear threatened to paralyze him, the craziest thought ran through his head. When the door opens in a dark room, the hallway's light spills into that room. The opposite was taking place down here, where the darkness ruled. It spilled into and over the light, consuming it, extinguishing it.

When he smashed into the railing of the staircase, he screamed and fell, bumping his elbow on the bottom step.

The darkness oozed around the corner of the tunnel and moved lazily toward him. It would swallow him whole and cause a madness only contemplated in Hell if he let it touch him.

Not sure how his legs continued to hold him up while enduring this level of fear, Logan pushed himself up the spiral stairs, feeling the entire time that his escape efforts were fruitless. Whatever God had allowed to let live in this underground Hell would get him no matter how far he ran or for how long. It was in the darkness of the night when he slept, the gloom of a closet, the monster under the bed. In the darkness of the mind, it was the place where terror manifested itself at levels unparalleled by reality.

At the last turn on the steps, he snatched a look

behind him once more and saw darkness surrounding the lower steps. Nothing but blackness below him now, an absolute absence of light.

He ran, the flashlight's brightness in his hand like a beacon of sanity, a weapon to stave off the monster's darkness.

He ran as fast as his legs could take him through the barracks hall.

Those explosives needed to be detonated. Whatever that thing was down there needed to die. He'd never sleep soundly again, knowing it remained intact in the belly of the bunker.

Logan exited the end of the barracks corridor and ran out into the night, the cool air brushing his wet forehead and his soaked shirt, reassuring him he'd done it, he'd escaped.

The only way out was the army truck, though. There was no way he was walking those woods in the dark, armed with only a flashlight.

When he turned toward the truck, a weapon fired, chunking up the dirt in front of his feet.

He stopped abruptly and looked up at a face he recognized.

"Stay right where you are," Command Sergeant Major George Miles said. "Do not move, or I will put a bullet in your face."

The weapon fired again.

Chapter 38

LOGAN STARED UP INTO the face of the Command Sergeant Major of the US Military while raising his hands out to the side. The man held a gun on him, his face glistening with sweat.

"What?" Logan gasped, trying to formulate words. "What are you doing? We have to get out of here."

Miles burped out a short laugh and sized Logan up. "You loaded the truck with gold for me, eh? Great job."

"What?"

"You still haven't figured it all out yet, have you?"

"What?"

"You're like that guy in *Pulp Fiction*, always saying *what*." Miles shook his head. "Where is everyone?"

"Dead, they're all dead."

"Atkins?"

"Dead, too."

"You saw him die?"

Logan nodded. "Saw them all die." He shot a glance at the barracks windows, imagining the darkness oozing over them and swallowing Miles whole.

"Did you kill them for the gold?"

Logan frowned, wondering where the man would get that notion. Why the hell would a state trooper murder people for some loot? Snatch some cash after a large drug bust before it hit the evidence room, sure, but kill to steal gold? If he were a cold-hearted bastard, he wouldn't have lasted long as a trooper.

The gold had never interested Logan. Sure, wealth could be good, and it would certainly help make for a more pleasant life, but he was here for Anna—*had* been here for her—and now he wanted to be as far away from this place as possible.

"I don't care about the gold and didn't kill anyone."

"You'd have made a good cop, but you aren't detective material."

Logan stumbled on his feet, his body filled with adrenaline and fear. "What makes you say that?"

"You didn't catch any of the clues. Trooper, I *sent* those men in to get the gold while all this time you thought they'd abandoned their posts." Miles shook his head. "If a little old woman could escape this terrible place, then an armed soldier certainly could. Carry as much gold as one could handle and keep a percentage for himself." Miles lifted one shoulder. "At least, that's how I figured it would go. But hardly anyone was coming out."

Miles stood dangerously close to a broken

window at the side of the barracks. If he kept him talking long enough, that darkness from Hell might seep out and seize him.

"What about that HAZMAT team?" Logan asked. "They had two men survive."

Miles laughed. "You believed that story? There was no HAZMAT team in the bunker taking pictures. Those photos came from Anna's phone."

Logan blinked. How did he miss that? "What about the Air Force? What if they had bombed the place? You would've missed out on the gold then."

"That was the original plan. Bomb the place once the gold was removed as it would cover our tracks, but when my men weren't returning with it, I knew they'd grabbed some for themselves and deserted for real, so I had to call off the Air Force and make it look like they were at fault."

"But I watched the cameras. I saw all those people down here in the clearing."

"My people, my soldiers, whom I sent in for that exact job. Well, that and grabbing the gold."

Logan shook his head, keeping an eye on the window beside Miles. "But they were all dead. They didn't desert you. That thing murdered them."

Miles shook his head, his gun hand lowering from the strain of holding it for so long. Even Logan's arms lowered a bit.

"There's nothing down there, Logan. I don't believe in fairy tales or ghosts and goblins. No monsters are lurking in back alleys or boogeymen.

There are just bad men and evil women doing terrible things to each other. Trust me. I've seen war. I know the horrors humans perpetrate on each other. I know what that looks like."

It was Logan's turn to shake his head. "No, I saw it with my own eyes. Whatever's down there doesn't belong here. It's not of this earth. A monster that became the darkness, swallowing men whole."

Miles stared at him for a long moment. "Wow, that's quite something. I'm assuming it ate Atkins, then?"

Logan nodded. "Atkins was taken and eaten. He's gone."

"Damn, we were supposed to split the gold. Guess I'll have to take it all for myself." He smiled wide, his teeth showing.

"Was this all about the gold?"

"Back to my reference about you not making it as a detective. Of course, this was all about the gold. Sure, some people disappeared many years ago, but then the government, the people I work for, sealed the file to the level that this place was steeped in mystery. No one could even locate the barracks. The maps were sealed, the road bulldozed, and history erased. Then Anna popped up, claiming to have been on a US military site in the woods of Oregon, and I had to see it for myself. Was it true that a trillion dollars in gold was stashed here? Or was it only a billion?" He laughed loud and hard, then pointed over his shoulder at the bars stacked in the rear of the truck. "And to think we brought you on as the fall guy."

"The fall guy? How's that? You said Anna requested my presence, which we both know is a lie now."

Miles nodded energetically. "Of course, it's a lie. Once the gold was removed and the place was bombed, if anything went wrong, we needed a civilian, or a cop, to appear greedy. None of the high-ranking officers would ever act in such a selfish manner."

"But when I asked for the keys to a vehicle so I could leave, you gave me permission."

Miles glanced down at the ground as if disappointed in his student. "Logan, you could've left without an issue. You were the fall guy. We drive off with the gold, then my reports follow, naming you the thief and murderer. After all the trauma of losing most of my men, I retire and end up on a beach somewhere, end of story. Although, after what's happened here now, you're no longer needed alive."

"How's that?"

"Well, everyone's dead. I'll take this truck with its bounty and drive out of here. You folks stashed the explosives in the bunker for me and loaded my truck with my retirement fund as I watched from over there." He stepped a few feet back to close the truck's doors. "I'll stash my loot, report for duty, and wait a few years before starting to cash these babies in. Then it's beaches and margaritas for the next twenty years. Whores, too."

"Sir, whatever's down there comes directly from Hell. At least kill it first."

Miles clamped the door shut, then spun around and pulled a device from his pocket. "Oh, cut the religious bullshit. There's no Hell, and there's no Heaven." He held up the object. "This is the detonator for every single crate of explosives in that bunker. When I'm over there"—he pointed at the clearing—"that should be far enough away to push the red button, and then that'll be the end of this shit." He moved a step closer as Logan glanced at the barracks. Where was the darkness? Why wasn't it coming out to grab Miles? "I'm just sorry you got caught up in this mess. Now, reach into your pocket and give me the keys to the truck. Do it slowly."

Logan couldn't believe this was happening but did as he was told. When the keys were in his hand, he dangled them out at the length of his arm.

Miles took them and then raised his weapon again.

"Wait a second." Logan stepped back, his own hands up. "Why kill me?"

"You're kidding, right? I can't have you running around with a story that differs from mine."

"You'd kill a state trooper?"

"You think I care what you do for a living? What a joke. It's a fucking job. It doesn't give you a free pass here, I'm afraid. I'd kill my own mother for that gold in there. Now start walking."

"Walking? Where am I going?"

"In there." Miles pointed at the side door of the barracks. The door that led to the hallway, that led to the top of the metal spiral staircase. The door that led to Hell.

"No way, no fucking way."

"Okay, then it's a bullet in the face."

"Wait a second," Logan gasped, barely able to catch a breath. "I can't go back in there. *It's* in there."

"It's in there, it's in there," Miles repeated in a childlike voice. "Fuck off with the baby shit and start walking." Miles was close to him now, so he pushed Logan, who stepped a few feet back. "Just enter the building. That's all I ask. You don't have to go back down to the bunker."

Logan moved toward the door, his mind racing on ways to get out of this mess. A bullet was so absolute, whereas the hallway of the barracks might not have that beast thing yet.

He glanced inside the doorway and aimed his flashlight down the hall. The light revealed the dirty floor and the walls, but no darkness slithering up from the depths of Hell. For whatever reason, it wasn't crawling with the darkness like what he saw in the belly of the bunker.

So he stepped inside.

Miles shoved him hard from behind, so hard that Logan tripped over his own feet and fell onto his ass, a grunt escaping his lips.

"The fall guy," Miles shouted and laughed. "Literally. Isn't that hilarious?"

He raised the weapon and aimed.

Logan brought up his hands like that would stop a bullet.

The weapon fired twice in quick succession, then twice more. Both of his feet jerked like they were punched.

Miles was shouting something about how good a shot he was as Logan stared at the holes in his shoes. The bastard had shot him in each foot. He would never walk out of here now, not unless he crawled all the way while bleeding.

Then Miles moved back from the door and trotted toward the truck. Frantic, Logan spun around and crawled out of the barracks hallway and onto the grass by the door. Then he stripped off his shirt and tore it into lengths as the pain and blood flowed.

He needed tourniquets on his ankles. He needed to stem the blood flow long enough to get back to the medical trailer at the temporary command post. Then he'd have a shot at surviving this ordeal.

The truck's engine fired up, then the gears ground once before he heard the engine rev as Miles pulled away from the barracks and headed toward the clearing.

A thought struck Logan. Before heading into the bunker with Anna, he'd glanced into the back of the truck and saw five or six crates of explosives still stacked up near the front by the cab. The last few had not been emptied as Atkins's men had been tied up shooting at the darkness at the end of the bunker. Had

Miles seen them and taken them off the truck? Or did he just see the gold and close the back doors?

The truck lumbered toward the center of the clearing.

Logan was already wrapping a strip of cloth around the first ankle when Miles made it to the tree side of the clearing.

The explosives in the bunker—and the truck— would go at any second.

He held his breath to manage the pain in his feet and the anticipation of what was to come.

Something clicked to his left, a loud sound emanating from the bottom of the bunker.

Then the truck lifted off the ground as the back of it tore apart, shooting gold across the open expanse of wild grass. The truck's cab was shredded into a mangled chunk of metal, entirely consumed by fire. The remains of the truck thunked back onto the ground, destroyed and engulfed in flames.

There was no way Miles could've survived that.

From under the ground, deep within the bunker, the rumble and firelight of the explosion below ripped upward, with flames shooting to the top of the metal staircase at the end of the barracks hall, which Logan had a clear view of to his left. A draft of a strong, hot breeze tossed his short hair upward, making him slam his eyes closed with its intense heat.

Something came to the surface with the fire, something smelling of burned mushrooms and melted flesh. The darkness he'd seen earlier, the one that had devoured the light, didn't ooze up the hallway—it raced along it toward him as if malnourished and now ravenous and in need of a meal.

Logan screamed as it shot toward him. Unable to move with the pain in his feet, he was a frozen impala waiting for the teeth of its predator to acknowledge the end was near.

In moments, the darkness was upon him, sinking into his consciousness, his flesh, devouring him whole, taking him back to its nest, its lair.

His body was gone now; his consciousness lost to float in the essence of the darkness. And in flashes of understanding afforded him, he knew how long the darkness had lived, how it loved fire, how it swam in flames and would continue to live as long as there was an Earth to inhabit. It had designed it all, even the sun, which would one day be the fiery cause of the earth's demise.

Humans had it wrong all this time. The suffering, the evil, the fear of the dark, all came from this entity, this malicious being. Earth was its playground, humans its bauble. It toyed with them in a most rancorous and pernicious manner because it created us from its own being to watch its children flaunt their desires, their whims upon each other, inflicting further pain and suffering as we traipsed through our lives imagining an all-forgiving God was waiting with open arms.

The joke was on us, and it knew it—just one more deception from the King of Lies.

When Logan's soul thought of God and contemplated prayer, the thing laughed at Logan's essence and allowed him one more shared thought.

Religion was its scourge for the imperfect, weak souls, something to cling to falsely. Still, more importantly, it was something that would cause more suffering and war than any other idea *it* had ever invented before. Religion was rooted in true evil.

As Logan's soul, his consciousness, endured these thoughts and understandings, losing itself in the essence of the height of evil, the epitome of all that was absolute darkness, he came to understand this entity had plagued the earth since the beginning of time, having created it in the first place as a sort of suffering carnival, going round and round, in a harsh and unforgiving universe that had created the darkness in the first place.

It managed it all on a micro and macro level, with every living thing an illusion once there and then gone. Even Anna's plight was an illusion, allowing her to leave the area only to draw so many more to fill its appetite for destruction.

Logan's final conscious thought before he lost himself to the insanity of his new reality was three words from a great philosopher he once revered and read with pleasure, Friedrich Nietzsche.

God is Dead.

Chapter 39

MICHAEL OLIVER FOLDED AND packed his tent, then stowed it in his hiking backpack. The sleeping bag was next, and it fit snugly at the bottom of the pack.

"How long before you're ready," Michael asked.

Sam Noah glanced up from his pack. "Couple of minutes at best."

Michael nodded. "I'll walk on ahead and take a piss."

"You do that."

Michael snickered at Sam's tone, then checked that the side pockets of his pack were secure before lifting it onto his back and strapping himself into it. One more look around the campsite they'd chosen for the night to make sure he'd left nothing behind— garbage included—then he made his way back toward the train tracks.

They'd had it easy for the first week as they traveled along highways and stopped in small towns for lunch and dinner. Even took a cheap motel a few nights in a row to have full showers and a bed to lie in.

Sam's idea was to head into the bush, navigate with compasses, and sleep under the stars. Three nights in, and Michael was already itching for a shower—literally.

They were still somewhere north of Crater Lake National Park in the Umpqua National Forest area, he figured, details acquired from the compass. They had enough food to last another week but would need a bank machine and another motel soon. He didn't know how much of this camping on the grass shit he could manage. The hiking to California idea was what sold him. The sleeping with the wildlife he could do without.

Although, for the first time since they started their *Walk The Earth Tour*, as they'd come to call it, last night was the first time he hadn't heard any animals foraging in the trees or wandering too close to their site, which was a relief.

He pissed by a tree, did up his pants, and strode onto the train tracks before turning around.

Sam was close behind.

"You checked the compass?" Michael hoped he had because he didn't want to pull his back out of his pack.

"Yeah, we're heading south, which is to the right."

They walked side by side for the first few minutes without saying a word. The silence of the woods was relaxing and unsettling at the same time. Being a city boy raised in downtown Portland and spending all his money at Powell's, he wasn't used to the endless trees, the enduring silence.

"So, you think we'll hit civilization again soon?"

Sam glanced at him. "You not into the wilderness?" He raised his arms out wide. "This beauty isn't for you?"

That condescending tone again, like Michael was a petulant child instead of a fellow graduate in need of a year off to find himself, to *walk the earth*.

"Showers, beds, beers, and a small list of nearly one-thousand things cause me to seek out the next motel. The wilderness is great, but if not tonight, I want to be out of it by tomorrow."

Sam shook his head, then rolled his eyes and finished by staring up at the early morning sky.

"Yes, by tomorrow night, we'll be back in a motel, walking on pavement, languishing in modernity."

Deciding to let Sam's derisive attitude go—he could be a bit of a narcissist at times—Michael grinned and walked faster, hopping from one railroad tie to another.

"Hey," Sam called. "Wait up."

They lunched late in the afternoon on a small wooden platform that looked like it was once a tiny railroad station. While walking the tracks, only one train had passed them a few hours before. It was a people mover, a passenger train, hauling car after car of travelers. Some stared out their windows and pointed, others waved, a few cameras flashed, and many others didn't see them.

Spreading out the nuts and berries, the bread, canned drinks, and granola bars, they feasted, knowing this was their last night without a bank machine or civilization.

According to the map, they would head east tomorrow morning, taking them to the Dalles-California Highway 97. They would take that highway south, and by day's end, they'd hit several towns or even hitch a ride early in a pickup or something similar and make it to Redding before sundown.

Sam called that *wishful thinking*, but Michael was sure they could be laid out in a motel in Redding, drinking beers and watching Netflix by dinnertime tomorrow.

Lunch completed, they packed the leftovers and the garbage, then chose to take a short nap.

"This wood is too hard for me," Sam said, hauling his pack onto one shoulder. "I'm sleeping on the grass behind it."

"Works for me, too."

Michael followed Sam around the back, sprawled out on the grass, and were promptly asleep minutes later, heads on their packs as pillows.

The oddest dream had Michael waking with the scent of something burning. He gagged momentarily, imagining the scent as part of the dream.

When he sat up, the smell was real and wafting to him in the breeze.

Sam was still sleeping to his left, his face slack, his right arm curled under his cheek.

Michael inhaled, trying to determine what that smell was.

Mushrooms.

Someone was sautéing mushrooms in the bush somewhere.

Even though they'd eaten a dry lunch with small gulps of water, the thought of a home-cooked meal made his stomach growl. What if the house was close? What if they offered them a few beers and somewhere to sleep for the night?

He checked the time and was surprised to see it creeping close to six in the evening.

The sun was lowering faster than he thought. If they didn't get a move on, they'd have to camp here for the night anyway.

"What time is it?" Sam asked.

"Almost six."

"Holy shit, man. We overslept."

"Yeah, and I think we need to pitch our tents soon. We lost half the bloody day."

"If we stop for the night now, Redding tomorrow night has lower odds."

"A bet on Redding, with the odds already as low as they were, isn't something I'd be willing to take, especially if it meant walking through these trees at night. I vote we spend the last hour or so of sunlight to scout out a place for our tents, sleep, and leave early with the early morning light."

"Can you smell that?" Sam asked, ignoring everything Michael had just said.

"Yeah, someone's cooking mushrooms."

"Damn, wish we knew where."

Letting Sam believe everything was his idea always worked well for Michael.

"We've got time." Michael got to his feet. "I agree with you. Let's see if we can find out if they're close, then find a place to camp." He glanced up at the sky. "Who knows? Maybe they'll have a spare room, a shower."

Sam shook his head again. "You're always on about a shower …"

That shake of the head—what Michael perceived as disrespect—was why he would never do anything remotely like this again with Sam Noah.

They shouldered their packs and moved deeper into the trees. In the distance, light shimmered as if someone had built a campfire.

"There." Sam pointed. "Someone's started a fire."

He moved quickly through the trees, taking no heed to Michael's advice of approaching slowly so as not to startle whoever might be camping out here in the middle of nowhere.

Up ahead, Sam slowed near a small building of some sort. When Michael got closer, he saw it was an abandoned cabin.

"Very cool," Sam whispered. "We could sleep in one of these rooms tonight. No need to unpack the tents."

They high-fived each other.

"Gentlemen," a woman said.

They both spun around and stared at the woman.

Michael figured she was in her late twenties or

early thirties and quite stunning for someone who wasn't wearing a bra. She literally stood there in a soft-looking summer dress, her nipples pushing through the fabric, her smile stunning, hair perfect. The tattoo on her left arm caught his eye. He loved when a woman got tats.

A goddess of the trees, a nymph of the forest, the woman in the woods.

"Uhm," Sam tried, then said, "hello."

"Gentlemen," she repeated. "You're on my property."

"Oh," Michael gasped, having held his breath upon seeing her fantastic form. "We're sorry. Just tell us which way to go, and we'll leave immediately—"

"Never." She waved a hand at him, her smile warm and inviting. "Please, we don't get much company out here."

Michael glanced around the area and saw a two-story building on the other side of the clearing for the first time. It looked like it had endured a fire at one point but was still mostly intact.

"You live in there?" he asked.

The woman glanced over at the building, then back at them. "Not really. I live behind and below it."

"*Below* it?" Sam asked, emphasis on the first word.

She nodded. "This used to be an army barracks. My sister and I bought it last year and have been fixing it up. We started with the old bunker as it was at least livable. Some of the rooms in the barracks needed a lot of attention, and places like this cabin won't be touched until next year, maybe even later."

"Wow, that's so cool," Sam muttered as if hypnotized by her beauty.

"We're getting dinner ready." The woman stepped back from them, then turned and started toward the barracks. "You two want to join us?"

They looked at each other, eyebrows rising and dropping in quick succession.

"You said 'join us'? You having a party? I mean, how many people are here?"

The woman glanced back at them over her shoulder. "It's just my sister and me. As I said, we don't get many men out here—I mean, many visitors, and it can get rather lonely." She stopped and turned to stare at them. "Well? Come on. Eat and drink and stay the night in the bunker with us. We'd be delighted to have you."

The way she almost moaned the words *have you* was all that Michael needed to be convinced. Evidently, Sam, too, as they both followed her at a distance.

Instead of a high five, they slapped hands once below their waist as they watched the woman walk toward the barracks, her hips swaying with each step.

"Holy shit is she hot," Sam whispered to Michael.

"I wonder what her sister looks like."

"Oh," the woman said over her shoulder. "We have beer, too."

"Really, we couldn't take all your supplies."

The woman stopped at the door to turn back. "Are you kidding? We bought this place and loaded a truck with supplies. We have cases and cases of beer, enough to last until next winter. Drink until your heart's content."

"Well," Michael gasped. "Put that way; we'd be happy to oblige."

The woman smiled again, melting Michael on the spot. She moved inside the building through a door on the side, her hand waving at them to follow.

"Sleeping arrangements might be tough, though," she said, loud enough for them to hear over her shoulder. "You may have to share beds."

Sam leaned closer to Michael as they entered the building behind her. "Does she mean share beds with them?"

"I sure hope so."

"This is a jackpot, man."

"I know." Michael straightened his face and stared at the woman's back as she moved along the corridor. "Just act normal."

Sam took the lead, moving fast as they followed the woman.

"So, what're your names?" she asked from up ahead.

"I'm Sam, and my friend here is Michael."

"Ahh, Michael, like the archangel." The woman stopped at the top of a staircase leading downward. "My name's Anna Valentina. Pleased to meet you both. Now, follow me into my bunker, my home. I love guests. Tonight, we'll live like there's no tomorrow."

Michael couldn't believe their luck. This couldn't be happening.

At the top of the metal stairs, he looked down into the expanse of the concrete underground. That mushroom smell was thicker in here. Without another thought, he followed Sam and Anna to the bottom of the stairs, then along a wide corridor to the right that was lit with candles on either side, past several rooms with doors that were missing, the walls scarred from some sort of fire, and into a massive door at the back wall.

Something rustled in the dark. The smell of burned mushrooms intensified a thousand times in this back room.

"Any lights in here?" he asked.

It all struck Michael as wrong on some level. Something was off here. The worst feeling swept over him, and he grabbed Sam to hold him back.

"We gotta go, man. Something's not right."

Sam jerked his arm out of Michael's grasp as the woman—Anna—appeared before them in the soft candlelight from the corridor. She was naked, her hands gesturing for them to come closer, to have carnal knowledge of her.

"What the hell, man?" Michael muttered, stunned at the sight before him. The woman was simply gorgeous. "What the hell?" he whispered again, appraising her.

"If you only knew," Anna whispered. "If you only knew …"

The darkness moved, coalesced around them, and then they were no more. There wasn't time to think, react, or even scream.

They were there one moment, gone the next, taken from the existence once granted by that very darkness, all in the name of suffering.

A deep, dark laugh echoed throughout the chamber as the darkness spread its wings and waited.

More would come in search of the hikers.

More always came, and the darkness waited.

It was the way of things and always would be.

Chapter 40

Two Portland-area residents have recently gone missing in the southeast Eugene area. Michael Oliver and Samuel Noah were last seen heading into the woods roughly forty miles southeast of the Eugene train station. During the course of the investigation, Eugene Police were in contact with several passengers on a southbound train who claimed to have witnessed these two men standing by the tracks close to a substation. The pictures used in this article are the ones taken by those passengers.

The authorities are asking for volunteers as search parties are being put together in an effort to help locate these two missing men. They will be meeting at the train station in Eugene before heading out in the morning.

It's understood that they were hiking and camping in the area and may run out of food soon.

If anyone has seen these men, please contact the Eugene Police at the number provided.

Afterword

Dear Reader,

Often, you'll find me writing novels with hope as the theme. My Sarah Roberts Series is filled with hope. In simplified terms, the bad guys take what they want, hurt others, and appear to be winning, but in the end, the good guys conquer.

With this novel, I wanted to create an environment where hope was fleeting, something we all cling to but ultimately watch as it seeps from our grasp. This novel, or at least the ending, is a total loss of hope, the end of everything, the antithesis of what we all hold dear. Hope is one of the strongest emotions —if not *the* strongest—even stronger than fear. When we're trapped by a force greater than us, and we're certain death lingers around the corner, hope makes us fight our way out against the odds. Some make it; most don't. Hope shelves fear. Removing hope only opens a void that can't be filled.

As much as I believe in God and have a spiritual approach to Him, I thought a novel revealing how Lucifer created the Earth for his own play toy would be delightful in its own sickness. A demonic being that reveled in allowing religion to flourish because of all the wars and suffering religion has caused.

This notion allowed me to explore the darkness and how the darkness under the bed, in the closet, in the dark of night, and losing sleep due to worry—borrowed trouble—was evil incarnate.

It also begged the question, "What if there was no God?"

Again, I believe there is, and I've stated that in multiple Afterwords in several of the over forty novels I've written before this one, but what if I'm wrong? What if a maleficent being created all of this to observe our suffering, revel in it, and laugh at our shortcomings?

I'm talking about the disease, famine—that bitch Mother Nature. I'm talking about war, rape, pestilence, and pandemics. Human lives lost, tortured, condemned, decapitated, and dismembered. In the end, is there a God? Or is this the work of something more malicious?

For the record, I believe in the Almighty, but I can explore elements of an existential crisis with fiction.

With Trooper Richard Logan, I wanted a character who thought like me. As a non-stop reader of fiction, and sometimes non-fiction, and a movie buff, I often think on fictional terms. Meaning I apply them to actual life events.

The way the darkness moved in that bunker, the way it rose up the metal spiral staircase and moved through the barracks toward Logan, swallowing him whole, was a nightmare of mine when I was seven years old.

I lived just outside Toronto then, in a four-level back-split house. My room was on the lower level but not all the way to the basement. In the middle of the night, in my dream, I had taken the stairs to the kitchen level and was about to turn to head to the uppermost floor where my parents were sleeping when I saw a tall black magician's top hat perched on the corner of our dining room table. As I stared at it, the hat melted into the table, dripped over the edge, and when the blackness hit the floor like a snake would slither, it oozed toward my feet.

In my dream, the thought of being touched by that blackness meant death. Feet jumping up and down like I was standing on lava, I screamed myself awake.

Of course, I ran from my room at two in the morning and raced up the stairs for the comfort of my parents' arms. But as I took the stairs and rounded that corner by the dining room table, I nearly pissed my pants as the dream had been that real.

To this day, that dream has haunted me like no other. We all get the shivers, goosebumps, and even the willies for things that cause our more delicate hairs to stand on end. The roving darkness that took Trooper Logan in this novel speaks to my inner dread. That sort of darkness is what causes nightmares in this author's blackest hour.

Before we go, I'd like to send out a *huge* thank you to author Rania Stone for her amazing help with some of the plot points in this novel. She read each scene, each chapter, and each word as it was written and discussed the novel late into the darkest evenings with me. I sometimes wonder how I ever did this writing thing without her.

Until the next novel, I thank you for reading, as I'm eternally grateful for every single reader who grabs a Jonas Saul novel.

Be well, stay safe and healthy, and we'll see you next time.

All my love,
Jonas Saul

About the Author

About Jonas Saul

Jonas Saul is the bestselling author of the Sarah Roberts Series—more than two million sold!—and has written and published over fifty thrillers. He signed with the Gandolfo Helin & Fountain Literary and Dramatic Rights Management team and has since signed several deals in Los Angeles, with MadRiver Pictures optioning his over-thirty books long Sarah Roberts Series (currently in development).

Jonas has often outranked Stephen King and Dean Koontz on Amazon over the past decade. He's regularly invited to be a guest speaker, teacher, or workshop presenter at international writing conferences and film festivals worldwide. He hosts an annual writer's retreat in Greece, where he currently lives. He focuses his teaching on how to get tension and emotion in every scene, on every page, how he made it as a creator/writer, the path to success in this business, and the pitfalls to avoid.

Jonas is also a professional freelance editor. He works for several publishers and does private editing for clients, with many testimonials on his website at www.imaginepress.org, which details each author's response to Jonas's editing skills.

At Imagine Media Group Literary, Jonas represents authors worldwide and is always open to reading the next bestselling manuscript at www.imgliterary.com.

To book Jonas for a speaking engagement at a writer's conference/festival, to have him on your jury at a film festival, or even to say hello, email Jonas directly at jonassaul@icloud.com.

For updates on releases, hit the "Follow" button on Amazon on any of Jonas's book pages or Bookbub.

Contact Jonas Saul

Linktree: Find me here
Email: jonassaul@icloud.com

Or send mail directly to Jonas Saul:

Canadian Address:

1865 Dilworth Drive
#366
Kelowna, B.C.
V1Y 9T1
Canada

www.ingramcontent.com/pod-product-compliance
Lightning Source LLC
Chambersburg PA
CBHW030948190726
48285CB00004BB/1282